More Praise for *A Love So Deep*

"*A Love So Deep* is a heart-warming love story between a man and a woman. It is a story of a friendship between two men. It is also a story about new and unexpected beginnings. The images are vivid, and I could feel the cold crisp morning, I smelled the Chivas at the Water Hole, I could feel the music at the church, and I could taste the meals Sister Mary Ross prepared. You might forget what someone says, but you always remember how it made you feel. A wonderful read."

—Doris Rose, reader, Sacramento, California

A
LOVE
So Deep

A Novel

ALSO BY SUZETTA PERKINS
Behind the Veil

A
LOVE
So Deep

A Novel

SUZETTA
PERKINS

SBI

STREBOR BOOKS

NEW YORK LONDON TORONTO SYDNEY

Strebor Books
P.O. Box 6505
Largo, MD 20792
http://www.streborbooks.com

ISBN-13 978-1-59309-141-5
ISBN-10   1-59309-141-9
LCCN 2007923864

First Strebor Books trade paperback edition September 2007

Cover design: www.mariondesigns.com

10   9   8   7   6   5   4   3   2   1

Manufactured in the United States of America

For information regarding special discounts for bulk purchases, please contact Simon & Schuster Special Sales at 1-800-456-6798 or business@simonandschuster.com

DEDICATION

In memory of my beloved mother, Ada Elizabeth Goward
and
To my father, Calvin Graham Goward, Sr.
Love never fails.

ACKNOWLEDGMENTS

To whom much is given, much is required. God has opened doors and placed many beautiful people in my path that are too numerous to name one by one. My literary journey has been blessed beyond my expectations, and I owe it all to Him.

To my Father, Calvin Graham Goward, Sr., I love you. You and Mom had a love so deep that shined bright throughout your fifty years together. To my daughter, Teliza; son-in-law, Will; and my granddaughter, Samayya, thank you for making Dallas take notice of me. I love you. To my son, JR, thank you for promoting me throughout the universe, whether you were in an airport in Los Angeles, on your job, on tour with me wearing the T-shirt bearing the cover of my book that the women literally tore from your body, or as the master controller of MYSPACE. You've made me proud, and I love you.

I'd like to extend a special thank you to my sister Gloria Jordan, who rushed out on release date for *Behind the Veil* and purchased the first copy in California. Thanks, sis. A special thank you to my cousin Doris Rose who loved my manuscript for *A Love So Deep* at first read and probably bought the second copy of *Behind the Veil* in California.

This journey would not be anything without the wonderful book clubs that so graciously invited me into their homes to discuss my work and fed me like I needed a meal. To the Sister Circle Book Club led by President Mary Farmer—Pam, Latricia, Lenora, Derian, Carlotta, and Jo Catherine—you were my initiation book club, and it was a blast from the discussion to the wonderful gifts. To my sistahs of the Sistahs Book

Club—Wanda, Valerie, Bridget, Tina, Melva, Tara, Melody, Angela, Jean, Latricia, Kim, Bianca, Bianco, and especially Donna Carroll who got everybody reading my book from Ohio to Charlotte—thank you for treating your president like a queen and making my book one of your favorites. To Jeannette Wallington and the ladies of Motown Review Book Club—Sherri, Francine, Valerie, Roberta, Yvette, and Yvonne—thank you for showing Detroit how to throw a real book club meeting. It was awesome. To Cornelia Floyd, Connie Marks, and the Triangle Ebony Readers, although my time with you will be later in 2007, I thank you for your support and encouragement on my journey. Finally to LaWana McNair, Keisha Haywood, Alisa Hester, Rikki Proctor, Camille McMillan, and Debra Kinney, thank you for a night to remember—book club meeting, jewelry party, Mary Kay party, and a pleasure party (that translates to SEX) all in one night. Wow!

I've been blessed to be part of New Visions writing group headed by best-selling novelist, Jacquelin Thomas, who has inspired and given me the best of her literary knowledge. Thank you and I love you. To fellow writers Karen, Titus, Angela, Monique, Sandy D and K, Cassandra, Lesley, Tanya, Pansy, and Valderia, some of whom recently had their own debut work published, I say stay on course. There's room enough for all of us.

Life on the road can be lonely, but with good friends and family by my side, the *Behind the Veil* book tour was a success. A special thank you to Yvonne Head for traveling to D.C. with me on the first leg of my tour, rallying all of her family together to purchase my book. We had a ball!! To my niece, Shonda, who invited her friends to come out and purchase my book at Karibu Books at Pentagon City, goes a great big thank you, sweetie. I love you. Karen Brown, you deserve a medal for BEING THE BEST TOUR PARTNER, although Mary Farmer was after your record. Thank you, Karen for being at just about every signing. Mary, you're a solid second place.

Angela Reid, friend and president of Imani Book Club, has always been there for me. From purchasing my books to sharing and providing book club insight to keeping the literary community informed, you're the best. To Tee C. Royal and RAWSISTAZ, I thank you for being so supportive of me.

A special thank you to Juanita Pilgrim who read my manuscript, enjoyed it, gave me her best critique, asked if I was writing it down, and demanded to see the new draft. While you were busy running Cumberland County, you gave to me, encouraged me, and told me that *A Love So Deep* was destined to be a movie. I love you.

To Dennis McNair, one of the best photographers in Fayetteville, North Carolina, thank you for always being there. Whether it was a Sistahs Book Club meeting or my fabulous book release party, you never said no. To Darlene McAllister and Ben Minter, you are the most creative team on the face of the earth. You've got gift, and I appreciate you both from the bottom of my heart for all the love you put into my book release party. Terrance Robinson, I thank you along with my son, JR, for putting up with my grueling production as we cut the musical single to *Behind the Veil*.

Donna Hill of Donna Hill Productions, you are the greatest. You know how to push and prepare a writer for success. I appreciate all you've done to enhance my career.

To Shunda Leigh, editor of *Booking Matters*, thank you for your wonderful publication and the opportunity to sell myself to the literary world.

To my publisher Strebor Books/Simon & Schuster, especially Zane and Charmaine, I thank you for giving me the opportunity and believing that my work was worthy of publication. For that, I am eternally grateful. To the other members of my Strebor family, especially Lissa Woodson and Tina Brooks McKinney who have been so supportive of me, I thank you from the bottom of my heart.

To my agent, Maxine Thompson, you're still the greatest!

With the expertise and skill of my editors Annette Dammer and Anita Diggs, *A Love So Deep* is at its best. Thanks Annette and Anita for being part of my journey.

A special thank you to Emma Rogers of Black Images Book Bazaar in Dallas; Ed and Miriam McCarter of Special Occasions; Urban Knowledge in Baltimore; Karibu Books; Jason Rosenburg at the Ft. Bragg Main Exchange; Barnes & Noble; and Waldenbooks for your support. You gave me space, a venue, and an awesome opportunity to show my face. I am forever grateful.

PROLOGUE

It was early fall, and weeping willows bowed to sun-baked lawns while giant redwoods spanked the skies, casting a lazy-like setting about the Bay Area. Maple trees were adorned with leaves of gold and reddish brown while squirrels scampered up twisted branches in preparation of the winter months that lay ahead. It was an enchanting feeling—a movie set backdrop. The summer was coming to an end, but its remnants were still very evident.

It was five in the morning when Charlie Ford, Dexter Brown, Bobby Fuller, with Graham Peters bringing up the rear, strode onto the Berkeley Pier, carrying tackle boxes, bait, chairs, and insulated coffee mugs filled with steaming coffee. The sun was not due to come up for another hour. The calm and peacefulness the water yielded was just right for the few fish that might nibble on their hooks.

Not much talk passed between the four men. This was to be a short trip—a two-hour excursion to help lift the spirits of a friend. Then it would be back to Bobby's house for his wife's hot, homemade biscuits with honey oozing from their sides along with a plate of soft-scrambled eggs, a couple pounds of bacon, and fresh brewed coffee to wash it all down. If they were fortunate to catch a few fish in the process, that would be all right, too.

Their poles were extended, lines laying in wait, birds chirping signaling the day to begin. An hour passed, and the sun rose like a yellow monster ready to devour the city. Its reflection illuminated the water a little at a time as it rose over the Oakland and Berkeley Hills to sneak a peek at the four men.

"Something's biting," Charlie yelled, reeling in a three-pound halibut. "Hey now, I got me a fish for dinner."

"Who you gonna get to clean and cook it for you?" Dexter chimed in. "See, I've got me a woman that'll clean my fish, fry it up in a great big pan, and serve it on a platter with homemade potato salad, collard greens, and hush puppies."

"But you don't have no fish for your woman to fry," Charlie countered, letting out a great big howl and slapping Bobby with a high five.

"I wouldn't eat the fish from the bay anyway. Heard there might be mercury in the water," Dexter said. "These puny little bass and halibut out in this water is just for sport—test your skills."

"Amanda!" Graham shouted, jumping into the water, causing the other men to gasp out loud in alarm. Graham gasped for air, his arms flailing around like he was cheering on his favorite offensive end, Jerry Rice of the Oakland Raiders.

"My God, Graham. What's gotten into you? What are you doing?" Charlie shouted at the top of his lungs, ditching his pole and jumping in. Graham could not swim.

Dexter and Bobby threw down their poles and ran to the water's edge. Sixty-two-year-old Charlie was the only one in the bunch who could swim, and he was giving it his all in the cold, murky water to save the life of his best friend.

Three feet out into the water, Charlie's muscular arms grabbed onto Graham, pulling him up. Bubbles came out of Graham's mouth. Charlie gave him a quick glance while paddling back to shore.

Anxious faces looked down at Charlie as he neared the shore. Dexter and Bobby extended their arms and pulled him onto the bank.

Graham's body trembled as he stood facing the group. His wet clothing stuck to him like Saran Wrap. His teeth clinked together in rapid succession, making a chattering sound. Bobby took off his jacket and placed it around Graham's shoulders.

Graham appeared tired and worn as he stared back at the alarmed men who were unable to utter a word. He looked at each one individually—Charlie, Dexter, and Bobby—then shut his eyes, clasping his hands over his face. He let out a sigh and his shoulders slumped with the weight of his grief. Amanda's death sapped the life straight out of him.

"What's wrong with you Graham?" Charlie shouted out of fear. "You could have drowned out there? Talk to me."

"Stop it, Charlie," Dexter cut in. "I know you're still hurting," he said, turning to Graham. "It's gonna take some time, but you hang in there buddy. It'll be all right after awhile."

"Manda, Manda, Manda," Graham moaned over and over again, his tears flowing like a busted fire hydrant. He fell to his knees, shaking his head, unashamed of his outburst. Life didn't seem worth living now that Amanda was gone. Charlie held onto him. His crying was so uncontrollable that his body shook violently as if he had been injected with a thousand volts of electricity.

"It's gonna be all right, man." Charlie hugged and squeezed his best friend. "If I could, I'd bring Amanda back, but that is not humanly possible. I loved Amanda, too. I wish I could somehow drain the pain from you, but for now, you'll have to trust that I'll be there for you."

"I can't go on without my beloved Amanda," Graham wailed.

Charlie, Dexter, and Bobby sat down on the bank next to Graham and wiped tears away from their own eyes.

CHAPTER 1

She was everywhere. Everywhere Graham turned and in everything he touched, she was there. Her reflection peered back at him when he looked in the mirror. She was a glimmer of light on a distant ocean. He felt her hand graze his while placing the oversized pillow on her favorite spot on the sofa. On the day he'd gone fishing, there she was in all her radiant beauty, staring back at him through the ripples in the water, and he had jumped in to try and save her.

♪♪♪

It was almost two months to the day since Amanda died. Graham had not ventured out of the house except for the day he'd gone fishing with his buddies. He sat home day in and day out waiting for Amanda to return so they could resume their life together. But with the passing of time, his obsession left him scraping the bottom of loneliness.

Today was going to be a new day, Graham promised himself. Self-pity had its place, but now he was ready to rise from its shadow. As he lay on the couch trying to make good on that promise, he was suddenly twenty again—a young man recently come to the Bay Area from St. Louis to follow a dream.

♪♪♪

Graham's best friend, Charlie Ford, had arrived in the Bay Area a year earlier. Charlie's Uncle Roscoe, or Roc as he preferred to be called, migrated to California after the war, finding work at the Naval Air Station in Alameda. Uncle Roc had invited Charlie to come out west after high school.

Graham and Charlie went way back. They met at junior high school. Charlie was one year older and seven inches taller than Graham, although Graham swore he was six feet tall when he had his Sunday-go-to-meeting shoes on. Charlie had coal-black, wavy hair that appeared an iridescent blue depending on the light. Graham had a thick crown of self-made waves with the help of a little Murray's hair pomade and a stocking cap. They were a pair. You'd rarely see one without the other. And yes, they could turn the charm on and were not accustomed to being without a girl wrapped in each arm.

Graham and Charlie played football in high school and were the main ingredient in a singing group they formed. Now Graham found himself in the Bay Area by way of Southern Pacific Railways with a shoebox filled with all his worldly possessions under his arm. Graham's mother, Eula Mae Perry Peters, had died suddenly of a brain aneurism, one short year after his father died. So Graham set off to see the world, leaving his two younger sisters behind with his Aunt Rubye to care for them.

It was Graham's first week in Oakland. The city was all a-buzz—a little like St. Louis, except that there were more jobs for Negroes and maybe a chance to strike it rich. Striking it rich didn't seem to be a likely event in Graham's immediate future unless he accidentally fell into it, but he did like the feel of the place he now called home.

Charlie subletted a small room from his Uncle Roc and asked Graham to stay with him until he got on his feet. There would be no problem with Graham getting a job. Hire notices were posted all over the black community. Everyone was looking for young, strong Negro men to work in the Naval shipyard, lifting heavy cargo.

But this was the weekend, and Graham was ready to see the sights. It had been a long, tedious ride on the train. The bright lights of the San Francisco Bay were a wonderful welcome mat for a young kid a long way from home.

"Come on, Graham," Charlie shouted. "The show's gonna start in about an hour. Man, you and me will be back in business in no time—all the babes we want."

"Church, Charlie? You've gotta be kidding. All of those clubs we passed on the way in. I'm sure we can find some good-looking girls there. I'm ready to unwind a little, kick up my heels."

"Relax, Graham. They say if you want a real woman, go to the church house. There's a convention going on at this big church up on Market Street that's about three blocks away and in walking distance. My man, Curtis MacArthur, swore up and down that there's gonna be a lot of babes at the convention. They come from far and wide. Graham, man, you can take your pick—short ones, tall ones, skinny ones, fat if you like, but there's enough to go around for seconds, thirds if you want. There's gonna to be good music, eating and even a little preaching, but this is the place to be if you want the cream of the crop."

"Charlie, you are crazy. You should have been a car salesman. Anyway, I don't have anything to wear."

"That's no problem. Uncle Roc got plenty of suits. They might be a tad bit too big, but they'll do for tonight." Charlie laughed and hit Graham on the back. "You're my buddy, and we're a team. Now what kinda friend would I be strolling with a fine babe on my arm and my best friend sitting back in the room all by himself?"

"You don't want me to answer that…?"

"Go on, tell me."

"What makes you so sure any of these girls are gonna even look at you? They're lookin' for preachers so they can become first ladies. No slick, jive-talking, unrepentant, tall, dreamy-eyed, dark-haired boy without an ounce of salvation got half a chance."

"I was counting on that tall, dreamy-eyed, dark-haired boy to do the trick." They both laughed until it hurt.

"You're right," Graham continued, "we are a pair, but you run on tonight. I'll catch you in church another time."

"Suit yourself, buddy. You're gonna wish you were there. And don't let me have to tell you I told you so."

"Get on and get out of here. I might take a walk later."

"Gonna try and sneak a peek, eh?"

"Catch you later."

Graham sat in the room contemplating life—what he was going to do tonight and then tomorrow. An hour had passed since Charlie left. It seemed the whole neighborhood had evaporated into the night—a hushed quiet that made Graham a bit wary. He jumped up and went to the window, but only the stars and the moon dared to stare back at him, the moon illuminating his face in the windowpane.

Graham grabbed his jacket off the chair and headed out the door. He wasn't sure where he was going, but he knew he needed to get out of that noiseless house—maybe hear a little music, ahh maybe some preaching, but he wanted to be where there was life and a little reminder of home.

He headed West passing a few couples out strolling. Then he noticed the cars—so many lined the street. He continued another block, and the cars—Buicks, Packards, and Fords, inhabited every available space on either side of the street. Yeah, he would own one of them one day. Then he heard it, felt it reverberate throughout his body. It reminded him of thunder, cymbals crashing. Yes, someone was having a good time, and it didn't sound like the blues they were playing back at Slim's in St. Louis.

As Graham neared the big church on Market Street, a flurry of activity surrounded it. The building seemed to sway on its cinder blocks, careful not to empty its precious cargo from inside. It was ten p.m., and although there seemed to be a lot going on inside the church, there was a lot happening outside as well. Small circles of young people milled about holding conversations. Suddenly, Graham was converged upon by a sea of purple and white choir robes which dutifully stretched into a single line waiting to march into the sanctuary. Graham looked around, but Charlie was nowhere to be found.

As Graham inched closer, a beautiful girl in her late teens emerged from the fellowship hall. She was about Graham's height, give or take an inch. She wore the prettiest white silk suit and a white pill hat with a bow made of lace attached to the front. The ends of her hair were turned up in a shoulder-length flip that accentuated her nutmeg-colored skin. But it was the nut-brown legs that made Graham come from his hiding place. Graham stumbled over a workhorse that had been placed over an open manhole. He regained his composure and followed her right into church.

He'd forgotten for a moment that he was not dressed appropriately, but that didn't matter. Charlie was right; "the crème de la crème" resided here. Someone called "Amanda," and the girl with the nut-brown legs waved her hand. What a pretty name. Graham would have to move closer if he was going to say anything to her at all. She looked his way and then quickly away, bobbing her head to the music as the choir marched in. She looked his way again, and Graham locked upon her gaze and didn't let go.

She seemed shy in a girlish sort of way, but Graham forged ahead. He pushed closer to her, the crowd unyielding until he was within an inch from touching her nose.

"Hi, Amanda," he said above the noise.

She sneered at him, wrinkling up her nose.

"Who are you, and how do you know my name?" Amanda Carter demanded.

"That's a secret," he said, even more mesmerized by her beauty. "My name is Graham." He extended his hand. "I'm going to be a preacher one day."

Graham saw the puzzled look on her face. "What does that have to do with me?" she retorted, leaving his hand in mid-air.

"Well...I...Would you like to go outside and talk for a few minutes?"

Amanda cocked her head back hesitating before she spoke. Her eyes cut a path down the length of his body and rested on his wrinkled khaki pants and blue pea coat that had doubled as a pillow on his trek to the west.

"Sure, why not," she said nonchalantly. "You seem harmless enough, but after this choir sings. They are so good."

Oh, if Charlie could see him now. Graham could tell Ms. Amanda liked the attention he was giving her, although she pretended she didn't. When the choir finished singing, they quietly went outside. They made small talk, but Graham was transfixed by her beauty (eyes the color of ripe olives embedded in an oval, nutmeg-colored face) and those beautiful nut-brown legs that he wished he could wrap his own around. Actually, he wanted to reach out and touch her, maybe place a kiss on those fine chiseled lips of hers that smelled of sweet berries when he got close enough to catch a whiff.

There was something about Amanda that was different—unlike those other girls who stumbled over themselves vying for the chance to be his lady. Graham Peters became a different person that night—his heart ached for Amanda Carter, a girl he had just met. If given half a chance, he would cherish her until the end of time.

CHAPTER 2

Two hours had elapsed when the telephone's ring brought Graham out of his reverie.

"Who's wanting me now?" he said aloud. "Don't they know I just wanna be left alone? Shut up!" he hollered at the telephone as the caller made no attempt to give up its quest to be heard. Graham made no attempt to answer. "All people want to do is give advice and get in your business," Graham grumbled. And he was having no parts of it.

Graham walked listlessly around the house, finally retreating to his bedroom. "Why Amanda, why?" Graham cried out loud, throwing his hands in the air. He sat on the edge of the bed, closed his eyes, and shook his head. He would not fulfill his promise to himself today. *Maybe tomorrow*, Graham thought.

Graham stood up and ran his hand along the dresser where Amanda kept her things. There were photos of their two girls, Deborah and Elizabeth, now fully grown with families of their own. The pictures were taken when they were five and six years old, respectively. Sitting next to the pictures was Amanda's jewelry box. It held everything from precious gems to costume pieces. Many were gifts the girls or Graham had given her. Amanda cherished each and every piece and would often tell people she couldn't part with them.

Graham rifled through the box until his heart stopped where his finger had also stopped. In the midst of all those trinkets was the rose pendant Graham had given Amanda on their first date as a token of his love and affection. Graham picked up the pendant and twirled it in his hand. He clutched it tightly, finally bringing it to his chest. The memory was so vivid—that first date. Graham fell on the bed and let time take him to the moment when he knew for sure that Amanda was his true love.

♪♪♪

It had been three weeks since Graham set eyes on Amanda at the big church on Market Street. Amanda lived not far from Charlie's Uncle Roc, but it was difficult to see her. Since Graham worked during the day at the Naval shipyard, it was next to impossible for Amanda to meet Graham. Mr. and Mrs. Carter kept a tight rein on their daughter. The best that Graham and Amanda could hope for was a phone call here and there.

As fate would have it, Graham got a weekend off and vowed to see Amanda. After giving Charlie what he owed for rent, Graham took five dollars from his remaining salary and set off to find something nice for her. A man bearing gifts had to amount to something. He'd show the Carters what he was made of.

There was an H. G. Grant store downtown that sold nice little trinkets; hopefully, he would find something befitting Amanda. He had called her the night before and asked her to meet him there for a fountain soda. Then he would give her the gift.

Graham circled the jewelry counter examining each piece. His eyes finally rested on the most beautiful rose pendant he had ever seen. He picked up the pendant and examined it thoroughly. A big, burly white woman peered at him from over the counter, sure Graham had no money to pay for the pendant. It made Graham's heart soar when he asked those steely-blue eyes how much the pendant cost. When she said $3.95, he handed her a five-dollar bill. It made his heart even happier when he saw Amanda walk through the door and head for the lunch counter.

Graham hoped she was as happy to see him as he was to see her. It was the longest three weeks, but sometimes things worth having took a long time to obtain. He saw her look around, then look at her watch, wondering if he would show. He picked up his stride, walked up behind her, and whispered, "Hi, Amanda. You look so pretty today."

Unable to contain her smile, Amanda blushed openly. Graham and Amanda stood at the counter and ordered floats, then sipped in silence. It was easy on the phone, but talking to each other in person posed a real challenge. Neither of them had felt this way about anyone else. They were both so young, however, nothing had prepared them for how they felt now. Graham sipped the last of his float and prepared to speak.

"I have a little something for you. I hope you don't mind."

"What is it, Graham?"

"You'll just have to open it and see," he said excitedly.

Amanda reached into the bag and pulled out the cardstock that held the rose pendant. Her smile turned to a frown. "I can't accept this, Graham. My parents would be furious."

"They wouldn't have to know; it's just between us. You can wear it whenever we're together. Do you like it? I picked it out special for you."

"Yes, I like it…I like it very much It's the best gift anyone has ever given me outside of my mother and father."

Graham was pleased with himself.

They sat staring at each other, each wanting a little more. A long A-line wool skirt now covered those nut-brown legs that Graham had admired. The wrinkled shirt and khaki pants Graham wore on the night he met Amanda were replaced with a red-and-white-striped, short-sleeved shirt that was tucked in a pair of starched blue slacks.

"I need to run home now. I'd like to see you again, though. Maybe we can meet in the park."

"How about tomorrow?" Graham said gleefully. "I have the whole weekend free. Mosswood Park isn't too far from here. We could meet about noon."

"I have to go to church tomorrow, but maybe I can get away around two o'clock."

"Okay, that would…"

"Graham, I have a better idea. Why don't you come to church tomorrow? That way, my parents would see you—even get to meet you."

Graham pondered this. Church was where he met her, but he certainly had no intention of venturing back there anytime soon. Graham saw the spark in Amanda's eyes, and somehow he knew that if he disappointed her, he would probably lose her forever. He must really be in love to agree to attend church services. There was nothing left to do but say yes.

♪♪♪

Graham was cute and even a little intelligent—well, maybe very intelligent in a weird sort of way. He was kind and attentive, although the extent of their casual relationship had been through the telephone lines.

Amanda's eyes searched the pews looking for Graham, not wanting to appear too anxious. He said he would come to the eleven o'clock service that had been in progress for the past ten minutes. Then she spotted him in the rear of the church. She slowly turned her head back toward the front, satisfied things were falling into place. She allowed herself a small grin—surprised by her own forwardness, her attempt to be a catalyst in bringing the two of them together.

She was in love and like a flower in bloom.

There were plenty of walks in the park after that day in church—the trip to the Santa Cruz boardwalk and many root beer floats were slurped from the counter of H. G. Grant. A few kisses were shared between them— sweet, tender kisses. And their bodies begged for more than Amanda was willing to give at the time.

There would be more than enough time for that, as Graham finally proposed to Amanda four months later, to the delight of both Deacon and Mrs. Carter. And to top it all off, Graham became a deacon in the big church up on Market Street—a place Amanda knew Graham had come to love. It wasn't just the people or the fact he met Amanda there, it was the love that transcended the place and how Graham was taken in among its members and made one of their own. And now he was going to marry the head deacon's daughter. He and Charlie could have never envisioned this back in St. Louis.

♪♪♪

Graham opened his eyes. The house was dark and still. He must have lain there a long time, because the street lamps provided the only light that shone in his empty house and empty heart. It was then he realized that the rose pendant was still in his hand. He slowly rose from the bed and put the pendant back in the jewelry box, closing the lid gently. Another day had come and gone.

CHAPTER 3

Particles of sunlight filtered through the venetian blinds. Graham lay outstretched across the bed in clothes that had hugged his body for the last three days, unwilling to let go of the body they held hostage.

For a brief moment, Graham thought about Charlie and some of the other buddies he had shut out of his life in the past month. Charlie was thick-skinned, didn't bruise easily, and was always ready to do battle with Graham. Maybe he'd give Charlie a call. Naw, then he'd have to sit and listen to all of the escapades that took Charlie longer to tell than it took to change four flat tires on a busy interstate.

Graham was restless and that only added to his loneliness. Graham jumped out of bed, stopping for only a brief moment to catch a glimpse of himself in the mirror. The mirror was unkind, but Graham didn't care. Who was going to see him today anyway? The large grandfather clock that sat in the corner of the formal living room chimed nine times.

Graham didn't bother to splash water on his face or pick up the toothbrush and toothpaste to chase away the germs and bad odor that had taken residence in his mouth. If life's urgency weren't so demanding, he'd probably forego that as well. He made a feeble attempt to wash his hands, and then sauntered into the kitchen.

The contents of the refrigerator stared back at Graham while he carefully weighed his options. Nothing seemed appealing until he saw the lone egg tucked in the back of the refrigerator. *An egg sandwich would do*, Graham thought. He bent down low, reaching in with his large hand to pick the egg up from its resting place. In his haste to get the egg, Graham's thumb pushed through the side of the thin shell, spilling yolk onto the shelf below. Graham retrieved his hand, slamming the refrigerator door shut in disgust, leaving the contents of the broken egg inside.

Graham had no taste for anything now and started to ease down into a kitchen chair when the doorbell rang. "Who the hell is it?" Graham stammered. The doorbell rang two more times until he could hear the tiny footsteps retreat. He went to the front window and looked out, catching the backside of Sister Mary Ross from the church. Graham believed Sister Mary was a little sweet on him. *She does have a nice behind for a fifty-four-year-old woman all bottled up in that too-tight paisley print skirt, but not as nice as Amanda's,* he thought. Maybe he'd hook Sister Mary up with Charlie. But she'd probably smother him to death.

Sister Mary left another package on the front porch—probably more food. She had come by last Tuesday and Thursday also with a hefty plate of food. Graham's first impulse was to leave it on the porch, but instead, he was compelled to go outside and get the package, since Sister Mary was kind enough to think of him and bring it by.

A blast of hot air met his unwashed face. He picked up the package along with the daily newspaper from the cement porch and hurried back inside. The brown paper bag contained a large plate of succulent turkey breast surrounded by homemade mashed potatoes and gravy, homemade macaroni and cheese, collard greens, and two pieces of cornbread. But nothing teased Graham and made his mouth water like Mary's thin-crust, sweet potato pie that none in the immediate community could emulate. Two slices sat atop the canopy of wonderful food.

Graham tossed the plate into the refrigerator. He was not in the mood for turkey breast at that hour. But he sat down in front of the two pieces of sweet potato pie—Sister Mary's famous sweet potato pie that was about to bring him joy. He placed his fork in the pie, gently cutting a piece from the pointed end and slowly lifting it to his mouth. He sat it on the edge of his tongue, savoring the taste for only a moment, then repeating the cycle until the first piece of pie had been consumed. As he started to cut into the second piece, Graham laid his head on the cluttered table, closing his eyes, allowing time to travel once again to a happier moment in his life.

♪♪♪

Amanda was so beautiful coming down the aisle. The Victorian-lace gown with its long, flowing train caressed Amanda's body with the elegance of a princess. Sister Mary's cousin, Loretha, a talented seamstress, had outdone herself this time. And Loretha couldn't contain her smile as she marveled at her own handiwork.

Amanda's best friend, Nadine Parker, was her maid of honor while Charlie stood as best man for Graham. Deacon Elroy and Martha Carter were proud parents that day, looking longingly after their only child who was leaving their house for his. They say Deacon Carter had to be nearly pried away from Amanda's arm.

Not a soul from Graham's family attended the wedding. His Aunt Rubye didn't have the fare for herself and his two sisters to come out West. Graham would have to share with them later how wonderful that day had been. The date was April 7, 1946.

They didn't have a honeymoon. However, Graham promised Amanda that he would one day take her wherever she wanted to go. After the reception held in the great fellowship hall, with a hundred well-wishers partaking in the celebration, the couple quietly slipped away and headed for the San Francisco beach. They took off their shoes and wiggled their feet in the sand. They strolled the length of the beach, discussing the rest of their lives together, letting the breeze swish through them—symbolic of their new-found freedom.

Amanda was in college working on her associate degree in early childhood. She wanted to become a teacher. Graham promised that she could continue until she received her degree. He had no plans of standing in the way of his new wife's goals and aspirations.

They got back in the car Graham had purchased a few months ago, with the money saved working overtime at the shipyard, and drove to the pier to catch the cable car. Things were looking up. He thought Charlie might be a little jealous now that Amanda had come into his life to stay, however, Graham reassured Charlie that he was his best friend and always would be.

They rode the cable car to Lombard Street, the crooked street that San Francisco is famous for. Coit Tower stood high on a hill to the north, and Alcatraz sat in a blanket of fog surrounded by the bay. The time had come to commence their love that was to last a lifetime. They headed toward home.

♪♪♪

Graham tried to raise his head, but thoughts of Amanda lured him back to the vision of their wedding night. They went to Graham's apartment, now their apartment, and embraced for the longest time. They pulled back and looked into each other's eyes, caught up in the moment. Their lips met, tasting and teasing seductively.

Graham held his love, flesh of his flesh, bone of his bone. The softness of her skin tantalized him while her round black eyes peered at him seductively. Amanda's dimple, tucked in her left cheek, smiled at him as he placed another kiss upon her lips. Graham wrapped his arms around her petite, nutmeg-colored frame, ready to release her from her white Victorian lace dress, so he could gaze upon and feel those nutmeg-colored legs of hers and everything else she had to offer.

Amanda was nervous, maybe a little shy, for the moment had come that she had waited for the last seven months. Although she felt the heat of passion many times before during their courtship, Amanda found that tonight she was unprepared to take their passion to a new level, a level where fire and desire would become consumed until they wanted no more. She was a quick study; and she slept like a baby afterward.

The next day, Graham couldn't take his eyes from his bride. Pride welled up in him like ten helium balloons. She seemed so at ease as she went about the day, as if she had been accustomed to the routine. Maybe she had attended one of those sophisticated schools of etiquette, but the most likely candidate was her mother, whose tutelage Amanda received each day of her life.

Graham raised his head from the table now, full of the memories that kept Amanda near him. He felt nauseous. He had not eaten a real meal in days—his only sustenance the two pieces of Sister Mary's sweet potato pie. You couldn't tell it by the pile of dishes that stood a mile high off the Formica counter. Graham had tried to eat but ended up leaving most of it on his plate or throwing it away. His daughters had called checking up on him, but he always told them he was doing fine.

He started for the refrigerator to retrieve the plate of food Sister Mary had sent, but the sharp smell of chicken grease brought back a month of Sundays and Amanda sweating over a large, black cast-iron skillet—grease popping across its surface like Orville Redenbacher popcorn.

♪♪♪

Amanda was a good cook and crisp, fried chicken was one of her specialties. Their house could have passed for a fast-food chicken joint the way folks flocked to it when they smelled Amanda's deep-fried chicken bubbling in the hot grease. Its golden-brown skin waited to be spanked by fat and thin lips that hung open in anticipation. Charlie was at the table as often as Graham and would have had to have a life-threatening illness to miss Amanda's fried chicken. According to Charlie, it was *the best in the West*.

Sundays after church, the Peters' house was the place to be. Amanda would cook four chickens to the delight of all invited to their table. With the exception of Graham, Charlie, Deacon and Sister Carter, all others had to rotate turns, because Amanda and Graham just couldn't feed everybody at the same time and on the same day. And after Amanda had the girls, the Sunday list got smaller still.

But Graham remembered it so vividly—the first full night they were together after they had married. Amanda promised to fix him a wonderful dinner. She even put out a few pieces of china her mother and father had given them as a wedding present and placed a long, slender candle in the center of their tiny wooden table.

Graham was listening to the radio. The commentator talked about a boxing match that took place a couple of nights before. Negroes were anxious to have a black hero in this event. As Graham sat listening, the smell of the hot chicken frying wafted under his nose. He rose to follow its scent. There in her petite splendor was Amanda slaving over a big, black skillet frying up some of the best fried chicken he'd ever taste in his life.

Amanda's back was to Graham, and the roundness of her well-defined hips and those shapely legs beckoned him forward. He tiptoed quietly behind her, placing his hands on either side of her curvaceous hips, letting his hand glide down and around the mound of flesh that had his lips watering.

"Stop it, Graham, you're going to make me burn myself," Amanda said, playfully swatting Graham's hands.

"The chicken was smelling so good, and I couldn't resist coming in to get a better whiff, but what I got instead…"

Pop!

"Ouch, 'Manda. That hurt."

Amanda turned to look at Graham, her hair swinging as she did. She still wore her hair in a flip, just like she did the day Graham met her, with her bangs pulled back with a yellow headband. "You're such a baby, Graham, but I love you." And she planted the sweetest kiss on his lips.

Graham did not want to remove his lips from hers. He could have stayed there all night holding her close and tight. "Better not let the chicken burn," he said finally, still caressing those fine hips of hers. Amanda playfully smacked his hands again, so she could remove the chicken from the bubbling grease.

Amanda arranged the chicken neatly on a platter just as she had seen her mother do. She pulled a dish of baked macaroni and cheese from the oven. There were fresh green beans simmering in a pot along with some thinly sliced onions, new potatoes, and bacon pieces. Homemade cornbread rounded out the feast. She set the dishes of food on the stove since the small wooden table would not hold it all. Graham was in awe. He had not experienced love in this form since he left Aunt Rubye's house. Now he had a wife who made him feel special and loved and looked good enough to eat, as did the food she set before him.

They ate from the china while sipping wine from the long-stemmed goblets Nadine had given them. This was their first whole day and second night together as newlyweds. They looked across the table at each other in silence, passing messages between them that only they understood. The mood was peaceful, and nothing could take away from how they felt at this moment.

"I'd like to dance, Graham. Turn on the phonograph and play some Mahalia Jackson."

"She's a gospel singer, 'Manda. We can't dance to that."

"She's my favorite singer. I hear she might even sing at Carnegie Hall one day. Anyway, I don't care what she's singing as long as we can dance to it."

"Okay, 'Manda. Anything for you."

"You mean that, Graham?" Amanda stepped back and put her hands on her hips and tossed her head up and down, looking at the full length of her man.

"Yes, Amanda, anything for you within reason. You know I will lay down my life for you, even go the last mile for you as long as this love of ours stands the test of time."

"I'll always love you, Graham Peters…from your young, boyish and handsome face with the cutest little eyelashes curled tight at the ends to the soles of your size-nine feet. Come here."

And with that, she took Graham by both hands bringing him close to her, twirling him around and then letting him take the lead as Mahalia sang, *"I believe for every drop of rain that falls, a flower grows. Out there in the dark somewhere, a candle glows. Every time I hear a newborn baby cry or touch a leaf or see the sky, I believe, I believe."*

CHAPTER 4

Graham was unaware of how many days and nights had passed. The last that he could recall was slow dancing with Amanda to one of Mahalia Jackson's songs.

What time is it? Graham wondered, stumbling out of bed scratching his head. The clock on the nightstand with its illuminated hands read ten o'clock. Next to the clock stood an opened, half-empty bottle of Johnny Walker Red. "How did this get here? I don't drink," Graham said aloud, snatching the bottle from its resting place and bringing the neck of the bottle to his mouth. "Ahh, that was good." And Graham fell back on the king-size bed and went to sleep.

The continuous banging at the front door roused Graham from his slumber. He slowly, mechanically, walked in the direction of the noise, knocking a picture off the wall but managing to remain on two feet.

"Graham, are you in there?" the voice on the outside shouted. "If you are, open up this door."

"Go away," came the feeble reply.

"Graham, if you don't open up this door, I'm going to get the fire department and the police and have them knock this door down. Now, I mean it. Open up this door!"

Graham stood staring at the door. He wasn't sure what he should do. He was in no mood to have a conversation with anybody, and he certainly didn't feel like having one with Charlie.

"All right, Graham. I'm going to count to ten, and if this door is not

open when I get to nine and a half, I'm going to call the cops. One…
two…three…four…five…six…" Graham moved closer to see if Charlie was
still counting. "Seven…eight…"

Graham cracked the door open, and before he could shut it, Charlie
forced the door open, almost toppling Graham in the process. Graham
regained his footing and stood in the doorway with a scowl on his face like
one of the Three Stooges after he had been hit over the head with a baseball bat. Then Graham followed Charlie into the room.

♪♪♪

It was dark when Charlie first entered the house, but he didn't need his
sight to determine that things weren't quite right. The stale, rank odor
that permeated the house sought refuge in his nostrils.

Charlie was appalled at the sight before him once his eyes had adjusted
to the light. He dropped *The Oakland Tribune* on one of the mahogany
end tables that sat on either side of the overstuffed beige loveseat. What
had happened to his dear friend, his best friend, Graham Peters? The four-
day stubble that covered Graham's chin and crawled up the side of his face
to his temples was ghostly white, adding at least ten years to his age. His
usually well-manicured mane was mowed down by several nights of fitful
sleep, along with the absence of a comb or brush. Graham's white shirt
and khaki pants were dirty and disheveled, and the smell that emitted from
Graham's unwashed body told the story only too loudly.

When Charlie walked into the kitchen to help Graham sit down, he was
confronted with yet another appalling sight. Dirty dishes, some of which
still contained food, were piled two feet high in the sink, contributing to
the pungent smell that had invaded the house. Charlie opened the refrigerator, hoping to find something to prepare for Graham to eat. There were
several plates of uneaten food. There was also what appeared to be remnants of a slab of bacon. But what made Charlie recoil in disgust was the
sight of a broken egg whose yolk clung to the insides of the refrigerator
like icicles with its cracked shell resting on the shelf below. Charlie closed
the refrigerator, opting to go out and buy something instead.

Charlie went around the house opening several windows. The fresh air found the stench a worthy opponent. Something would have to give soon, because Charlie was beginning to gag from the funk, and tears were forming in his eyes because of the heartbreak he found here.

Charlie looked at his friend curled up in a ball, refusing to speak because Amanda had left him by himself. Charlie wanted to curse Amanda, blaming her for Graham's slow demise. When she left, she took Charlie's best friend's heart and stomped on it like ripe grapes ready to be turned into wine. But if Amanda had a choice, she wouldn't have left Graham, and Charlie knew that. In fact, Charlie missed her as much as Graham did.

Charlie couldn't take anymore and stood before Graham, pleading with him to take his life back. Graham looked up at him, and then lowered his eyes without speaking.

"Graham, I'm not going to tolerate much more of this outta you," Charlie hissed. "Get up, get up now and let's take a nice, long, hot bath. It'll make you feel better."

Graham scowled at Charlie, hoping that would be enough for Charlie to leave him alone. But Charlie had been with Graham almost his entire life, and he knew what made Graham tick. Graham may have been inaccessible to any type of reason at that moment, but Charlie was not going to sit idly by and let Graham wither away.

"Look, Graham, I know you're hurting, but you've got to grab hold of yourself, man. You have so much more of life to live. It's me and you again even if we are a little rusty behind the ears." Charlie laughed at his own memory of them in their young days—woofing the women. Charlie thought he saw a hint of recognition in Graham's eyes.

Charlie walked across the room to sit next to Graham. "Whew, buddy. I'm gonna run you some bath water. We can reminisce later."

Charlie rose from his seat and turned back to look at the half shell Graham had become. "Why don't we go to church tomorrow? It'll do you some good...do me some good, too. You know, I haven't seen the inside of a church since Elizabeth got married." Graham sat there in his pitiful state, and Charlie proceeded down the hall to the bathroom.

♪♪♪

Graham's eyes scanned the room like a surveillance camera, not sure what he would find. Everything his eyes rested upon reminded him of Amanda. Graham got up from the chair and went and lay down on the couch in the living room. He closed his eyes and was quickly drawn to the day he and Amanda had moved there.

It was a brisk autumn day. The large brown, yellow, and red maple leaves were falling everywhere, scurrying about, not sure whether to stay or float away into the yard of the new next-door neighbor. Amanda was so excited because they were finally going to move into their own home in a small quiet little neighborhood that was far enough away from Mommy and Daddy but close enough that if they needed to get to her parents, they could.

Amanda bought gingham curtains for the kitchen and bathroom windows, and her good friend, Loretha, volunteered and made comforters with matching curtains for the rooms of Amanda's daughters, Deborah and Elizabeth. Amanda and Graham purchased their first set of furniture from the Sears and Roebuck catalog. It would be delivered later that day. Deborah and Elizabeth were with their grandmother, Martha, which left Graham and Amanda to themselves.

"You want to christen the living room?" Graham teased, giving Amanda a sly, seductive wink.

"Graham, you're so naughty. We can't. We don't know what time the Sears truck will bring our furniture. And…"

"So, it's not a bad idea, hmmm?"

"Graham, behave. We've got a lot of work to do. Help me put up these curtains."

"I'll help you if you give me a great, big kiss first."

"I know you, Graham Peters. You are up to no good. With our luck, we'd be well into making our third baby. What if one of our new neighbors stops by to introduce themselves?"

"We're married, ain't we?" Graham tried to be comical. "Well, *this* married couple makes love in the afternoon. And anyway, they can't disturb us if we don't let them."

"Graham, you're so crazy."

"But you like it. Come here, baby. Time out for all this talking. If we start now, we'll be ready and energized by the time the Sears truck rolls up."

Amanda sashayed slowly toward Graham letting those strong, nut-brown legs do their thing as Graham became hypnotized and mesmerized by her rhythm. They lay on the blue shag carpet letting their passion take over. Graham planted kisses on her mouth, down her neck, then on her breasts, lingering to savor the sweetness her nipples produced. Amanda took Graham's face in her hands, planting kisses on the top of his head as he moved slowly downward. Their bodies moved to a rhythm that was all their own.

♪♪♪

Graham inched further down into the couch, thoroughly enjoying this part of his dream when a light tap on his shoulder dared to disturb him.

"Water ready," Charlie said in a soothing voice.

"Leave me be, Charlie. This ain't none of your business."

"Oh, we do talk. You don't say. Well," Charlie said, starting off slow and ending on a high note. "Get your stinkin' ass in that water now! If you don't, I'll have to treat you like a little kid and bathe you myself."

Charlie had half a mind to walk out the door, but the fishing trip flashed before him. And he thought better of it.

Charlie busied himself, trying to restore Graham's house to some semblance of order. He watched Graham from the corner of his eye. He briefly looked away and saw the large pile of dishes again.

"What you been eating, Graham?" Charlie asked, not expecting an answer. "Maybe you can make it your business to get up off of that couch and fix me something—well after you take your bath, that is."

Charlie ran hot water in the kitchen sink until it was nice and sudsy. He scraped the remains from the dishes and placed them in the hot water to soak. Newspapers littered the room and methodically Charlie went about picking and straightening up. It felt good helping out his friend in this time of crisis. *Graham wasn't so depressed that he wasn't eating and reading the paper*, Charlie thought. He'd give Graham some time, in fact, all the time he needed.

Charlie plugged along until a shadow in the doorway forced him to stand still.

"What would you like to eat?" whispered the voice. "Well, think about it," Graham said when it was apparent that the cat had Charlie's tongue. "Think about it; I've got to take my bath before my water gets cold."

"It's good to have you back, Graham."

"It's good to be back, Charlie. You don't give a man a choice, but it sure does feel good."

Charlie heard Graham shuffle down the hall. "Grits, eggs, bacon, toast… and coffee—yeah, a strong pot of black coffee," Graham yelled. Graham smiled to himself and shut the bathroom door behind him.

CHAPTER 5

Graham looked in the mirror, admiring his fresh look. It made him feel like a million dollars. Amanda didn't peer back at him today. He looked for her, but she didn't appear—like she knew Graham needed this time.

Graham rose early this Sunday morning, anxious for the new day he'd promised himself. He put on his best Brooks Brothers suit, a gray pinstripe, double-breasted piece. It made him look devilishly handsome. He plopped his feet in a slick pair of Stacy Adams his daughter Deborah had given him last Christmas. He hadn't heard from either of his daughters in a week—probably tired of putting up with an old fool who didn't want anyone's help, even theirs.

Graham patted his hair in place, examining it for the sixth time. When Amanda was alive, it was she who gave him the nod of approval, and as long as he had Amanda's thumbs up, nothing much else mattered. Graham could hear the sputtering of an automobile and then the blast of a horn. Charlie had arrived to take him to church. Amanda would have chuckled at the idea of Charlie escorting Graham to church.

Graham took one last look in the mirror, then headed out the door. It was a beautiful day outside. The birds chirped loudly, adding music to the already colorful backdrop the city lent. The sun in its splendor, radiating showers of love everywhere, put a smile on Graham's face. Even Charlie, sitting tall behind the wheel of his red Honda Accord XL, seemed to be mesmerized by all that God had made. Charlie's long arm outstretched beyond the open window, beckoned the sun to come sit in the palm of his hand.

Charlie gave Graham the longest smile when Graham approached the car to get in. It had taken some doing—some prayer and a little cussing, but Graham Peters was on the road to recovery. Even though forty years had passed and new lives had been formed, loves garnered and lost, Graham and Charlie looked like the old duo from St. Louis ready to set out on a new adventure.

The church on Market Street was about a twenty-minute drive from Graham's house. Charlie would have to step on it if they planned to be on time. Graham sat silent reflecting on the last time he had been to church. It was the day he had buried Amanda.

Graham's heart was pounding so hard he felt it could be heard across town. They parked the car outside the church on Market Street, and Charlie jumped out and extended his arm to Graham, hoping the support would make Graham feel more comfortable. Graham's knees could scarcely keep him up. The parking lot was full and it seemed that everybody who was anybody decided to make this church the place to worship.

As the pair came close to entering, Graham hesitated, not sure that this was a good idea after all.

"C'mon, Graham. Everything's going to be all right," Charlie said.

"I can't do this, Charlie. I just don't feel right. I can still see Amanda lying…"

"Well, praise the Lord. It's Deacon Peters and his friend Charlie," Sister Mary Ross said upon opening the door and finding the two of them standing on the steps. "Ya'll go on in and make yourselves comfortable in the Lord's house."

"Thank you, Sister Ross," Graham replied, catching another glimpse of her backside once she passed by them.

"If I didn't know any better," Charlie chimed in, "I think Sister Mary is a little sweet on you, Graham."

"You're exaggerating, Charlie. But did you get a look at that…?" Graham gestured with his hands pointing to his backside.

"You mean her ass?"

"We're in the house of God, Charlie. Let's go in before I change my mind." They looked at each other and chuckled.

As the pair made their way down the aisle, heads turned forty-five degrees left and right, depending on what side of the aisle they sat. Eligible bachelorettes, young and old, did double-takes when they realized who the handsome gentlemen were that graced their sanctuary. A couple of Charlie's past flames nodded their availability, flashed elongated eyelashes, tossing their weaved manes for further effect.

But it was Graham who stopped short before the pew Charlie had selected. Right before him sat his children—Deborah and her husband, Grant, alongside Elizabeth and her husband, Riley. They stared at one another, disbelieving their own eyes. Graham was ashamed at how he had treated them—the daughters he loved with all his heart. They turned around and stood with tears staining their faces and embraced their father who had somehow come back from the dead.

Pastor Fields, now in his eighties, stood before the congregation, flashing his new set of dentures and directing the parishioners to join in a hymn of praise. *The wooden pews that held the hymnals and Gideon Bibles still look the same*, Graham thought. It had only been two months.

Graham reached for the hymnal, but the tempo and the beat of the music led to a hand-clapping celebration of praise. "This is a time for rejoicing," Reverend Fields shouted. "The Lord has brought our lost lamb back into the fold." Graham and Charlie looked from one to the other, not sure if Reverend Fields were talking about them or some other lost sheep.

The rhythmic thumping and clicking of Mother Hattie Mae Johnson's and Sister Betty Boyd Floyd's high-heeled shoes on the worn-out floorboards left a cloud of dust in its wake. The bass of the Hammond organ pumped by the long slender fingers of Reverend Fields' granddaughter, Charlotte, intermingled with the percussion of the snare drum and added to the frenzy of the dancers, the Spirit-filled dancers, lost in their reverent praise of the Almighty.

Charlotte made the organ roar, and the worshippers jumped from every pew surrounding Graham and Charlie. Graham was enjoying himself and felt a sly grin slide out the corner of his mouth. He looked over at Charlie who seemed terribly uncomfortable and afraid—afraid he'd get caught up, because he had too much running and womanizing left in him to give up all to follow Jesus. Yes, Graham had missed the congregation, and he felt a tear fall down his cheek remembering that it was in this very church that he met Amanda with no intention of ever coming back. He was home.

As Reverend Fields rose to speak, images of Amanda lying before the crowd at her homegoing enveloped Graham. His leg began to tremble, first slowly, then picking up the pace. His foot tapped on the floor, creating a melody all its own—shoving Graham's anxiety out in the open. He couldn't shake the image of Amanda in her coffin and dropped his head to avoid looking straight ahead.

"We are all going to meet Our Maker one day," Reverend Fields exhorted, extending his index finger toward Heaven. And Graham fled, with Charlie close at his heels, followed by Deborah, Elizabeth, and their husbands.

They caught up with him in the vestibule, Graham now sobbing uncontrollably. "Why did your mother leave me?" he wailed. "God, why did You take her away from me?"

"Daddy, it's going to be all right," Deborah said, forever the family spokesperson. "Liz and I miss Mom, too. You have to know that her spirit lives on inside of us."

"Yes, Daddy, Deborah is right," Elizabeth interjected. "Mom lived a good life, but she wants us to honor her by going on and living our lives to the fullest. We weren't trying to get you to forget Mom; she'll always be in our hearts. If not for yourself, you have to be strong for the rest of us—me, Deborah, and your grandchildren."

Graham pushed back the tears. "I know you girls are right, and I apologize for the way I've been acting. If it weren't for Charlie here, I wouldn't be here now. You all bear with me. I'm doing the best I can. I just saw your mother lying in there all over again, and I guess it spooked me. You're right; I'll be fine."

"Everything all right?" Sister Mary asked, as she appeared through the double doors of the church, pushing a tissue at Graham. "If there's anything you need, just call on me. I can stop by your house later this evening and bring you some dinner, Deacon Peters."

"That ain't a bad idea, Sister Mary," Charlie chimed in. "You got enough for all of us?"

Graham smiled in the direction of his daughters. He was so proud of them. They had been a rock after Amanda's heart attack; and all they wanted to do was care for him. Charlie breathed a sigh of relief.

CHAPTER 6

All the progress Charlie had made, which amounted to one small victory in getting Graham out of the house, was undone in the course of one hour. It was going to take a miracle of major proportion to untie a knot Graham might ball himself into if left alone again, and Charlie knew he couldn't let Graham go there.

Charlie and Graham took off down the street promising to meet up with Deborah, Elizabeth and their families, along with Sis. Mary, for dinner at Graham's later on. The sun was straight overhead, illuminating the scene that had left Graham breathless earlier that morning. It had been a long time since Graham and Charlie had hung out together. When Amanda was alive, life centered on her and the family.

Charlie drove into the heart of downtown Oakland casually waving his hand as he passed familiar faces. This was his territory; and he came alive as if his very presence was the indication for life to begin. Even for a Sunday afternoon, activity seemed to evolve—perhaps the knowledge that with sundown another week of labor would begin.

"Hey, Graham," Charlie said enthusiastically, slapping Graham across the ribs, "let's hit the Water Hole for a couple of drinks."

"Man, you know that's not my scene—haven't even seen the inside of a bar since I can remember. And…we just left church. I'm a deacon and a Christian."

"Yeah, yeah. Remember, I know you. C'mon, buddy. We can have a couple of brews—maybe shoot some pool. You need to relax, unwind a little."

"I don't know. Maybe you should take me home."

"What's at home, Graham? You've got no one to go home to."

Graham shot Charlie a hateful glance, so hot it could have melted butter. "If I was driving this car, your ass would be on the side of the road."

Charlie chuckled. "No need to get on the offensive, Graham. Just want to see you enjoy life a little—spread your wings. You've been cooped up in the house for too long. You could stand a little excitement."

They drove along in silence for the next few blocks. Urban dwelling had changed a lot of things. Drug dealers cruised neighborhoods looking for buyers. Lazy, afternoon hookers strolled the streets looking for a stray trick. Kids toted guns at school daring the teacher to make them follow the rules. Children played in playgrounds oblivious to their surroundings—then begged to be an errand boy in the gang. Life certainly had changed since the days Graham and Charlie had first arrived in Oakland.

Charlie made a sharp turn to the right and then another into the small, cramped parking lot that served the Water Hole. A red cherry sat in a tall cocktail glass with the colorful words "The Water Hole" splashed across the bar's large Plexiglas sign. Three or four older gentlemen graced the walkway outside, dibbling and dabbling in small bits of chatter. They all had some history, a story to tell and appeared to belong to a society of brotherhood. Each wore a polo cap of assorted colors and fabrics which sealed their bond.

"Hey, Charlie," one of the men shouted with a smile as big as a watermelon.

"What's happening, Moe? Good day to be alive!"

"You bet! Even with all the aches in my body, I feel good."

"Shelly's inside. Been askin' for you. Who you got here?" Moe asked, turning to get a better look at Graham.

"I'm Graham…Graham Peters." The men shook hands.

"He's my best friend," Charlie added. "We go way back."

"We ain't never seen you around here," Floyd put in. "You must be one of them special friends 'cuz we thought we knew all Charlie's friends."

"Graham is a Christian man. Just lost his wife. We're here to cheer him up," Charlie said, feeling the need to explain and justify their being at the Water Hole.

"Well, it's nice to meet you, Graham," the group said in chorus.

"Nice to meet you, too," Graham replied, finding no other reason to continue the conversation.

Charlie led Graham into the lounge that was dimly lit but littered with people throughout. Graham could hear soft music playing in the room they had not yet entered—the room that stragglers went in to shoot the breeze, drown their sorrows, or just pass the time away. Scantily clad waitresses scuttled throughout the room taking orders for drinks.

A high-yellow woman who appeared to be in her early forties made her way through the cluster of men as soon as she saw Charlie and Graham enter. "Hey baby, you buying me a drink?" She placed a quick kiss on Charlie's lips, brushing up against him slightly, and turned to get a better look at the man who accompanied him. "And, who might this fine gentleman be?" Shelly asked as her eyes moved from north to south, taking in all of Graham's five feet, eleven inches.

"Shelly, Graham. Graham, Shelly. This is my boy from way back."

Shelly took a once-around Graham stopping within inches of his face, his mouth, and his lips. Graham backed up, and said, "It's nice to meet you, Shelly."

"Look, why don't we go and sit at the bar," Charlie chimed in, becoming a little irritated at the attention Shelly was giving Graham. "Two Chivas, Harry. One for me and the lady. Graham, whatever you want, it's on your buddy, Charlie."

"A Coke will be fine," Graham insisted.

"No, Harry. Give my buddy a beer. It'll take the edge off of him."

Graham sat still, not bothering to look at Charlie. He wasn't sure how he allowed this to happen, but here he was where he didn't want to be. This was the last time Graham was going to let Charlie muscle him into doing something he didn't want to do.

"Where have you been all of my life?" Shelly purred, pulling on Graham's tie like he was a tuna fish fresh out of water.

"I've been with my wife and children," Graham said, hastily rescuing his tie from a surprised Shelly.

"Well, what are you doing here? You don't seem to be enjoying yourself," Shelly plowed on.

"His wife just passed," Charlie said, becoming even more perturbed that he had to explain it yet again.

"As in died?" Shelly asked, trying to make the connection. Her eyes widened and her mouth became a huge circle. "Ohh…Sugar, you must be awfully lonely…"

Graham jumped up from the stool and went hurriedly to the men's room. He was tired of hearing Charlie make explanations for his being in that dump. He didn't even want to be here. God, Amanda must be shaking a big finger at him. He could hear her say, *Couldn't wait for me to leave you before you went running back to that life of sin. Didn't I mean anything to you?*

No, baby, Graham said to himself. *It's not as it appears. I will always love you.*

Graham did his business and went back to the bar where Charlie and Shelly were deep in conversation. He'd try and stick it out, but this was the last time.

The small band picked up their instruments for the beginning of a new set. A long-legged, dark-skinned woman came to the stage. She appeared to be in her late forties or early fifties with a complexion as smooth as silk, and was wrapped in a black skin-tight dress that hit just above the knees. She plucked the mike gracefully from the stand and sat on the edge of a tall brass stool, poising herself for the first number. The band checked their pitch and then immediately went into some soft jazzy numbers. It was her intro—and Graham couldn't take his eyes off of her.

"I'm Rita Long, and this is my band, Midnight Express. I'm going to sing, and if you feel like clapping your hands, do so. If you feel the groove, let your groove thing swing. If you feel like making love, do it on your own time because right now, I want all of your attention."

"You got my attention!" yelled a large, burly man in the crowd. "You got my attention."

Couples jumped to the floor when Rita began singing. She started with a jazzy number called "Route 66." It had an upbeat tempo that made you just want to get up and click your heels. Charlie was on his second Chivas, and Shelly felt like dancing.

"Hey, Graham, why don't you dance with me?"

Graham waved his hand no, but no sooner had he done that, Shelly wrapped her hand around his wrist, snatching him up from his propped position at the bar and propelled him onto the stage. Graham was dumbfounded and stood in the middle of the crowd looking like the village idiot. "Dance!" someone shouted. "Dance."

Shelly took Graham's arm and flung him around—just like Amanda had done so long ago. *What was it with women?* He knew how to lead and be led; Graham just wasn't sure that he wanted Shelly to be the one to lead him. Shelly twirled him gracefully, showing him the steps that could possibly make him swing champion one day. After Graham got the hang of it, he actually started enjoying himself. He and Shelly must have danced the next four songs non-stop. Then Ms. Rita Long broke it down real slow.

Shelly pulled him close, brushing her ample breasts on his chest. That stirred something in Graham that he did not want stirred. He glanced over at Charlie who despite his fourth drink was not taking too kindly to Graham monopolizing all of Shelly's time.

"Why don't we sit this one out?" Graham suggested.

"Sugar, I was just beginning to enjoy the way your body was feeling next to mine."

"What about Charlie?"

"What about Charlie? Charlie's my good-time man—I like you."

Shelly held Graham in a vise grip, and even if he wanted to, Graham would not feel the padding of his seat for a while. Shelly held him hostage for the next four songs, grinding her body into Graham—inviting him to take a sample. But Graham stole quick glances at the lovely Ms. Rita every chance he got. She seemed like a real lady—like his Amanda was, only he found Amanda in the House of the Lord and Rita was at The Water Hole.

Graham finally sat down exhausted and drained with Shelly at his heels. She seemed to be a nice girl, but she definitely wasn't Graham's type. Her ample bosom and honey-blonde features didn't arouse him. Anyway, she was Charlie's girl, no matter what Ms. Shelly said.

Disappointment was all over Shelly's face as her attempts to charm Graham went unnoticed. "Let's go, Charlie. I'm bored here. Let's go back to your place."

"I've got to drop Graham off first, but after that, it's you and me, girl."

Graham didn't understand Charlie. But he had to admit, at age sixty-two, Charlie hadn't missed a beat. Graham wished, though, that Charlie could have settled down and been a real husband to Ernestine who had really loved Charlie but could not make Charlie love her back. *Women would always be in his blood; and no one woman would ever do.*

CHAPTER 7

It was after seven p.m. when Charlie finally dropped Graham off. There was no sign of life, and it was then that Graham remembered that the girls and their families as well as Sister Mary Ross were supposed to come by for dinner. Shame consumed Graham like the devil controlling a tormented soul. He had wanted to spend time with his girls, if only to make up for time he had mistreated them.

Graham noticed the note sticking from the door. In his haste to retrieve it, his shoe stubbed the side of a paper sack that was obviously left by Mary Ross. Graham lifted the sack from the porch, and shame rolled up over him once again.

The note was signed by Deborah stating that she and Elizabeth had come by to sit and comfort their father; however, he must have found comfort elsewhere. They were sorry they had missed him, but they would get in touch with him later in the week. Deborah acknowledged that Sister Ross had come by and left him a care package and how grateful she and Elizabeth were for all that Sister Ross had done in the wake of their mother's death. It was signed, *Love, Deborah*.

As much as he would have liked to been in the company of his daughters and their families, Graham was glad he was alone. He needed some time to reflect on the past twenty-four hours and the past two months. Graham walked to his room and took off his suit—hanging it neatly for the next time.

Snapshots of Rita Long hung about his eyelids. Visions of her chocolaty smooth satin skin danced circles around Graham. She probably didn't notice him, but he recalled every curve in her body, the shade of her lipstick, the color of her nail polish, the length of her eyelashes, the size of her breasts, and the shape of her lips when she sang "If This World Were Mine"—and he reached out to hold her, if only for one night.

"Amanda, Amanda, baby, don't be mad at me," Graham said aloud. "I was only looking…but she was very pretty. I felt guilty looking at her, you know—knowing that you are the only love for me, but I couldn't help but think that somehow Ms. Rita Long could share some of my love, too.

"I think you'd like her, 'Manda. She reminds me of you, although I've only seen her one time and have never spoken to her. Remember how enamored I was of you after seeing you for only half a second with those nut-brown legs and your pretty black hair turned up in a flip that bounced to the music?

"Forgive me, 'Manda. I've got to see her again. Nothing serious. Maybe some small talk, a walk in the park, a ride to the beach or out to dinner. I hope you don't mind. I love you, wherever you are. And for the record, it felt good being back in church. It really felt good."

Yes, it was a fairly good day, and as Graham prepared for bed, Rita Long flashed before him again. He didn't know why he couldn't get her off his mind, but there was something about that woman. Maybe she reminded him of Amanda, but there would never be another 'Manda as long as he lived.

With that Graham fell asleep, lost in his world—a world that existed without Amanda this night.

CHAPTER 8

Amanda went to dialysis several times a week before she died. Deborah and Elizabeth had jobs and families to attend to, so the chore was left to Graham. Going to the dialysis clinic with Amanda had become a ritual that forced him into early retirement. Now without Amanda to cuddle, retirement left Graham empty and lonely.

As Graham began to contemplate the rest of his life, thoughts of Rita Long surfaced again. He tried to shake the images that tried to engulf him, but something in the way she moved and caressed a song until there was no more life to it made Graham shiver. *It wouldn't hurt to go down to The Water Hole and hear her sing again*, Graham thought, *a little music to soothe the soul.*

Just as Graham reached for his coat to embark upon his new journey, there was a soft knock at the door. Graham wasn't expecting anyone, but he moved toward the door to see who his unsolicited guest was.

"Well, hello, Sister Ross. You're out early this afternoon."

"Hello, Deacon Peters. Just wanted to see if you got the food I left for you yesterday and if you might need something else."

"I'm doing just fine, Sister Ross. And yes, I received the food." Graham had other things on his mind and a visit with Sister Mary Ross was not it. Rita Long was waiting for him at the lounge, but Graham forced his anxiety about seeing her again to the background.

Sister Mary wore a straight, pastel-yellow shirtdress with a matching belt. She wore a pair of low, yellow sling-back shoes that held her shapely legs covered in mahogany-colored pantyhose. A white sweater made of acrylic was draped across Sister Mary's shoulders with the arms tied in the front like a makeshift collar.

"Well, Deacon, do you mind if I sit a spell? I had to walk two blocks from the bus stop, and I'm all out of breath. I could use a cold glass of water," Mary said, coughing for added effect.

"Please come in," Graham said, minding his manners but not offering Mary a seat. It was clear that Mary had other ideas on her brain and leaving wasn't one of them. He didn't want to be rude because she had been so good to him, but another day and another time would suit him fine.

Mary looked around the family room and made herself comfortable in the beige overstuffed loveseat that faced the fireplace. The mantle was filled with memories of the Peters' household.

"It's been awhile since I've been to your house, Deacon Peters. Amanda and I weren't as close as I'd like to have been. This room is so warm and cozy. I could be right comfortable here." Graham rolled his eyes. "Do you ever light your fireplace, Deacon?" Mary asked as he handed her the glass of water.

"Very seldom. Look…Sister Mary, I was on my way out. I've got to take care of some business. I really don't mean to rush, but…"

"That's all right, Deacon Peters. Maybe you can drop me off at my place. It's about fifteen minutes by car."

"I guess that won't be a problem." The longer she stayed, the longer Sister Mary would cut into his "Gotta See Rita Again" time.

"Well, thank you for the water. I can come by tomorrow; I'm cooking a big pot of chitlins and neckbones. It'll give you something different. You need somebody to watch after you."

"You've done enough already," Graham admonished. "There's no need to bring me anything else. Deborah and Elizabeth are stopping by later in the week to take me to dinner."

"Well, all right. Ahh, Deacon Peters…may I call you Graham?"

Graham stared at Mary trying to read into what she was saying.

"Graham," Mary plowed on without waiting for a reply, "you're a nice man. I know that it's been only two good months since Sister Amanda passed, but do you think we can…maybe…ahh…go out to a movie or dinner sometime?"

Graham was surprised at Mary's boldness where he thought there was none. She had totally caught him off guard. Sister Mary wasn't bad to look at and she did have that fine behind that made the hair on his chest stick out, but Graham's mind was traveling elsewhere, and Sister Mary Ross hadn't even been part of the equation.

Graham didn't want to hurt Sister Mary's feelings, but he saw no other recourse at the moment. A few days ago, life was empty and bleak, and now life was shouting out promises beyond his wildest dreams. But there would be no harm in going out to eat with Mary—he'd meet her somewhere and have a quick bite—nothing like a real date. "We'll see, Sister Mary…"

"You can call me Mary."

"Okay, Mary. We'll see."

♪♪♪

The drive to Mary's house was quiet and without incident. Mary eyed Graham from the corner of her eye, secretly taking in his form as he lazily drove the black Buick Regal with its white leather interior.

Mary wondered what business Graham had to take care of that demanded he leave his house in an abrupt manner that screamed emergency. The fragrance from the cologne that drenched his body was certainly much too sensual for an afternoon of taking care of business. He looked so striking in his off-white Polo sleeveless vest worn on top of a beige shirt and khaki slacks. A white golf cap sat on top of his head and completed the look that made Mary want to reach out and grab Graham and plant the juiciest kiss upon his lips.

Mary had dreamed off and on for the past ten years what it would be like to make love to Graham, Deacon Peters, despite the fact he was happily married to Amanda. Mary secretly held on to the hope that one day she'd have Graham, and she was not about to let the opportunity slip through her hands. She was a patient woman. Why, she had waited a lifetime! She could have married several times, but the prize she wanted was five feet eleven and already married. Her fire and desire rose like yeast bread every time she saw Deacon Peters. Her heart ached when she looked upon what didn't belong to her. Mary would wait as long as it took. Graham might not be interested now, but in time, he would be hers.

"If you need to go take care of your business first, I don't mind," Mary said, planting the first seed. "I could go along for the ride—it'll do me good to take a break from that house of mine."

"I'm sorry, Mary, maybe next time. I have some personal business to attend to and it may be awhile. But maybe we can get a bite to eat one evening, if your schedule permits."

"My calendar is open seven days a week, except for the hours of eight to one on Sundays. My God is first and foremost in my life and His time is sacred, but the rest is yours."

A small chuckle seeped from Graham's lips. He was tickled by Mary's outward display of affection for him, but her dwelling was the end of the line. "I'll call you in a few days," Graham said, pulling to the curb in front of Mary's house. "In a few days."

CHAPTER 9

Sister Mary Ross was harder to shake than lint balls on an old pair of pants. Graham felt a sudden sadness for Mary. It wasn't that she was unattractive or a bad cook. The truth was Graham's mind had been trapped by the subtle melodies of Rita Long.

The Water Hole lay in sight. One more stop sign before he'd be able to lay eyes on the scrumptious Rita.

The parking lot was sparse due to the earliness of the hour. The afternoon crowd was mainly made up of regulars.

Graham rushed from his car into the dimness of The Water Hole, not wanting another minute to lapse in his quest to fulfill his dream—just being in the presence of this woman who had taken liberties with his mind. A few solo acts sat at the bar, engaging the bartender in useless chatter. Graham gazed slowly around the room, not wanting to miss a spot, then to the stage with no sign of Rita. It never dawned on Graham that Rita and company wouldn't be performing until later that evening.

Graham sat dejected, angry with himself for operating blindly because his hormones were working overtime. He needed to get hold of himself and stop acting like a depraved old man in heat.

Graham was thankful there was no one he recognized, because he didn't feel like talking. He raised his hand, extending his index finger, hoping to catch the eye of the bartender. When he approached, Graham leaned slightly forward. "Let me have a shot of Johnny Walker," he whispered, a little tension in his voice.

"C'ming up," the bartender responded.

Graham nursed his drink dry. After forty-five minutes of wasted time and a dream unrealized, he decided to leave. Graham slithered off the chair and crossed the still densely populated room looking for the men's room. Although Graham's eyes were adjusted to the dimly lit interior of the lounge, he somehow had not gauged the collision course he found himself on.

Graham bumped head-on into a tall, thin dark-skinned woman as he had looked every which way except for straight ahead, hoping to get a glimpse of the fabulous songstress.

"Excuse me, Miss," an embarrassed Graham said, reaching out to steady the slightly shaken shapely woman, her face obscured because of the lighting. "I'm terribly sorry."

"It's okay," said the soft, seductive voice, tapping Graham's hand in reassurance.

The door to the men's room flew open, casting a fragment of light that briefly illuminated the face of the seductive voice. Graham's knees began to knock together as if a sudden artic chill had entered the room. She stood directly in front of him, albeit a tad bit shaken. Now he looked like a fool even though his chance encounter was too good to be true—totally unexpected. Graham vowed not to let this be a missed opportunity.

"Ms. Long...I'm truly embarrassed," Graham stuttered. "I heard you sing yesterday, and I've been mesmerized ever since. In fact, I came this afternoon hoping to hear you sing."

"That's nice of you to say..."

"Graham, Graham Peters."

Rita shook Graham's extended hand. "I appreciate you coming by, but I don't perform until this evening."

"I'll definitely be back. I've not heard such good jazz in a longggg time."

"Look, my band and I are getting ready to rehearse. Why don't you stay awhile and give me a nod on my selections?"

"Oh, yes," Graham said, unable to keep the excitement out of his voice. "I'll be there in a minute. Again, I apologize for my clumsiness."

"I'm fine. It's not every day I get to meet a fan *this way*."

"The pleasure is all mine."

They both smiled, and Graham walked into the men's room with an enormous grin on his face.

CHAPTER 10

Graham emerged from the men's room, fresh and excited. The old saying, "The whole world is a stage" came to mind. Graham felt as if he had a bit part in a play that was sure to be held over for weeks with the hero and heroine becoming stars of their own off-stage play.

Graham bounded effortlessly back into the lounge finding a table close to the stage. It seemed the chatter had increased in the fifteen minutes since he'd been gone. Graham sat in his seat twisting his body unconsciously left, then right in anticipation of seeing Rita again.

One of the scantily clad waitresses approached Graham, who ordered another whiskey. Preoccupied with his thoughts of Rita, Graham hadn't realized the waitress was trying to engage in small talk until she finally moved on.

There was a sudden clanging and bumping of what sounded like instruments. A tall, dark, lean man with a short goatee moved on stage hugging his electric bass guitar close to his chest with an amplifier in the other hand. A short, round fellow dressed in a white linen Cuban-styled shirt with khaki pants strutted behind the man with the guitar and swung a pair of drumsticks in his right hand. Another high-yellow man, tall in stature with extra large hands, strolled to the other side of the stage and picked up a cello that had leaned on a back wall waiting for its owner to reclaim him. And there she was, Miss Rita Long, her endless legs covered in denim jeans that must have been a size eight and her dark glistening skin two shades lighter than the ebony piano whose keys were now being tickled by the pianist.

All eyes were cast toward the stage—all movement frozen in time, waiting for the first warm-up note to release them from their trance. Graham was as entranced as the rest, but it would take more than a note or two from a guitarist's guitar, a cellist's cello, or a piano player's keyboard to break his spell.

Rita sat sideways on a stool placed center stage. She leaned slightly to her left, her right leg extended and her toe touching the floor. Her left leg was bent slightly with her left foot perched on the bar that encircled the three legs of the stool. Rita gave Graham a quick wink and immediately went through a brief repertoire of songs she and Midnight Express would sing that evening. She sang with elegance, grace, and style. Graham drank it all up without any distractions, nodding his consent to every song.

An hour passed. Midnight Express brought their rehearsal to a close—Graham's cue to leave. For sure, he'd be back tonight. He couldn't get enough of her—the voice helped him to forget how empty his life had been the last two months.

Only two shots of whiskey, but Graham felt a little tipsy. He'd ask God's forgiveness, for surely God understood his grief and the short detour to this dump. The Water Hole held a new treasure Graham wanted to claim.

As he tested his footing, a bold, blonde honeysuckle figure approached him from the side, tapping him on the shoulder.

"Oh, Shelly," Graham stammered.

"Why, Graham. You've made your way back to The Water Hole. I thought Charlie said you were grieving. I noticed you were mighty engrossed with the delights of Ms. Long."

"Look, Shelly, I don't know what you're talking about. I came here to get away from home. A little music never hurt anyone."

"That's true, however, I got the distinct feeling this was not your kind of groove. By the way, where are you on your way to?" It was time to set up her rook for the checkmate.

"Home. I'm on my way home. I'm a little tired," Graham lied.

"Well...well," Shelly continued, "why don't I go with you? Looks like you could use some company."

"No, I'm tired. And by the way, where's Charlie?"

"Charlie's your friend."

"That he is, however, I thought he was yours, too."

"Whatever."

There was pity for Shelly in Graham's eyes. He didn't understand what Charlie could possibly see in her other than a cheap date every once in a while. Whatever it was, Graham wanted no part of it. He disconnected his eyes from Shelly's and walked out, leaving her to contemplate just what had gone wrong with their conversation.

CHAPTER 11

It had been an exciting afternoon filled with unexplainable emotions and then some. Graham was becoming his old self, and he whistled a tune as he drove merrily toward home.

Charlie was always fun to have around, but this solo act was more enjoyable to Graham. He wasn't subjected to listening to a long list of Charlie's conquests and what Charlie thought he ought to be doing to get himself out of his doldrums. He loved Amanda, always would. And Rita Long, as mesmerizing as she was, would never take Amanda's place.

Graham's whistling had now become a hum. He waved to Sarah Baker, a retired schoolteacher, as he passed her watering her lawn this late fall day. Harry Byrd, who worked at the Naval yard with Graham before he retired, was painting his garage door when Graham drove by. Graham gave him a hearty wave and his hum became a broad smile.

Turning onto Chester Street, the tall oaks that stood at least forty feet high were inviting. Their autumn leaves welcomed Graham home. As he approached his house, Graham saw the black Lexus SUV parked in the driveway.

"Deborah must be here to check on me," Graham said aloud. He looked at his watch. It was 5:25, and he had every intention of being at The Water Hole at 7:30.

"Hey, Daddy," Deborah said, coming out of the house. She embraced him, and he hugged her in return.

"Hey, baby. Dropping by to check on your old man?"

"Yes, and I've got a surprise for you, too."

Graham's brow wrinkled. "Surprise? You made me a cherry cheesecake or some of your good ole macaroni and cheese just like your mama's?"

"No, Daddy. Come inside and see."

Deborah linked her arm through Graham's and walked into the house.

Graham could hear laughter in the kitchen and moved forward to see who was behind the commotion.

Graham stopped and stared, letting his head fall down slightly. He raised it, softly smiling. "Hi, Mom. It's so good to see you. I haven't seen you since…"

"Yeah, son. I miss my baby, too, but I know she's gone to be with the Lord."

"Hi, Daddy."

"Hi, Liz."

Graham embraced them all, and tears began their roll down his cheeks. Graham felt terrible for lusting after Rita Long. Amanda had been the love of his life for more years than he had fingers and toes, and this family gathering only served to remind him just how deep that love was.

"I stopped by Grandma's to see how she was doing. Daddy, she was more worried about your state of being than hers," Deborah said.

Martha was very dear to Graham, and he replaced his own beloved mother with that of his mother-in-law who had such a giving and wonderful heart. From the first day he stepped inside the big church on Market Street so many years ago, and was finally introduced to Amanda's parents, he felt as if Mr. and Mrs. Carter were his own. Just then, he thought of his sisters. They had come to Amanda's funeral. It had been fifteen years before then since he had seen them.

"Mom," Graham started, shaking old memories away, "if it was last week or the week before that, you'd probably have held your head down in shame. Today, I feel pretty good. Went to church for the first time yesterday…"

"Yes, he did," Deborah and Liz said in chorus.

"…And it was good being back amongst the saints. Reverend Fields preached a good sermon." Graham was quiet for a few minutes. Then he spoke. "I'm really sorry, Mom, for not checking on you and Dad. Amanda would be quite upset with me, I'm sure. I was so consumed by my own grief that I couldn't see others were equally grieving."

"It's okay, Graham. You're still my favorite son-in-law."

"Your *only* son-in-law."

The girls laughed.

Martha looked around the kitchen taking in every inch of Amanda as she scanned the room. From the two-tiered yellow gingham curtains to the apron, potholder, and towel set with the field of summer flowers on them. "'Manda is all in this room," Martha finally said, unable to control the urge to speak.

Graham looked at her and then turned away. Martha was right. Amanda was everywhere, and it was only as late as yesterday that he decided life had to go on. Graham looked at his watch, a feeling of guilt washing over him. Rita Long had to wait for some other time.

CHAPTER 12

The week progressed nicely. Thanks to his mother-in-law's appearance, Graham brought his life back into perspective. Grief for Amanda still lingered; however, Graham's outlook on life was taking on a new shape.

Dexter and Bobby came by to see if he wanted to go fishing, and agreed upon a date for early Friday morning with a promise of a no-repeat of their last outing together. The guys agreed that there wasn't going to be a Charlie to fish his non-swimming behind out of the water this time. As the guys reminisced about that day, it was hard for Graham to fathom that he had tried to kill himself—to follow Amanda to the grave. What could he have been thinking? It would be all about the fishing this time.

♪♪♪

Just as Graham settled down to have a bite to eat, the doorbell rang, interrupting what promised to be a quiet breakfast. "Lord, don't let that be Sister Mary Ross," Graham muttered aloud. "She'll be staying on the porch today."

After a relentless onslaught of rings that reminded Graham of hail pelting the ground, a familiar rat-a-tat found Graham's ears. "Charlie. What does Charlie want this early?" Graham stood and strode briskly to the front door, unlatching and unlocking so that his best friend could come in.

Upon opening the door, Charlie stood frozen on the porch. He let his eyes rove around, not really able to see much from his vantage point.

"Why are you still standing there? You were ringing the bell like you needed immediate refuge or the men's room."

"You all right?" Charlie asked at last, still standing at attention and never moving from the spot he had positioned himself. "Checking to make sure you haven't suffered a relapse and are still on the road to recovery."

"If you're going to come in, come in because my breakfast is getting cold."

"Got an extra plate?"

"Sister Mary hasn't come by today, thank goodness. So you'll have to watch me eat." They both let out a howl, and Charlie walked into the house at ease.

"Heard you been down to…The Water Hole," Charlie started, pulling up a chair to sit in. With no immediate response from Graham, Charlie plucked a toothpick from his front pocket and stuck it in his mouth. He watched Graham bite into his biscuit, butter oozing from its sides.

Thoughts of Rita Long lay in the recess of Graham's mind, but Charlie caused those dormant thoughts to be aroused. And as if on cue, Graham turned to Charlie, licking jam that had crept from the side of his biscuit onto his finger. "Yeah, I was there," Graham said, very nonchalant.

"Don't be on the defensive. I just thought you were not impressed with the place. You made such a big fuss about it!"

"And I'm still not impressed."

"So what made you go back there…and the next day, mind you?" Charlie asked, ignoring Graham's previous answer.

"Is this some sort of interrogation? It appears you already have the answers to your questions."

"All right, Graham. It does appear that I'm being a bit nosey, but…"

"A bit nosey? All up in my business. What you need to do is get rid of that blonde honey you call a girlfriend or whatever she is to you."

"All right. Give Shelly a break."

Graham put down his fork. He placed his elbows on the edge of the table and held his chin in his balled-up fist. He dropped his arms, folded them and stared straight into Charlie's eyes, got up and stood directly in front of him.

"Charlie, you're my best friend. Known you darn near most of my life. Been through a lot of things together. I'd like to see you find real happiness, if not true love, before I die." Charlie didn't move a muscle. "You've been wandering in the wilderness so long—in and out of bad relationships, accepting less than you're worth. For what—a laugh or two, a smile, acceptance? How do you measure life, Charlie? By how many women you wine and dine a week? How much alcohol you can consume in a day? How much sex you can have in a year? Huh, Charlie…?"

"Enough. You didn't have to go there."

"You'll stay out of my business next time," Graham muttered to himself.

Charlie paused for several minutes, then continued. "I was in love once, but she didn't even notice me. Never gave me the time or day. She slapped me in the face when I tried to get close. I'd watch her from afar, dreamed about her day and night, and when I realized I couldn't have her, I married Ernestine."

"You never confided that tidbit to me. Secrets…I thought we didn't have any of those."

"You had your life with Amanda. No one was interested in how ole Charlie felt about life. Besides, you'd probably slap me upside the head and give me another one of your great lectures." Charlie and Graham began to chuckle.

"I was always there for you, Charlie. Still am."

"I know, and that was a long time ago. You're still my brother." The two men embraced. "Let's go to The Water Hole."

"Hold on, and let me get my cap."

CHAPTER 13

"Hey, Rita. The crowd should be good tonight."

"Well, I hope so, Clyde. You know I always love to play Oakland just for that reason. I'm going to hate for Sunday to roll around. But I'll be back in two months, if you still want us."

"Who wouldn't want Midnight Express and the lovely and talented Ms. Rita Long? Girl, you make my customers happy, and in turn, they make me very happy."

Rita slapped Clyde on the arm. He was an old and dear friend and a true confidant. Clyde Smith had been the proprietor of The Water Hole for more than two decades. The Water Hole had become a landmark in West Oakland, and many had passed through the frosted, colored-glass doors looking for a good time or to have their blues assuaged.

Many small-time performers had graced the stage at The Water Hole, some using it as a stepping-stone to a lucrative recording career. Rita adored her small following of fans and never really aspired for the big time, although she was well known up and down the West Coast.

Rita hailed from Seattle, Washington, the sultry city on the Puget Sound, a place known for its haven of lush evergreen trees. She was an only child and grew up in a very nurturing family, a family where love abounds.

Marriage tested Rita's love for family. William Long had been a handsome man—dark like Rita and standing at six feet five inches tall. His rugged good looks commanded attention wherever he went. William played a few seasons for the Los Angeles Lakers, but after sustaining a severe knee injury, his career came to an abrupt halt.

William had become accustomed to the glamorous life an athlete's salary afforded him. While he had not yet risen to star status, William was very well on his way to being the next Wilt the "Stilt" Chamberlain or Bill Russell. Then his career was cut short. For a young man under thirty with a sizable salary, William lavished his wife with expensive gifts. Rita would later learn, other women were also benefactors of his generous spending.

William met Rita on a trip to Seattle while attending the wedding of one of his teammates. Rita was a friend of the bride, and gave a rousing rendition of "Close to You" at the nuptials reception. At that moment, William knew he wanted to get closer to this lovely woman whose poise and grace, along with her beautiful voice, had him mesmerized. It wasn't long before they became an item—an AP photo—and with William's basketball star on the rise, they held their lavish wedding on Valentine's Day with over one thousand in attendance.

And then the unexpected injury, the hospital stay, the prognosis, and the end of a career that had threatened to give Wilt Chamberlain's and Bill Russell's legacy a run for their money—and another legend for Michael Jordan to look up to. Rita watched day and night as William sunk from a vibrant, super athlete to a dismal, sullen, belligerent, and vengeful tyrant. He spent less time with Rita and more time with the bottle, and then he began to spend a lot of time at the gambling tables in Vegas, or wherever a high-stakes card game was going on, while dropping large sums of money in his wake. Finally, it was other women. Sometimes Rita wouldn't see William for a week at a time, and when he did decide to show up, he stumbled into the house in a drunken stupor.

It was the physical and mental abuse that took its toll and led Rita to seek an attorney to rid herself of the only other person outside of her parents that she loved. Rita couldn't understand why William preferred to bounce her off the wall instead of picking up a Wilson basketball and taking out his aggression on it. She loved this man more than life itself.

Through it all, Rita continued to sing, and she ended up with a cozy settlement to the tune of $10,000 a month.

Rita could have chosen her own lot, but she was comfortable sharing her gift of song at the small clubs up and down the Pacific Northwest with little or no fanfare, and a following all her own. So she found herself once again in Oakland giving her fans a little of what they craved and keeping a little for herself. But it was the attractive, sexy older gentleman Rita had bumped into a few nights ago, who claimed to be present at all of her sets, that caught her rapt attention—a spark that ignited a low-burning ember.

The soft sound of the brush caressing the drums met Rita's ears as she entered the lounge. She smiled. The band was already warming up; the guitar being tweaked, and the low mellow hum of the cello put Rita in a real funky mood. She smiled again. Tonight, she felt like singing.

♪♪♪

Graham wasn't sure what possessed him, but he let Charlie talk him into going to the health club and getting his Tae-Bo on. But it was obvious that Graham enjoyed it—in fact, he hadn't had that kind of fun in years. And that's not taking away from the wonderful years he and Amanda had shared. Something about the muscular sistahs, bodies encased in sculptured frames only Picasso's brush could capture, who stood gawking at the pair of over-fifty gentlemen. Graham couldn't count the number of high-fives passed between him and Charlie.

Graham and Charlie strolled into The Water Hole at 3:35. They sauntered into the dark lounge like a precision drill team. Music met their ears. But it was the distinguishable Ms. Rita Long's voice that caused Graham to experience a twinge of anxiety.

The duo found a small table and planted themselves there against the protest of Charlie who was a die-hard bar man. "Tables are for lovers," Charlie snapped.

"And bar stools are for fools with a tired rap," Graham countered.

Charlie smiled. "Are you in love?"

Before Graham could reply, the waitress appeared at their table. She slid a small piece of paper into Graham's hand as in a well-rehearsed scene in a spy movie. Graham hesitated, then slowly lifted his eyes in the direction of the waitress, passing between them a silent message of acknowledgment. He wasn't sure what he was acknowledging, but revelation was a short minute away.

"May I take your order, please?" the waitress asked, carrying out her duty as if nothing else had transpired.

"Coke for me," Graham said.

"And a…"

"Chivas," the waitress said, patting Charlie on the back. "I'll be back in a sec."

The paper grew moist smothered in Graham's hand. He wanted to open it, lay eyes upon the content, and hoped it was the bearer of good tidings. Making excuses to go to the men's room were getting a little old, but the mystery that lay inside the folded sheet of paper got the best of him.

Charlie looked at Graham once again. "Are you all right?" Charlie asked, frown lines plastered across his forehead. "You seem agitated and restless."

"Yeah, yeah. I guess I was thinking about Amanda," Graham lied.

Charlie relaxed. "Well, Ms. Long has been eyeing you for longer than a minute. Now, she's a fine woman. Comes to Oakland quite a bit. Used to be married to that basketball star on the Lakers years ago. What's his name?" Charlie questioned himself, snapping his fingers in hopes of jogging his memory.

"Not William Long?"

"Yeah, that's him. Heard he treated the lady pretty bad, although she bears no visible scars."

Graham digested Charlie's words. He took a quick glance in Rita's direction; and she appeared to be staring straight into his soul. Then Graham remembered the paper that was still folded in his hand. "I've got to go to the restroom. Be right back."

"There you go again. You need surgery for that leaky bladder of yours."

Graham turned around and gave Charlie a half-smile. "If the faucet is running, you've gotta do whatever it takes to turn it off."

"Handle it!" Charlie put in. "And no pun intended."

Graham raced to the restroom eager to put some distance between he and Charlie. The temperature of his hand caused the paper to be matted. Graham found a stall and gently shut the door, trying not to attract attention.

He fumbled with the paper and then quickly unfolded it. Not able to wait any longer, his eyes went directly for the signature line that read "Rita."

The fluttering of the heart could mean only two things: either you are getting ready to experience a heart attack and possible death or you've just simply died and gone to Heaven. Graham squeezed the paper tight, then willed himself to open his palm so that he might read the rest of the note.

Hi there. I was afraid I wouldn't see you again. I looked for you Monday evening, but was disappointed when you didn't appear. Maybe we could have a drink after I rehearse. Give me a nod if we're on. Rita.

He wanted to jump for joy, climb the highest mountain. Nerves took over and then a sly grin. Graham shut his eyes for a second, looked at the paper again, crumpled it in his hand and screamed, "Yes!"

"Are you all right in there?" came a concerned voice from another stall. Embarrassed by his outburst, Graham flushed the unused toilet and practically ran from the room. He slowed his gait when he noticed Charlie watching him. Had he somehow changed? Had Charlie picked up on it?

Graham reached the table and faced Charlie head-on. "I feel better now." Charlie sat and stared with a puzzled look on his face.

Midnight Express was already ten minutes into rehearsal. The patrons streamed in slowly—many of them retired folk who were there to pass the time. Colorful conversations and laughter were there for the asking. Some folks stopped talking, then patted their feet while the group rehearsed. Others rolled on with their conversations, heads bopping to the beat.

Graham eased back into his chair, positioning himself so he could have a good view of Ms. Rita Long whenever he dared take a peek at the stage. Getting up enough courage to look, the stage appeared to be much closer than it was the other day. Gravity pulled Graham's eyelids up, and Rita came into view. She appeared to be only an arm's length away. She seemed to sing straight into Graham's heart, closing her eyes periodically as the lyrics drove her to the zenith.

There was a slight nod of Graham's head. Rita momentarily opened her eyes, caressing the song—a song Graham had unconsciously claimed as his and Rita's. Charlie caught Graham's slight movement, but said nothing and held it amongst the other mental notes he was stockpiling.

Rita came from out of her trance-like state slowly, moving into a soft banter. "I promised to spend my whole life with you," she sang, "neva leave you, nor forsake you… but you let me down, left me all alone. And I got a new friend now who promised he'd never leave." And she nodded her head in Graham's direction. He understood, taking a handkerchief from his breast pocket to wipe the sweat away from his forehead.

Excitement and energy mounted as Graham anticipated his rendezvous with the lovely Rita. How to dodge Charlie was the larger task.

Rehearsal ended twenty-two minutes later. Graham sat in his seat, unsure of his next move. Charlie was engaged in light conversation—a few buddies from the hometown, laughing and talking about old times.

A sudden shadow crept over Graham making him feel uneasy. The sudden hush and the three pairs of eyes now peering in his direction confirmed that he had just become the center of attention.

"Hello," Rita whispered softly while Graham scrambled to his feet. He could not erase the smile that stretched across his face. Charlie silently mocked him, slightly jealous for not being privy to what was going on in front of him.

"Hello, Rita," was Graham's reply. "Would you like to have a seat?"

"That would be nice." Rita eased into the seat Graham held out for her. Realizing that their presence bordered on intrusion, Charlie's homeboys bid farewell.

"Rita, this is my good friend Charlie."

"Hey, Charlie." Rita touched his arm. "Charlie has been a regular at The Water Hole as long as I've been singing here, I believe," Rita said, turning to Graham. "Everyone has always been so good to me here; it's like home."

"It's good to see you too, Rita. Who would have thought that after all this time, I would be graced with your presence at my very own table?" Charlie reached into his shirt pocket and pulled out a toothpick, something he seemed to do a lot when his nerves were pricked.

Graham detected a hint of cynicism in Charlie's voice. Did Charlie like Rita once? Graham couldn't remember Charlie ever mentioning Rita Long in that vein even though it would be hard to not want to get to know her. Charlie was too busy with the easy-women hustle. A real woman would have eluded him.

"I enjoyed your set," Graham said nervously trying to find something to say. He hadn't courted in over forty years, and this was all new to him.

"Well, I hope you'll catch the real act tonight, and I promise you a real treat."

"I'll be here. Would you like something to drink?"

"A club soda is fine." Graham signaled for the waitress who he sensed felt a partnership in whatever was going on.

"Uhh…how long will you be here this time, Rita?" Charlie asked.

"Through Sunday, then we'll head back to Seattle."

Graham slightly jerked his head upward. The "through Sunday" caught him off guard. He had just met this woman who had stirred something inside of him. Surely, she didn't mean *this* Sunday. That was four days from now. How could he possibly get to know someone in that short period of time?

"I'll be back in a couple of months. I have to go home and take care of some business, and I have a couple of engagements in Seattle and Portland."

"Well, don't stay away too long. I think my friend has a craving for you."

Rita smiled and Graham puckered his lips as if to say something but thought better of it.

"Two months isn't that far from now."

Things weren't going exactly how Graham had envisioned. He wanted to be alone with Rita in hopes of getting to know her better. Charlie insisted on staying at the table, and Graham was forced to make the best of the situation.

Light jazz was piped in through the sound system. David Sanborn, Najee, Grover, and Miles kept the patrons entertained. A sudden inspiration hit Graham who now summoned enough courage to ask Rita to dance.

Without hesitation, Rita jumped from her seat into Graham's waiting arms. They were swinging, then shuffling, finally ending up in the dance couple's embrace—the song made only for them, lost in their own thoughts. All eyes were on Rita and Graham, and soon other couples joined in. Charlie sat in his seat and scowled.

"You're lovely."

"Thank you," Rita said modestly. "I thought we'd never get away from Charlie."

"Me neither. He seems to have eyes for you."

"I think he's just surprised. I've known him a long time, and I think he might have been sweet on me at one time. Nothing ever came of it."

"I see."

They danced in silence, each consumed in their own thoughts—thoughts of Charlie.

Charlie was a handsome fellow, and there was a time when Rita wanted the likes of a Charlie Ford to take her home, pamper her, make love to her, and introduce her to all of his friends. It was plainly obvious that Charlie was a good-time man—a man about town who loved the women; but Rita already had had her good-time man.

William had been trying for years to get back with Rita. She was a real woman, and unfortunately William realized that just a little too late.

"Look, don't worry about Charlie," Rita said, breaking the silence. "Besides, we didn't get up to dance to talk about him. You seem like a nice guy. I've noticed that you've been by yourself."

"Yes," Graham hesitated. "I'm a recent widower."

"Oh," Rita said, allowing some air to escape from her mouth. *Rebound,* she thought.

"Believe me, I've grieved awhile. Didn't want to have anything to do with anyone. It was Charlie who saved me from myself. Amanda, that was my wife's name, released me too. We shared a wonderful life together, and I thought that there could never be anyone else. Then…I came in here, and I heard your magnificent voice."

Rita smiled. She pulled back slightly and gave Graham the most gracious smile. "There was something about your posture and the way you looked at me the first time we met. I couldn't put my finger on it, but something inside me wanted to get to know you."

"I have a confession to make. The Water Hole was the last place I wanted to come to. I had not graced the inside of one of these places since Amanda and I got married. That doesn't mean that our life was boring, but our life was with our family and the church.

"Charlie and I have been friends since junior high school. I followed him here to California, and friends we will always be. In fact, we're like brothers. This lifestyle has always been a part of his life. That first Sunday that I saw you, Charlie was helping me to get my life back on track. Imagine Charlie helping me to get my life on track."

"He's a good friend, that I can see."

"He really is, and I'd do anything for him."

"I'd like to get to know you better."

"I'd like that very much. I'll drive my car tonight, and maybe we can go somewhere after you've finished for the night and get something to eat."

"I'd like that. Well, that song has finished, and Charlie is looking a little bit lonely."

"He'll survive. He always does."

CHAPTER 14

Graham was ecstatic. Couldn't wait for tonight to come. Rita Long consumed all of his time, his thoughts, and every daydream. Graham thought he heard Amanda's voice lurking in the shadows, but the reassuring calm that came over him more than confirmed that, in his mind, Amanda had given her approval. And, as if he knew what Amanda might be thinking, *No, Sister Mary Ross never stood a chance.*

Although Amanda loved the Lord and was a good Christian, she and Sister Mary Ross were never the best of friends. Amanda had known that from the moment Mary Ross set foot in the church on Market Street, she had hopes of snagging Graham for herself. But Amanda had given Graham the best years of her life, along with some good sweet loving and two beautiful daughters. And Graham had been satisfied.

Now Amanda was gone, and as fate would have it, another blessing stood before him. She was sweet, beautiful, and had a voice like a sparrow. Boy, she could sing. Graham glanced at his watch. It was almost six. He wanted to get a good seat up front so that Rita would never be out of his sight.

He looked in the bathroom mirror once more. "Looking good there, old fellow." Graham picked up the bottle of Armani aftershave that Deborah had given him for Christmas and splashed some on both cheeks and down the front of his neck. Graham had aged, but he still looked good. He examined his gray pin-striped, double-breasted Brooks Brothers suit he had just worn on Sunday. Rita probably hadn't even noticed.

Graham did a once around in the living room, threw a kiss at Amanda's picture that sat on the mantel over the fireplace, gave a nod of approval to the mirror, and proceeded to do the George Jefferson walk—waddling out of the door. He looked back reassuring himself that all was well, should the night turn into more than expected. This was a move even Graham had not anticipated before this afternoon—*that is* allowing someone else other than his wife to come into his home. Just in case, he was ready.

The sun had set, and the random cars that passed by their occupants on their way home from a hard day's work made Graham come alive. *Nighttime is the right time*, he had heard someone sing. Something about the night air, the night grooves, a nightclub, and listening to your favorite singer sing songs of love and tenderness—messing with your love groove, your smooth move—that did nothing but pump up Graham's adrenaline.

The hardest part of the evening was making Charlie understand that he wanted to go to the club alone. And the sad part was that Charlie made him spell out why, as if he didn't have a clue. Charlie had a cauldron of women that he could choose from, but why was it that he always seemed to be interested in the one Graham was interested in?

It was the same with Amanda those long years ago. Graham noticed how Charlie hung around all the time, and after the wedding, Charlie was a ghost for several months until he could no longer stay away. And then they couldn't get rid of him—always hanging around at dinnertime and at other family gatherings—but Charlie would always have a girl with him, even if the girls were not the same from week to week. Charlie was family.

♪♪♪

The crowd was alive. If hump day was a day set aside for celebration, there was no more room to accommodate those who were trying to get over the hump. It was definitely the Fourth of July in the place tonight. It was much more festive than earlier in the day. Graham scanned the place hoping to avoid familiar faces, especially Charlie. Though the lighting made it difficult to see, there was no evidence of Charlie or Shelly anywhere.

Graham proceeded through the dense crowd, a mix of the young and old. The younger women wore stiletto heels with skin-tight lycra skirts and halter-tops that looked like designer bras and left very little to the imagination. The older women wore Rena Rowan and Ralph Lauren pantsuits accessorized with designer costume jewelry. It was no secret that those women who were unescorted, young and old, were looking for a good time, a playmate, or a way to a better life.

Graham was sorry he had not come earlier. He hated competing with the crowd for a seat. Now surely he would not get a table, let alone a seat. Just as he was about to give up and stand by the wall, the waitress who had placed the note in his hand earlier and wore close to nothing grabbed him by the arm. She wore a sensuous smile on her face.

"Got a special place for you tonight."

Astonishment crossed Graham's face.

"Ms. Long reserved a special table for you and asked me to make sure you were taken care of as soon as you came in."

Speechless was not the word. Graham couldn't pry his lips apart. There was a gleam in his eyes that the waitress understood.

"You don't have to say anything. I'm just as surprised as you are. I've been working here nearly four years, and in all that time, I've never seen Ms. Long make a fuss over anybody."

"I'm sorry," Graham stuttered. "Thank you. Your name?" Graham couldn't control his breathing, exhaling large doses of air. He was just like a school-boy on a first date.

"Natalie."

"That's a pretty name, Natalie."

"Thank you."

Graham followed Natalie to the middle of the room, then front and center where a small table was set for two. Adorning the table was a single candle and a bottle of champagne sitting in a bucket, chilled to perfection.

"Please thank Ms. Long for me," Graham said, looking up at Natalie, "and tell her that I will chat with her after her sets."

"I'll be sure to tell her." And Natalie moved on to the next customer.

Graham quickly sat in his seat not daring to look around, feeling more pairs of eyes than he could count. He twiddled his fingers, then caressed the neck of the champagne bottle. Graham wasn't sure whether he should open it or wait for Rita. Waiting for Rita might take awhile, so he busied himself with opening up the corkless bottle of champagne and poured himself a glass.

Norman Brown's "After the Storm" filled the room. Graham felt on top of the world. He felt his head nodding to the smooth jazz as he finished off his first glass of the bubbly. Graham poured another glass deciding to take it slow—sipping and nurturing the taste of the champagne, wanting it to last as long as he hoped the night would. He caressed, fingered, stroked, and smoothed the glass of bubbly, finally taking a sip only to repeat the sequence again.

"May I sit down," a familiar voice said, startling Graham as she came from behind him. "You seem awfully lonely sitting here."

"Not anymore, and it would be my pleasure to have such a beautiful woman as yourself share this table with me." Graham immediately jumped to his feet, pulling out the chair for Rita. "After all, it is I who owe you gratitude. My timing was off, and if it hadn't been for you, I would not have had a place to sit."

"No need to thank me. The pleasure was all mine. I have fifteen minutes before I go on, so I decided to surprise you and come and say hello."

Graham could not peel his eyes from Rita. Her hair was brushed in an upsweep with small tendrils falling about her face. Her dark cocoa complexion glistened under the candlelight, and her teeth sparkled like diamonds.

Rita wore a silver-and-black dress belted around the waist with a strapless left shoulder. The bodice was made of silver lamé with small, beaded flowers sprinkled throughout. The full skirt was made of black satin that fell three inches below her knees. It was made for swinging. Her three-inch satin T-strap heels were set off by rhinestone buttons that joined the "T" to the shoe, and the rhinestone earrings that hung down the side of her face like upside-down Christmas trees accentuated her keen facial features. She looked as if she had been chiseled from marble. She was flawless in Graham's eyesight, and if she never sang again, gazing upon her beauty was enough for him.

"I'm glad you surprised me. I feel I can hang on until the show is over."

"You're too kind," Rita said softly in her most sensuous voice.

"It's only the truth. How about we drink to us?" Graham whispered, pouring Rita a glass of champagne.

"I'd like that."

"To us." And the glasses rose to their lips while their eyes locked onto each other. They sipped, and then she was gone.

CHAPTER 15

Rita and Midnight Express started off with some real jazzy and swinging numbers. Couples hit the dance floor, lost in their own little worlds. Waitresses flitted back and forth in an attempt to keep glasses full. Women without partners danced by themselves, or with other women if the song dictated, especially when the Electric Slide was in order. The men who were not dancing held up the bar, engaging in light conversation with old buddies or women who sought other than a dance.

Graham finished his second glass and was making himself comfortable when Shelly appeared. "May I sit?" Shelly asked. Dropping her head slightly to the side, she bent over just enough for Graham to gaze upon her ample bosom.

"No, that seat is taken."

"Well, I don't see anyone sitting here." Shelly sat anyway. "If they come back, I'll be more than happy to get up."

"Suit yourself."

Shelly reached for the champagne, but Graham politely lifted her hand from the bottle before she could get a firm grasp. "What kind of man are you? Selfish little bastard. I've never been treated this way before. It's evident you've never been with a woman of my caliber."

"Maybe next time you can save face when someone tells you the table is occupied. And no, I've never been with a woman of *your caliber*, whatever that might happen to be."

"You bastard," Shelly hissed as Charlie rushed over to assist.

Charlie had sat in the corner observing his friend who for the last two months had all but given up on life because the love of his life, Amanda, had died. Now Graham was a revived gigolo and getting more action than Charlie had seen himself in months.

"Hey, buddy. I'll take care of her," Charlie said, giving Graham a wink and pulling Shelly away from the table. "Handle your business."

"I will," Graham mumbled back.

"No one asked for your assistance," Shelly grumbled as Charlie led her away. "I can take care of myself and take your hands off of me."

"Shelly, cut the crap and be glad somebody is paying you any attention." Charlie loosed his grip on Shelly instructing her to sit at the bar, which she did without resistance. Shelly glanced back at Graham who had already turned his attention to Midnight Express and the lovely Rita, who was well on her way to making this night one to be talked about for a long time.

♪♪♪

Graham tapped, sang along, and drank, enjoying the mood and the unforgettable love songs Rita cajoled her audience to partake in. Those in love seemed drunk from the fires that erupted when Rita sang. Yes, Rita sung the folks happy tonight. And those without a special someone now looked for someone they could get close to and ride the waves of love and lust—flying high from the melodies that Ms. Rita Long flung their way.

Graham waited patiently for Rita to come from her dressing room. He was smitten with the same fire. Rita was in his blood. People continued to chat long after Midnight Express completed its set. Charlie and Shelly had long since bid farewell, and Graham felt more at ease.

Rita emerged wearing a black, low-cut, cowl-neck slinky number that set off all of her curves. Graham hid his disappointment. It was not the gorgeous silver-and-black dress she wore earlier in the evening when she called out his name and sang songs of love to him, making him wait in anticipation to be close to her. However, disappointment evaporated quickly when she got up on him, so close he could smell her sweet perfume, making him want to drop his head in her bosom.

Rita looked down her long, thick eyelashes that spread out like fans. Graham finally looked up, willing himself up from his chair. Their faces were close enough to rub noses like Eskimos, and their breath left traces of fog between the fenceless boundary that separated their lips.

"You were wonderful tonight. I couldn't keep my eyes off you."

"Thank you. I'm glad you enjoyed it."

"Why don't we go somewhere that's a little more private? And this time, I'll buy the champagne."

"I'd like that. Let me say goodnight to Clyde and the Midnight crew."

"I'll be waiting right here when you get back." The grin on Graham's face was as wide as a six-lane highway. No one could blame him; love had struck again, and it felt mighty good. Mighty, mighty good.

CHAPTER 16

They drove through the heart of Oakland, going east on Interstate 580, eventually leaving the highway at 105th Avenue and venturing into the Oakland hills. The skyline provided a breathtaking view with thousands of tiny lights illuminating the sprawling city. And further west was the San Francisco Bay. The city was home to the Oakland Raiders and across the bay, the San Francisco 49ers. The Oakland/San Francisco Bay Bridge walked across the bay, a string of lights denoting its location. Aircraft came from all destinations across the U.S., Canada, and other foreign soil announcing their desire to land at either Oakland or San Francisco International airports.

A full moon illuminated the sky signaling the completion of its rotation for the month. Graham parked the car along the side of the road in the utmost part of the Oakland Hills that overlooked the city. He rolled down the window and sat close to Rita, little spots against the giant moon. *Rita feels so right*, Graham thought. He wondered what his daughters would think. It had been only two months since Amanda died.

Panic struck him straight in the heart. *What was he thinking? What would people think? And why would a beautiful woman want to be with a sixty-one-year-old man with one foot in the grave and the other on a banana peel? I've been with no other woman but my wife for the last forty years*, Graham thought. *Am I doing the right thing?*

Graham's mind was racing. Now Amanda stood before him peering down at him and Rita while they watched the moon. *'Manda, baby*, Graham's subconscious began, *I love you, and now that you're gone, I don't know how I'm gonna make it. I thought that I could love no one but you, but someone else has found their way into my life, and I think I'm in love with her.* Graham was frightened by his own admission.

No disrespect, 'Manda, because you were my life, my reason for being, the mother of our children who gave me everything I could ever hope for in this life. I could never love another the way that I love you. But I hope you understand, 'Manda, that this thing with Rita will not replace the memories of you and our love, but will help me to go on and lead a normal life until I see you again.

I do believe I'm falling in love with Rita, and it's only fair that I give her the best of what's left in me, if that's what she wants. Say you understand, 'Manda. I've been toiling with this a few days. I know that Deborah and Liz probably won't understand. They'll say, it's too soon, that I'm disrespecting you, God, and the church. I know they'll say that I'm an old fool, but if I have your blessing, it won't matter what anyone else thinks. I'll wait to hear from you, 'Manda.

Rita placed her hand on Graham's arm. "You okay, Graham? You seem far away. You seem a little jittery all of a sudden."

"Oh, I'm fine. Just thinking about how blessed I am." Graham turned to face Rita who made him drunk just gazing upon her. "You're a beautiful woman, Rita Long. I'm not sure that I deserve you."

"And what makes you say that?"

"Oh, I don't know. I guess I was just thinking…"

"About your wife?"

"How did you know?"

"It's only natural. A lot of things cross your mind. Am I doing the right thing? What will people think? I was thinking, what would my mother and father say? It's part of the human drama. I experienced a different death, but yet somewhat the same. You grieve, you resist new love, you question God, you resist, your heart softens, you give in a little, you resist, you give in some more, then some more, you give in, then you question if what you've just done was the right decision. Been there, done that."

"Girl, you are too much for me. How did you become so wise?"

"Life's lessons."

Graham was silent—a fresh breeze hitting his face from the open window. His eyes roamed Rita's face and she twitched under his gaze. He moved closer to her and opened his mouth, then moved back an inch. "May I kiss you, Ms. Rita Long? I'd love to kiss those sweet lips of yours."

They giggled like teenagers until silence overtook them. Only the sounds of passionate kissing beat out the silence, the backdrop for a new kind of melody. They needed each other, and Graham knew that he would have to talk with Amanda again about this new event in his life.

♪♪♪

After an early-morning breakfast at a local IHOP, Graham drove to Jack London Square where he and Rita walked along the marina. It was cool, and Graham took off his jacket and placed it around Rita's shoulders. They walked slowly, sucking in the brisk air and the gentle breeze that rose from the water. The silhouette of the boats docked along the marina swayed in the water, casting shadows wherever the tall lampposts illuminated them.

Rita and Graham stole kisses as they walked, not wanting to miss an opportunity during the short time they had together.

"I still owe you that bottle of champagne."

"Maybe tomorrow. It's probably time for us to call it a morning; it's three a.m." She smiled.

"You're probably right, in fact, I know you're right. What was I thinking about…keeping a pretty girl out all night?" They laughed softly.

"You're an incredible man, Graham. I'd really like to get to know you better."

"I'd like to get to know you better, too, Rita Long. But right now, I had better get you back to your hotel."

They walked silently, hand in hand toward the car, Rita's back protected from the chilly breeze by Graham's jacket. Rita paused, turned and smiled at Graham.

"New beginnings," said Rita.

"There is life after death," Graham whispered only loud enough for Rita to hear.

The pair stood, silently sharing this most perfect moment. Resurrection was at hand.

CHAPTER 17

Thursday came and went. It was midday on Friday before Graham realized he had missed his fishing trip with Dexter and Bobby. Had they called? He would have to make it up to them. Now it was Saturday.

The last couple of days were completely consumed with Rita. She and Graham couldn't get enough of each other. Graham was now a regular at The Water Hole with his own reserved table. He hadn't missed a night of Rita's performance. After hours, Graham and Rita talked late into the night over a light meal or on the phone after he'd dropped her off at her hotel. They shared thoughts on the future and snuck a telephone kiss here and there. They were in each other's system.

Graham gave no further thought to what others might think or say. Rita had come into his life, and that was that. Even Charlie noticed the difference in Graham and purposely remained distant, feeling somewhat abandoned. It was just a phase. Surely, there would be someone else when Rita ventured to another city.

Rita would leave on Monday. It was now Saturday afternoon. A nagging thought had plagued Graham for two days. He wanted to bring Rita home. The home he once shared with Amanda and his girls. The home that held memories of him making love to the woman who captivated him for the last forty years. Memories of children born, of barbecues and great get-togethers, graduation picnics, memories of quiet nights of just he and Amanda, and memories of family and friends coming by to pay their last respects to a virtuous woman who gave him all the love that any one woman could give a man. He had a dilemma.

He wanted to share more of himself with Rita. He wanted her to know that his feelings were more than a lonely man in need of love. He wanted her to know what made him tick. Graham wanted Rita to know that he was falling in love with her, wanted to be with her, wanted her to stay with him so that he could take care of her and shield her from harm, and to make love to her.

These thoughts plagued him all night. Amanda must have been busy with her angelic duties or didn't care, because she had not paid him a visit on the matter. Graham grabbed his coat and hurried out the door. He'd let nature take its course. Whatever nature dictated, he'd follow.

♪♪♪

When Graham arrived at The Water Hole around 6:30 p.m., the parking lot was already half full. Charlie's car was parked at the far end. Graham had ignored his friend the past few days, and when he got a chance, he'd go to Charlie to set things straight. Right now, he needed to be alone with Rita. Surely, Charlie could understand that.

"Hey, Graham!" Clyde yelled, giving Graham a high-five. "Got my girl's nose open."

"Clyde," Graham whispered a little embarrassed at Clyde's announcement. "I'm in love with her."

"Oh," Clyde said. "It's worse than I thought. Congratulations, man, 'cause she must be in love, too. I haven't heard her sing like this in a long time. Go on in and have a good time. Talk with you later."

"Yeah, Clyde."

Graham was anxious to get away from Clyde. Graham was never a loud person. That was probably why it was important for him to separate himself from Charlie these last few days. Charlie was Mister Goodtime. Always the jokester, he never seemed to have a serious bone in his body. It was all right when they were growing up as kids and teenagers, and Charlie was his best buddy, but Graham didn't entertain all the silly antics that were so characteristic of Charlie.

Everyone was dressed to the nines. It seemed the brothers had purchased every three-piece suit that was for sale: Black-and-white pin-stripes, blue-and-white pin-stripes, with fly-away collars and button-down jackets hiding matched silk vests accentuated by either Christian Dior or Calvin Klein ties. Likewise, Macy's, Nordstrom, and Saks Fifth Avenue must have taken in an estimated $5,000 in African-American plastic to dress the sistahs who were laid out at The Water Hole on this evening.

The lighting was dim as Graham made his way through the dense crowd. He spotted Charlie, who turned his head when Graham looked his way. Talking with Charlie would be on his priority list. Some couples were already on the dance floor getting their groove on. Graham wanted to get to his table so he could get his own groove going.

No visitors stopped by Graham's table to chat other than Natalie, and that was only to see if she could freshen his drink. Graham looked toward the bar, catching Charlie staring at him while a toothpick dangled from his lips. Graham motioned for him to come and sit. Charlie remained positioned at his post.

A rather plump, caramel-popcorn-colored woman strolled up to Graham's table. "Sweetie, you wanna dance?"

"No, I'm fine. Maybe another time."

"Come on, honey. I just love this song, and it's going to be over in a minute."

"Really, I'm not...on the other hand, I think I could stand to work up a little sweat."

Shelly stood a few feet away with hands on her hips and watched as Graham and the pleasingly plump lady whirled onto the dance floor. After a minute, suddenly tiring of her watch, she strolled over to Charlie at the bar, gingerly planting a kiss on his lips that he did not return.

Graham danced for three numbers and rather enjoyed himself but begged out with the announcement that Rita Long and Midnight Express would be on in a few minutes. Graham scrambled to his chair and wiped his forehead of sweat with a handkerchief. He picked up the chilled bottle of champagne and cradled it in his hand. He was drinking an awful lot of the stuff lately but a little wouldn't hurt.

The crowd was thunderous as they gave a hearty clap to Rita and Midnight Express. Whistling sounds could be heard above the clapping. Everyone seemed alive and vibrant. Local talent stopped by to catch a glimpse of Rita and drink up the sounds, old and new, she threw their way. Swirls of smoke like cumulus clouds enveloped the place as Newports, Camels, and Marlboros dangled from the sides of mouths that all the while engaged in conversation that had lips moving ninety miles an hour. Glasses clinking as Johnnie Walker and Southern Comfort hit the rocks only added to the sound of gaiety.

Rita belted out song after song utilizing every inch of her vocal chords, provoking some to take a walk down memory lane, others to whisper sweet nothings in their lover's ears, and some to just move with the groove.

During intermission, Rita came and sat with Graham whose eyes swallowed her whole in all her radiant splendor. Rita had chosen a swanky, slate-blue chiffon, sleeveless dress with matching sling-back pumps. A bold, platinum necklace with a two-carat diamond-teardrop pendant hung proudly around her neck with a half-carat each, teardrop pendant earrings secure on her small ear lobes. Rita wore a fiery-red lipstick that made her dark complexion come alive, and her long, thick lashes played foreground for the silver-blue background that enhanced her almond-shaped eyes two-fold.

"You look good enough to eat, and I'm hungry." Graham laughed nervously, trying his stint at being funny.

"They don't call me the chocolate diva for nothing, but I hope you'll settle for a Snickers bar instead." Graham and Rita broke out laughing.

Rita sat down and took a sip of Graham's champagne. "Where has Charlie been? I thought the two of you were best friends."

"We are, but I believe Charlie is a tad bit jealous. I'm going to talk to him. I do rather like having you all to myself, though. That might sound selfish, but that's how I feel."

"I'd be telling a lie if I said I didn't like having you to myself. I'm sure Charlie will come around—especially if he's a good friend like you say."

"Don't worry about Charlie. He'll be all right next week."

Graham watched Rita as she searched his eyes for the meaning of that statement, but he offered no further explanation and turned his attention to the dancers on the floor. Graham and Rita made small talk, taking small sips of champagne and gawking at each other as if trying to set a Guinness Book world record for the time a couple could stare at each other.

"Gotta run, sweetie. The band's getting ready to go back on in a couple of minutes."

"Don't be longgggggg," Graham admonished.

Rita blew him a kiss, and he watched her cross the dance floor and disappear behind the curtain to rejoin the band. Graham couldn't wait for tonight's set to be over. He was going to ask Rita to come home with him. It was decided. Amanda had given him her blessing; at least Graham believed she had.

The next couple of hours were a blur as the dizzying dancers grooved to the soulful sounds of Midnight Express, and laughter and chatter surrounded Graham. Charlie lowered his head on the few occasions Graham happened to look in his direction. It didn't matter. Graham wasn't interested in making amends tonight. He wanted to be distraction free when it was time to whisk Rita away to the night he had planned.

Rita announced her last number and gave a rousing rendition of "The Look of Love." Every inch of the dance floor was covered by panting lovers drinking in every word Rita sang hoping to hold on to some of the allure—long enough to take it home, or wherever they might end up, so they could continue their session, lost in their passion, in the electricity of their love making.

Nerves wracked Graham's body. His hands began to sweat and his stomach felt queasy at the thought of asking Rita home. He wasn't sure why his body decided to act up on him now. But he was sure of one thing. He wanted to forge ahead with his plans, and that included an intimate evening with Rita.

Graham was poised when Rita emerged from behind the stage still dressed in the slate-blue chiffon dress Graham had admired all evening. She pecked him on the lips, and Graham blushed.

"You were wonderful as always," Graham acknowledged.

"I'm glad you enjoyed it," Rita whispered. He had her rapt attention.

Graham pulled himself together internally and externally, licked his lips, and turned toward Rita. He caressed her chin and turned it in his direction. "I'd like to take you home tonight."

Rita's body refused to move. "I'm not sure that I heard you correctly, but there was no mistaking your words. Go home tonight? Are you sure about this? Are you ready for that step, Graham?"

With a grin on his face, he touched her lightly on the arms and looked straight into her eyes. "I've been ready ever since I met you."

Now it was out. Graham breathed a sigh of relief, not quite believing he had actually said it. He was relieved, though, when he saw the bright smile that lit across Rita's face, even at three in the morning.

♪♪♪

It was too dark to see much, but from what Rita could make out by the light of the moon, it seemed to be a cozy neighborhood. Most houses in California were made of stucco, but in the Pacific Northwest, the majority of homes were made of wood, possibly due to the overabundance of trees. And although Graham had been down Chester Street more times than his mathematical skills could compute, it seemed to light up as he and his new queen paraded down the street in Graham's 1988 Buick Regal. Most house-lights were out in the neighborhood, and the nosy neighbors were asleep.

Graham turned into his driveway, tapping the remote for the electric garage door he had installed a year ago. They sat more than a few moments after Graham cut off the ignition unsure, if not nervous, about the step they were getting ready to make.

"It's now or never," Graham said more to himself than to Rita while he opened the door on the driver's side.

Graham walked around to the passenger's side gently opening the door to assist Rita. Rita seemed reluctant. When her feet touched the ground, she froze almost as if she had stepped in a puddle of quick-drying cement. A reassuring hand took hers and led her to the door.

Graham gently guided her into the house, the moment of apprehension now behind him. He wanted Rita to be comfortable and made every effort to afford her just that.

Graham took Rita's wrap and purse and set them in the coat closet. He was nervous, as well as she, and Graham excused himself to allow enough space for him to catch his breath.

♪♪♪

Rita slowly pivoted on her toes taking in every inch of the warm surroundings in which she found herself. She could feel the love and warmth that permeated here.

Rita slowly walked to the fireplace and lifted Amanda's picture from the mantel. She studied it a moment, curious about the woman that had been Graham's wife. Rita looked into Amanda's eyes trying to understand what she was trying to say. It was easy to understand, just by looking at the photo, why Graham loved this woman so. There were other pictures—two girls, obviously Graham's daughters whose ages ranged at different intervals depending on which picture you were looking at. An old photo, probably taken in the early 1920s, was of a couple that had just gotten married. The couple might have been the grandparents of the children. It was hard to tell since the picture was somewhat faded.

Graham stood in the shadows watching Rita as she blazed a path across the mantel, acquainting herself with Graham's past and some of his present. Feeling a presence in the room, Rita turned to find Graham staring at her.

"What was she like, Graham? Amanda, what was she like? I can tell she was a wonderful person, just by the smile on her face."

Graham looked at Rita thoughtfully, scratching his head as he walked toward her, lifting the photo from her hand. He looked down at the picture and gave Amanda a hearty smile. "She was a wonderful woman, the love of my life for forty years. We adored each other. There wasn't a day that went by that we wouldn't say how much we loved one another. I was salt; she was pepper. I was bread; she was butter. I was a cold glass of milk; she was a chocolate-chip cookie. We had a love so deep that only Heaven or hell could separate us." Graham paused a moment and let his head drop. "Heaven won…but I know Amanda is having a ball."

A tear rolled down the side of Graham's face. Rita took her index finger and wiped it away like the stroke of a painter's brush.

"Can you imagine her having all that fun without me?"

Graham let the tears roll. Rita took him in her bosom and rubbed his well-manicured head until it was practically matted down. They swayed in the quiet of the room until Graham abruptly lifted his head, somewhat embarrassed by his display of emotion. Rita, sensing his uneasiness, kissed him lightly on the lips and stepped back.

"It's okay, sweetie. It's okay to cry. Take as long as you need because your love was deep, and you just don't stop loving because they've gone on to be with the Lord. I'll be right here waiting."

Graham looked at Rita longingly, pulled her ever so gently toward him, and kissed her with all the passion he had left in his body. They formed a lover's embrace that lasted for what seemed like hours until they finally collapsed onto the beige overstuffed loveseat, exhausted from getting to know each other without committing their bodies for sexual pleasure.

CHAPTER 18

They sat for more moments than they had kissed, examining each other as if each were the potter and in turn the clay. The soft light Graham had managed to turn on highlighted the soft lines in Rita's face. Her supple skin gave no clue to her age, only the light banter that drew on experience of many years past, years that only one who had lived them could attest to. Like a great archeological find, Rita outlined the curvature of Graham's face, unmasking ancient secrets held within.

All was silent but the purring and smacking of lips as they caressed each other like it was their last time. They weren't sure where they'd go from here. Holding each other close, an occasional peck on the lips and cheek was the ultimate foreplay. And they were getting to know each other very well.

"How about a little something to drink? I have a real nice champagne or Zinfandel if you like."

"Why don't I have a glass of Zinfandel, Mr. Peters?"

"One glass of Zinfandel coming right up for the sweet lady. You just keep that pose for me, and I'll be right back."

"I'm not going anywhere."

♪♪♪

Graham appeared in the doorway with two flutes of Zinfandel on a round silver tray with a single red artificial rose that he plucked from one of Amanda's flower arrangements. Rita was impressed and smiled widely. This man was special, and all her inhibitions and anxieties fell by the wayside.

They sipped and laughed. They sipped and pecked. They sipped and talked. They sipped the sweet drink until their glasses were empty and she fell asleep in his arms.

Rita and Graham lay together fully clothed on the overstuffed couch until dawn. Even the loveseat pillows that cushioned their bodies were submissive to their demands, which were…none. It was love in bloom, the beginning of a metamorphosis that seeks no boundary—a caterpillar's cocoon that emits a beautiful butterfly in an array of dazzling colors that flits about the earth taking in all of God's wonder.

Stale breath and eyes encrusted with what Grandma called *sleep*, did not alter how they saw each other upon opening their eyes. Rita and Graham basked in the afterglow of the newness of their love, relaxed and somewhat amazed at how easy they melded together. Their love seemed genuine, although it had been shy of a week since they met—a week that might have been spent deep in self-pity if Charlie hadn't coaxed Graham to accompany him to The Water Hole.

They lay around touching and feeling until Rita announced she'd like to go to her hotel room to pick up a few things. Graham found it hard to pull away from Rita, and Rita found it hard to resist Graham's arms that protected her from harm and danger. But they managed and were soon facing the world outside—a world that judged, a world that might judge their being together, a world that might judge her as an opportunist or a gold digger, and a world that perhaps would judge him unfaithful to his dead wife.

♪♪♪

It was Sunday. Buicks, Fords, Toyotas, and Mercedes whizzed by with well-dressed worshippers on their way to Sunday services. Women in an array of well-designed hats, some of which were too large to fit in the interior of a car, made ready to make their entrance into the sanctuary. Folks toting the King James version of the Bible hugged them proudly as if that would keep them close to the Lord.

Graham thought back to last Sunday when he had entered the church on Market Street for the first time since Amanda's death. He didn't know how to feel, what he felt as he walked along the path where Amanda took her last ride. An image of Sister Mary Ross loomed in front of him. Graham shook his head to dislodge the vision that tried to trespass on his thoughts.

Graham was sure Liz, Deborah, and their families were at church. He'd go next Sunday. The church on Market Street had been his mainstay for the last forty years.

Graham continued forward to his destination, happy for the first time in two months.

"Sky's kinda cloudy," Rita uttered. She was a stickler for detail and was more than just a casual observer. Her mama told her once that the naked eye could capture more than a snapshot could.

"Yeah, it is."

"Cloudy. Hmmm. It makes me kinda sad, you know."

"Oh." Graham wasn't sure he got it all. He was trying to follow; he was so in love, he wasn't sure what kind of day it was.

"Listen to me, Graham."

"I am, baby." Rita liked the sound of that; and so did Graham. She had the biggest smile on her face.

"A cloudy day because we're going to have to part soon. I've got to go to Seattle."

Graham had temporarily forgotten. He panicked and put his foot on the brake too fast, making a loud screeching sound that caused the Sunday drivers to stop and stare. "Tomorrow...you're leaving tomorrow. What am I going to do?"

Almost as if Rita had been thinking about it for some time, she murmured, "Why don't you come home with me?"

"Me, go home...with you? I don't think I can do that right now."

"You asked me to come home with you. And I did."

"I know, but it's different having to go several hundred miles away—away from your comfort zone. What will I tell my daughters? Charlie?"

"Charlie? So Charlie matters now?"

"It's not that. Charlie and I confide in each other. Even though we haven't been together for the past few days, he knows that I'm not far away. I'm not sure Charlie and the girls would understand."

"Lighten up, Graham. I'm not judging you. It's okay. *I really need to go home alone.* I've got a lot to take care of. Watch out! You're going to miss your turn!"

Graham held the wheel tight and quickly turned it to the right. The wheels let out a squeal, leaving tire tracks for at least twenty yards. Both Graham and Rita shifted back and forth in their seats until Graham gained full control of the car. Rita's hand was still latched onto the door handle when Graham spoke again and continued the conversation where they had left off.

"Please don't think ill of me, Rita. It's…such a giant step for me to take right now, but if you give me a raincheck, I promise I'll cash it in the very near future."

Rita released her hand from the handle and slowly turned toward Graham. She shook her head, then let out a chuckle. Before she could respond, Graham cut in.

"What's so funny?"

"Graham, Graham," Rita said, tapping his arm gently and still giggling. "Honey, what am I going to do with you? Do you realize that you nearly took a few months off my life going around that curve? You could have crashed."

Graham looked puzzled.

"Never mind. But you should have seen your face when I asked you to go home with me. You'd of thought you saw a ghost."

"I believe I did. Amanda's ghost." And they both laughed until they had popped every stitch.

♪♪♪

Rita hurriedly changed her clothes. Wasting one moment of precious time would be bad for her health. She went to the closet and pulled out the dress she would wear at her last performance. She didn't want it to end, but she'd be back.

Rita and Graham spent the morning leisurely riding up the coast and made a stop in Sausalito for a light lunch. Their day had been perfect. A cloudless sky spread as far as the eye could see. The view of the Golden Gate Bridge with its wings spread across the great expanse of bay left a lasting snapshot for Rita to remember, although she'd seen this bridge many times before. She was in love—in love with a man who gave life new meaning and who made her body quiver, although they had never given themselves to each other fully.

Graham was the embodiment of a real man—not that *men are from Mars* crap. He knew how to treat a woman, make her feel like fine china, and was always the perfect gentleman in every way. No doubt it was the reason Graham and Amanda's love had stood the test of time.

A fleeting thought crossed Rita's mind. *What would it be like to be Mrs. Graham Peters? Would Graham compare her constantly to Amanda or would he accept her as she was—a new challenge, a new face, a new life with substance of its own—with no hint of the previous, just the present.* Silly thoughts. She'd known him barely a week and already her wayward mind was running rampant with thoughts of marriage. But she could feel it deep down inside—way down into the heart of her soul, that she and Graham were meant to be.

Graham whistled jovially, finally arriving at Chester Street. He made a right turn and continued straight until his house was in view.

It was an old family neighborhood made up of single-dwelling homes—tract homes that were probably built in the early 1960s. Fences were affixed around the perimeters of most of them with small yards boasting healthy, thick St. Augustine grass. Rose bushes, chrysanthemums, and petunias in all variety of colors rested in gardens or flower boxes, adding a splash of color to many of the homes. Weeping willows that looked as if they belonged in some ancient animated fairy tale with branches burdened with heavy layers of moss lined the street in the yards of every other house. Young men who looked to be in their early teens gathered for a game of basketball. Other than that, the street remained rather quiet—the church-goers not yet released from their awe-inspiring services.

Rita felt much more comfortable as she entered Graham's house a second time. Their night together came back to her, and at that moment, she wished she had made love to him.

Graham escorted Rita into the house as if it were an ordinary occurrence, comfortable in the fact that Rita did not seem ill at ease. He placed Rita's things in the hall closet while she stood by his side. He turned to face her. Rita stared back into Graham's eyes, taking his hand in hers and squeezing it tight. Graham cupped Rita's chin with his free hand and placed a tender kiss on her lips. When he tried to withdraw, they stuck together like sweet, sticky bubble gum.

"I love you, Rita."

"I love you, too, Graham."

They kissed again, backing into a wall that kept them from falling. Graham let his hands roll over Rita's shoulders and down her arms, not quite sure where he should go next. He could feel his passion rise and moved quickly away from Rita lest she expose his secret.

"Let me get you some lemonade, my sweet. Pretty hot outside."

Pretty hot inside, Rita thought to herself. She fanned herself pretending to mock Graham's sudden inference to being hot. If he felt like she did, he'd know that the throbbing between her legs would take more than a glass of lemonade to cool off.

"A glass of lemonade will be fine. You better hurry; I think I'm going to faint from the heat."

They laughed.

"Sorry, these old houses don't have air conditioning. It gets hot, but the ocean breeze somehow cools us off."

"Baby, get me that glass of lemonade and stop explaining." They laughed again.

Rita watched as Graham poured the lemonade into the glass tumblers. Even the rhythm with which he poured turned Rita on. He had so much finesse and certainly would be a lucky catch for any woman, regardless of his age. Rita walked up to Graham and gently traced his back with her hand. Graham passed Rita her lemonade, pulled her to him, embraced her, and covered her full lips with his own. Then they sat, she sitting sideways on Graham's lap, laughing and having the time of their lives.

They were so engrossed in their moment in time that neither Graham nor Rita heard the front door open. Upon taking a moment to exhale, they looked up, and before them stood seven pairs of eyes. The door closed with a bang.

Rita jumped up from Graham's lap like a guilty party at the scene of the crime. Graham grabbed her arm, pulling her toward him as he stood.

"Daddy, what is this?" Deborah exclaimed, her eyes contorted and fingers pointing toward Graham and Rita.

"Hold on, now."

"Liz, can you believe this? Mama's not even cold in her grave, and this…"

"Watch it, baby girl, before you say something you'll regret later."

"Grant, take the kids to the car. Liz and I will be out in a minute."

"I'll be there in a moment," Liz said to her husband, Riley.

The room was silent until the children, Grant, and Riley had closed the door behind them. After the door was completely closed, Deborah swung around and faced her father with hands dancing in the air and slender fingers pointed at the accused like small daggers ready to claw.

"I want an explanation, now, Daddy. Who is this woman disrespecting my mother's house?"

"Deborah Ann, I've warned you. This is my house, and I won't have you or anyone else come up in here and disrespect my guest."

Deborah rolled her eyes Heavenward trying to fight back the tears. "Disrespecting your guest? Our mother just died, and you've got this two-bit floozie…"

Graham reached out a raised hand toward Deborah. "Don't, Graham," Rita begged. "I'll leave. I understand."

"No, Rita."

"Get out, Rita or whatever your name is!" Deborah shouted.

"Stop it, Deborah," Liz cut in. "Why don't you give Daddy a chance to explain? I'm sure there's a logical explanation for all of this." She gave Graham a menacing look.

"We don't have all day. Our families are waiting out in the car. Came by because we were concerned about your ass…"

"We just got out of church, Deborah."

"Shut up, Liz. You're not even helping."

"I'm waiting, Daddy, or are you my daddy?"

"That's enough, Deborah," Liz said. "I want to hear what Dad has to say, too."

"Can we sit down like adults? Yes, I'd like to give you an explanation." Turning toward Rita, Graham gently took her shaking hand and asked her to sit. "This is Rita Long, a friend of mine."

"Umph," Deborah muttered.

"We met this week, and we found that we had a lot in common. You both know that I loved your mother with all of my heart and soul—I still love her the same. I didn't think that there would ever be anyone who could ever take her place." Treading cautiously, Graham continued, "I believed never would." Graham could feel Rita flinch. "I lost my best friend, my reason for living and these past two months have been so hard on me…"

"Like it hasn't been hard on anyone else," Liz uttered through her teeth.

Graham ignored the comments and plowed on. "I wanted to give up on life, but your uncle Charlie put the fear of God in me—I know what you're thinking, but he did. And I realized that my two daughters, my son-in-laws, and my precious grandchildren still needed me. So I listened to Charlie and I got up and went to church last Sunday, because I knew that was where my strength lay.

"God also put someone in my path that could understand what I was going through."

"Yeah, right," Deborah moaned.

"Rita isn't just anyone, she's a special person with a gift for listening," Graham said, ignoring Deborah.

"Well, Ms. Long, what do you have to say for yourself? Where do you come from? What do you do?" Deborah asked, hands on her hips in her

Sunday go-to-meeting outfit that was ready to come off at any time. "You see, my mother, Amanda Peters, was a virtuous woman, well respected in her church and in the community. She loved my daddy, and she'd never do anything to hurt him. She was his sunrise and sunset; you get my meaning, Ms. Long? Their love was deeper than the ocean."

Rita and Graham glanced at each other.

"My mother has been dead for only two months—the memory of her passing is still fresh in my memory, and I just wonder why my dad brought you into this house, this house that's filled with memories of my mother."

Deborah sat down. Holding her face in her hands, the tears streamed down her face. Liz rushed to her side, rubbing her back to comfort. Liz looked at Graham without a word.

Deborah rose from the chair, waved her hand around the room, and looked straight into Rita's eyes. "Ms. Long," Deborah said, pointing, "see these curtains and all the flower arrangements and knick-knacks that are all throughout this house? They're Mama's. She loved pretty things. Ask Daddy."

Rita stepped forward, now only inches from Deborah. "I can't fully understand your pain…"

"Hell no you can't!" Deborah shouted.

"But I want you to know that your father and I are just friends. I'm just a friend who lent a shoulder, a shoulder so that he could shed some of his burdens and move on with his life."

Liz and Deborah stared at Rita like she was a freak at a traveling carnival.

"Whatever you may think of me, I hope you understand that I'm not trying to take your daddy away from you or disrespect your mother's memory. I'm just being a friend."

"What do you do, Ms. Long? How did you meet my dad?" Liz asked rather politely.

"I'm a singer," Rita nearly whispered. "We met at a local club."

"Oh, no, no, no, no, no, no, no, no!" Deborah yelled, voice trembling and arms swinging wildly in the air. "A nightclub singer? Daddy, are you for real? What are the people at church going to say?"

"I really don't give a damn what anybody says," Graham said. "I've put up with just about enough of your outbursts. I've tried to tell you how I feel, but I'm not going to be disrespected in my own home."

"Daddy," Liz interjected, "I've listened and have gone over every detail in my head. Why now? Did it have to be so soon?"

Graham grabbed Elizabeth and hugged her. She cried uncontrollably. Rita felt terrible and would never come have here if she knew she'd be playing out a scene from *All My Children* or *One Life to Live*. She couldn't take much more. On the edge of her last nerve, she was ready to leave—perhaps never to return. Rita watched Graham and his daughters. She understood their hurt, their pain, and their love for a mother who had been more than faithful to them; however, the treatment she received was uncalled for, and it was leaving a scar on her heart.

Everyone's head turned when they heard the familiar voice—a voice that no one wanted to hear right here, right now.

"How you all doing? Just came by to see if Deacon Peters needed anything. Why are you all looking at me like that? The door was open."

"Sister Ross, right now is not a good time," Graham uttered as gently as he could. "Why don't you call tomorrow? We're having a family meeting."

"Oh, I see," Mary Ross said. "I can wait in the living room until you all are finished."

"Sister Ross, please go home," Deborah said, none too kind.

And Sister Mary Ross left the kitchen briskly. She was just about on her way out when she turned on her heels, spotted the comfortable overstuffed loveseat and plopped on it. Being ignored for a minute too long, Sister Mary eased up from the chair and found her way back into the kitchen.

♪♪♪

Rita watched blindly as Deborah continued her attack on Graham, willing her ears to shut and block out all the senseless chatter. Sister Mary Ross, who'd been shown the door over ten minutes ago, had the nerve to throw her arms on her somewhat shapely hips and strike a pose—ready to come to Deborah's defense if needed. Mary was a little common, Rita thought, but it was plain to see that she'd relish being in Rita's position if given half the chance.

There was something different, Rita noticed, about Elizabeth. Rita could almost see Amanda in Liz, although the only thing Rita knew about Amanda was what Graham had shared with her. Liz had a calming spirit, humble, almost angelic, and while she shared her sister's concern, Liz assumed the role of mediator. She was compassionate, yet stern.

Rita looked down at her watch and gasped in alarm.

"I'm sorry for all that I've caused, but I really must go, Graham. I'm late for my rehearsal, and I'm sure the band is wondering what's happened to me."

"Okay, Rita, let's go," Graham said. "We've got to be going; however, if you want to continue this discussion," Graham said, directing his remark at Deborah, "we can get together later." Graham turned to Rita and offered his apologies for his girls.

"No need to apologize for us," Deborah ranted. "I've been going over all of this in my mind, and I just don't understand…"

"Another time, Deborah. I must get Rita to rehearsal."

As Graham and Rita tried to plow through the group, Deborah tapped Rita on the shoulder. "I have just one question for you. Where did you say you worked?"

"I didn't," Rita said smugly. "But if you'd like to know, we're appearing at The Water Hole."

"Don't start, Deborah," Liz cut in, anticipating her sister's next outburst. "Let them go."

Rita kept her eyes straight ahead as she and Graham moved from the kitchen to the living room and away from the lynch mob that besieged them. Just as Graham pulled open the door, Rita suddenly realized she'd forgotten something.

"Graham, I forgot my things in the closet."

Rita's timing was all wrong. This time, only three pairs of eyes stared back at her, but they were the unfriendliest eyes she'd seen in a long time. They followed Graham as he proceeded down the hall, until his eventual return holding a garment bag that belonged to Rita Long. Now the three pairs stared at the two sets of eyes that dared anybody to say a word.

Deborah's head moved like a mechanical bull that was just getting warmed up. The steam from her nostrils began to flare. The pinkness of her gums harbored a set of teeth well taken care of through the years. But sometimes the well-manicured mouth speaks before the mind knows what it's going to say. "Hold up, hold up. Wench...did you sleep with my father?"

Rita summoned all of her social decorum and her mama's wonderful home training. Sistergirl had crossed the line, and she was asking for a sho 'nuf smack-down. Rita could care less whose daughter she was. But Rita was a lady in every way, and fighting wasn't in her, although little Ms. Deborah Peters-Hill had provoked her to the brink. "You've already asked your last question."

"It's none of your damn business," Graham jumped in, his tone angry. "I should have put a stop to this ridiculous circus earlier."

"Deacon Peters!" Sister Mary exclaimed.

"Sister Ross, goodbye," everyone said in unison.

"I'm not having any more of this," Graham continued after Sister Mary Ross was out of earshot. "If anyone in here does not like what I'm doing, you can march out of here right now and not come back. I won't even be mad."

"Stop it, Graham," Rita pleaded. "Stop it." She turned to Deborah and Liz who hadn't said a word in the past two seconds. "Your dad is a good man who loved your mother with all of his heart. His heart has been broken, in case you haven't noticed." Rita watched as the girls rolled their eyes like disobedient teenagers. "But he deserves better than this.

"Your dad has been so lonely since your mother passed, and the only thing he's guilty of is allowing someone to nourish his soul, albeit through song. I saw your dad sitting at a table silent and unmoving in an audience of party-goers who were having a good time in a place your father didn't relish. But his best friend Charlie tried the best he could to help your dad out of his funk and ended up at The Water Hole.

"We talked, and I saw something in him, this wonderful quality you don't find much of these days. I was attracted to him. After a while, he seemed to light up and thaw out a bit. Graham told me about his wonderful family, Amanda, Elizabeth, and Deborah. I heard how your dad met your mother, how she was love at first sight, how the sun rose and set with her. I feel as though I know Amanda even though I never had the opportunity to meet this wonderful woman.

"Your dad and I did not sleep together. When he picked me up this afternoon," Rita lied, "I brought my clothes for tonight's show with me. This is my last night in town, and we spent today soaking up God's beauty. It really is a beautiful world God has created. I really need to get going now, but I'd like you to know this, you can feel however you like about me. But cherish your dad, he won't be here always. He loves you, and most of all, he needs you."

Tears rolled the length of Deborah's face forming large drops that sought refuge as they ran the course from eyes that looked so much like Graham's to the edge of her chin that was so much Amanda's. Her fuchsia silk jacket that blanketed her black three-quarter-length chemise became a dumping ground for those tears.

Everyone in the room sensed Deborah's embarrassment after Rita's speech. Deborah stood in the middle of the room. No one was sure what her intentions were, but it appeared she wanted to go to her father—maybe ask for his forgiveness. She shifted first on her right leg, then the left, taking turns at ten-second intervals while all eyes awaited her next move.

Elizabeth remained planted with a puzzled look on her face. She glanced first at Rita, then toward Graham and finally allowed her head to fall slowly in shame. When Liz lifted her head again, her eyes were full, full of water from the tears she hadn't shed before. Tears she'd held at her mother's funeral—trying to be strong, the rock for everyone else.

Liz glanced out of the living room window. Riley and Grant were having one of those man-to-man talks on the sidewalk. Then a question came to mind. *What would Riley do if I passed away? Do I expect him to not seek companionship or get married again?* She looked into Graham's eyes and smiled. Liz reached out for her dad and hugged him with all her might. "I love you, Daddy."

"I love you, too, baby." And Graham rubbed the top of Liz's head like he did when she was a little girl.

"I'm sorry, Rita," Liz whispered.

Rita nodded her acknowledgment.

Liz and Graham clung together like paper and glue. Deborah stood alone, suddenly betrayed by her sister. She seemed deep in thought and no one was able to read her mind. She abruptly stood erect, straightening her face and clothes, as if reassembling a jigsaw puzzle that had accidentally come undone.

Deborah looked in Graham and Rita's direction, letting her eyes travel from one to the other. She didn't run to Graham like Liz, although her inner soul wanted to. Liz had given in too quickly. Words were trying to come. For some reason, they remained blocked.

"We've got to go," Graham said. "You all lock the door behind you."

Deborah and Liz watched as the couple got into their dad's car, waving to Riley and Grant before departing.

CHAPTER 19

Sister Mary Ross was armed with the hottest piece of news since the whole world found out Jesse Jackson was someone's baby-daddy. Mary Ross wasn't going to be able to keep this news to herself. She had to tell somebody—this was *CNN Headline News*, a nine and a half if using a scale of one to ten.

"Had the nerve to kick me out of his house…and he's the sinner. Hmph," Sister Mary Ross fumed out loud, stopping long enough to extract the last piece of sweet potato pie from her refrigerator. The kitchen was just large enough to hold Mary, the refrigerator, the kitchen sink, and the oven she used to prepare meals for her future intended, Graham Peters, but it wasn't too small to hold back what Mary was going to shout to the world. "Martha Carter won't like it all when I tell her what that son-in-law of hers has been up to. No, she won't."

What should be her first course of action? "Loretha would know the answer," Mary said out loud between bites of pie. "She won't believe this." Loretha was wise in her ways and was better than most shrinks when it came to giving advice.

Mary dialed Loretha's number—her hot fingers anticipating what her hot lips were going to say. Mary Ross was going to have Deacon Peters, and no low-life hussy singer from some hole-in-the-wall nightclub was going to steal from her what she had waited for a lifetime to take!

CHAPTER 20

Rita had been gone close to a week, and life as Graham knew it prior to Rita had resumed—except for the pity parties. Even Amanda had failed to make an appearance in Graham's nightly dreams. Graham and Rita spoke nearly every day for hours at a time, unable to get enough of each other. Graham was consumed with the very essence of Rita—like rain absorbed into the earth, saturating his already rich soil. Deborah and Elizabeth had taken some of the fire out of Rita's zest to get to know Graham better; however, Graham's adamant plea to be patient and let love abide, tore at Rita's heart strings.

They explored possibilities of a life together with subtle hints of marriage—in the very distant future. They talked about Graham leaving Oakland and possibly settling in Seattle. They talked about children, although both were well past their prime, and Graham was just fine nurturing his grandchildren and giving them all the love they needed. They spoke of consummating the love they shared for each other giving no care to what others thought—not that anyone would be privy to that bit of knowledge when it happened. Just like Deborah, Liz and Sister Mary Ross had speculated that the two of them had been together; let all of those sitting at the foot of judgment judge them—who cared? It was none of their business anyway.

There was an immediate matter Graham needed to take care of. He had not spoken to Charlie in over a week. Graham thought Charlie would have shown up at his doorstep by now, but it was quite evident Charlie was hurt by being "put off" by Graham.

Graham reached for the phone to call Charlie when the doorbell rang. He walked the few feet to the door, peeked through the curtain, and gasped at Charlie's lean figure standing on the front porch. Graham became tense and coiled his body, ready for Charlie's onslaught of questions and accusations. But he was glad to see him.

Graham's sweaty palm turned the knob to the front door. They found each other's gaze wishing the other would say something first, an awkward moment between best friends. "Hey Charlie, good to see you. I had just picked up the phone to call you."

"Umm," Charlie murmured. "May I come in?"

"Yeah, buddy. Come in. You're not a stranger here," Graham retorted.

Charlie shrugged his shoulders and smirked, his head tilted to one side. "I feel like a stranger."

Graham remained quiet as he moved aside for Charlie to enter. Charlie let his eyes roam about the room as if it was his first time setting foot in Graham's house.

They went into the kitchen, their customary hangout. Charlie's eyes continued to rove about—like a spy trying to uncover an encoded secret, a bloodhound on a hot trail. Charlie's behavior amused Graham somewhat; however, he was in love with Rita Long and that was that. He was now a single man whom had long ago left the playing field but found himself in left field ready to play ball. He couldn't help it that after all this time Charlie wasn't able to do any better than Shelly.

"Word on the street is…," Charlie began.

"Word on the street is what, Charlie?" Graham asked mockingly, putting up an invisible shield to block what he was sure would come next.

"Word is… you slept with Rita."

Graham took his time and stood up from the table, assuming a position that made clear he was about to lay his point on thick. "Word is…it's a lie. And you can go and tell whomever you got that piece of misinformation from that that's the word and that whatever I chose to do and with whomever I chose to do it with is no one's damn business. Now that I've gotten that out of the way, how you've been, Charlie?"

♪♪♪

Charlie couldn't believe that he had been in Graham's house all of five minutes and had gotten slam-dunked on his first lay-up. The game was over, history, and there would be no referee to hear his protest. He'd leave the subject of Rita Long on the back burner for now. He'd be ready for Graham the next time—for sure it would come up again. Graham was truly the victor this time, however, next time Charlie would be ready with a block, steal, dribble, and ten baskets.

Charlie wasn't sure why it was important to know what had transpired between his best friend and Rita—maybe it was the fact they had been friends for nearly fifty years and had always shared secrets. Well, maybe not all secrets, but nevertheless, they had shared almost everything. *Yeah, almost everything*, he thought. But now he felt his friend had kicked him to the curb, and Charlie had a sudden urge to get them back on track.

Charlie diverted his attention back to Graham whose smug look and taste of victory were written all across his face.

CHAPTER 21

Sister Mary Ross couldn't wait to get to the church house. There would be fireworks tonight; she felt sure of it. Well, she was going to be right there, telling her side of the story when the time was right. The *word* was out—so expedient was the church grapevine that it didn't miss any area code or prefix in its attempt to inform the masses. Every deacon, deaconess, missionary, minister, and congregational member of the church on Market Street, including Pastor Fields, had become privy to Sister Mary Ross' bit-of-gossip—whether by first, second, or third person.

The saints were gathered for Wednesday night Bible Study, but their minds weren't on the powerful story of Saul, once a persecutor of Christians, whose name was changed to Paul after a great light blinded him while on the road to Damascus. Many had come to get the real scoop on Deacon Graham Peters who was said to be seen in the company of a nightclub-singing floozy—and right in his own home, dishonoring the sanctity of his recently departed wife's spirit. Two months had barely passed, and now the gossip threatened to taint not only Deacon Graham's reputation but the church's good name as well.

"Samson and Delilah. Nothing like a woman to bring a man down."

"Chile, have you ever heard of such? From the church house to the nightclub."

"And so soon after his wife's death. He probably was cheating on Sister Amanda all along."

"They ought to throw him out of the church. Such a disgrace."

"Sista, he can ask for God's forgiveness. God forgives seventy times seventy."

"Yeah, that's what they say, but don't sound like the deacon is thinking about repenting. Sounds like he is dipping and sticking."

"Sista, shut your mouth and don't be so loud. You ain't heard no such thing. But I'm going to tell you what I think. I think Sister Mary Ross over there is a little sweet on the deacon. You know, she's the one who supposedly saw the two together and ran back and told everybody."

"Sounds like you might believe that rumor."

"Well, Mary did see them together. And what was she doing over at the deacon's house, anyway?"

"You think there's a little jealousy somewhere?"

"That's what I'm thinking."

Tongues ceased to wag and all became deathly quiet as Deacon and Sister Elroy Carter entered the sanctuary. Most pretended to read their Bibles as they awaited Reverend Fields' arrival. Many in the congregation held their heads down avoiding the Carters' eyes that they believed might have held the look of shame. Yes, the Carters had heard the rumors, too, not sure whether to believe what they heard from the lips of Sister Mary Ross. The congregation wanted to know, and the Carters, bless Amanda's soul, would have to hear along with the rest of them.

♪♪♪

Reverend Fields coughed when he entered the sanctuary causing the congregation to stir—putting their sanctimonious attitudes in check. He looked over the crowd; there hadn't been this many people at Wednesday night Bible study or even a business meeting in a long time. Reverend Fields knew why they had come. *God strike them dead*, he thought, all the while asking God to forgive him of his evil thought. Well, he'd let them fidget in their seats a little while longer, because he was going to let God orchestrate this meeting. After all, this was Bible study and not the gossip hour.

Reverend Fields picked up the glass of water from the tray set out for him. The reverend rarely ever took a drink of water unless he was in the midst of a sermon and his throat became parched from the several octave levels he'd taken the congregation on his wild ride to the truth of the gospel. All eyes were on him, and he took a sip from the glass, prolonging their agony just a few minutes longer. He swallowed hard, put down the glass and began to pray.

Bodies leaned in close so as not to miss anything Reverend Fields might say, especially as it pertained to the sins of the deacon who was not there to defend his position. Reverend Fields prayed for the lost and the lonely, the homeless and motherless, the drug addicts and convicted felons, those in need of a financial blessing, and those in need of just a word from the Lord. The reverend reminded the crowd that God sat high on the throne and looked down low and could see the *SINS* of the *WHOLE WORLD*—implying that Deacon Peters wasn't the only one in need of God's help. "You who are without sin, cast the first stone," the reverend demanded, peeking ever so quickly from behind his once tightly closed eyelids to see if he had elicited any furrowed eyebrows. Seeing none, he said, "Amen.

"We're going to defer tonight's scheduled Bible study lesson on the Apostle Paul to talk about forgiveness." There was a rumble from the congregation, but Reverend Fields ignored it and plowed on.

"We serve a good God, an awesome God. If it had not been for Him, many of us wouldn't be here today. God loved us so much that He gave His only Son to die for the sins of the whole world. Imagine that—the whole world. I can't say how many billion or trillion people that might be. It doesn't matter how good you are or how bad, God gave each and every one an equal chance to repent of their sins so they can join the Savior in His heavenly home when the time arrives."

Reverend Fields looked out into the crowd. Disinterested faces met his eyes, but he didn't care. The Lord told him to share this message with his people, and that's what he was going to do. He continued, "I want you to go to the book of Mark the sixth chapter and the twenty-fifth through twenty-sixth verses. It says, 'And when you stand praying, forgive, if ye have aught against any: that your Father also which is in heaven may forgive you your trespasses. But if ye do not forgive, neither will your Father which is in heaven forgive your trespasses.'"

"We want to know what you're gonna do about Deacon Peters!" someone shouted out.

"Yes, I was there," Sister Ross chimed in, standing up and facing the congregation with a smug look on her face. Now they were getting to the heart of what everyone really came to hear. "I saw the deacon and that nightclub floozy with my very own eyes, all huddled together professing their love for one another." That wasn't quite the way it was, but no one knew differently.

"You are out of order, Sister Ross, and so is anyone else bent on disrupting Bible study."

"Well, Reverend, what are you going to do about Deacon Peters?" an elderly, portly gentleman, Deacon Harris, asked. Head of the Deacon Board, Harris was set in his old-school ways. "You do wrong; out you go. I say we dismiss Peters from the Deacon Board and any other auxiliary he's on. This is a disgrace to the church."

Voices rose from every corner in the sanctuary acknowledging agreement with Deacon Harris.

"Just a minute, folks. Since you want to talk about Deacon Peters, we'll talk about Deacon Peters. He has done nothing wrong. Sister Amanda has departed this life leaving Deacon Peters a widower. While I don't understand how and where he met this woman you all speak of, we can't conclude anything until we speak with Deacon Peters first. There is nothing wrong in his seeking out the company of another woman; the deacon is a free man. And as I said earlier, if any of you are without sin, then cast the first stone. But Deacon Peters has not sinned."

"Well, you're missing the point, Reverend," Sister Mary Ross interrupted. "No disrespect to you, but Sister Amanda has been gone for a little over two months. Out of respect to the church, his family..." At this, Amanda's mother stood.

No one expected it, and all eyes were on Sister Martha Carter as she rose. Deacon Carter looked a little uneasy—not sure what his wife was about to do. Martha had put on some weight in her latter years, and her generous serving of hips held her left hand steady as she propped it on her left hip and proceeded to the center aisle. Her head leaned forward as if ready to do battle.

"I've sat and listened to just about enough of this, Sister Ross. You don't care what the church thinks of Amanda's good name. You and my daughter never did see eye-to-eye, and Amanda believed you were a little sweet on her husband."

The crowd gasped. Sister Mary moved closer—but a safe distance from Martha. "You don't know what you're talking about, Martha. It's that no-good son-in-law of yours and his disgraceful ways that's the topic of this discussion."

"My granddaughters have told me how you seem to be hanging around Deacon Peters' house all the time. Every time they go by, you show up on the pretense of taking him meals he doesn't even eat! Got your nose all in his business. And if you continue this charade…trying to trample my son-in-law's good name through the mud, I'm going to have to ask the church for forgiveness. Because there's no telling what I might do to you!" Deacon Carter jumped up to quiet Martha.

"I'm all right, Elroy," Martha said, holding up her hand for him to leave her alone. "And another thing, Sister Ross, Deacon Peters had a good, virtuous woman for forty years and just maybe he's looking for another. But rest assured, it won't be you. I'm through, Reverend. I apologize for the disruption, and I ask for the saints' forgiveness."

Reverend Fields clapped his hands, happy that Sister Martha had told old Sister Mary off. The reverend swiftly raised his hands. "That's enough, Sister Carter and Sister Ross," the good reverend said, oblivious to the fact that Sister Carter had already relinquished her stand. "This is the House of the Lord. We are going to pray and dismiss Bible study until next week. I'll be speaking with Deacon Peters, but in the meantime, I want you to read the book of Proverbs 31 and Psalms 34:13—words for each of us for everyday living. God bless you all and good-night."

♪♪♪

The sanctuary of the church on Market Street was as quiet as an empty schoolroom. One by one, the congregation single-filed out—no after-church fellowshipping, no whispered words, even on the sly.

Sister Carter looked in the direction of Sister Mary Ross who deliberately kept her head turned in the opposite direction. Sister Carter had won this round, and Mary Ross wasn't ready for further battle right now—at least not just yet. Everyone was looking at her like she was the buffoon, causing a ruckus where there shouldn't have been one. *In time*, Sister Mary Ross thought, *I'll have Deacon Peters all to myself.*

♪♪♪

Elroy and Martha huffed and puffed as they made their way to their pale yellow 1975 Coupe de Ville. The Carters had outlived their only child, Amanda. Now in their early eighties and with a good life behind them, Martha wasn't about to let no "old maid, never had a man, jealous to the bone" wannabe talk about her daughter and son-in-law with disrespect. She wasn't having it.

Martha hoisted her body into the front seat, looked over at Elroy, and patted his hand. They had many good years together, and they loved each other every day of their married lives. Martha had groomed her daughter well, because her life with Graham resembled, if not exactly mirrored, the one her parents had lived before her.

"Honey, what do you think about all that Sister Ross was saying tonight?"

"Baby, first off, I was scared you were going to whoop her ass."

"Elroy!" Martha tried to contain her grin but was barely able to hold on to it. "I'm eighty-two years old. Now, what would I look like trying to fight that heifer?"

"I know I wouldn't have been able to hold you back if you got started." Elroy broke out in a grin and Martha followed with a loud outburst of the most hilarious cackle Elroy ever heard. "I'd say, Lord forgive them for they know not what they do." Martha looked at Elroy, Elroy looked back at Martha, and they screamed with laughter.

"Forgive us for we know not...? I guess you trying to get the reverend's sermon in since Sister Mary just took over—just disrespected Reverend Fields."

"Now, baby. You had your Academy Award moment, also. Sister Mary was scared, baby. She was sho 'nuf scared of you."

"Elroy?"

"Yes, baby?"

"We need to talk with Graham. I don't care how much I hated Sister Mary Ross for slinging mud at my family in the church house tonight, it tore at my heart. Yes, my heart was hurting. I can't see Graham with nobody but our Amanda. I realize she's gone to be with the Lord, but she ain't been in that ground long enough for Graham to go looking at another woman."

Martha threw her hands up in the air. "It hurts to know Graham has already gotten over Amanda. When Mary Ross was up there running off at the mouth, I just got mad. I don't know if I was mad at Graham or at Sister Ross. But I got her told like Amanda should have so many years ago. 'Manda would have been proud of her old mother."

Elroy was silent for a moment, listening attentively to his wife's ranting and raving, her hurt and pain. "Graham has done nothing wrong, Martha. He's a man…"

"Hold it. I don't know what being a man has to do with anything. Respect is respect."

"Hold on now, Martha. Let me try and explain it without you fretting so. Like I said, Graham's a man, a lonely man." Martha's cheeks started to expand—trying to hold off her displeasure with Elroy's reasoning. Elroy ignored her. "When the opportunity presented itself, Graham was vulnerable and fell like a rat with a pound of cheese sitting in front of it. How much you wanna bet Charlie Ford is at the center of this? Mark my words. Don't you remember the state Graham was in before coming to church last Sunday? He didn't look like a man who was after some other woman's skirt tail, and if he was, he had all of us fooled."

"Yeah, Graham and Amanda's love was so deep." Martha sighed, letting go of her steam. "I believe he still loves her, Elroy."

"I'm sure he does, too, honey."

"I love you, Elroy. You've been in my life a long time. There will be no other."

"Girl, I don't want no one but you. Let's go home now. I got one Viagra pill left, and I feel like getting my groove on."

"Hush now, Elroy. Don't make me do nothing I don't want to do."

"Girl, I want you to do everything you can remember to do, and meet me with your black drawls on."

"Baby, you so nasty."

"You my baby."

"I'd say we're doing pretty good for some eighty-year-old kids. 'Kickin' it,' they say."

"Give me some sugar, man. I love you to death, Deacon Carter." Martha placed a great big kiss squarely on Elroy's lips.

"I love you, too, Sister Carter," Elroy purred, gasping for air but ready for another generous portion of Martha's sweet lips.

"Well, hurry up and drive me home so we both can get our groove on."

CHAPTER 22

It didn't take long before the backlash and remnants of the storm that breezed through last evening's Bible study reached Graham's doorstep. And depending upon whose version you heard, Sister Ross was either trying to incite a mutiny, or she didn't have anything on the deacon that really amounted to anything and grossly disrespected the reverend up in his house—the Lord's house. However, there was no mistaking the one element each version consistently reported. Sister Ross' interest in this was solely personal, because she had a crush on the deacon.

Graham chuckled as different people called either to express their disgust or trying to be the first to say they had no part in the diabolical events of the evening. The latter claimed that although Deacon Harris had stood against him, the remainder of the Deacon Board stood in solidarity with him. Graham let them talk, one by one, though the truth of the matter was he could care less what any of them thought, and that included the good reverend. Hypocrites.

His mother-in-law and father-in-law were another matter. He loved them as much as he loved Amanda. Amanda encompassed everything they were, and Graham couldn't remember a time the Carters weren't there for them—whether it was babysitting when he and Amanda wanted to just get away for a while, helping them out financially, or just sharing their love. Graham had not intended to hurt them, even though he knew he had done nothing wrong. His timing might be a little off, but he had conferred with Amanda about all of the decisions he made regarding Rita

Long. If Amanda wasn't upset, why should the rest of them be? He'd handle it; a visit was imminent, but he'd handle it.

Graham got up from the sofa and moved from room to room, briefly stopping to admire some object that reminded him of Amanda. When he picked up her picture from the fireplace mantel, Graham recalled how he found Rita admiring it while she thought no one was looking.

Images of life with Amanda came floating back to Graham—images he thought he'd conquered so he could go on with life. He would never stop loving her. She had been his soul mate for forty years. Amanda left a void that hurt Graham deeply, a void he thought he would never fill—until last week.

Graham set Amanda's picture back on the mantel and headed for the kitchen. He needed to talk to Deborah and Liz. He needed to tell them how much he loved them and how much he loved their mother. He would never do anything to disgrace Amanda's good name or that of their children. He was falling in love with Rita Long, and there seemed to be very little he could do about it.

♪♪♪

The heels of Sister Mary Ross' worn feet moved back and forth in her dark living room as she contemplated the events of the evening. Never before had she been so humiliated, and to her utter dismay, the allegiance she had forged with the majority of the church members was now past tense as they dismissed her like day-old bread.

Mary looked around her, although in the dark, and with what little light filtered in from the hallway. She led a drab existence—an interior decorator's dream challenge if one could turn puke-green walls and worn brown-tweed Herculon furniture into something of beauty.

A picture of Jesus hung on the living room wall, and an old floor-model television hi-fi combination sat on the floor directly underneath. Carpet the color of split-pea soup ran throughout the house, resting against faded walls in the living room and kitchen. Mary's bedroom was painted pink and the guest bedroom canary yellow, picking up the puke-green in the bathroom. The furniture was so old, it had an old folks' smell that no amount of Febreezing would cover. The tiny, two-bedroom house was the only safe haven she could call her own.

There was a time when Mary had a few men's rapt attention. They would have asked for her hand in marriage. However, she abandoned all suitors in lust for a married man who was unmoved by her existence.

What had she done, Mary wondered? What had she intended to prove by denouncing the man she secretly loved? She wanted to be the one who came to his rescue when all others had forsaken him, but she had perpetrated the chaos. Her plan had been to be the understanding one, and Deacon Graham Peters would thank her again and again for her kindness and support.

Then Mary would fall into Graham's arms, and he'd take her to a secret hide-a-way where they'd embrace, allowing each other's healing touch to be absorbed into the bosom of their souls. Then Graham would slowly undress Mary, drenching himself in her beauty—overcome with her sensual lust, wowed by her tender lips and the perfect breasts that she kept hidden under her ultra-conservative clothing. Then Mary would undress Graham, first his shirt and then his slacks—after untangling her fingers from the fancy belt he wore around his waist.

Moisture between Mary's legs threatened to expose her burning desire for him. But visions of his chocolate-colored frame still well-defined after sixty-one years of wear, and the imagined erectness of Graham's manhood extended an exuberant invitation, and caused Mary to come before she had ever been touched.

Brrng. The telephone nearly caused Mary to fall where she stood— where lustful thoughts of passion had consumed her. She became acutely aware of a stickiness between her legs when she took a few steps to retrieve the phone from the floor, where it had laid since the night before when Mary's fingers had caressed every digit at least thirty times on at least thirty different occasions.

Mary picked up the receiver but couldn't talk for feeling dirty—almost sinful for allowing her fantasy to make a mockery out of her. She had the remnants of a wonderful dream—thirty years of pent-up release, but no man to make it real. She raised the phone to her ear and held it as the caller kept shouting, "Hello!" at the other end of the line.

Mary heard Loretha's voice as Loretha tore into Mary for making a complete idiot of herself at Bible study. But Loretha's voice wasn't what Mary wanted to hear, and without saying a word, she politely laid the receiver on the hook, yanking the phone cord from its receptacle with a swift snap of her wrist. Mary had had enough for one evening, and she silently prayed that Graham would come to her and make love to her—if only for one night, if only for one night.

CHAPTER 23

A surprise phone call from Rita sent Graham reeling. She was arriving in Oakland that very afternoon to handle some personal business and would be in town for a couple of days. It had been nearly three weeks since they had last seen each other.

Graham acted like a schoolboy with a crush on his fourth-grade teacher. He needed to spruce up the house, get a haircut and shave. The cleaners held his nice khaki pants and a multi-colored Angora sweater Amanda had given him a few birthdays back. He wanted to look his best for Ms. Rita Long, the new queen of his heart.

Then he remembered Amanda's parents were coming by to talk. This was the first opportunity they had to chat with their son-in-law since the ill-fated Bible study a couple of weeks ago that half the community was still talking about. Graham would stop by their house while he was out running errands. That way, he wouldn't run the risk that they'd run into Rita.

Halloween was near. Colorful artwork comprised of ghosts, goblins, witches and pumpkins screamed through bedroom windows that neighboring children made while at school. Every other house on Chester Street it seemed was decorated in some form or fashion with relics of the pending kids' holiday. Graham would get candy for the trick-or-treaters while he was out and about.

Graham hurried from the house and jumped in his car, anxious to clear up his calendar so that all of his free time could be spent with Rita. He headed first to the cleaners, then he'd get a haircut. If time permitted, he would stop by the Carters or cancel until another time.

"Must be a happy man." The attendant chuckled, plucking Graham's ticket from his hand and checking the number so that he could retrieve his cleaning.

"Oh, it's a good day," Graham replied as he continued to whistle. "When life is good, you can't help but look up toward the heavens and give God a thumbs-up or a shout-out. I prefer to whistle."

"That'll be eleven dollars and may God continue to bless you."

Graham gave the attendant $15. "Keep the change. I'm already blessed; have a good day."

♫♫♫

The attendant walked to the door after Graham. Graham still whistled. The attendant shook his head. The words, *into each life some rain must fall*, came to him. He had just received some terrible news the day before. His wife might not be able to carry their baby full term. He was upset with God and blamed Him for what might be. And then this man comes into his cleaners whistling because life was good. The attendant shook his head. "Humph. God sure is good. God is good."

♫♫♫

The barbershop was full when Graham reached it. It was 11:30 in the morning, and the noonday crowd was gathering. The shop was located in the heart of downtown Oakland in a small storefront. Manny, the owner, had been cutting hair for the last thirty years in the same location with almost the same loyal following. Some came to Manny's to get their hair cut; others came to get the daily gossip.

Graham peered through the glass and saw Roscoe hugging up a corner. It was plain to see that a good story had just been told from the contorted facial expressions on the men as they grabbed their middles and slapped their feet on the floor. The composition of men ranged from young to over sixty. Manny's was the place to hang out.

A picture of Martin Luther King, Jr. hung proudly on one of the narrow blue walls with a picture of Malcolm X a step down to the left. On the opposite wall rested a poster of Huey Newton flanked by two other members of the Black Panther Party—a relic from the '60s and '70s movement. Underneath the picture was a worn-out cardboard sign that read: "Haircuts $10.00, Style Cuts $15.00, Edge-Up and Mustache Trim $10.00." Behind the row of barber chairs filled with colorful human characters, a large, oblong mirror hung with pictures of kids now grown, if not dead, pasted around its perimeter. Three barber licenses, issued by the State of California, hung neglectfully either on the mirror or on the wall to its right and left, making it legal for all three barbers to cut some mean hairstyles this crowd craved.

The loud roar was even more audible as Graham stepped into the filled-to-capacity room, but it suddenly became quiet as Graham's presence was made known. He felt like he was the major character in their story, and they had just been busted. But after a brief exchange of howdy-do's, the place became lively again—this one telling a story and another one telling his story with a series of high-fives adding to the excitement.

"I want a nice fade," Graham said, as he eased into Manny's chair.

"Ain't seen you in awhile. How are you doing?" Manny said, draping Graham's shoulder with a towel.

"I feel pretty good. Don't cut off too much on top."

"Ohhhh. What's that all about? You usually want it cut close."

"Nothing."

"Must have something to do with all the rumors swirling around. Ain't mad at ya." They sat in silence as Manny whizzed away.

Manny dusted off the back of Graham's neck and pulled the towel from around his shoulders. Graham felt like a million dollars, and he only hoped Rita would approve of all that he had done to make himself presentable for her. The door chimed, and everyone looked up as Charlie Ford came through the door.

Charlie's eyes found Graham's. Graham nodded, paid for his haircut, and prepared to leave. Graham knew Charlie was still a little miffed since their last meeting, and he didn't want to get into any discussion about it, especially with other ears around. Graham looked at his watch and back at Charlie who was moving his lips to say something.

"Hey buddy, you in a hurry?"

"I'm on my way to my in-laws' house; they're expecting me any minute," Graham lied.

"Well, how about meeting me at The Water Hole later on? I hear it's gonna be off the hook."

"Give me a rain check on that Charlie. I've got some other plans for tonight."

"I hear Rita's in town."

Graham flinched as Charlie tossed the words, *Rita's in town*, out to him. How in the hell did he know? He just found out himself early this morning. "Yeah, I know," Graham threw back, trying not to let Charlie see how much he'd irritated him. "We're getting together later."

Charlie lifted his left eyebrow digesting Graham's last statement. "Seems you're not the only one she's meeting," Charlie smirked as if having the last laugh.

"I'm not sure I know what you're talking about. After all, this is a free country, Charlie. Rita is free to see anyone she likes. She's probably seeing a lot of folks today. I'm well aware she has some business to take care of—not that it's any of your business."

Charlie fished a toothpick out of his shirt pocket. "Well, I'll let you sizzle on that little appetizer for a while. After all, I owe you. If you should change your mind, you can find me at The Hole."

"Well, I really must go. I'll chat with you later, old friend," Graham said with a tone of animosity. Graham looked around the now-quiet room—from one person to the next—wondering if they too held some hidden knowledge they weren't sharing. *The hell with them all*, Graham thought. He pushed past Charlie and walked out into overcast skies.

♪♪♪

Water cascaded over her shapely body, massaging the taunt muscles in and around her shoulders. Rita lathered her shoulder-length mane, stimulating her scalp with long sculptured nails as they raked the crown of her head. She let out a small moan of satisfaction as the water continued to wash over her. Eyes closed, Rita allowed herself to immerse in the floral water garden that promised to soothe her achy limbs and prepare her for the day that lay ahead.

Thoughts of Graham swirled through her head. Rita had fallen in love—smitten by the bug she held at bay for more years than she had realized. Visions of her and Graham together had consumed most of her waking hours and just as many countless, sleepless nights. She now longed for the feel of him, his scent that made him so irresistible, and tonight Rita would let him know just how irresistible.

Another matter of great concern had brought Rita to the Bay Area. Old events and lives in her past frequently reared their ugly heads, often disrupting the peaceful life Rita had built. Each time she tried to shake it, the old haunted her in the new, but she resolved this would be the last time she'd let the old venture into her life again.

Rita stepped from the shower, gently toweling her body with the oversized, white, fluffy towel with the big "H" raised on the bottom. She liked staying at the Hilton because of its proximity to the Oakland Airport. Sitting at the vanity, Rita gazed into the mirror that was more than kind. It did not betray all she had been through in life; she was still an attractive woman.

Rita picked up the blow-dryer just as the telephone began to ring. It rang twice more before Rita attempted to move, but then it was silent again, and Rita commenced to dry her hair. She had not informed Graham of the time of her arrival or where she would be staying, so the call could not be from anyone she was dying to speak to. Only Clyde knew the real reason for her sudden trip to Oakland.

Quickly picking up her pace, Rita pulled a tan, cashmere, midi-length skirt from the closet, followed by a long, multi-toned, loosely fitting, coat-like cardigan in shades of brown and cream. A long, ash-brown, cowl-neck knit tunic lay on the bed and was the perfect complement to the other two pieces. Rita found her knee-high, tan-suede, pointed boots and sat them next to the bed. She'd put them on last—no need to tire her feet so soon.

A slight breeze filtered in the room and caused Rita to shiver. She rose to retrieve her robe from the bathroom.

Brrng, brrng, brrng.

Even though the phone startled Rita, she didn't want to be bothered. She had no desire to engage anyone in conversation before she was ready to do so. She let it ring.

Rita thought about calling Graham, if only to let him know she'd arrived safely. However, she thought better of it. She'd only end up having to answer a lot of unnecessary questions like *What time did you get in? Why didn't you call me sooner? Can I pick you up?*. No need to put herself in that position when all of that could be avoided. She'd take care of business and then she'd see Graham. First things first.

Rita quickly put on her clothes and looked at her watch again. It was 12:45—time to be on her way.

The garage was nearly empty when Rita went to get in her rental. She slid into the black BMW 318i with cream leather interior and sun-roof top, along with all the other amenities that made this car fit for a queen. Rita moved out onto Hegenberger Road and drove toward the old Nimitz Freeway, now called I-880, and headed toward downtown Oakland. There was a fair amount of traffic going northbound, but she had more than ample time to make her 1:30 appointment.

Rita dreaded her impending meeting. Life's circumstances somehow had a way of reaching out and grabbing you—pulling you back to places you hoped to never revisit. Such was the case, and if there had been any other alternative, any other way at all, she would have taken it rather than be where she was at this moment.

Signs of the Embarcadero whizzed by on her left as Rita pushed the BMW farther toward Oakland's epicenter. Downtown Oakland loomed in the distance, tall buildings rising from the ground like age-old stalagmites. It would be another few minutes before she would exit the freeway. Her meeting was at the Starbucks nestled among several rows of stores and restaurants at the Oakland City Center near Preservation Park. Rita exited the freeway and made a right onto Broadway, making a series of turns in an effort to find a convenient parking space.

A vacant space was not to be had. Businessmen and women walked briskly in and out of office buildings. Some stopped at a café or bistro to catch a late lunch; others ran a quick errand during a long session break at a conference they attended at the Marriott Oakland City Center. Rita looked at her watch. She had another five minutes.

Rita drove down Twelfth Street and hung a right on Martin Luther King Jr. Way. She drove alongside Preservation Park, a beautiful setting comprised of restored homes with a fountain at its center. It depicted a nineteenth-century Oakland neighborhood. Preservation Park sat on a plot of land once neglected but now renovated. Emulating the glory days of Oakland, it boasted architectural history that included Victorian- and Italian-styled homes. Several homes that still rested on their original foundation had historic value. Many used the park for a variety of nonprofit events. Rita turned down Thirteenth Street and at last found a lonely parking spot on Jefferson.

The large Louis Vuitton purse hugged Rita's side as she made her brisk getaway from the car. She was now ten minutes late and still had to walk a couple of blocks before entering the City Center Plaza. A string of quaint shops and small eateries occupied the little square. When Rita spotted Starbucks, she stopped and looked over her shoulder, then ahead again, recording the scene in her memory. Then she stepped into the coffee shop, the aroma of the various café flavors swirling about her nose. She scanned each table until she spotted him sitting off in a far corner, reading the early edition of *The Oakland Tribune*.

He looked much different than she remembered. He sat slouched down in his seat in a coffee-ground-colored trench coat and a black turtleneck sweater. Dreadlocks replaced his usually close-cropped haircut, and he seemed tired about the eyes, though they were somewhat shielded by a pair of reading glasses. But she still recognized him—and he was still somewhat handsome.

Rita stood clutching her purse tightly, not sure if she wanted to go through with her meeting. As she contemplated what she would do, he looked up from his paper, glanced at his watch, and put the paper down, never taking his eyes away from her. He was also growing a beard, she noted, that appeared to be in its infancy. A large café latte sat on the table and the crumbs of a blueberry muffin scattered about the saucer it had lain in. She saw a look in his eyes and began to move in his direction as if the question were settled. Rita took the seat opposite him, not quite sure what to say.

"You look good, Rita. It's been a long time."

His voice was gruff in a sexy kind of way—the voice that once aroused her to unknown depths. Disconnecting her eyes from his, she answered him in a low whisper. "Yes, it has been a long time, William. In fact, I had not expected to ever see you again."

"Well, I'm glad you came. If I didn't need your help, I wouldn't have asked. Would you like something to drink?"

"No thanks. I would like to know, though, what this is all about. How come you couldn't tell me on the phone? It cost money for me to come down here."

"Look, Rita. I…well, I…I just need you to do this one thing for me. I can't explain right now. I've been carrying this insurance policy on you for years, and I need to cash it in for the cash value."

"Is it some kind of business venture or are you out of money?"

"Did you bring the $15,000?"

Rita was silent for a moment, a little put off by his forwardness. "I did, but…can't you tell me what it's for? You sounded so urgent and made it seem imperative that I come right away."

"It is urgent, Rita. My life is depending on it. I can get $10,000 from this policy once you sign it and hopefully everything will be all right."

"Are you gambling?" There was silence again. "Remember, I was married to you once."

William sucked his teeth and looked into her eyes, those beautiful eyes he had hurt on so many occasions. "I need the money for a deal that could go bad, and if I don't hurry up and handle it, it will cost me a lot more than it will right now."

"Some things never change."

Rita sat with her hands folded. She lowered her head and reached back into her time capsule searching for one of those happier moments with William. There were a few.

"Where do you want me to sign?"

William pushed the insurance policy in front of Rita, moving the now cold latte off to the side. "Sign by the 'X.'"

Rita picked up the papers and examined them, running her fingers across her name on the face of the policy. "The end," she murmured under her breath—her words not lost on William. "You know, William, most policies are surrendered upon death of the insured." Rita looked up when William didn't respond. "I guess I should feel fortunate in that I'm able to sign my name on the dotted line and able to walk out into the sunshine even though I don't get to keep a cent."

"Enough, Rita. Just sign the paper, please. And don't forget the…"

"Don't worry, William. I'm not going to run off without giving you the money."

William sighed. Rita signed the papers ignoring William's audible exploits. Putting her pen down, Rita reached for her purse and pulled out the cashier's check she had tucked away for safekeeping in a hideaway compartment. She held it in her hand, toying with it as if indecision had set in about actually giving it up. William watched Rita until their eyes met. And she handed the $15,000 over without fanfare.

"Thanks," he said.

"I've got to go now. I have nothing else to give, William. I hope everything works out for you."

"You just got here. There's no need to run off unless you gotta meet that old man you've been hanging out with."

"I don't know what you're talking about," Rita stammered, her voice showing signs of irritation.

"My, my, my. I've never known you to lie, Rita—not you, the epitome of the All-American girl."

"And now we've become arrogant since we've gotten what we wanted.

What I do with my time and who I see is none of your business. You ceased to exist a long time ago in my life, and whatever you think you might know is again, none of your business."

"Okay, Rita. Calm down. Everyone is looking this way. I didn't mean to get you all riled up. I've just watched how you cuddled up to lover boy at The Water Hole." Rita fell back in her seat in disbelief. William had observed her without her knowledge. "Oh, I live in Oakland now, in fact, I've been living here for the past few months."

Rita's hands went to her face. A slight smirk passed over William's face as he sat back and wallowed in her obvious discomfort. Rita stood and William rushed to his feet ready to offer assistance if needed.

"Stay away from me, William. I've given you what you've asked for, and I can't help you any further. Stay away."

"Do you love him, Rita?"

"It's none of your business. Have a nice life, William."

Rita walked as fast as her pointed-toe, suede camel boots would take her. She felt a small trickle of water run past her cheeks. It couldn't be true. William could not have been in Oakland and she not see him. She had been puzzled with his choice of cities to meet in. What was he up to? She had not seen William in over fifteen years. Her life finally had meaning, and she was sure she'd met the man who truly loved her for who she was. Surely, this was not to be the onset of a nightmare. Rita needed Graham in the worst way, if only to hold her.

William watched from the window as Rita flew past and then out of sight. She was still a good-looking woman, but more than that, she could be a great asset to him in the future. There had to be a way to make Rita see that. She was wasting her time with the widower. Once he had been all she needed. William looked at the cashier's check and Rita's signature on the insurance policy. Yes, she could be a great asset to him down the road, and he'd do all within his power to make that a reality.

CHAPTER 24

The day had not panned out as Graham anticipated. His patience grew into irritation waiting for Rita to call, especially since Charlie announced three hours earlier that Rita was in town. He didn't quite know what to make of it. Was Rita hiding something from him? How did Charlie figure into the equation? There was certainly a cloud of curiosity surrounding Rita's visit to Oakland.

To top it all off, Graham had run from one dead end to another. He tried relentlessly to catch up with his in-laws but to no avail. They hadn't quite caught up with the twenty-first century and probably never would; they had refused to get an answering machine. They claimed that if people thought whatever they had to say was important, they would call back until they were able to reach somebody. Graham's only hope was that they wouldn't stop by today. It was not a good day to talk about Sister Mary Ross' accusations.

There had been five messages from Sister Mary Ross when Graham returned home. Each message pleaded with him to meet her for either breakfast or dinner—to talk about things. There was nothing he wanted to talk to Sister Ross about. *The nerve of that woman*, Graham thought, shaking his head like he'd come out of a bad dream.

Now his stomach was all tied in knots—all because of a woman, a beautiful woman he had met less than a couple of months ago while grieving the loss of his beloved Amanda. And he was in love—fell for her like a ton of bricks from a demolished building.

♪♪♪

The air seemed thick as Rita moved blindly and hurriedly sought refuge in her car. She couldn't believe William had been spying on her right under her very nose—right in the very room where she performed, where she sang out of her heart—songs that made people laugh, songs that made some sad, songs that called to lovers in the night like they had called her.

Rita was agitated and annoyed, her anxiety level driven high. The BMW was in sight. She picked up her pace, hoping to put more distance between her and the unsettling meeting of a few moments ago. Rita miscalculated how low the car was to the sidewalk, nicking her suede boots, causing a small tear as she swung the car door open. That only irritated Rita more.

"Damn," she said out loud. "This is all your fault, William."

Behind the wheel, Rita rested her arms on the steering wheel. She was not going to let William's revelation unnerve her. She had to get a grip; she had a new man—a man who loved her—all of her.

Going to Graham's right away wasn't such a good idea now. Rita needed time to relax and think things over. She wasn't sure what seeing William meant. It was best to not worry about it. After all, she and William were divorced.

Rita looked across the dash. It was 2:30. Maybe she would stop and get a cup of coffee before calling Graham. That would calm her nerves.

♪♪♪

The Oakland A's were in a slugging battle with the Seattle Mariners. It was Eric Chavez against Ichiro Suzuki. Graham sat slumped in the over-sized chair, his angora sweater and khaki slacks now wrinkled. He was in front of the tube watching his favorite team, the A's, beat up on the haggard Mariners. His favorite pastime was ceasing to placate him.

"Top of the ninth inning," the announcer said, "Mariners, three; Oakland, seven. It's a great day to be in the Bay Area." Graham nodded—his mouth partially open.

The telephone rang, startling Graham awake. He dropped his arm carelessly along the side of the chair, jerked the receiver from its hook and fumbled to keep it from falling.

"Hello," Graham said in a flustered voice, not yet fully awake.

"Hi, Graham, this is Rita. Wanted to let you know I made it safely, and I'll be there shortly."

Graham hesitated, and then spoke slowly, careful not to show any signs of irritation. But it was in his tone, hidden but yet felt. "Can't wait to see you," Graham said with an air of indifference. "When should I expect you?"

Rita sat up straight, almost knocking over her cup of coffee. She looked down at her cell phone to reassure herself that the number she had just dialed was indeed Graham's. There was something in his voice—agitation, maybe even jealousy. What was it? Rita hesitated too long, and she could hear Graham calling out for her.

"I'll be there in about an hour. I've just about concluded my business. Uhh…"

"Yes?"

"Are you all right? Is something wrong? You seem distant. You do remember that I said I had business to take care of, which was my reason for being here."

"Yes, yes, I'm fine."

"Oh," Rita said. "I'm at Barnes and Noble at Jack London Square. Would you like to meet me down here? Maybe we can get a quick bite to eat at T.G.I. Friday's or Jack's Bistro."

"No, why don't you come on over? We can sit and talk, and then I'll take you out for a nice dinner at Kincaid's Bayhouse. I hear the seafood broiler and the crab cakes are finger-lickin' good."

Graham's mood seemed to lighten and Rita's along with his. She didn't offer anything else. Her business was just that…her business. "That sounds like a wonderful idea."

"I'll be expecting you," she heard Graham say as she clicked the off button. Rita pondered her phone call and then took a sip of her hot cappuccino dosed with a hint of vanilla. The chatter from the small cluster of groups pigeonholed in the coffee shop grew louder and drowned out the confusion wreaking havoc in her head. She drank up, anxious to get to her next destination.

Rita finished her coffee, purchased a couple of books she had been dying to read, and headed for the door. For a moment, she felt a strange vibe—a force trying to get her attention. She looked about, turning her head from left to right. Nothing out of the ordinary, yet she felt uncomfortable.

It was 3:30 p.m., and a few tourists straggled about. The BMW sat on a corner two blocks from the bookstore. Rita walked briskly, constantly searching and scanning her surroundings, becoming totally aware of all that encompassed her in a 100-yard radius. She pulled the keys from her purse and rubbed against the small canister of mace that lay at the bottom. *There is no reason to be alarmed*, she thought. But just in case, her secret pal and weapon of choice was at her fingertips.

She arrived at her car without incident and hurriedly drove away. William's words came to haunt her: *I've watched how you've cuddled up to lover boy at The Water Hole*. Rita shivered at the thought. *He's been watching me. Hmph, maybe I need to get some real protection.*

Her body relaxed as she entered Chester Street. Not much had changed since she was there last. She saw Graham's Buick Regal in the driveway and a car she didn't recognize. The car didn't belong to Deborah or Liz. It was an older model. Graham hadn't told her anyone would be there.

Rita approached Graham's house and parked the car on the street. She wasn't sure why she didn't pull into the driveway, just a feeling.

She shrugged it off and walked casually to the front door. Before she could ring the bell, the door flew open. An anxious pair of eyes, set in an obviously bewildered face, met her. Rita was unable to read Graham, but somehow she knew it was associated with the yellow Coupe de Ville sitting in the driveway.

From out of nowhere, a large, stately woman appeared behind Graham. "Aren't you going to invite her in, son? Don't let her just stand out there on the porch."

Rita glanced between the two of them, unsure if she was willing to endure another episode that might send her blood pressure skyrocketing. Whoever this woman was, she seemed pleasant enough. She had an air of familiarity about her, though, and she called Graham "son." Then it dawned on her. Yes, it was Amanda's mother. The striking resemblance was carved in the chiseled contours of the woman's face, from the high cheekbones to the cleft of her chin. It made Rita recall the day she held Amanda's picture in her hand while Graham stood off in a corner, observing her.

But Rita was not up to a confrontation with this woman about being in Graham's life so soon after Amanda's death. It had been more than she could endure at the hands of Deborah and Liz as they hurled their angry insults at her. Rita thought about making a fast exit, but she heard the woman shout out for her to come in.

"Hello," came a voice from somewhere behind Graham.

"Hello, Rita," Graham said in a voice huskier than usual. He took Rita's hand and ushered her into the house. "This is my mother-in-law, Martha Carter."

"Nice to meet you, Mrs. Carter." Rita extended her hand and Martha took it, cupped it in her own left hand, and patted it with her right.

"It's nice to finally meet you," Martha said to Rita with a slight bow of her head.

Rita wasn't sure if the woman was trying to be sarcastic or she genuinely meant it. Martha's lips were set in the shape of a crescent moon and her teeth, real or false, glowed like they'd just been polished.

"And this is my father-in-law, Elroy Carter," Graham continued as they moved farther into the living room.

They exchanged similar greetings. Rita noticed Mr. Carter had the same painted smile on his face, although she did not detect any hint of pretentiousness.

"Anybody want tea or coffee?" Martha called out, trying to break the tension in the room.

"There isn't any made, and…"

"Son, entertain your guest. I'll take care of it. You all look as if you need something. I know I do. No sweets in here, either," Martha droned as she opened up the refrigerator and kitchen cabinets. "I've got a sweet tooth, and I guess I'm just going to have to wait until I get home."

The group began to giggle until the giggles became a crescendo of crazy laughter with all of Martha's crazy antics. And like a defroster unfogging a steamy window in blinding rain, the tension seemed to ease.

"You've been the topic of many conversations in our town lately, Ms. Rita," Elroy said when the laughter had died down. "Now I understand why."

Rita blushed and became ill at-ease again. She arched her eyebrows in confusion, unsure what direction the conversation was going. Graham had said very little since she arrived. He almost seemed intimidated by his in-laws. Rita looked at Graham, hoping he'd pick up the conversation and keep her from the witches' pyre.

"I've got coffee for everyone," Martha said before anyone got a chance to say anything further. Cups and saucers rattled on a gaily painted tin tray Martha carried along with a coffeepot and four spoons. She gave each a set of utensils and poured Elroy's coffee first, Graham's next, then Rita's, and finally her own. She placed the tray on the coffee table and took a seat on the couch next to her husband.

"What did I miss?" Martha asked.

"Nothing, Mom," Graham finally replied.

Needing to say something, Rita blurted out, "I am a dear friend of Graham's. I was in town on business, and I came by to see how he was doing."

"Honey, we know who you are," Martha piped in. "You're a very beautiful lady. I see why my son-in-law is smitten with you."

"Mom…"

"No, Graham. Let me," Rita cut in. "Mr. and Mrs. Carter, I understand how you might feel seeing Graham with someone else besides Amanda."

"I never said he shouldn't be…"

"I want you to know that he is a good man, and I understand how your daughter fell in love with him. Graham still loves Amanda dearly, although she is not physically here. He's told me all about their wonderful life together, his wonderful children, his wonderful in-laws and how Amanda was his whole life. While it seems I might be slightly jealous or wanting the same thing for myself, I'm not. I met a man drowning in his sorrow, hurt beyond repair, it seemed. I met a man who could only talk about one woman, and her name is Amanda. I met a man whose love is so deep it seemed impossible he could love another. Somehow, we found our way to each other; I call it a blessing from God.

"I've suffered some of life's tragedies, but I was able to move on. I was married once," Rita hesitated, "to a very popular man who mistreated me. I wanted to wallow in self-pity, but I picked myself up and made a new life for myself. I've been divorced over twenty years. I've dated off and on but never had a serious or meaningful relationship. And then, I finally met someone…someone I was drawn to for a reason unknown to me. But when I met him, I immediately knew that there was something special about him.

"If Graham was smitten, he couldn't have realized it when we first met. The man I met was drowning in sorrow. I drew strength from him, and he from me. But I knew he would be all right."

"My, my, my," Martha said, breathing a sigh of relief. Martha fanned herself and took another sip of coffee. "We didn't come by, sweetie, to render judgment on you. The fact of the matter is, we came by to talk to Graham here, about what happened in Bible study a few weeks back."

"Yes, Lord," Elroy put in.

"You were part of the discussion, but Graham was the major topic, and the church folks seemed to have come armed to do battle."

"You should have seen my Martha," Elroy teased. "She knocked out Sister Mary Ross with a one-two punch."

"Hush up, Elroy."

"Sister Mary Ross?" Rita chimed in. Rita looked over at Graham who sat still with his mouth closed, seemingly enjoying the festivities.

"Yes, one in the same. Mary had called all the saints to tell them she had seen you at my son-in-law's house and…well you were there, you know the story. Anyway," Martha sighed, "that information was routed out to the whole church network, and instead of having Bible study that next Wednesday, we had Let's Oust Deacon Peters Day."

"I'm so sorry, Graham," Rita said, dejected, not sure she wanted to hear the rest of the story.

"I'm fine. You might want to hear what happened."

Rita turned her attention back to Martha, who was dying to get the rest of the fiasco out of her mouth.

"Sister Mary Ross, as Martha said," Elroy butted in, taking the lead and not waiting for Martha to give her account, "started talking about how she saw the two of you hugged up together and Amanda hadn't been dead but a minute. She asked Reverend Fields what he was going to do about it. Then Deacon Harris called for Graham here to be put off the Deacon Board. This is where it gets good."

Rita noticed the grin running across Graham's face.

"Then Momma gets up out of her seat cuz she done had just about enough."

"And you sat back in your seat like a scaredy-cat," Martha said.

Graham chuckled.

"All right, Martha," Elroy said. "Let me finish. Martha commenced to telling Sister Ross off. Told Mary Ross in front of the whole congregation that she didn't care nothing about how the church felt, because Mary had an eye on Graham for herself, which was why she was making all that fuss in the first place. The church was *r-e-a-l* quiet.

"Then, Sister Ross hollered back at Martha, and at one point I thought Martha was going to knock her down. But this is the good part. Martha told that nosey woman that if Graham was going to be with someone, it wouldn't be her."

"Mom," Graham spoke for the first time, "Did you really say that? And you stood up for me? I really appreciate that."

"Look," Elroy said, not wanting to be slighted in giving the whole account, "Reverend Fields got up and started clapping his hands, and Bible study was over for the evening."

Martha grinned at Elroy. "See, I love that man. We've been together longer than time itself. He still has a little spunk left in him."

Elroy coughed and continued, "God has blessed us—He's given us long life, a wonderful daughter and son-in-law, grandchildren, and a life she'd never trade for anything."

Martha looked at Graham and Rita. "It's obvious you are in love—not just mere acquaintances. Amanda was the apple of Graham's eye. He loved my daughter for all those many years and was a true gentleman, father, and friend. It *is* difficult seeing Graham with someone else, but you seem nice enough, unlike the description my granddaughter Deborah painted of you."

Rita flinched.

Martha bowed her head, and then lifted it. She turned toward Graham and Rita with all eyes looking at her. "I was concerned when my grand-daughters told me what happened the other day. And, of course, there are always two sides to a story. But, I'm Amanda's mother, and knowing the love that flows within this family, our history, and what all else, I'll admit I was hurt that Graham had brought someone into this house so soon after...A-Amanda was gone. Yes, I was angry and I wasn't going to have any of it, but I became angrier still when I heard Sister Ross disrespecting my family before the whole church." Martha began to sob and Graham went to her.

"I'm all right," she admonished, shooing him away. "While I don't apologize for my granddaughters, Rita, I do understand their hurt and pain. We are all part of a grand family chain. We had each other for a long time, and it was devastating for all of us when Amanda died. Our family was so close, and the thought of outside intervention was non-existent. And now a new face dares to replace one of familiarity, a face that had been with the family for sixty odd years, that is now but a shell buried away in a lush garden overlooking the city." Martha clasped her face in her arms, and all drew around her to offer comfort.

This is a wise, old woman, Rita thought to herself. Much like her own mother. She was instantly drawn to her—maybe it was her wisdom, definitely her grace and wit. But Martha had the strength of a thousand women, and time had not held her back. Rita rubbed Martha's shoulders.

"I understand," Rita said. "I understood before I ever entered this house, because Graham had already made me aware of who Amanda is in his life."

Martha looked up with a smile on her face. "Sweetie, I know the state my son-in-law was in after Amanda died. For weeks on end, he was a pitiful wreck. I heard he wouldn't eat, sleep, or even clean himself up. He didn't want any of us around—just wallowed in self-pity like the rest of us didn't miss our sweet Amanda. He almost drowned himself in a lake thinking he had seen her reflection in the water. I know he missed, and still misses, Amanda dearly."

Graham came and stood behind Rita and placed an arm around her, the other around Martha. "I know I've been rather quiet. Actually, I had hoped to avoid a confrontation by searching you and Dad out earlier today. In fact, I was afraid if you came by and Rita was here, there would be a repeat of the debacle with Deborah and Liz. I couldn't chance losing Rita. But now I understand it had to be this way."

Graham looked at his in-laws. "You will always be my family. I've just been fortunate enough to find someone to possibly share what time I have left on this earth. I can't explain the timing, but I do hope you can forgive me if I've in any way disrespected you or disgraced the memory of Amanda. That was certainly not my intent. I'm not even sure where our relationship will go, but I appreciate this moment, this time in which we have been able to sit down and talk about what's in our hearts. I will always love Amanda, but I've come to realize that I do have room in my heart to love again."

Martha smiled and rubbed Graham's hand while Rita squeezed the other. "I know you love Amanda, son. Elroy and I were a little shocked at the news that you might be seeing a woman so soon after Amanda's death; however you, me, and Elroy don't have a lot of time left here on this earth." That elicited a snicker from the group.

Martha's voice became serious, whispering almost as she continued to speak. "I want to see you happy, Graham. It seems Rita makes you happy."

"She does."

"Elroy and I are in our eighties, and we don't have a lot of time left to be worrying about what you youngsters are doing as long as it's right. God has blessed us, and we got a little livin' left in us. And a little more lovin'."

"Martha," Elroy shouted.

"How old are you, Rita?"

"Forty-five."

"A little young," Martha said, giving Graham a sideways glance. "But age is only a number if you truly love someone. Look, I just want you both to be sure what you're doing. I know it doesn't look good so soon after Amanda's death, and it will still be hard for me to see the two of you together, but Amanda is gone, Graham, and you served her well and in an upright manner.

"You seem to be a nice lady, Rita. I will try to talk to the girls, but I can't promise any miracles. I'll do my best. Just don't disappoint me."

"Thank you," Rita said. She gave the old woman a kiss and went over and hugged Elroy. "While I don't quite know what to say, I'll say this. I'm just Rita. I have a good and kind heart. I'm not here to take Amanda's place. I felt her warmth when I stepped in this room for the first time, when I looked at her picture, and at all the things in and around this house that told her story. Thank you for giving me a chance."

"Well, sweetie, it'll take time, but this is a start. Elroy, let's go. I'm sure these two would like to spend some time together."

"It was nice meeting you, Rita, and we've got to get together and go fishing real soon, Graham."

"I think I can handle it now, Dad."

"Elroy, get my door," they heard Martha say as the couple stumbled to their car. And a burden fell from Graham's shoulder.

CHAPTER 25

D usk had fallen and a full moon was in view. The clock ticked on the mantel and lent the only noise to a melancholy evening. Graham and Rita sat silently on the loveseat, reeling from the unexpected meeting with Graham's in-laws.

The moment was tender and innocent as they held each other's hand and reflected on what had transpired. Relief was written in their body language and love written in their hearts. It was a sign from God that everything would be all right.

Rita stroked Graham's arm. Her business with William kept nagging at her.

Rita had a dilemma. If she was going to forge a relationship with Graham, she didn't want it to start off with secrets. But was it a secret? She didn't want to keep anything from Graham, but this was her business. Did Graham need to know? If William showed up again, what would she say?

A voice that belonged to Martha rang in her ears, admonishing Rita not to disappoint her.

She still could not bring herself to say a word.

♪♪♪

Graham was lost in his own thoughts. Although unplanned, his in-laws stopping by and what had transpired during their visit could only be a blessing. Their unwavering love and understanding meant more to Graham than life itself. All he had anticipated would happen once his in-laws confronted him gave way to a new meaning of love, trust, and faith. And to know that Martha stood up for him, no matter how she may have really felt deep down inside, said more to the character of that great lady.

Although Graham's mood had mellowed, the nagging feeling that something else was up remained. Rita gave no hint to that possibility, and since there was no time for conversation because of the untimely visit from Graham's in-laws, Graham would have to continue to speculate. It was probably all in his mind, but the mere thought that Charlie was privy to information unknown to him, and the aloofness in which Charlie delivered his message, left an air of uncertainty.

Graham turned to look at the full length of Rita. She was truly a stunning woman—from her shoulder-length mane to the points on her tan-suede boots. They exchanged a quick glance, and Rita sensing Graham's hesitation, came over and placed a tender kiss on his lips.

Yes, she was remarkable. Graham closed his eyes and pulled Rita to him with the force of a gale wind. She leaned into him, and Graham gingerly tasted her lips before thrusting his tongue into the fullness of her mouth.

She incited him. He teased her. Consumed by the moment, their lips remained locked as each competed to be the first not to come up for air while their tongues searched and tasted.

It was becoming sheer madness—his cologne intoxicating her and she holding on for dear life. Her sculptured nails ran through the thick forest of hair on his head. She panted every now and then when the electricity was more than she could stand. He was lost in the heat of passion wanting to consume every bit of the sweet, chocolaty morsel that had aroused more than just his manhood.

Rita let the coat-like cardigan slide off of her shoulders and onto the floor. Graham pushed back and surveyed her petite frame with the healthy portion of breasts protruding from the knit cowl-neck tunic. He reached out and drew her to him—the sweet smell of honeysuckle exuding from her hair intoxicating. He began to massage her breasts through the sweater, stimulating Rita all the more. The more aggressive Graham became, the more Rita gave in.

Rita's hands crawled down the length of Graham's angora sweater. The soft feel prompted Rita to play there a while, making it hard for Graham to concentrate. And without any persuasion, Rita followed Graham to the room, the room where only one other woman had lain with Graham, made love to Graham, conceived his children, and gave him her all. Rita didn't hesitate. The emotion she held inside was bursting at the seams. And likewise, Graham didn't want to waste another moment getting to know this woman better.

They removed their clothes in silence trading kisses at five-second intervals. When Rita was down to her Victoria's Secret, tan lace, push-up bra and bikini panties and Graham in his Joe Cool boxers, she crawled upon the bed and lay on her side, beckoning Graham to come closer. She moved her tongue in and out in a sensuous rotation. Graham reached for Rita, trying to sequester his overpowering passion. He wanted to leap upon the beautiful goddess that lay before him.

Graham brought Rita's face to within a half inch of his. He thrust his lips upon hers again and kissed her with all the passion he possessed. He removed his tongue and slowly let it slide down her chin, down her neck, encircle her shoulders, and finally catching sight of her very firm breasts just south, pushed away her bra until he had one pointed, tender nipple in his mouth and the other between his fingers. Rita moaned with pleasure at fever pitch until Graham had to stop and look up to see if she was all right.

Rita pushed his head back down, and he continued to suckle each breast in turn. He released his hand from her breast and traveled farther south finding the very essence of her womanhood ready and in wait of him. Graham was intrigued that his own inhibition did not prevent him from making love to Rita. Although he and Amanda had an active sex life up until she died, he found himself wanting to please Rita from the top of her well-coiffed mane to the tips of her gaily polished toes.

Graham felt her wince as he explored the whole of her. His hands traced her hips and again moved to the mound of all her glory. She moaned and hissed when he touched her, and he breathed heavily as he fought the premature urge to come before he was ready. He parted her shapely legs, bringing her knees up to his chest. He found her waiting, and he went in. They moved to a rhythm that was all their own, stirring up emotions and passion inside of them that was dormant but had now come to life.

Soon they lay spent from their lovemaking. Being with Rita awakened a new surge of energy—a new life for Graham. For Rita, it was being without a real man for the last twenty years and finally finding someone she wanted to give her soul to.

A new woman had brought a new passion and a new thirst for life. A new man had brought love and a desire to conquer the world. Oh, it seemed so right—a good fit like the right glove to a hand.

"Together," Rita sighed softly, as she rubbed Graham's temples and kissed him softly on the lips.

"For all times," Graham murmured, a smile crossing his face as he continued to tease Rita with his tongue, stroking the fires of desire once again.

Rita silently prayed that it would be for a time. Graham thanked God that love had found its way—again.

CHAPTER 26

William pulled his fingers through his locks and tumbled out of the coffee shop into the brightness of the day. It had gotten to him seeing Rita in such close proximity. She was more beautiful now than when they were together. That was a long time ago, but he was going to change that. Rita was going to be his, by hook or by crook.

William had fallen on hard times and much of it was caused by his own unscrupulous behavior. When he and Rita split up, he was still living the big time, running women and horses. He'd spend days at a time in Vegas hoping to hit the big one—to carry him over during the lean times or just to continue the life to which he had become accustomed.

After the divorce was final, William had lost Rita for a time. As Rita's career blossomed, her name became somewhat of a household word in the music world up and down the West Coast. Although she remained somewhat in the shadows of the big-timers, William began to hear about her successes and eventually followed her career, every once in a while venturing to one of the clubs where she was performing. He would always sit in the back remaining incognito, although, there was one time when he thought Rita might have recognized him.

As William's popularity waned, the women drifted away. He earnestly held down a couple of jobs, but the sting of being out of the spotlight was too much for him. He wanted to be a star, and selling insurance or having a nice cushiony office job as Assistant Director for Promotions for IBM weren't going to produce the kind of life he sought.

He stopped going to work and started drinking more, gambling harder, until most of what he had left after the divorce was consumed. And he lost track of Rita.

He was virtually alone until he found Angie. A friend had talked him into going to a karaoke bar for some fun. And there was Ms. Angie Black, all dressed in white singing "Unbreak My Heart" along with Toni Braxton. William wasn't sure what drew her to him—maybe she reminded him of Rita so many years before, singing at his friend's wedding.

Angie took William home, believing she had found the man of her dreams. She took care of him while he bungled job after job. After six years of scuffling and taking care of a man who had no "get up and go," who believed the power was in the bottle and sometimes drugs, who'd rather lay up and let her go to work, pay the bills, and buy the food, Angie bade farewell to William. Told him she was going to Oakland to live with her sister, Latrice.

Four months after Angie left, William headed for Oakland, hoping to find her. William was able to get Latrice's number from one of Angie's girlfriends. When he got to Oakland, William found out that Angie had found a friend and was living with him.

William became angry, almost violent, pleading with Latrice to give him the address so he could talk with Angie. When Latrice refused, William threatened her, and she snatched up her mobile, fingers poised to dial 9-1-1.

William left as quickly as he had arrived. A run-in with the law was the last thing he needed his first night in Oakland. He got a room at the California Hotel on San Pablo Avenue. While talking to a few stragglers in the lobby, he met a guy who wanted to know if anybody wanted to go to The Water Hole for a drink. A drink was just what William needed, and he accepted the man's invitation to the club.

When William got there, the place was alive and jumping. The jukebox was going and the band was on their intermission break. Everyone was dressed to the nines. Double-breasted pin-striped suits hung from some of the brothers and Stacy Adams shoes adorned their feet. The women sported designer suits, except for the younger set who wore skin-tight lycra dresses and tops that bared their midriffs. William's grin grew wide.

He sat at a table in a far corner by a wall. His ride, Maurice, was off somewhere getting his hustle on. William wasn't dressed like those around him, but he could on any given day. And he didn't plan on going anywhere, because he was digging the scene. The three scotch and sodas he consumed only helped to warm his heart and put him in the groove.

It wasn't until the band came on to do their final set that William came out of his trance and grew conscious of his surroundings. Right before his very eyes was his ex-wife, singing her heart out to folks who didn't know her like he did, who lusted after her, who screamed for her to sing on until she was spent.

William sat transfixed as she belted out number after number. The way she swayed her hips and sent sensuous glances to one side of the room made it appear she was singing to someone in particular. William scanned the room to see if there was some crazed individual longing to be with his wife, hoping that she would go home with him and do things that only she and he used to do together.

The set was over and Rita disappeared from sight. Moments later, she reappeared and William watched her with rapt attention. Rita sauntered to a table in front of the stage and pecked the cheek of a man who seemed much older than she. William continued to watch them from a distance as they said good-bye and the gentleman left with another gentleman— about the same age with a yellow girl hanging on his arm.

William stood back. He didn't know what to make of it, but he'd be back at The Water Hole tomorrow for sure.

And William came and watched for the next two nights as Rita swooned and cooed her lover with song. He also noticed that the other gentleman seemed a little put off by the couple's obvious affection—maybe he liked her, too. He would have to do a little snooping around, but for sure, Oakland was going to be his stop for a while.

William drove his broken-down Acura Legend away from downtown contemplating his next move. The money Rita had given him would cover his gambling debts and give him a clean slate. But what William hoped for more than anything else was respectability—just the way it used to be. When William Long's name was called out during a game in the old days, people listened, sent up high-fives, and gave a resounding round of applause. Now his name was as common as the next—couldn't even buy a job at the corner grocery store.

He entered the neighborhood of fellow former player, Troy Kemp, who had not quite measured up in the NBA. He lived in what could have passed for a mansion sitting on the edge of a slum. *A refuge for the time being*, William thought. Trash and broken bottles littered the streets. Empty, brown, crumpled-up paper bags made a chain-link fence around the neighborhood liquor store. Brothers who had not known what it was to work an eight-to-five job stood outside the liquor store sharing a piece of a promise and a half-empty liquor bottle. William drove on, making a promise to himself that this stop would not be for long.

CHAPTER 27

"Your lips are like cotton candy," Graham whispered, tasting Rita's lips once again.

"Your lips are sweet as honey," Rita cooed, enjoying Graham's playful prowl.

Graham leaned over her, placing kisses all over until he heard her moan in satisfaction.

"Better not get anything started, even though I could lie here and never get up," Rita said. It was Graham's turn to moan.

"And if we don't get up, somebody will be hungrier than they are now."

"Just hungry for you."

"Oh, baby, don't go there. I may never let you leave Oakland, especially my bed."

Rita and Graham laughed like two lovesick newlyweds wishing the moment would last forever.

"Baby," Rita said slowly, "have you regretted making love to me?"

"No, why do you ask?"

"You won't believe what I was thinking."

"What?" Graham asked, lazily rubbing the length of Rita's arm.

"Amanda."

Graham sat straight up, leaning back on his arms. He looked around the room as if Amanda's spirit had suddenly materialized. Then he looked at Rita, who stared straight into his eyes. "Amanda? What...about Amanda?"

"Well, I...I was wondering if she was sitting way up there in the sky looking down at us…upset with herself for leaving you and not being the one you were making love to tonight."

Graham dropped his eyes.

"I was wondering if she'd accept me like her parents did, knowing that I had your best interest at heart, and that I would never try and take her place, but love you for the rest of your days."

"Amanda is gone, Rita. I have just come to that realization myself after all I've been through these past few months. It has nothing to do with you being in my life. It has everything to do with knowing that Amanda is not coming back to me, and that what we shared was wonderful, wholesome; and no one can compete with that. I truly believe that Amanda would be upset with me if I just sat around and pouted, let life drift away to the point of decay that even turns the vultures' noses up."

"You have a way with words."

"I'm serious, Rita. I loved Amanda—and still do. But I love you, too. And right now, I'm alive—more alive than I've been in a month of Sundays. And, if you don't stop looking so good lying there…you, you goddess of the hearth, I'm going to have to delay dinner at Kincaid's and dine on the feast that layeth before me!!"

"You sweet, sensuous man. Come here!" Rita squealed with delight.

Graham fell upon Rita, and their bodies entwined. They held each other close—so close it seemed their breathing stopped. They kissed passionately, rocking back and forth on the French provincial, queen-size bed that offered only comfort as the couple slipped further into the depths of what was fast becoming another evangelical ride to the mountaintop.

CHAPTER 28

It was 6:30 when Graham rose from the light slumber that overcame him and Rita after a healthy second helping of lovers' delight. Now sitting up, he looked down at her—so peaceful with an angelic expression on her face. Her right arm hung carelessly off the side of the bed while her body formed the shape of a geometrical design with her head and feet marking points on a linear equation. Graham was in love.

He shook her gently, not wanting to scare her. First her right eye, then her left fought to peel back the lids that shut out the miracle of day. Rita fluttered her eyelashes as she tried to focus—her eyes seeking a sense of familiarity. She slowly lifted her body, catching a glimpse of her disheveled head in the dresser mirror before finally spotting the object of her daydream. Rita was in love.

They showered together, unable to get enough of each other's touch. They kissed and touched. They kissed and rubbed. They kissed and held each other. They kissed and toweled off one another. They kissed as they put on the clothing they had carelessly tossed about the room. They kissed between searching for her purse. They kissed after he picked up his keys. They kissed and touched. They kissed and rubbed until someone managed to unlatch the front door on their way to get a bite to eat. They were in love.

Rita and Graham walked to their respective cars. Rita agreed that after dinner, Graham would follow her back to her hotel room so she could pick up a few articles of clothing and whatever else she needed to tide her over for a couple of days. It would be so simple to give up her hotel room, however, Rita wanted the option of its availability on the rare chance she might need it. And with the way things were going, she doubted very seriously she would need it at all.

Graham was already in his car when Rita noticed a folded piece of paper under the windshield wiper. Someone must be advertising a big event in town. Rita took the piece of paper from the window and tossed it onto the passenger seat, along with her purse, without looking at it. She leaned her head back against the headrest; she was hungry and couldn't wait to taste the crab cakes at Kincaid's.

Graham and Rita arrived at Kincaid's twenty minutes later. They elected valet parking, and after leaving their car keys with the attendant, hurriedly went inside the restaurant. The place smelled of smoke—possibly the remnants of grilled steak and seafood—that caused their palates to water. Men in expensive suits, an aged woman with several large diamond and emerald rings weighing down her frail fingers, and a huge, burly man with the stump of an unlit Havana cigar stuck in the side of his mouth waited to be seated. There was a crowd tonight, but the wait would be worth it.

They were finally ushered to a table in a cozy corner of the restaurant. Small table lanterns were lit and the overhead lights turned down low. It was the hour of the day when lovers sipped their favorite chardonnay and carried on light conversation in low romantic whispers. They were given a menu, and the waitress promised to return in a minute.

Rita excused herself to go to the restroom and passed a large party of diners celebrating what seemed to be some sort of office get-together. The men in the expensive suits had joined the party sitting at a round table with two overbleached blonde women in their late twenties. Someone told a funny joke and the crowd began to howl.

The restroom was in the opposite corner from where they sat, and she lost sight of Graham when she rounded the corner. Before entering the restroom, Rita felt as if someone was watching her. She looked, but didn't see anyone she remotely knew. She shrugged her shoulders and went in.

When Rita emerged from the restroom, the laughter from the large group of diners met her ears. She now realized they were roasting one of the employees, and everyone was getting into the act. Then she spotted Charlie at one of the booths, sitting with a lady friend who was way over-dressed in a mink fur coat and hat—unseasonal for that time of year. It was a bit chilly, typical for the Bay Area in the early evening, but in the thick of October, the leaves were still yellow and brown.

If Charlie saw Rita, he pretended not to, although he was sitting in the direction that had her in full view. Rita decided not to go over to his table; she would spare Charlie the embarrassment of having to introduce her to his new woman, who just might be intimidated by her intrusion. Rita still could not get over the feeling she was being watched. She twisted her neck in all directions, was grateful there wasn't a trace of William, and deduced her fear to her imagination.

When she returned to her seat, Graham was sipping chardonnay—the stem of the glass resting on the palm of his hands. He got up when Rita returned, and sat when she had comfortably settled in her seat. Graham had a faint smile on his face. He took Rita's hand off the table and kissed her fingers gently. Rita blushed.

"The waitress came by for our order, and I told her to return in a few minutes."

"Thank you," Rita whispered seductively.

"When we're an old mar…I mean…when we've been together longer, then I might take the liberty of ordering for you."

"You are the last of the purely great breed of gentlemen."

"I do my best."

"I saw Charlie sitting at a booth on the other side when I came from the restroom," Rita said, changing the subject.

"Charlie, here?"

"Yes, he was sitting with a woman I didn't know, but he didn't see me." The look on Graham's face turned to one of puzzlement.

"Something wrong?" Rita asked. "You have a puzzled look on your face."

"Just thinking."

"What is it, Graham? One minute I was telling you about seeing Charlie, and the next you climbed into some cocoon. Did I say something wrong?"

"Charlie didn't say anything to you?"

"Like I said, he didn't see me or pretended not to see me, although I was in plain view of him. And, I wasn't about to go up to his table and say hello."

"Where did you see him again?"

"Across the room and around the corner."

Before Rita could say another word, Graham jumped up from his seat and proceeded in the direction Rita had pointed out. He was gone all of one minute before he returned and sat down.

"Didn't see him. He seems to have left in a hurry."

"Hmph, that's strange. It didn't appear he had eaten yet."

There was a long pause before Graham spoke. "Rita, how did Charlie know that you were here today?"

"What are you talking about, Graham?"

"I saw Charlie this morning at the barbershop, and he made it a point to let me know you were in town."

Rita watched Graham, searching his face for the accusation, finally realizing the source of his strange mood earlier in the afternoon. It was apparent Graham was upset Charlie knew she was here and that he had just found out, as if her coming to Oakland was a big secret. She didn't know how Charlie knew, but it was Graham she was worried about—his not trusting her.

"I don't know how Charlie knew I was in town. The first time I saw Charlie since I've been in town was ten minutes ago—and then from a distance. I'm not sure what you're trying to insinuate, Graham, but it has me a little perturbed. Don't you trust me?"

"Of course, I do, Rita. It's…it's just that Charlie and I have been sort of on the outs. And it has been mainly about you. Charlie has always been jealous of me for whatever reason, and although we go back fifty-something years, he has not changed."

"What's that got to do with us?"

"It was the way Charlie said, '*I hear Rita's in town.*'"

"Maybe he heard it from Clyde. I called Clyde this morning to let him know that I would drop down there today or tomorrow to sign a contract for our next gig. That's the only explanation I have, Graham. Whatever silly game Charlie is playing, if that's what he's doing, I am not aware of it. I had some personal business downtown, and that was that."

A smile lit up Graham's face. "I'm sorry, Rita. I guess I was a little jealous that he knew something only I should have known—and that tone of voice…just set me off."

"Don't worry about it, baby. I like my man a l-i-t-t-l-e jealous." Rita stroked Graham's arm. "We can kiss and make up tonight." But Rita was more than worried—and not about Charlie.

CHAPTER 29

William walked up the stone driveway that led to Troy's house. The house sat back from the street and was well hidden by the clump of maple trees that shadowed the house. It was a two-story, split-level, stucco dwelling boasting four bedrooms and four baths, a large formal dining room, family room, a twenty-by-twenty, brick-laden kitchen with built-in grill, a game room made for previewing NBA game tapes and entertaining sports enthusiasts from all spectrums of athletics, two wet bars, and a ten-by-fifteen laundry room that could house a small twin bed if needed. Troy never forgot where he came from, so he built his house on the border of the haves and have-nots. Not many of his old NBA buddies stopped by anymore, though.

William used the key Troy had given him to let himself in. He dropped the insurance papers on the sofa table in the foyer under the tall, oak mirror with a heavy Greek pattern outlined in gold foile running around its perimeter. An empty feeling engulfed William as he was consumed by the vastness of the place now devoid of human life. In fact, Troy rarely stayed there, spending a lot of his time with a special lady friend who was well on her way to becoming the next female Johnnie Cochran.

William threw down the keys on one of the glass end tables in the family room and headed for the well-stocked wet bar. An open bottle of cognac caught William's eye, and he lifted a high-ball glass from its glass shelf and poured until the glass was full.

William retreated to the white leather couch and took a sip of his drink. Engulfed in the leathery bowels of the pillow-cushioned couch, he looked up at the white-speckled ceiling and about the room. There was no mistaking the influence of a masculine touch. While Troy was no longer making NBA money, he didn't deprive himself of the finer things in life. It was a playa's way, however, Troy was fortunate to be able to capitalize on his degree in business from UCLA, having become one of several whose name was readily sought out as a top agent to the athletes.

There were pictures on the wall of Troy and William's playing days with the L.A. Lakers. There was a trophy wall that held Troy's trophies—from MVP of his high school basketball team to leading scorer at UCLA. Those were the glory years. The Lakers had promised the same, but somehow he became lost in the shuffle—couldn't pull his game together—wrought with disputes with the coaching staff, and to hear it told, some teammates. After four years on the team, Troy found himself on the NBA blacklist—and finally on no list.

There was a panel to the left of the trophies that held pictures of Troy and some of his female conquests. William shook his head in remembrance of some of the crazy antics and misguided, bizarre, and hurtful things he had done. Each came with a price in the end. Now this beautiful room with its white Italian leather sofa and chairs, huge maple entertainment center with a sixty-four-inch Sony television set and built-in music system for easy entertaining became a reminder of where he had been and all he had lost.

William picked up the remote, flicked on the television, and abruptly turned it off. He pulled the cashier's check from his pocket and got up to retrieve the insurance policies from the table where he had deposited them when he first entered the house.

William stared at Rita's signature for the longest time—almost burning a hole through the paper with his intensity. Rita was doing well, and she would be just what he needed to get out of his slump and on top again. Maybe, he would be her manager—getting her professional and box-office gigs—none of that hole-in-the-wall, juke-joint stuff. Rita would be on world tour sharing the stage with Whitney Houston or Brian McKnight. She was a singer in her own right—that's what drew him to her; and they could enjoy the lavish lifestyle they once had...enjoying the finer things of life. A home in New York, one in L.A., and a cottage on the French Riviera.

William jumped up. He had to get a plan and put it into action. Recapturing Mrs. Rita Long would be part of the plan. William wasn't sure how he was going to do it, but it would be a mission he'd accomplish. He'd watch her for a while, even if it meant taking a couple of trips to Seattle. In the end, she would be his again, and together they would conquer the world. And she'd have to dump her new friend, because the future didn't include that old man.

But first, William had to find a poker game. A little gambling wouldn't hurt. He knew just who to call on—*his* new friend. *Umph*, William thought, *he'll fit nicely into my plan.*

William put the papers away, finished off his cognac, picked up the keys, and headed out the door. Today was a good day.

CHAPTER 30

Sister Mary Ross was used to rejection and being ostracized by most of the members at the church on Market Street was not a big thing…just one more rejection to add to her resume. Yes, Mary Ross was the queen of rejection, and even with the limited amount of mathematics she possessed, she had yet to figure it out. You could ask anyone who knew her what it was about Sister Mary Ross that got on their nerves. The answer would always be the same…her big mouth. When asked what they liked about Mary Ross, the answer was always unanimous…her sweet potato pie.

But Mary's latest rejection was more than she could endure. She had waited more years than she was willing to admit for Deacon Graham Peters, and now that he was available, there was no way she was going to miss her opportunity to be Mrs. Graham Peters, especially for the likes of a juke-joint singer.

Deacon Peters deserved better. After all, he was a decent, Godly man who loved the Lord, who loved his church and family, who paid his tithes and had bought his wife beautiful designer hats. Graham's temporary fall from grace was just that, temporary. And she, Sister Mary Ross, would be first in line to forgive him from his transgressions. One of Reverend Fields' favorite scriptures when he was admonishing the saints about their walk with the Lord was "We have all sinned and fallen short of the glory of God." Donnie McClurkin's number one gospel song, "We Fall Down But We Get Up," only confirmed the weakness of man and God's grace through forgiveness.

A sudden idea came to Mary. Oprah Winfrey had just aired a show on makeovers. There were troubled mothers, sisters, and daughters who were at their wit's end and had tried everything from counseling to old-fashioned beatings to get their loved ones to dress more appropriately. There were husbands who got tired of looking at their hum-drum wives who had lost the twinkle and spark that caused their husbands to look at them in the first place.

After Oprah's fashion designer and hairdressers got through with these women, they became a page from *Cosmo* and *Ladies Home Journal*.

"That's it, I'm gonna change my look. Then Deacon Peters…no, no…Graham, will notice me then."

Mary Ross staggered into the pink bedroom with the puke-green carpet and closed the door shut. On the back of the worn wooden door hung a floor-length mirror. Mary plopped in front of it as if it were a new discovery.

She stuck out her tongue and wiggled her fingers, her thumbs extending from each ear. Childhood memories came flooding back—a time long ago when she and her cousin Loretha use to play hide and seek and would put their thumbs in their ears, buck their eyes, wave little fingers, and scream to the hunter, "You can't catch me!"

"Hmph," Mary Ross muttered aloud, "those were the good ole days."

Mary looked in the mirror again, this time standing tall. She put her hands on her hips and swayed from side to side. Then she collapsed her left knee, letting her hip drop a little and shaking it like she'd seen the dancers do on *Live at the Apollo*. She turned clockwise until she had a sideways view. Mary admired herself and let out a giggle. She dropped her chin a little and put on a sexy smile. Then she made a 180-degree turn so she could determine which was her best side.

"Not bad," Mary remarked.

Mary took off her shirtwaist dress until she was down to her white nylon slip with the fancy lace running around the bottom. She took the slip off until the mirror announced she was down to her last two garments.

"Not bad, but it needs some revitalizing."

Where was the phone book? She remembered seeing those Victoria's Secret catalogs sitting on Loretha's kitchen table the last time she had visited. Mary knew there had to be a Victoria's Secret somewhere in town. Wherever it was located, Mary would have to pay them a visit. *Nothing like sexy underwear to excite the man of your dreams*, Mary thought.

A puzzled look came across Mary's face. What was she missing? She searched the mirror for answers, but wasn't quite sure what she was looking for.

She was on her twentieth pose when it finally struck her. If it hadn't been for the mirror, the answer staring straight back at her, she would not have gotten it at all. So…it took a while, but she was going to call Suzie's Cut and Kurl right away and make an appointment for first thing in the morning.

"I might even get it cut," Mary blurted out to the ceiling. "I know Lord… I promised not to cut my hair, but this is an extreme emergency. And yes, ain't nobody gonna reject Mary Ross then."

Mary was excited and she continued talking in rhythm just as if the Lord had given her a new song to sing.

"*I'm going to Macy's, maybe Nordstrom, better yet that expensive store… uhhh…Neiman Marcus. I'm going to buy me a new dress, a new pair of shoes, who knows, maybe a new pocketbook, too. Hmph, I might even stop by one of those nice furniture stores and buy some new furniture and spruce up my place. After all, if I'm going to bring my baby—oops, Graham, back to the house, I want him to feel comfortable in his new surroundings.*"

Mary stomped her feet and raised her hands. "You go, girl," Mary shouted, parading around the room like she was a Victoria's Secret angel. "Watch out, deacon. I'm about to knock the socks off your feet and the pants off that fine behind…in time."

Mary gathered her things and prepared for a day of shopping. "Gotta put Fashion Fair on the list—maybe I'll have one of those girls make me up real pretty."

CHAPTER 31

Rain was forecast for later that evening. A few dark clouds eased across the horizon, trying to make good on that threat. William drove his Acura until he pulled in front of The Water Hole. Fridays were always busy, and even though it was yet early, the parking lot was full of happy hour revelers.

Clyde maintained a back room for special clientele at The Water Hole—those who had a few extra dollars to drop and loved a good game of poker. Admission into the group was always by invitation. He had to control the flow of traffic because gambling was illegal, and Clyde had run a respectable establishment for thirty years without ever being closed down. He wasn't about to let any riff-raff come up in his place and destroy what had taken him a lifetime to achieve.

William looked around and saw no one that he knew. Nice soft jazz played in the background, and a crowd of business types sat at the bar and tables chewing the fat with co-workers about the past week's antics.

William took a seat at the bar's far corner and ordered a cognac. He was good at holding his liquor. After downing the first glass, he ordered another. He watched people saunter in—men dressed in dark tailored suits, the women in everything from business suits to leather ensembles with high-heeled shoes. Some gorgeous women flocked through the door and gave cause to more than just one glance from William, but he had a mission and becoming involved with another woman now was out of the question.

A healthy well-dressed sister approached the bar. She was with four other ladies apparently just off from work. Her sculptured hair-do was piled high on her head, giving height to the rest of her body draped in a black, ultra-conservative, full-figured Yves St. Laurent suit and accentuated by a multi-colored scarf wrapped about her neck and tucked inside her jacket to hide ample cleavage. She spied William sitting off to himself and unabashedly approached him. Without batting an eye, she left her group as they found seats at a cozy table next to the hors d'oeuvres.

"This seat taken?" the woman asked, cocking her head to the side as her eyes burned into William.

"It doesn't appear to be," William responded, dropping his hand in the direction of the seat to indicate the same.

"Hmph, my, my, my…we are Mister All That, and I do love a man in dreads."

William returned her gaze and raised his eyebrow without uttering a word, nursing his drink with one hand.

"You mind buying a sister a drink?" the healthy sistah purred, flashing two rows of polished dentures.

"And what would you say if I said I did?"

The woman looked at William for a long hard minute—then did a once-over. She ordered her drink and pulled her plump body from the bar stool she found herself leaning against and turned away, cocking her head just a little. "You aren't the only decent-looking brotha in here, and you ain't even all that!"

Before William could come back with a line on the plump lady, she called out, "Angie, over here."

William and Angie froze, neither able to believe that the other stood or sat before them.

"Y'all know each other?" the plump woman asked as their continued silence more than confirmed the obvious.

"Oh, girlllll. I'm sorry, I didn't know this was your man. He's a little stuck up."

"Shut up, Adrienne," Angie said, softly, unable to take her eyes from William.

Angie looked splendid in a black-and-white tweed ensemble by Vera

Wang accentuated by black faux fur around the collar and cuffs. She wore a skirt at least three inches above her knees that was in no way tasteless. Four-inch black Paolo pumps, with white piping highlighting the front perimeter of the shoe, adorned her size-eight feet. A small black leather handbag swung from a silver rope chain and rested on the crest of her hips.

William was mesmerized, but still felt the brunt of Angie's rejection. It no longer mattered, because he could not lose focus on what had now become really important to him—reclaiming Rita. Who knew? Angie might play an important role in his plan.

"How are you doing, William?" Angie queried somewhat reluctantly.

"Fine now. I'm doing great. I'm making it on my own." William noticed Angie perk up at his last announcement.

"Where are you staying?"

"In Oakland—out a ways," William said, not wanting to give up too much information. Since he had Troy's house practically to himself, maybe he'd take Angie out there, have sex—no strings. Whatever the outcome, he'd take it slow. It had to fit into the plan—a plan he had yet to devise.

"Well...let me give you my number so that if you get the urge to call..."

"I thought you had a new man?"

"Just a friendship. Nothing serious. But really...if you want to just get together, just to talk, maybe we can hook up."

William looked at the piece of paper Angie held and then at her. "Maybe, we can get together later. I've been working on a hot project that's consumed much of my time," he lied, "but I'll give you a call." William took the piece of paper, folded it, and put it in his wallet.

"It was good seeing you, Angie. I'm off to a..." He thought better of telling her that he was getting ready to play poker. After all, his gambling and other obnoxious habits were the reasons she had left in the first place.

"Well, it was good seeing you again. You're looking well, and I do hope you'll call."

"I will."

William watched as she sauntered off to join the group of ladies already on their second helping of finger food. Angie did look good, but he'd be damned if he was going to let her know it.

♪♪♪

William caught Clyde's eye and signaled his desire to go to the back room. Clyde crooked his head to the right giving William the go-ahead to advance to the poker game. To get to the room, William had to exit through a side door next to the stage, then head down the hall and into the door on the right next to Clyde's office. William disappeared so quickly, Clyde wasn't sure if William had actually passed through the side door or out of the building.

As William approached the door to the special room, he could hear laughter vibrate against the thin walls of the building. There was a pause, then more laughter and a loud exclamation from someone who no doubt had folded their bad hand. William knocked on the door and proceeded in.

All eyes rested on William—a cloud of smoke meeting him at the entrance. He tried to clear the air with his hand. It was a fascinating group of men, although William was somewhat disappointed that his newly found friend, Charlie, was not among the players.

They sat, a group of six, at a large round table cluttered with brightly colored chips and half-filled glasses of Johnny Walker, Chivas, and the big Jim Beam, having already negotiated their seat at the table. The men came in all shapes, sizes, and colors.

A light caramel-colored man with sandy-red hair seemed to be the leader of the six-man crew. He was rotund with thick hands that sported a military ring. He wore a camel-colored jacket and a brown turtleneck knit shirt underneath. His thick, red mustache sat on top of a set of thin, lightly freckled lips that shouted out orders with which everyone else complied.

To the right of him sat an older man, dark complexion and in his late sixties. The butt of a cigar jetted out the side of his mouth, housed in an area where several missing teeth once stood. He probably had been playing poker at The Water Hole as long as it had been in existence.

To the left of Red sat a chain-smoking, back-in-the-'70s wannabe playa sporting an outdated Jheri-curl and a two-carat diamond stud earring in his left ear. He wore a black leather jacket and a scoop-neck black knit shirt that lay snuggly over his muscular body. A thick gold rope chain hung around his neck, and his fingers were manicured to the bone.

A medium-brown man sporting a brown-and-tan stevedore with a feather stuck in its side sat next to the *The Playa*. He wore a two-tone-brown, starched cotton barbershop shirt with intricate embroidery on the pockets.

A dark-skinned man, who appeared to be in his forties, sat next to the gentleman with the feather in his hat. He seemed to be in a world all his own—not paying any particular attention to the conversation before him. He wore a white, crisp-cotton, button-down shirt over a white V-neck T-shirt that protruded outward due to an extended belly that had seen too many beers. Two empty beer cans sat in front of the dark-skinned man while cigarette smoke whirled about his face.

Next to *Cigar Man* sat a rather distinguished, well-groomed-looking gentleman with salt-and-pepper hair. He wore a sky-blue, wool sport coat over a black designer dress shirt. Black and blue formed a unique geo-metric pattern on the man's tie, which was loosened and hung lazy about his neck. Smart cufflinks and a Rolex watch rounded out the top half of his well-put-together wardrobe.

Before William could get a word out, Big Red spoke up.

"Hey, man. Good to see you, again. Grab a seat; I'm getting ready to deal a five-card draw. Stakes are higher tonight." He laughed. It was contagious as the other five picked up the laughter in chorus.

William did another once around the room, nodded, and sat next to Salt "n" Pepper—far enough away from Big Red, yet close enough to be part of the group. They played for two hours before Charlie appeared, soaking wet from the downpour predicted for the evening.

Charlie squeezed in between William and Salt 'n' Pepper acknowledging William with only a nod. William's luck wasn't running as well as he had hoped, and he was about to cash out when Charlie appeared. It would be worth a couple more rounds of play now that Charlie had arrived. If the opportunity presented itself, he would set the bait for the future use of Charlie in his plan. He heard, *I raise you fifty*, and went back to concen-trating on the game at hand.

CHAPTER 32

Rita picked at her crab cakes as she and Graham sat in silence. They exchanged a quick glance, Graham managing a smile while hiding behind the nagging feeling that something was not quite right. Rita managed her own smile, then looked away to avoid any further questioning from Graham about her sudden trip to Oakland.

Rita looked out the window—the rain now sheets of nasty water that splashed violently on the pavement.

"You seem distracted."

"No, just enjoying my time with you."

"I wish I could believe that."

"Believe it. I love you, Graham, and I want to spend the rest of my life with you."

He smiled. She smiled back.

"Let's get your things from the hotel. Leave your car here, and we'll pick it up on our way back."

"Splendid idea."

"I thought so, too." Graham motioned for the waitress. "Check, please."

"I can't wait to get back to your place."

"We are in sync tonight, however, I was thinking about stopping off at The Water Hole a moment. Surprise them."

"We don't have to; I'd rather just go to your place and make love to you, if that's not being too presumptuous of me."

"Presumptuous? It fits into my plan quite nicely. We'll stop at The Water Hole first for only a few minutes, though. I need to check something out."

Rita said nothing. The same awful feeling that had consumed her earlier in the evening was present again. Rita didn't know what to make of it, but for now, she'd be safe at Graham's side.

♪♪♪

Rita glanced about the room looking for no one in particular. She relaxed and exhaled when she saw no familiar faces. The mix of sweet fragrances rushing from human flesh intoxicated Rita as the parade of party-goers passed in front of her on their way to have a good time.

Rita turned just in time to see Graham enter the building. They had come in separate cars, and Rita had managed to get to The Water Hole ahead of him.

Graham reached for Rita's hand and led the way into the dimly lit club finding seats in a far corner of the room. Although Rita could have a seat anywhere, she opted to remain out of sight. If Clyde had any inkling of her presence, he'd have her up on stage in a heartbeat.

It was local talent night, and a young woman with a sultry voice was on stage. She sang a few contemporary jazz numbers and sounded much like Anita Baker. Her physical likeness to Anita was uncanny, except she wore her hair in small locs pulled back by a band made of Afrocentric material that matched the garment she had wrapped around her. She was good.

Rita sipped her wine and caught Graham's eyes as they bore into hers. He was a wonderful man, and there was no denying her love for him. He took another sip of his drink, his eyes never leaving her. All of a sudden, Rita had an urge to pour out her soul to Graham—to release the tension of the day—and what was really going on in her life.

Graham saw erratic movement in her eyes and became alarmed.

"Are you all right, Rita?"

"Yes," she stuttered. "Why do you ask?"

"Your eyes were dancing around like they were on fire."

"Say what?"

"Yeah…your eyes seem troubled—like you were in deep contemplation and toiling with whatever has your attention."

Damn, Rita thought. *Why does he have to be so perceptive? I've got to control my emotions.*

"You know," Graham rambled on, "your eyes and body language can convey a lot of things."

"Who made you the smart one?"

"Look, Rita. Look into my eyes and tell me what they are saying."

Rita blushed and a big smile flew across her face. "You love me, Graham Peters. Tell me I'm right."

"Oh, you're right, all right. You hit the nail on the head. But you didn't get it all."

"All? Graham Peters, I am not a mind reader."

"Look into my eyes, Rita. Read my eyes—see all they're saying."

Rita pretended to gaze deep into Graham's eyes, but when she locked on, she had to pull away. The message was strong and vivid—just like the singer who sang another of Anita's songs, "Caught Up in the Rapture of Love." Graham's eyes spoke volumes about his love for her—his deep abiding love. And…she saw that he wanted to hold her, never letting her go. He wanted to shield her from all harm and danger. He wanted to make love to her—love that knew no boundaries, love that turned heartbeats into soft music, love that turned a cold chill into a raging fire.

"Whew," Rita said at last. And they chuckled, lost in the sounds of those around them and the songstress who dared them to ride along.

"You must have seen a lot," Graham chided. "I thought I was going to have to call the paramedics to bring you back to life."

"Funny." Rita tapped Graham lightly on the arm. "What do you see when you look in my eyes now?"

"I see a beautiful woman."

"No, silly. Look into my eyes."

"I see someone who loves me as much as I love them, who will go to the end of the world with me, who'll be by my side no matter the journey. I also see a mysterious woman who holds many keys to doors yet to be unlocked."

Rita abruptly moved her eyes away.

"What's wrong?"

"I love you, Graham, with all of my heart. You're the bookend that has eluded me for so many years. I believe we have what it takes to stand the test of time."

A wide smile crossed Graham's face. It was contagious. A smile that crossed a country mile was all over Rita's face and every ounce of her being. Then she spotted him out of the corner of her eye, staring straight at her and Graham.

The awkward and strange feeling came over her again. Was William at the restaurant tonight? She had to will her eyes to remain as Graham had last seen them. She didn't want him to read fear and the possibility of exposure in her eyes. Rita had to get out of there.

"Sweetie, was I right in reading that you wanted to make love to me?"

"That's always in my eyes."

"Well, why don't we make good on that desire of yours, because I can safely tell you this, my eyes are saying the same thing."

Graham grinned again. He took Rita's hand and ushered her toward the door while William watched from a safe distance—almost in silhouette in the dim light of the club. Someone spotted them and called out, "There's Rita Long. Girl, sing us a song."

Rita smiled politely at the friendly face of a cigar-toting gentleman, the cigar sitting at the vertex of the "V" his middle and index fingers had formed. Rita put her finger to her lips and softly mouthed the word "no," only causing the gentleman to say her name louder.

The crowd turned in her direction and began to clap and chant Rita's name. Graham gave her a friendly nudge to go up front and sing her heart out. It was intermission, and Rita's appearance would certainly be the highlight of the party-goers' evening.

Rita wanted to run, but the smile on Graham's face and the cheers from the crowd made it all but impossible to refuse their request. Then she saw William come from the side of the stage, clapping along with the others. She thought she saw him mouth the words, "I love you."

Rita walked in staccato to the stage, not wanting to be here at this moment. She turned around one last time to look at the begging crowd before climbing up the stairs to the platform. Rita stiffened, then walked the few feet to the microphone, releasing it from its stand.

She stood contemplating what she would sing—the unfamiliar band waiting their cue to follow. Rita lifted her chin, stared into the crowd, and closed her eyes.

"I've been so many places in my life and time. I've sung a lot of songs and I've made some bad rhymes."

Rita continued to blare out the lyrics of the popular tune. Couples latched onto each other while Graham stared at the woman who had grabbed his heart, who had become his obsession, who held such a strange mystique and now sang such a sad, sad song.

Only moments ago, they were full of joy and jubilation—ready to lie in each other's arms and make love. She sounded sad and far away, but Graham let it go, not finding any explanation that would explain this seemingly sudden onset of pain. Rita looked out into the audience—her eyes vacant and absent of expression.

Rita finished the song and rushed from the stage amid a thunderous applause. Graham sensed her urgency and rushed forward to assist her. When she reached Graham, Rita took his hand and squeezed it tight.

"Let's get out of here," she said.

Her adoring fans were cheering her on. Just as they were about to leave the building, a younger woman in a black-and-white tweed suit approached them.

"Ms. Long, you were wonderful. I wish I had a voice like yours."

"Well, thank you…"

"My name is Angie, Angie Black. Some of my co-workers and I came down to catch the local talent tonight."

"Do you sing, Angie?"

"Some, but I'm not that good. Oh, I wish I had a voice like yours."

"Well, maybe the next time I'm in town, I can look you up."

"Oh, God, that would be great! I have a business card somewhere," Angie said, digging frantically in her small compact purse. "Here it is. You can call me anytime. I can't thank you enough."

"You already have."

Graham took Rita's hand once again, and they dashed out into the night in a downpour that refused to let up. And along with the falling rain, a stream of tears flowed down Rita's face.

William watched the whole scene. It was coming together better than he had anticipated. As William stood watching Rita's exit, a heavy hand fell on his shoulder, startling him a bit.

"You're still in love with her."

William said nothing but turned his head slightly in order to see his casual observer better. He dropped his shoulder, and Charlie's hand slid back to his own side. William turned and went back to the bar leaving Charlie to muddle over what had just happened.

♪♪♪

Rita sat behind the wheel of the BMW too exasperated to put the key into the ignition. Her life had been uncomplicated for the last fifteen years, now all the peace and tranquility she enjoyed seemed threatened by William's sudden desire to rekindle a burned-out flame. What they once had would never be again.

The day's events crossed Rita's mind like a prop plane flying through the sky. She was not beholden to William. There would be no more money no matter how desperate his situation. He was more than likely throwing it away anyway.

The sight of William galled Rita, and the fact that he had now made Oakland home complicated matters more. Rita sensed William wanted more from her than the money she had given him. It frightened her because he had made it known that he wanted to get back with her. William would always know when she was in town, especially when she gave a performance, and keeping William's present fixture in the community from Graham—a community both William and Graham shared—was becoming a difficult task.

She jumped at the loud beep of Graham's horn. Rita hurriedly turned on the ignition to keep Graham from thinking something was wrong and get out of his car. She needed this moment for her private thoughts—a time for reflection. Tonight had not gone exactly the way she planned, and her last glimpse of William, staring at her as if she were some kind of Madonna, unnerved her.

As Rita turned her head to back out of the parking spot, she spotted the folded piece of paper she had thrown on the seat beside her. After finally navigating her way onto the street, Rita reached over and picked up the piece of paper and put it in her purse to read later. Right now, she had a date with Graham, and she needed him to take all her blues away.

CHAPTER 33

Sister Mary Ross dropped her packages on the living room floor, puffing as she sank down into the nearest chair. Shopping was a chore and made Sister Mary hungry. She was too tired to get up and go into the kitchen and decided to catch her breath and rumble through all the pretty things she'd picked up.

Dumbfounded was Sister Mary Ross when she entered Victoria's Secret. She had never ventured into the lingerie store before, and to find it filled with so many fabulous colors and styles of panties and bras was overwhelming. Lacy, padded, and provocative were the adjectives to describe the high-priced lingerie Mary thought only models wore. Only white cotton underwear ever touched her body because white was pure, but she was ready to get worldly for her man.

Fancy sleepwear made Mary blush as she brushed her face against a few of the furry pieces. Unable to resist the silk-like material of the others, she took them between her fingers to feel the texture of the rich fabric. Mary grabbed a few pieces, deciding it was all or nothing.

Next she ventured to one of the display tables and hesitantly picked up a gorgeous, peach, lacy bra that one of the salesladies claimed would give her breasts a nice full lift. She held it up imagining what her breasts would look like in it. As if on cue, an image of Graham leapt before her, gazing at her 38D's that filled its cups like homemade cupcakes. Graham was licking his lips while his eyes bulged from their sockets from the sight of it all.

The vision was clear, and Mary not only took the peach bra, she selected a black one and picked out matching panties and camisoles for the both of them. Mary was pleased, and marched up to the cashier to pay for her purchases.

She felt younger at this moment than she had her whole life. She was beginning to understand what Loretha meant by making yourself presentable, pretty, because you feel like a whole new person.

Mary was going to get her man. Although it had begun to rain heavily outside, it was not going to deter her from her planned rendezvous with the best department stores in town. She headed for Macy's across the Bay.

Mary's wardrobe was plain and simple. Pastel-colored shirtwaist dresses consumed one-half of her small walk-in closet while two suits, one white the other black, occupied a small space at the far end. Several blouses in varying colors hung proudly in front of the dresses, each waiting its turn to accompany whichever suit Mary wore each Sunday. Sling-backs and one-inch pumps dotted the sparse closet floor accompanied by an able-bodied pair of Nike sneakers.

People scurried in all different directions. Men and women in their business suits, others in the uniform of their profession, raced to catch the city bus, cable car, or BART. Market Street was a main arterial through downtown San Francisco, and when Mary stood in front of Macys, it shadowed over her like a towering giant. Ross' department store was the extent of Mary's shopping excursions, and those excursions were few and far between.

Counters and aisles were threaded throughout the store like a giant maze. It made Mary dizzy and unsure which way to go. She turned right, then left and found she had made a complete circle becoming totally disoriented in the process.

Then she spied the counters of fine perfume—Chanel, Givenchy, Tommy, Perry Ellis, Calvin and Donna—packaged in exciting bottles that glittered on glass countertops like jewels in a treasure chest. It held Mary captive, and she took the liberty to sniff each one. Finally settling on a 2.4-ounce bottle of Pleasures by Estee Lauder, Mary walked into the maze to find the women's department.

She was amazed at the large selection of women's clothing from blazers and vests, dresses, coats and jackets, hats, scarves, gloves, and jeans—which didn't interest Mary at all. She scanned one section at a time feeling the fabrics as she passed. She had never bought a *designer* dress or suit, and now she stood among several racks of fine dresses and suits by Ralph Lauren, Rena Rowan, Jones New York, and DKNY.

Some of the pieces were more stunning than she had imagined. A double-breasted, tailored, navy blazer by Ralph Lauren with its signature gold buttons that ran down the front caused Mary's mouth to gape open—especially the price. It was sporty and elegant, and if Mary was going to give herself a total makeover, she would need a classic blazer like this one in her wardrobe.

But it was the slinky, black-crinkle velvet dress by Ralph Lauren that caught her attention. Mary knew immediately this would be the dress that would win Graham over.

Packages hung from every arm. Mary found a diamond heart pendant that was the perfect complement for her dress. A pair of ankle-strap pumps by Antonio Mellani completed her outfit. A couple pairs of slacks and a smart tweed suit in a drab olive rounded out her purchases.

Now Mary sat in the middle of her living room surrounded by her new finery. In the morning, she was going to the hairdresser for a brand-new hairdo.

By this time tomorrow, Mary planned to be in the arms of her man.

CHAPTER 34

Rita was up early busying herself in the kitchen. The whistle on the teakettle broke the silence just as Graham rounded the corner. *She was beautiful*, he thought as he watched Rita flitting around. Her long, satin, egg-shell-colored negligee flowed effortlessly with every movement—an angelic being.

"Breakfast?" she asked, turning ever so slightly and catching her man gazing at her.

"I'd love some."

It was remarkable how much Rita reminded Graham of Amanda at that moment. In the same kitchen and with the same easy movements. It was almost eerie to look at her. It was certainly a testament to Graham's taste in women—although forty years had lapsed since he'd first asked Amanda to be his lady, then his wife.

Graham watched as Rita moved from cabinet to cabinet, assessing the provisions available to make breakfast. Rita pulled down a box of instant grits along with a box of pancake mix. She reached in the refrigerator for a carton of eggs and began the process of fixing Graham's breakfast.

The kitchen came alive, and the wonderful smells engulfed the room and a broad smile crossed Graham's face. He walked up behind Rita and put his arms around her waist while she stirred the pancake batter and poured it onto the hot grill—just the way he had put his arms around Amanda when she fried chicken the very first time as his wife. Rita shooed him away just as Amanda had done, and Graham glanced about the room as if Amanda might possibly be overseeing things.

The bacon sizzled and the pancakes danced in hot grease. Graham snuggled up to Rita who offered little resistance. It drove Graham crazy. He sniffed at the faint smell of her perfume and slowly began to kiss her on the neck and then along her shoulders, dragging his tongue along the journey, following the road map to succulent breasts that he tenderly planted kisses upon. Rita trembled as he continued to warm her with his kisses. Then he loosened the lonely button on her robe and reached between it and her negligee, gently caressing her breasts as his hands glided effortlessly over the smooth fabric.

"Ouch," Rita shouted, swiftly pulling her arm away from the grill.

"I'm so sorry, Rita. Let me put some ice on it," Graham said, grabbing Rita's hand. "Just a little burn, but we don't want it to welt." He kissed her on the nose.

"Look, you're going to have to make up your mind. You're either going to eat breakfast or make love to me."

"You drive a hard bargain, madam; you know what I'd rather do."

"Eat your breakfast," Rita said as she placed plates on the table. Rita reached over and placed a quick peck on Graham's lips. "I'm not going anywhere."

♪♪♪

Graham quickly washed dishes while Rita finished her last cup of coffee. They sat silently for a while enjoying the peace and solitude. Rita brought her empty coffee cup to the sink to be washed and placed a friendly kiss on Graham's cheek. Graham dropped the dishcloth into the water and quickly scooped Rita into his arms, encircling the whole of her, and he placed hot, passionate kisses upon her face.

Their bodies joined together, becoming one fluid pattern as Rita returned searing hot kisses upon Graham. They moaned and swooned until they fell against the kitchen table in an uncontrollable outburst of passion—passion that bubbled like crude oil—sweat pouring from their bodies. Their bodies moved in a continuous rhythm. Rita's head fell backward as

Graham sprinkled her body with kisses and then exchanged places and repeated the same exercise all over again. Then Graham slid the thin straps from Rita's shoulders, letting the bodice of her negligee fall around his hands—fighting to release them so he could take each breast in his hands as he swooped down on them with his waiting tongue—gently tasting them, making love to them as if nothing else mattered.

Graham tended to Rita like a sculptured piece he had worked on for some time, chiseling each section slowly and meticulously, becoming drunk from the very essence of his creation. Rita rubbed Graham's head, caressing his shoulders, pulling gently with her fingers the pajama top that already lay open, exposing his well-kept body that had more than a lifetime of appeal. Their bodies were past their prime, but they had many more years of sexual dexterity left in them. Graham lifted Rita and carried her to his bedroom where they spent the better part of the morning getting to know each other better.

♪♪♪

The doorbell startled Rita and Graham. They had fallen into a light sleep and lost track of time. Graham rolled over and peered at the clock on the nightstand. It was two in the afternoon, and time was slipping away fast. Rita would be boarding a plane back to Seattle in less than twenty-four hours.

It must be the parcel postman at the door, Graham thought, trotting toward the front door to silence the menacing sound of the doorbell. Graham was bathed in the scent of a lover's potion, his face glistened with the sweat from the inferno he had found himself. In his haste to get to the door, Graham was clad only in his blue silk pajama bottom with his upper body exposed to the world—a forest of ashen bushes. His bare feet marked the path—the path of his eventual return to the woman who lay waiting for him in all her splendor.

Graham jerked on the doorknob, realizing he needed to unlatch it first. He had made sure the door was secured this time so as not to have a nasty replay of events like the Sunday Deborah and Liz had barged in. He had almost lost Rita that day, and to ensure it wouldn't happen again, Graham took the liberty of having the locks changed without the girls' knowledge. After all, it was his home, and if their keys didn't work, they had another place they could go. However, neither Deborah nor Liz had been back to the house since that day. Nevertheless, Graham was taking no chances.

"Just a minute," Graham shouted through the door, finally unlocking the last lock, anxious for all the commotion to be over. So anxious was Graham that he never thought to peer out the window to get a look at his visitor.

With the last lock unlatched, Graham swiftly pulled the door open to find a well-coiffed woman in her mid-fifties standing on his porch. Her dark auburn hair was cut short and tapered in the back. Several small rows of precision curls circled the small of her head while crisp, starched, and neatly cut bangs hung an inch above her eyes. Two-carat diamond studs sparkled from the lobes of each ear only to enhance the barber's meticulous handiwork.

Graham's eyes fell the length of the woman who wore a slinky black velvet dress with shoes that were a perfect complement. Perfect breasts rose and fell and tugged at the bodice of her dress while just enough material was allotted to accommodate her dangerous, ample hips. *A perfect "ten,"* Graham thought, if he was judging a beauty pageant. And rounding out the perfect wardrobe was a small, black designer bag that hung from her shoulders.

Her face was beautiful—straight from the pages of *Essence* magazine's Health and Beauty section. Rich earth colors complemented her eyes with a twinge of reddish-brown blush highlighting her cheekbone—defining features that had once been lost on her. A black eyeliner pencil was used on the base of her eyelids to make her features stand out and her face round and full. A nice earth-tone lipstick completed the look that made this woman divine.

But the face looked familiar—a sly, seductive smile taking shape. And now, Graham suddenly realized he was naked from the waist up. The way the woman twitched back and forth, it appeared Graham might have evoked some fantasy this woman was concocting. Then he looked harder into the eyes that met his, those steely, confident eyes that said she was here for something and was not leaving until she got it. And then that smile.

"Sister Mary Ross?" Graham gasped, his mouth flying open upon discovery. "Is that you?"

"You don't want to keep a woman standing on your porch like this do you?"

"Ahh, Sister Ross…"

"Mary, Graham. Please call me Mary. We've known each other long enough that we can be on a first-name basis."

"Mary…this isn't a good time. You see, I'm not dressed," Graham stammered, wanting to cover his chest but unwilling to leave her there while he went to get his robe for fear she'd follow.

"Surely you're not going to let me just stand outside."

Graham was silent.

"Well, if you're not going to invite me in, I'll invite myself."

"I wouldn't do that if I…"

Mary breezed past Graham getting up enough nerve to let her hand graze across his chest, allowing it to linger in his ashen forest longer than she dared. Graham tried to grab her, to keep her from going farther into the house, but it was too late.

Mary circled the living room, finally turning to rest her eyes on Graham who stood in the middle of the room like a lost sheep. His body was well kept, although the hairs on his chest gave his age away. Mary's eyes continued to roam the length of Graham's body, finally resting on the silk pajama bottom with the convenient peephole, staring at it as if wondering what lay beyond its door. There was lust in her eyes, and if she hadn't been half the Christian she claimed to be, she would have been all over Graham within seconds.

But Mary was unsure what to do. Even though this luscious creature stood statuesque in front of her—an Oscar waiting to be picked up—she could not reach out and grab it. She had never been with a man, at least not like that, and Mary became exasperated by the thought. Now she looked foolish—all up in this man's house—a man she had loved most of her adult life but always from a distance. And she knew she looked good; she could see it in his eyes—the way he gawked at her.

"Graham," Mary started, choked up at what she was about to admit. "I'm sorry. I had no right coming here, barging in on you like this."

She is finally making some sense, Graham thought. "It's okay, Mary."

"Let me finish. I've been in love with you, Graham Peters, for a long, long time." Mary avoided the startled look in Graham's eyes—and then the look of disgust. "I remember when I laid eyes on you the first time I went to church with my cousin Loretha. It was love at first sight, but you were married to Amanda.

"I waited, hoping that maybe you and Amanda would break up, and then, just maybe I would have a chance. But as you very well know, that wasn't to be. There were days when I hated Amanda—even envied her all those years for having what I believed I should have had. I don't know what made me think that, but I did.

"And then," Mary paused, not sure if she wanted to divulge what she was thinking, but allowed it to seep through her lips anyway, "Amanda died, and I suddenly felt this was a blessing from God. I had another chance."

Mary watched Graham's expression change. She hurried on—afraid he would throw her out. She needed to explain, and maybe Graham would have some compassion and embrace her after all. It was worth all she had gone through.

"I'm sorry," Mary ran on, not giving Graham an opportunity to get a word in, "for all the mess I've caused—you know…with the church and your in-laws. I wasn't thinking." Mary looked thoughtfully at Graham. "You didn't deserve any of that. I just became unglued when I saw you with that other woman."

Graham began shifting absently from one foot to another. Mary noticed it as well, paused and continued on.

"Anyway, from somewhere deep inside an idea came to me—an answer to a prayer, maybe. In any event, I knew what I had to do to get your attention. So I pulled off the layers of my old self and found a new me—one I rather like. It makes me feel good, Graham. And I had hoped by coming here today, you would see the new me that I've discovered, but I've realized a little too late that I've gone about it the wrong way."

Graham spoke for the first time since Mary had entered his house.

"You are who you are, Mary. A leopard is a leopard whether you change his spots or not. It is that thing within our hearts that we have control of…that we can affect change. Your scheming and conniving still spells Mary Ross though your outward appearance looks different."

"I'm willing to change," Mary charged. "Please give me a chance. I'm sorry, sorry, sorry. Any other woman would have pounced on you as soon as they saw you as you stood before me. I must confide in you…I've never been with a man before. I had hoped you would teach me."

Graham's jaw dropped. "Sister Ross, Mary, you didn't just say you haven't…"

Mary cut him off, not wanting him to repeat those awful words she had just uttered to him. It reminded her of how truly lonely and desperate she was and how the one man she had dreamed of day in and day out could fix it for her now—but shunned her advances.

"It was partly because I was walking my spiritual walk."

Graham shook his head, not believing a word she said. "But surely, there was someone who was interested…that could have loved you enough to…"

"To marry me?" Mary sneered. "Is that what you were going to say?"

"Yes, marry," Graham said, his patience wearing thin. "You are a beautiful woman, Mary. I'm sure if you gave someone half a chance…"

"You just don't get it. You haven't heard a word I've said. Why won't you have me, Graham? I have waited all my life for the right man—you."

"And again, you may never know who the right man is if you don't give anyone a chance."

"It is you, Graham Peters. My spirit told me so."

"Your spirit lied," Graham said without malice. "Amanda was the one, and our forty years of marriage said the same. Our love was so deep, Mary, that it would take Heaven or hell to separate us." Graham sighed as visions of Amanda rushed through his head. He looked thoughtfully at Mary, but did not have the heart to say to this woman all he would have liked, realizing she did not know what real love was all about.

"What about now—now that Amanda is gone?" Graham heard Mary say.

"What about now?"

"Has the spirit lied to me, again? No, I feel it strong—deep down in my bosom."

"I'm in love with another woman, Mary."

Mary's eyes jerked upward. "Your spirit line is all crossed up," Mary managed to say, not ready to give up on love. She turned and looked at Graham, again, in that lustful way. Graham had all but forgotten that his body was practically exposed to her.

"Mary, I appreciate you confiding in me, and I'm sorry if you've gone to a lot of trouble to please me. But I'm not in love with you."

"But Amanda is dead!" Mary shouted. "And I know you find me attractive."

"You've crossed the line, Mary," Graham said with constraint in his voice. "It's time for you to go."

"I'm not leaving. I love you, Graham Peters. Make love to me."

Graham jumped out of the way just as Mary lunged at him. "Please take me in your arms and hold me like you do in my dreams," she demanded, her breathing labored. "Kiss me, take me in your arms, and make sweet love to me."

"No, Mary!" Graham shouted as Mary continued on while wobbling on one foot.

"I've rehearsed this moment in my dreams almost every night since Amanda died, and I'm not going to stand by and listen to you tell me you're in love with someone else." With that, Mary fell into a bookcase on the wall that led into the kitchen.

Suddenly, Mary's arms were in the clutches of Graham's hands. Mary's eyes were wild—the glamorous look she came with now gone. Her curls were unraveled, her makeup smeared, her dress rearranged as she fought for Graham's affection. "Make love to me, Graham," Mary shouted over and over as Graham ushered her to the door.

"What's going on in here," a third voice resounded over Mary's chant for love and affection.

Mary froze and looked from Graham to the woman who had ventured out of nowhere wearing a negligee that revealed more than she wanted to see. Her shoulder-length hair was wild about her head like a freshly tossed salad.

Rita looked from Graham to the woman who Graham had by the arms, then raised her hand to her head, running her fingers through her hair.

"It's you, the lady from the church," Rita said softly, disgust in her eyes.

"You are going to the devil, Graham Peters. They didn't believe me, but they are the ones who'll be sorry. I think I'll go and tell Martha and Elroy right now so they can see for themselves. Then she'll have to apologize for that show she put on in church."

"What are you going to tell them?" Graham asked. "That you were try-ing to get in my bed but found someone else already there?" He realized as soon as it left his mouth how that may have sounded to Rita, and her expression said the same, but he would explain it to her later.

"The Carters already know," Rita blurted out, the hurt registering on her face. But she believed she knew what Graham was trying to say, and he would have to pay dearly for that slip of the tongue. "In fact, I met them yesterday, and we had a nice chat."

Graham smiled at his baby. She was truly remarkable.

"I wasn't talking to you," Mary interjected.

"Well, I'm talking to you. Was there anything in particular you came by for today?"

Mary sneered at Rita and then at Graham. "I didn't come to see you, however, since Deacon Peters is apparently not free at the moment, I'll be leaving."

And then suddenly Mary realized she had taken a cab over. It would be a little awkward asking Graham to take her home this time, but he owed her big. Instead, she asked for the phone and dialed. "Cab, please. Five-five-five-four Chester Street."

CHAPTER 35

Mary sat in the back of the cab trying her best to soothe her wounded heart. She was unable to comprehend Graham Peters' apparent dislike of her. Not only had she gone to a lot of trouble to make him notice her, she had receipts piled an inch deep on her dresser that totaled more than a thousand dollars to attest to the fact. She knew she was still attractive—fifty-five years of life and time had been good to her. And after shedding those old boring clothes she'd worn for the last thirty years, why did Graham Peters deny she was a suitable mate for him?

Who did that nightclub floozy think she was talking to anyway? And how disgusting, walking around the place like she owned it in that ugly see-through gown or whatever they call it. Didn't Graham understand that she loved him? She couldn't have made it any plainer. She had made a fool of herself one too many times and in front of that straight-from-the-gates-of-hell, no-count, nightclub-singing sinner who didn't even look as good as she did. And besides, that woman Rita, or whatever her name was, was too thin, and nobody wanted a bone but a dog.

♪♪♪

"What are you looking at?" Mary lashed out at the cab driver who peered in his rearview mirror. She let her head fall all the way back into the seat and mumbled to herself, although the cabbie heard every word.

"That fine, handsome body—all up in my face. God, what did I do wrong?"

"Are you all right, ma'am?" the cabbie interjected.

Mary didn't answer.

The meter in the cab continued to click as miles translated into dollars. Home was the last place Mary wanted to be and directed the cab driver to take her to T.G.I. Friday's at Jack London Square.

Mary watched the rows of buildings whiz by—some were old landmarks like the H.C. Capwells Building that was now the new Sears building and the Paramount Theatre that had seen its share of patrons over the decades from serving as a movie theater in its infancy to housing many award shows, musicals, and the Ebony Fashion Fair show. Some of the buildings seemed as lonely as Mary—standing tall on their cement blocks watching over the city by day and by night; watching the seasons change month after month, year after year; braving the elements whether it was the sun tanning their metal or brick frames or the rain beating down on them like a liquored-up man in a drunken rage. A stream of downtown dwellers moved in and out of shops—shopping for bargains or just out for a stroll— glad that the downpour of yesterday was now only a remnant, although an occasional splash from a passing car served to remind some of how hard a downpour it had been.

A tear fell from Mary's eye. She felt like a fool, but feeling sorry for her- self was a temporary fix and a nice meal would placate her for the time being in her failed mission to capture Graham's affection. So she hit a stumbling block in her relentless pursuit of the one she loved; Mary would not give up. She smoothed her dress and ran her fingers along the designer bag she had bought to impress her man.

Interstate 880 lay ahead, and when the cab drove underneath, Mary's excitement rose. Jack London Square was just ahead, and in a few min- utes, Mary would be sitting in Friday's feeding her face with a slab of ribs, her favorite when she dined there. Mary was accustomed to eating alone, although she occasionally was able to coax her cousin Loretha away from her sewing machine to go out for a quick meal.

It was mid-afternoon and not many patrons were in the restaurant. Mary was seated right away and her mood changed immediately. A chubby wait-ress stuffed in a white shirt and black denim shorts waltzed to the table to take her order.

"A combination appetizer and a glass of water with lemon for starters." Mary beamed.

The waitress shuffled off, and Mary sat tapping the tabletop with her lightly manicured fingers to a tune she hummed under her breath. Pictures of famous ballplayers hung on the walls along with other pieces of nos-talgia that reminded Mary of different times in her life that were good and sometimes sad. But she liked this place—a place where the atmosphere accepted her for who she was, whether alone or in the company of others.

The voice startled her from behind.

"Care if I sit down?"

"Uhh, no…no, please…please sit down," Mary said nervously, blushing at the same time.

"Tell me, what is a beautiful woman like you doing eating by yourself?" Mary blushed again and unconsciously patted her hair.

"Or maybe I've got it all wrong? All dressed up, you must be meeting someone."

"It's okay, Mr. Ford. You're embarrassing me."

"I'm sorry, I wasn't trying to embarrass you, Mary. Can I call you Mary?"

Mary looked at Charlie as if noticing him for the first time. He was handsome for an older guy in a rugged sort of way. He must be about Graham's age, and they were best friends. Mary recalled Charlie was there when Graham and Amanda got together, he was the best man at their wedding, he was the godfather of Graham and Amanda's girls, and he was Graham's life support when Amanda departed this life. Mary knew little else about Charlie since he didn't spend much time worshipping at the church on Market Street.

Now he came out of nowhere, interrupting her private thoughts, causing her to temporarily forget why she had come to the restaurant in the first place. He wore a yellow polo shirt that was unbuttoned at the top exposing just enough to attract attention. The shirt was bright against his mocha-colored skin giving him a playboy look that was brought out by the cropped, short wavy hair on his balding head.

"So what are you having?" Charlie continued.

"I'm having the rib platter. I always order it whenever I come here."

"You come here often?"

"No, but when I do, I almost always order the ribs."

"Maybe I'll have that, too."

"Good choice. How is it that you happened to be here?" Mary inquired. "It appears we're both by ourselves."

"I like to come to the Square, and since I was a little hungry and alone, this was my place of choice."

"Oh," was the only thing Mary could find to say.

"You, Graham, and I will have to get together one day and make it a lunch date. We can make it a singles' day out."

Mary squirmed in her seat while Charlie's eyes pierced her skin. She suddenly became uncomfortable.

"What do you say, Mary? I think it's a good idea."

"Maybe," Mary said, her voice low.

"Well, I think it's a good idea. I haven't seen much of Graham lately—I believe he's been hanging out with a new lady friend. I'm surprised—so soon after Amanda's death. Don't you think so?"

The air became deathly silent. Casual conversation and waitresses taking orders cut through the thick air that surrounded the table. Mary looked deep into Charlie's eyes—a frown as long as Lake Pontchartrain crossed her face—replacing the smile that welcomed Charlie to the table moments earlier. What was this man up to? After all, he was Graham's best friend, and this man knew Mary Ross knew that. Did he know about her going to Graham's house today? Was he trying to humiliate her because he found out what happened at the church? An uneasy feeling overtook Mary's spirit, and suddenly the good-looking man in the polo shirt became less attractive.

"Excuse me, Mr. Ford. I have to go the ladies room."

"Sure, Mary. And please call me Charlie. I hope I didn't say anything to offend you."

"No," Mary managed weakly. Suddenly the new dress, the new shoes, and hairdo lost their luster.

♪♪♪

Charlie watched Mary saunter to the restroom. He wasn't expecting the comely-looking lady from the church up on Market Street to make him stop and take a second look. Her nice shapely behind didn't count; that had always been her main attraction.

It was as if layers of skin had been peeled back and Mary's beauty had come forth. There's something to the saying that clothes can make a person. In Mary's case it took a complete overhaul from head to toe, transforming a homely creature into a thing of beauty. And Charlie noticed.

Charlie's mind was racing, and then it clicked. Mary Ross was fast becoming the vehicle he needed to implement his plan—a plan yet to be finalized.

CHAPTER 36

Soft, mellow jazz engulfed the room—the swishing sound of the drummer's brush simulating mock anticipation of a lover's call while Grover whispered in his tenor voice, "The Look of Love." The look of love was plastered on their faces and contentment oozed from their souls. Rita lay snug in the crook of Graham's arm—Graham encircled her body with his arms. With eyes closed, the melody entrenched their minds, souls and bodies.

And as all fairy tales come to an end, Rita knew it was time for her to depart. She had an early plane to catch to Seattle in the morning, and she needed to go back to the hotel and pack her things. She tried to remove Graham's arm from around her; however, his vise grip was so tight, Rita thought he had her in a death hold.

Rita struggled to free herself when Graham suddenly released his hold on her. She stared at him, not sure what to make of it. She was probably overreacting—some moment from her past trying to resurface. Graham was a gentle man. *At least he was up until this moment*, Rita thought. It unnerved her a little, for surely this was not a sign of things to come. It was all right for a man to be a little possessive, but Rita would never again allow any man to possess and control her soul using her at will. Her concern melted when he spoke.

"What's wrong with my baby?"

She needed to let Graham know straight up how she felt, because there would be no nipping it in the bud later.

"You were holding me so tight, and…when I tried to get up, I had to struggle to get out of your grasp."

"What?"

"Sssh. I endured a lot from a man I once loved, and I will never, ever…"

"Baby, stop. Do you think I would ever hurt you? Never, ever. I'll call up Amanda if you want me to. She'll give you an outstanding character reference on my behalf."

They both laughed, and Rita felt a little ridiculous for having thought that Graham would try and hurt her.

"Amanda would have liked you," Graham continued. "I must have slipped into a deep sleep, because I was dreaming about holding you forever and never letting go."

"Don't play, Graham Peters. You had me a little distressed."

"Know this, my angel, I will never hurt or try to control you…only love you. And besides, you have yet to say that you'll be by my side for the rest of your life."

"I will, baby, I will. I've never met a man like you. You're warm, thoughtful, loving, caring, intuitive, sensitive, compassionate…did I leave anything out?"

"Was I a good lover—even for an old man?"

"A damn good lover, Graham Peters."

Graham pulled Rita to him and kissed her neck…behind her ears.

"You know?" Rita said, sitting up and pulling away from Graham.

"What, baby?"

"I was a little jealous today when that woman from your church came busting up in here. In fact, it ticked me off somewhat that you were giving Miss Thang an eyeful of what was only mine to enjoy." Memories of their last encounter were fresh in her head, along with every antic Mary had pulled since then. Rita wished she had been at the church when Martha had given this desperate Graham-chaser a piece of her mind.

"She did look real good today. I mean extra good. Her perfume smelled good…sensual…downright intoxicating. And that booty…"

Rita picked up a pillow from the sofa and hit Graham with it. "Graham

Peters, you're supposed to be feeling my pain, not flattering yourself about a desperate, ain't-never-had-a-man, call herself a Christian woman who is lusting for you."

"You have nothing to worry about," Graham said with a straight face.

"You saw how she was looking you up and down, and...and you standing out there bare-chested so she could see what my man was giving me."

"But don't you see? All she *could* do was look. You had the goods and the only thing Mary could do was walk out knowing that you and I were joined together."

"How were we joined, baby? Say it."

"At the hips, tits, lips, and fingertips."

"You are so bad."

"Well, Mary Ross had no business coming up in here."

"You let her in."

"I was in a hurry to get back to you, baby. I didn't even peek out of the window to see who it was. That was so stupid of me."

"Well, she'll have a lot to tell the church folks this time."

They laughed.

"Sister Mary needs to get her own man, because I'm already spoken for. I love you, Rita."

"I love you, too, baby. I've got to go. We'll talk every night and day."

"Will that be enough?"

"Maybe not, but it will have to do for now. I'll be back before Christmas."

"I guess I'll have to settle for that."

Brrng, brrng, brrng, brrng.

"That's my cell," Rita said, looking back at Graham before she rummaged through her purse to retrieve her phone. "Hello."

"Hey, Rita."

"Clyde?"

"Yeah, baby. I need a big favor."

"If I can."

"I had a cancellation, and I need an act for the next few weeks. How about it? Can you be here next weekend?"

"But Clyde, I'm on my way back to Seattle tomorrow, and I'm not prepared…"

"Stop your whining, girl. I know you and Midnight Express won't let me down."

"I don't know. The band may be off doing other things…"

"I need you, baby. I heard you were in here last night and tore the house up. Ran out before I could catch up with you."

"I was tired. And if I had relented, the crowd would have kept me there all night."

"See, that's what I mean. They love you here. Tell you what…give me a call tomorrow and let me know your decision. I'll give you time to round up the posse. But I need you, baby."

Rita sighed. "Okay. I'll let you know something then. Thanks, Clyde."

"Bye, love."

Rita closed the receiver and stood staring at Graham. "Clyde wants Midnight Express to headline for the next few weeks, beginning next weekend. I really hadn't planned to come back to Oakland that soon."

A sly grin crossed Graham's face. God was having favor on him. His prayers were being answered. "I think that's a wonderful idea. You could stay here."

"No, baby. That would be a bad idea. We can spend time together, but it would look better if I stayed at a hotel."

"That doesn't make sense. If we're going to spend time together, why can't we just be together—like now?"

"Graham, sweetheart, it wouldn't be right. I'll be here for an extended period of time—not just a day. Your family will be in and out, and if we're going to be together, forever, we have to make a good impression. That doesn't mean we can't make love to each other every night."

"You are making this hard, but you're right. That's why I love you. You use your head for more than a hat rack. Okay. Let's get your stuff so you can get out of here."

"Kicking me out now?"

They laughed.

"No, baby. I'd never do that. I just want you out so that you can hurry on home. And the sooner you do, the sooner you'll be back in my arms again."

"I will be back."

Graham helped Rita take her things to the car. It was early evening and unusually quiet in the neighborhood. A waning moon already hung in the clear eastern sky offering no hint of yesterday's downpour.

As Rita got into the BMW, she looked up slightly and thought she saw someone looking at her from a car parked across the street and a few feet ahead. She looked away, and when she looked in the direction of the parked car a second time, she didn't see anyone. Maybe she imagined it. She didn't want to alarm Graham and decided against saying anything to him.

It was the second time today she had reacted to what seemed like nothing. She didn't want to give Graham any reason to think she was unstable, although she was beginning to wonder if something was wrong—with all the strange feelings she was having. Did it have something to do with see-ing William this weekend? Rita let it pass. She bade farewell to Graham and was off.

♪♪♪

Mary returned to her seat. Unfortunately, her guest had not chosen to leave. He gave her a broad smile, his eyes never leaving her. Mary smoothed her dress down like a nervous schoolgirl. And the smile she tried to sup-press came rushing to the surface.

"You are absolutely beautiful," Charlie said. "And please forgive me if I upset you."

Mary waved her hand in absolution. "It's all right. I guess I'm a little sensitive about things and I tend to overreact." Mary blushed again.

His eyes were fixed on her, and Mary squirmed some more. It seemed Charlie was looking into the core of her soul as if trying to analyze and dissect every word she was saying. He took both of her hands in his and continued to stare, occasionally parting his lips as if to speak but without a single syllable escaping. Then his mouth flew open and he rambled some-thing that Mary was not sure she heard. "What?"

"I'd like to get to know you better, Mary." It was Mary's turn to stare at

Charlie. She wasn't sure what this man wanted. "There is more of you than meets the eye."

"I guess I should be flattered," Mary started, unraveling her hands from Charlie's, "but you know that I'm not a worldly woman. My life is my church."

Charlie sat with a vacant look on his face. He raised his right hand slightly and scratched his head, finally bringing his elbow down to rest on the table, culping his chin with his hands.

"I don't believe I'm a worldly man, Mary. I haven't been to church much, but maybe I can go with you sometimes. And look, we're already having lunch together—our first date."

Mary wanted to be flattered, but Charlie puzzled her. He knew she was in love with Graham Peters, but yet, he was trying to come on to her. Why?

"Mr. Ford…"

"Charlie."

"Okay. Charlie. I'm not sure why you want to be with me. I know that you are well aware that I'm attracted…attracted to…" Mary hesitated.

"Attracted to Graham?" Charlie prompted.

Mary nodded yes. "You were saying earlier that he has been seeing someone else." Mary lowered her eyes, and a small tear traveled down the side of her face. "I don't know why I'm telling you this, but…" Mary hesitated again, "I need to talk to somebody. I was over there this morning."

"You mean Graham's house?"

"Yes, Graham's house. I wanted him to see the new me. I shed my old clothes and got a new hairdo, and I had hoped he would notice. He came to the door in only a pair of PJ bottoms, and I could tell right away I had more than surprised him. I believe he even liked what he saw." Mary paused and noticed Charlie's intense interest in what she was saying.

"Continue," Charlie prodded.

Mary watched Charlie's expression as she spoke. "I could tell he did not want me there—like he might have been preoccupied."

"Was he alone?"

"Excuse me," the waitress said, interrupting a pivotal point in Charlie and Mary's newfound friendship. "Two rib platters." She sat the food on the table. "Can I get you anything else?"

"Ketchup," Mary shouted, happy for the interruption.

Charlie fingered his fries while Mary kept her eyes diverted, concentrating on the insatiable appetite she'd just acquired. Changing the subject, she said, "Go on and try the ribs. They're good."

"I will in a moment." With no intention of aborting his last question, Charlie inquired again if Graham was alone.

"He wasn't," Mary said in between bites of her ribs that she delicately tore from the bone. "But I don't feel like talking about that now. I'm starving, and your food is going to get cold if you don't eat."

"All right, Mary. The food looks good...smells good, too. We'll just have to make another date; I'll pick out the restaurant."

Mary sat the bone down on her plate and looked straight into the eyes of the mysterious Mr. Ford. Her gut feeling told her that Charlie had an ulterior motive for wanting to see her again—his sudden appearance at her lunch table, his coming on to her. Not only that, he seemed to be pre-occupied with what was going on at Graham's house. He was his best friend; didn't he know?

Charlie Ford had seen Mary on several occasions and had never once made an attempt to speak to her or give her a sideways glance—except maybe to look at her backside. She always caught men looking at one of her best attributes, and truth be told, Mary liked it even though she was married to Jesus. But for now, she was going to play along with Mr. Ford—find out what he was up to. Maybe she could bring the sinner into the fold.

"What makes you think I want to go out on a date with you?"

"Now, Mary. Aren't we having a wonderful lunch together?"

"But I was already here. I'm paying for my meal."

"Let me pay for your meal, and let's try this again. I really would like to get to know you better."

Mary was still for a minute. Then she looked in Charlie's eyes. "On one condition will I meet you again."

"What's that?" Charlie asked, sitting up in his seat now more attentive.

"That you go to church with me this Sunday."

Charlie coughed and threw his head back. "I'll go with you this Sunday."

Mary was shocked and her expression portrayed as much. It must be serious if this man was willing to go to a place that he was least likely to frequent. Mary was going to enjoy this. A few free meals, maybe a nice ride down the coast, but she was not going to lose sight of her own goal which was winning Graham's heart.

"It's a date."

Charlie smiled, and they ate their meal like two old friends who had been getting together for years.

♪♪♪

Charlie hadn't expected Mary to make going to church a condition by which he would see her again. He looked at Mary, who wore a slight smile on her face, and knew that if he didn't accept her condition, she would walk away—a risk he wasn't willing to take.

He was not going to let a minor oversight put a glitch in his plans. And he could come to like this woman; there was a freshness about her that he hadn't noticed before—a rebirth.

CHAPTER 37

Rita drove in silence reminiscing about the weekend's events. Her time with Graham was most memorable for her; they had finally made love. There had been touch-and-go moments, but Rita attributed much of that to her mood, probably induced by her meeting with William and his acknowledging that he wanted to get back with her. Then seeing him at The Water Hole caused her to experience an undue amount of anxiety. It was almost as if he were following her.

Unable to admit it aloud, it was good seeing William again, although all the feelings Rita ever had for her former husband were like her virginity— gone forever. He had aged, but hadn't she? It had been nearly fifteen years since she had seen him last. And he was still gambling; that's why he needed the money. It didn't take a rocket scientist to figure that out.

As Rita neared Hegenberger Road, the sky was illuminated from flood-lights that hung over the Oakland Coliseum. Oakland was battling it out with the Texas Rangers trying to clinch first place in the American League West. The playoffs for the World Series were just days away.

Rita was close to the hotel. She didn't have much to pack, and she planned on calling it an early night so she would be refreshed in the morning. She would be real busy upon her return to Seattle, especially if she was due to return in a few days.

Rita hopped out of the car, casually observing her surroundings. She quickly picked up her overnight and garment bags and headed toward the hotel entrance. It was quiet at the moment; no doubt many folks were glued to their TVs or out at the ballpark watching Oakland knock the Rangers back to Texas.

Just before entering the hotel, the sound of a car motor caused Rita to turn toward the street. She caught the back end of a slow-moving vehicle that seemed to be casing the hotel. Immediately, Rita remembered the car parked on Chester Street—the car she imagined had an occupant that might be watching her. She wasn't sure of the make and model of the car, but there were some similarities.

Rita all but ran into the hotel, and after reaching her room, secured the security latch for added protection. Safe? She wasn't sure, but she wasn't taking any chances.

The red light on the telephone blinked incessantly. Rita checked her voice messages and found she had four incoming calls. It couldn't have been Graham since she had just left him, and he had her cell number. Maybe it was her mother confirming the time of her arrival at Sea-Tac Airport.

Message One—*Beep*. "Hi, Rita. This is William. I know you're surprised to hear my voice. It was good seeing you today. Take care."

"Damn," Rita said, sucking her teeth. "Just what I need."

Message Two—*Beep*. "Hi, Rita. William again. I've been thinking a lot about you. You tore the house down tonight. Girl, you still got it. I love you. Here's my number if you decide to return my call, 555-4433."

Message Three—*Beep*. "Rita, I want to see you again. I know there's someone else in your life, but, if you give me a chance… We have history. I believe I know you better than anybody—your moods, your thoughts, the curve of your hips…"

Delete. "You don't know anything about me, William," Rita shouted out loud. "You were never there for me. You didn't have a clue what my likes and dislikes were then and you sure as hell don't have a clue now. Shit, you didn't even know what made me feel good—what it really took to please me, you son-of-a-bitch."

Message Four—*Beep*. "Rita…"

Delete. "Leave me alone, William. Leave me alone."

Rita hung up the phone and sat on the side of the bed. She needed to tell Graham that William was now living in Oakland and there might be reason to be concerned for her safety. But she couldn't just now—it would make the whole weekend seem like a farce, especially since she had kept the reason for her visit to Oakland a secret. Finding the right time to tell Graham was high on her priority list.

Rita picked up her purse. It might be a good idea to record William's number in the event she would need it. She had no plans of getting in touch with him, and she was definitely not giving him any more money. Still, there might be an occasion that having William's number would prove valuable.

She pulled out the piece of paper that was stuck under her windshield and wrote William's number on it. Rita unfolded the paper for the first time and gasped when she saw the words scrawled in large letters across the paper by a black magic marker: *I'VE BEEN WATCHING YOU!*

Rita grabbed her chest, her heart palpitating fast. Who left this message? Did it have anything to do with the strange feelings she'd had lately—that someone was watching her? Now, she wasn't sure if she had been imagining things or not. And there was the car parked down the street from Graham's house. Had someone followed her to the hotel?

Rita reached for the phone. She turned the paper over and dialed William's number. She had no idea why she decided to call him, but calling Graham would just cause her more undue stress. He would want a lot of answers to questions she was not ready to answer.

"Hello," said the gruff voice at the other end.

"This is Rita."

"Rita. I will say I'm surprised to hear your voice," William said, with a certain smugness.

"This is not a social call," Rita cut William off, getting right to the point. "I want you to stop following me and putting messages on my car windshield. Stop being a coward…"

"Whoa, whoa, slow your roll. What in the hell are you talking about?"

"You know very well what I'm talking about, William. Do I have to itemize it for you? The hand-printed message left on my rental vehicle. You had to have been following me in order to know where my car was parked."

"Rita, I'm telling you, it wasn't me. I did not write anything nor did I put anything on your car. Why would I go to the trouble of leaving you phone messages, if I was going to go through all the hassle of following you and leaving you a ridiculous note? That would be a little too obvious, don't you think?"

"How did you know where I was staying?"

"I see you've forgotten that you let that little tidbit slip before your arrival in Oakland."

Rita let out a sigh. She let what William said sink in. It made some sense, but Rita just wasn't sure. Who else would have put the note there? Was it meant for someone else?

"I've been having some strange vibes. I believe someone is following me," she said. "And after seeing you in the club last night, I thought for sure it must have been you."

"Look, Rita, I'm not going to lie to you. You sparked something in me when I saw you yesterday. Maybe I'm intrigued because after all these years and seeing you again up close, I finally saw what I really lost. I was a no-good-for-nothing loser who didn't realize God had already blessed me with something special in my life. And yes, I can admit that now." William paused. "Even when the basketball failed me, I had a precious gem that loved me and would have stood by me through the thick and thin, if I had only been the man I should have been. I have regretted the bad decisions I've made—the women, the booze." William hesitated, then continued. "And it didn't help that your old boyfriend was hanging all over you."

Ignoring his confession of guilt twenty years too late, the question that had lingered in Rita's mind sat on the edge of her tongue ready to jump—and it took a leap. "You're still gambling, aren't you?"

"My life has been one disappointment after another, Rita. I could lie and say that's all behind me, but there's no point to it. Before I came to Oakland, I was living with a woman who cared for all my needs for several years. She had had enough, left me, and came to Oakland. I followed when

I was able, but I was not able to persuade her to take me back. I've been staying with Troy Kemp. Remember him?"

"Yeah, Troy. How is he doing?"

"Troy is fine. He spends a lot of his time with a lawyer friend of his—I think it's serious. Troy didn't suffer any backlash from being axed from the NBA. He's got his life together and doing quite well. I'm the one with the problems."

"You never answered my question."

"Sometimes it's hard to break old habits, Rita. Yes, I'm still gambling, but I want to get my life on track. I know you have sacrificed for my selfishness, and I've never really done anything for you."

"Don't worry about it, William. I hope you can get control of your life. I remember the person you were once, and while a lot of time has passed, it's never too late to get help, if you need it, and start over. As long as you can accept the fact that your basketball career is over—has been over—and can let it go, then will you move on."

William sighed. He knew Rita was right. Not being able to play basketball, not becoming the star he had always envisioned, killed him as a person. But that was all in the past. He was brooding about what had happened over twenty years ago. Many people during William's twenty-year hiatus had suffered the loss of a dream but were able to move on to something else and become successful.

"I miss your wisdom, Rita. If I had just listened…"

He was getting sentimental on her, and Rita didn't need that.

"I'm sorry to have bothered you. I guess I feel better knowing that you had nothing to do with this note."

"I don't want to hurt you, Rita."

I'm not going to let you, Rita thought.

"Well, I guess I better go."

"Are you all right?"

"I will be. My doors are bolted."

And then he surprised Rita. "Would you like me to come over?" William said carefully. "It would put your mind at ease, and I won't bother you."

"No, William. That won't be necessary."

"Rita, it's no trouble. We were husband and wife once."

"Yes, William, we *were* husband and wife. I love Graham Peters, now."

"Well, why didn't you call him to let him know that you're all in a tizzy, because you believe someone is following you and leaving you messages that's got you shaking in your boots?"

"That's enough, William," Rita hissed. "I called you because I wanted to know if you were the pervert who left the note on my car. And that was the only reason."

"No need to call me names."

"I didn't want to worry him."

"And you thought I wouldn't be worried? No, because you thought I was the cause of your concern, and you planned on telling me off."

They laughed. This was the first time Rita felt at ease talking with William, realizing she'd made a mistake thinking William was the culprit.

"It's still not a good idea, William."

"I'm coming over. The least I can do is make you feel at ease until you have to catch your plane."

Rita paused for several minutes. "I can't. We can't put back the pieces of our lives that took only a short time to unravel. I've made peace with myself—had even vowed to not let anyone else in my life…until now. I'm sorry I called you, William, but I do appreciate you listening."

"Are you afraid that if I'm in the same room with you…that you might want to get closer than close? Are you afraid that after all these years, there's still an ember burning inside of you for your ex?"

"Don't be so presumptuous, William. You're certainly not all that, otherwise our lives would have been different. And, it's too late for that now. I have someone in my life."

"Have it your way, Rita. I'll wait. You'll come. I've got nothing but time."

"Suit yourself. I've got to pack."

"I know you. I hear it in your voice. But you'd rather take your chances by yourself than trust me to protect you."

"We've already gone through this, William. Good night."

"If that's the way you want it, good night, Rita." *It's just a matter of time before you'll be mine again. I've got plans for us, and you and your beautiful voice are going to take us there.*

And the line was dead. Rita crossed the room to the window pulling back the gold, rustic-looking curtain to get a view of the street. No stray cars hung about like thieves in the night, but a steady stream of late-night winged birds flew in and out of the Oakland Airport—Rita silently waiting her turn.

♪♪♪

Settled in his comfortable chair, the phone cradled in the curve of his neck, Graham flipped the television channels until he came to the baseball game. The Oakland A's vs. the Rangers; this was the game to watch. He hung up the phone. After three tries, Rita's line was still busy.

CHAPTER 38

It was Sunday morning, a day when many hearts and minds would turn toward God. Fragments of light filtered through the blinds—Graham was thankful for the light of day. He had awakened from a paralyzing dream with chills and a thin veil of sweat coating his forehead and chest. Amanda was looking down on him, flashing an elongated index finger at him—a warning rather than a forget-me-not.

Graham grabbed at his throat, struggling to disengage himself from some unforeseen force that had him bound. Amanda had appeared at the tail end of his dream, and after her admonishment, she evaporated like water on a sidewalk under a one-hundred-degree Hawaiian sun. Pulling the sheets from the bed, Graham wrapped himself in hopes of calming his chattering teeth.

What did it mean? Graham looked at the clock. It was 6:45. Rita would be boarding her plane shortly. He hadn't been able to reach her at the hotel, and she hadn't called, either. Graham gave her space, choosing to feast upon the memories of the day stuck to him like a sticky lollipop. They had consummated their friendship with more than a gentle peck on the lips, and it had consumed Graham in fires of passion he hadn't felt in a while. So much so, he slipped into a deep sleep, missing the A's topple the Rangers in a ninth-inning, come-from-behind grand-slam hit by Canseco.

Graham sat up, looked at the phone, resisted. She would call; he could depend on it. Seconds then minutes passed and pent-up emotions flooded his psyche, recalling moments that caused Graham to wonder if Rita was holding back something from him. It nagged at him, even Rita's explanation. Her pronounced agitation on last evening wasn't lost on him. Had Amanda been trying to warn him about Rita?

A smile found Graham's face. It was 6:29, and the sound of the phone ringing became music to his ears. A quick goodbye and a sweet sensual telephone kiss passed between them—Rita vowing to give Graham a call when the plane had landed safely in Seattle.

Graham bounded out of bed and unwrapped himself from the tangled sheets. He picked up the radio from the nightstand and tuned it to station KDIA—the Bay Area's own gospel on Sunday mornings. He and Amanda had shared many Sunday mornings with KDIA's own Al Moreland who would invite folks to come down to Pearl's Grill for some Louisiana coon. And he could spin the meanest gospel hits—James Cleveland, Jesse Dixon, the Dixie Hummingbirds, and The Mighty Clouds of Joy. God rest his soul, Al had gone on to be with the Lord some years back.

Yes, Graham was going to church today. He'd show those two-faced church folks that whatever they thought of him didn't matter. His business was between him and God. He felt good today, and he was going to give the Lord the time He deserved. Maybe that was what Amanda was doing— admonishing him to go to the house of the Lord because he had strayed a little.

Thoughts of Deborah and Elizabeth clouded his head. Graham hadn't seen either of them since that Sunday when they found Rita in the house with him. Liz had called once, but Deborah was somewhere seething and still making her case. Graham loved his daughters, but he wasn't going to allow either one of them to dictate how he would live his life. He had been a good husband and was still a good father—faithful to Amanda for all of their years together. Who were they to chastise him and give him grief? Daughters or not!

♪♪♪

Graham walked up the few steps to the door of the church. He adjusted his tie once more. The last time he was there, his legs wanted to buckle, but he could feel Amanda giving him a gentle nudge so he wouldn't be late. Being late would be sure cause to make him a spectacle; however, Graham knew it didn't matter because he had been the hot topic for the last month or more. And saints were sometimes worse than sinners—they never let you forget.

Graham stood in the vestibule and peeped through the window of the door that led into the sanctuary. There was a line of parishioners waiting to be ushered in. The deep, rich, wine-colored carpet that ran from the vestibule into the sanctuary made him feel at peace coming into the Lord's house.

Elation! Sister Mary Ross wasn't the gatekeeper today, and he wouldn't have to ignore her or make a scene. However, Graham could not dismiss Mary from his mind. He was unable to shake the image of her—dressed up in new designer clothes, a new hairdo, a new look that defined the essence of someone Graham hadn't recognized to be Mary Ross—a rebirth. Maybe Amanda was warning him about Mary. But he was ahead of the game. Mary Ross in her many disguises would have to get up early in the morning to pull the wool over his eyes. And he was ushered to his seat.

Heads bobbed back and forth like Pac-Man, the old Atari game. Graham sat at the end of a row undaunted by the continual stares—happy to be back in the house of the Lord. Stares became smiles that became contagious. The happy worshippers lost interest in Graham, immersing themselves in the hymn for the morning—fans moving in unison while the congregation sang "Nearer My God to Thee."

When he got up enough nerve, Graham scanned the sanctuary, his eyes finally resting on Deborah. He let out a deep breath. It was obvious she had been looking in his direction, because she quickly looked away as soon as his head zoomed in on her. Graham didn't miss the little nudge in the arm Deborah gave Liz—Liz looking up and releasing a small smile.

Riley and Grant nodded in Graham's direction. They understood. It was a man's thing, but since they had to live with their wives, a nod was all they could give their father-in-law.

Graham spotted Martha who was all decked out in lavender—a fancy, lavender-and-white flowered hat sitting regally on her head. Surprise was etched on her face, but the smile that accompanied it was a sign that Martha was glad to see Graham. She continued peeping as if half expecting to see someone else. Graham realized Martha was wondering if Rita was coming. "Home," Graham mouthed, hoping Martha understood.

Mary Ross. Graham might not have spotted her if it had not been for her constantly looking back down the aisle as if she half expected him to be there—or so he thought. She was amazing—her sparkle brighter than it had been the previous morning, standing in his living room with the sleek, black velvety dress on. Mary appeared ten years younger.

Their eyes locked, but Mary's didn't linger. This puzzled Graham since she had made it clear to him that she wanted him and would do whatever it took to make it happen. Maybe Mary was suddenly embarrassed by her outright display of desperation. Graham felt sorry for her, but he didn't have time to dwell on it as all attention was averted to the praise dancers, who dressed in white chiffon blouses with long blouson sleeves and white, flowing, floor-length skirts that resembled upside-down funnel clouds. They looked like Heavenly beings sent from above to usher in the Holy Spirit.

"Order my steps in Your word, dear Lord," crooned the recording artist. Arms, heads, and fingers so graceful as their movement mimed the lyrics to the song. The essence of a well-trained ballerina to the defined ethnic movements of the Alvin Ailey dancers encompassed these spiritual, earthly beings who gave reverence to the Lord.

A thunderous applause met the young ladies as they bowed at the end of their tear-wrenching dance interpretation. Saints jumped to their feet, raising their hands high above their heads, crying out "Hallelujah, Hallelujah" so filled with the Spirit that had touched nearly every soul in the sanctuary. It was a contagious event with every seat empty, including Graham's.

As the roar of the crowd died down, many worshippers who had found themselves in the middle of the aisle, lost in the Holy Spirit, settled back into their seats. Late entrants to the service were allowed to come inside by the ushers.

Mary turned around again—this time her frown becoming a slight smile, then a full-grown grin. It was obvious she had recovered from her own one-act play yesterday—with the illustrious Deacon Peters in all his glory now just a fleeting memory. Graham turned in the direction Mary had been looking and was just in time to catch a glimpse of Charlie heading down the aisle—bypassing a seat next to him in favor of one next to Sister Mary Ross.

Silence fell like an object caught in quicksand. Even the keys on the organ that Charlotte had been caressing throughout the service fell silent for a minute too long—the interruption in the music causing folks to choose between stopping to see if something was wrong with her or continuing to stare at the *slight* distraction that sat next to Sister Mary Ross. Graham sat stoically in his seat—his eyes cast in their direction. Mary glanced once more in his direction and quickly turned away when she was satisfied Graham had an eyeful.

The remainder of Sunday service was a blur. It became a chore not to stare at Mary and Charlie, so Graham did until service was over. Graham wasn't sure when Reverend Fields got up or sat down, or for that matter, what the sermon was all about. An attempt to remember was clouded by a vision of the two people who sat a few feet in front of him.

Fellow deacons mobbed Graham the moment service came to an end. Glad to have him back in the fold, the deacons welcomed their missing brother with open arms, some offering a seat at their Sunday dinner table, while others offered a warm hand and a promise to get together soon.

But Graham was looking past them trying to catch a glimpse of Charlie and Mary. He and Charlie had been on shaky ground lately, and after their brief meeting in the barbershop on Friday, it seemed their friendship had taken another small beating. But Mary Ross? What was Charlie trying to prove?

After shaking the last brother's hand, Martha and Elroy were at Graham's side. Graham hugged his in-laws, giving Martha a kiss on the cheek.

"Looking like a beautiful spring garden this morning," Graham said to Martha.

"Son, this is the day that the Lord has made. I will rejoice and be glad in it." Martha raised her hand up to Heaven and gave the Lord a great big *Hallelujah*. "It's so good to see you today."

"Sure is," Elroy said.

"Thank you. I wish my daughters felt the same. They have pulled my grandkids into this."

"Now don't you go worrying yourself about it," Martha said. "They'll come around. Just give them some time."

Graham nodded knowing that Martha's statement was probably correct, but he was not interested in prolonging this conversation. Graham shifted from one leg to the other, anxious to leave the sanctuary in hope that Charlie was still on the church grounds, but Martha wasn't quite through.

"The girls and their families are coming by this afternoon for dinner." Martha paused. She saw the hurt in Graham's eyes. "You can come by if you like."

"Yeah, Graham. It would be good to have you for dinner. In fact, you haven't been over since…A-man…" Elroy paused, unable to push Amanda's name out of his mouth.

"I know, Dad. I promise I'll come by soon. Today is not the day. I don't want to spoil dinner for everyone. My being there would cause a scene, and I'm not up to it today."

"Well, make sure you do soon. And bring Rita with you," he half whispered. A smile flew across Graham's face. "You should have brought her to church."

"She's back in Seattle, Dad."

"Between me and you, son, the church might not have been ready for it."

"Probably not, especially my girls."

"But tell me something," Martha butted in. "Charlie and Mary? Now that is a tongue-wagger. They strolled out of here like they were a couple. And I can't believe the good Christian Sister Mary would even consider fraternizing with the sinner, Charlie. That's a true example of unequally yoked. I'm not a gambling woman, but I bet Reverend Fields' next sermon will be about being unequally yoked."

"You know it," Elroy concurred. "Mary causing all that ruckus up in here. Just goes to show what she was really up to."

"Revenge," Martha said. "Revenge 'cause she couldn't get the man she wanted."

"Well, she can't go and discredit someone else without discrediting herself," Elroy said. "But she sho look better. I had to do a triple take."

Martha popped Elroy on the shoulder and the group snickered until Reverend Fields walked up alongside them. Reverend Fields extended his hand to each of them. Stopping before Graham, he gave him a gentleman's hug.

"Glad to see you, Brother Peters. We miss you down front with the other deacons. If there's anything I can do or if you just need to talk to someone, don't hesitate to call me."

"Thank you, Pastor."

"I mean that. And enjoy your afternoon."

Goodbye hugs were passed among the group. Reverend Fields went one way, and Elroy and Martha exited through a side door admonishing Graham to visit soon. Now, Graham was free to leave—possibly too late to catch Charlie. They needed to talk, and today would be a good day if only Graham could catch up with him.

Graham passed through the doors of the sanctuary into the vestibule when he spotted Liz standing off to the side. She looked like a model in the midst of a photo shoot surrounded by church ministerial pamphlets and leaflets scattered on sofa tables strategically placed throughout the room. Liz watched Graham whiz through—moving fast like he had somewhere to go. Liz rushed forward stretching out her arms to embrace her daddy, her children at her side.

"Daddy," Liz called out in a voice barely above a whisper.

"Granddaddy," Elise and Riley, Jr. said in unison.

Graham hesitated, then opened his own arms wide. "How are my babies?" Tears welled up in Graham as he encircled his daughter and grandchildren in his arms.

They stood that way for nearly three minutes—one large umbrella protecting the family from the elements. All that could be heard was soft sobs coming from the huddled group.

"I love you, Daddy. Please forgive me."

Graham tried to speak but was restricted from parting his lips because Liz's taut finger was placed against them.

"I've neglected you, alienated you from your grandchildren. You've been a wonderful father, and I don't have a right to impede your happiness."

Liz took her dad's face between her hands and kissed him on both cheeks. Graham felt the warmth of Liz's affection and in someway felt exonerated. Now tears of joy fell freely from his eyes.

"We love you, too, Granddad," Elise said, hugging her granddad harder than the rest. She was her grandfather's favorite.

The sweet words of a child—music to Graham's ears. "I love you, too, babies. Maybe we can take in a baseball game."

"Yeah. Did you hear that, Mom?"

"Yes, baby. We'll have to get together with Granddad this week—if that's all right with you, Dad."

Graham looked at his second-born. She looked so much like Amanda. Her innocent, electrifying smile, the shape of her teeth. "Of course it's all right."

"Okay, Dad. I'll call you later in the week. Gotta go. Riley is waiting for me in the car. We have dinner reservations."

"Yeah, your grandma told me. Have fun. I love you."

They gave each other a departing kiss and then Liz and the kids were gone. Graham lingered in the vestibule a few minutes longer, overcome by the love he had received.

Caught up in the moment, Graham had completely forgotten about Charlie—that was until he exited the church and nearly fell on top of Charlie and Mary, who were standing at the foot of the church steps. Graham looked from one to the other absently, kicking a small pebble that lay close to his foot. The sight of Mary and Charlie together rendered him speechless.

It was comical, almost downright funny…the two of them locked hand in hand. But it was just yesterday when Graham had lain eyes on the transformed Mary Ross—a revitalized beauty who had risen from the dead. Graham wasn't quite sure what to make of it. Was this an attempt on Charlie's part to make him jealous? It was probably the consensus of everyone who knew Mary Ross and had seen her in the past few days that Mary had emerged from her cocoon—a not-so-attractive caterpillar making her entrance into her second life as a beautiful monarch.

Mary wore a sharp, two-piece wool navy suit with bold brass buttons running north to south on the three-quarter-length jacket. Graham's head moved in the direction of the buttons, pausing momentarily upon her breasts that peeked slightly above the fly-away collar on her jacket. A pair of navy, high-heeled, T-strap Aigners accompanied Mary's outfit, along with a matching bag that hung from her shoulder. Her face was well-defined—slate-blue shadow dusting her eyelids with a hint of charcoal eyeliner setting the boundary between lid and lash. A brick-red blush highlighted her cheekbones, making it difficult to ignore the sculptured look of her precision haircut. Whatever Charlie's intentions were, Sister Mary Ross was ready to give him a run for his money.

CHAPTER 39

The wheels of the 727 jet squealed upon hitting the tarmac at Sea-Tac Airport. Droplets of rain tapped the plane's window—a sign that Rita had indeed arrived in the Pacific Northwest.

Washington State was well known for its long periods of relentless rain backed by a nervous chill that frequently brought out everything from fur-lined boots to full-length mink coats. And the forecast for the week ahead was temperatures well below the fifties, making for a very brisk October.

Rita sat looking out the window, waiting for the plane to taxi to the gate. Her thoughts bounced from Graham to William as she went over the events of the past few days. It weighed heavy on her—heavier than the rain that was once droplets and now a heavy downpour.

"Glad you're home, baby," Mavis said. Mavis placed a gentle kiss on her daughter's cheek. She was well aware what took Rita to Oakland. Mavis tried desperately to talk Rita out of going—wasting her time and money on a no-good ex-husband who had caused her nothing but pain and misery.

It was Mavis and George Duncan who had helped Rita pick up the pieces, although Rita was much stronger than they had given credit. They had nursed her through the pain of break-up and humiliation.

Rita was a survivor, and she rose from the ashes—never looking back. She came out of the marriage with a nice settlement that would more than take care of her needs since Rita was not an overly flamboyant person or an excessive spender. But she did have an ache in her heart for William, and while she did not run right away when he called, she knew she'd help him in the end—even at the protest of her parents she loved dearly.

"Glad to be back, Mom. You're so radiant today."

Rita looked at Mavis—black streaks running through her silver mane with loose-fitting curls that bounced like a toy Slinky off her shoulders. Rita picked up one and let it fall, the curl recoiling from all of its pent-up body. Mavis wore a black polka-dot-on-crème satin blouse tucked into a pair of straight, black, wool slacks that sculpted her slender frame.

"Did you see him?" Mavis inquired, picking up her coat as they headed for the baggage claim area.

"Yes, Mom. I saw him. He's aged some…but that's to be expected since I haven't seen him in awhile."

"And that was too soon."

Ignoring Mavis, Rita continued. "You won't believe this, but he's wearing dreads and glasses."

"I'd like to drag him by those dreads and hang him up somewhere until the crows pick his body."

"Aw, *Mother*. I know you hate William, but must you talk like that?"

"Maybe you've forgotten what he put you through, but your father and I have vivid memories, and I hate him…"

"Hate is a strong word, and I forgive him. He wants me back in his life."

Mavis stopped in her tracks, not caring that she was blocking traffic in the middle of the hallway. Two other flights had recently landed, and the rush to get baggage and be on their way was evident from the flow of people who moved in the same direction.

"And I know you told him no way, no how." Mavis was pointing her finger and moving her arm like she was finger painting. "That's the only answer. Your father and I could not bear to go through what we did when he hurt you before."

"Mother, stop being so dramatic. You and I both know that he'll never get the chance to do that again. Remember me telling you about a new man in my life? Well, I love him…he's the missing link…my gift from God."

Mavis sighed. "So you're serious about this boy wonder?"

"Very serious—serious enough that if he asks me to marry him, I'll accept."

Mavis gasped. "My Lawd, girl. I had no idea it was *that* serious. Wait until your father hears this."

"I know it seems hard to fathom since I've had no real man in my life all these years—an escort here, an escort there, and some good conversation in between. I was afraid of being hurt because William did such a good job of hurting me."

"That's why we didn't want you to go to Oakland, baby. I figured he'd try to worm his way back into your life with you doing good and all. And you giving him all that money was nothing but an open invitation to do just that."

"Mom, I'm a grown woman. I can handle William."

"Please don't tell me," Mrs. Duncan cut in, "that he awakened some sleeping giant." Mavis paused to look at Rita as they continued down the corridor. "Get over it!"

"Mom, you're not hearing me."

"I hear you all right, and I hope that alarm that's going off inside of me is false."

Rita allowed herself to be amused at her mother's ramblings. It was good seeing William, but she knew there was no chance for their lives to be entangled again. Rita was truly happy for the first time, and she thanked God for blessing her with a wonderful man like Graham.

"So tell me," Mavis said, "about this new man in your life."

"He's handsome, gentle, kind, loving, thoughtful…"

Mavis feigned a cough. "All right, I get it. But he must possess some other qualities."

"You never let me finish." Rita sighed. "He's a good kisser—lips sweet as honeysuckle."

"It's apparent you know those lips well."

"I do."

"And…"

"He's a widower with two adult children." Rita wasn't about to tell her mother that one was a witch and the other was tolerable and what they had put her through. "And…he's sixty-one years old."

"Sixty-one, mature, and minus the baby-mama-drama syndrome."

"Mom, you are crazy, and what do you know about 'baby mama' anything?"

"Girl, I have lived life. We may have not called it that as I progressed through the years, but I've seen enough to know what 'baby mama drama' is no matter how old I get."

They shared a laugh. "Watch your step, Mom," Rita admonished as she and Mavis rode the escalator to the lower level.

When they reached the bottom, they searched for the turnstile that would bring Rita's luggage from the belly of the plane. A large crowd had assembled—Mavis and Rita were nearly the last two to arrive. They stood back from the crowd that had already claimed their space along the perimeter of the turnstile—a few pieces of luggage finally emerging.

"Graham lives in Oakland and so does William."

"Have you told Graham about your ex-husband?"

"Graham is aware of William but unaware that I came to Oakland to meet with him. I just learned William has been in Oakland for some time and has even been to the club where I perform."

"He's what? Rita, listen to your wise old mother. You can't go back there. I know Oakland is one of your favorite places and the people there have certainly been good to you, but with William there and darn near stalking you, you'll only be asking for trouble. It wouldn't be fair to Graham."

"Mom, you're overreacting, and what do you care about Graham? Anyway, William has never followed me or made contact with me until now."

"And how long did he plan that? You can't be too sure, Rita, and I just don't like it. You need to talk with your father about this, and certainly your new friend, Graham. He needs to know, Rita."

"I know, Mom. I plan on telling him."

"When it's too late?"

"Lower your voice. Everyone is starting to look at us."

"Who cares? Somebody's got to talk some sense into that thick head of yours."

"You act as if William might do something to me."

"Rita, you're my only child. Don't think I'm not aware about all the bruises and black eyes you suffered at that maniac's hands."

Rita stiffened. She had guarded that secret well, at least she thought she had. Only one other person knew besides the doctor, and he was the abuser. How could Mavis have found out?

"I believe William has changed."

"I don't care how old you get, you have eggshells for brains when it comes to that man. I don't understand it. Tell me, what's he doing now?"

"What do you mean?"

"Why did he ask you for all of that money? I say he's still gambling. I'm right, aren't I?"

"You might be, but I'm not sure, but you have certainly made your point perfectly clear. There's one of my pieces; I'll be right back."

Well, I'm not going anywhere, because I haven't finished. Rita left Mavis tapping her toes against the floor while Rita retrieved her bags from the turnstile. She turned toward her mother with bags in tow and stood and watched the steam rise from her mother's nostrils. It was right comical and downright cute.

"Rita, hurry up. You've got me all riled up now." Mavis watched Rita shuffle through the crowd with her luggage in hand. "If I had a gun twenty years ago, I'd a popped a few rounds in that arrogant, self-absorbed, jerk back then," Mavis muttered under her breath.

CHAPTER 40

Graham found himself sitting in the backseat of Charlie's Honda, Charlie at the wheel and Mary riding shotgun. Charlie and Mary were engaged in juvenile banter—girlfriend, boyfriend kind of stuff, purposely alienating Graham from the conversation. Eyeing and hissing, lip smacking and "ohhs" and "ahhs" passed between the two passengers in front, giving the illusion they were a new couple getting to know each other—teasing here, teasing there—playing the dating game.

Graham was unsure why he had accepted their invitation to lunch. Curiosity had gotten the best of him. When had Charlie and Mary gotten together? It was just yesterday morning that Mary had come to the house trying to seduce him. Charlie seemed to have some kind of chip on his shoulders, and he and Graham had barely spoken to each other, let alone had a decent conversation in months.

In fact, ever since Rita had come into his life, Graham had sensed Charlie had amassed a certain amount of jealousy toward him. It was so thick, you could cut it with a knife. And why would Charlie be jealous when over the years the local scuttlebutt was always about Charlie and his many women?

It was true that Charlie could have just about any woman he wanted. They used to fall at his feet, but he wasn't ready to settle down. That was until Ernestine came into his life. But he wasn't ready for Ernestine, either. Ernestine was different and did not fit into the lifestyle Charlie had carved out for himself. And then he lost her, Ernestine, the one woman who could have made Charlie most respectable.

Now as the car rolled along, the only view Graham had was the back of Charlie's and Mary's heads. Graham began to suspect that he was being set up. He wasn't sure how Mary fit in, but Graham's intuition led him to believe that Charlie was the mastermind behind his unconfirmed suspicions.

"We ought to go back to Friday's," Mary finally said, pawing all over Charlie.

Charlie smiled. "We haven't been to Shenanigan's. They have a wonderful brunch. I've worked up a hunger after Reverend Fields' two-hour message." Charlie and Mary laughed so loud, Graham put his fingers in his ears to drown out the noise. It wasn't even that funny, although he didn't remember a thing Reverend Fields had spoken about.

What was Charlie up to? He would have never given Mary Ross the time of day, no matter how good she looked. Religion was not in Charlie's vocabulary despite his showing up at church today, and Mary Ross was one of God's loyal angels. Besides, Graham had tried relentlessly over the years to reel his buddy into the umbrella of the Lord and failed on every attempt, except when he and Amanda and both girls were married and for Amanda's funeral. No, something was not right, and he would play along until Charlie's hidden agenda was exposed.

Graham broke his silence. "Why don't you drop me off, Charlie? I seem to be a third wheel."

"No, buddy," Charlie rushed to say. "Mary and I are just getting to know each other. Sorry if we seem preoccupied. I'm surprised I hadn't noticed her earlier."

"Yeah, right," Graham muttered under his breath. "Maybe it's because you're allergic to church. Right, Mary?"

Mary stared straight ahead not daring to take a peek at Charlie who sat silent, mulling over Graham's snide comment.

"Well, Mary is a beautiful woman."

Mary blushed.

"And, I'll go to church every Sunday just to be near her."

"They say the Lord works in mysterious ways," Graham said under his breath.

"I'm sure you've noticed Mary of late. She's a single man's dream."

Here we go, Graham thought. "No disrespect to Mary, but while I will admit that I have noticed the change in her, Charlie, and find her to be rather attractive, she's still Mary."

"For your information, Deacon Peters…"

"Call me Graham."

"Slam, Graham, thank you, ma'am…whatever. I know you find me attractive. I saw how you were mulling over my body with your eyes yesterday. If that…that woman hadn't been in your bed already, I might have been in it instead."

The car careened to a screeching halt as Charlie nearly ran a red light. Charlie and Graham passed glances in the rearview mirror—Charlie locked on until Graham finally looked away.

Mary twisted around in her seat frowning at Charlie. "What is it, Charlie? You darned near turned the car over. I told you yesterday that they were together."

"Well, you didn't quite put it that way."

"There was no mistake in what I meant. Graham had on only a pajama bottom, and that…that woman had on this see-through nightgown. Aghh!"

"Enough!" Graham cut in. "It's nobody's business what went on at my house."

"I'm not interested in knowing what went on there," Charlie said, tossing another look at Graham in the rearview mirror. "All I know is, I'm the lucky one. If Graham had not let you go, Mary, I wouldn't have had the opportunity to get together with you."

Mary batted her eyes. "Oh," Mary said satisfied, while Charlie kept Graham in his view with one eye while maneuvering in and out of traffic.

"Well, Mary, I do wish the best for you and Charlie on the occasion of your blossoming relationship. You are a beautiful woman, and if I wasn't already in a committed relationship, I'd probably give ole Charlie boy a run for his money."

Graham caught Charlie's look in the mirror. Graham wasn't sure if it was a look of surprise, satisfaction, or entrapment, but Graham was enjoying the game. But it was Mary's look that said it all—the pleading as she whipped her head around, flashing her eyelashes in Graham's direction as if she couldn't believe her ears. Her eyes were full of hope. But Mary surprised Graham as she reached up and gave Charlie a peck on the cheek to the surprise of Charlie, who had yet to make any sexual advances toward her.

Graham continued to watch, not sure if Mary was pretending or actually believed he and Charlie were fighting over her. He'd even test his theory if it meant not hurting Rita, but he wasn't about to risk losing his precious jewel.

♪♪♪

"The car isn't far," Mavis said, putting on her trench coat. "Why don't you stay here; I'll bring the car around. Your father would have been here if he didn't have to go to a board meeting this morning. You know he's on the board of Seattle-First National Bank, and they called a special meeting to discuss an emergency matter."

"That's not necessary, Mom. I'll go with you. The rain seems to have let up some."

"After you're settled, maybe we can get together for brunch. I want to show you the menu and program for our gala fund raiser for our Women's Center on Friday. Maybe you can say a few words to the group; after all, it's because of all that you've been through with William that I became involved in the first place."

"I'll have to decline, Mom."

"But why? And miss the opportunity to showcase my beautiful daughter? I was hoping you could fit a song in there."

"Mom, I really hate to disappoint you. I won't be able to go to the gala."

"Rita! You've known about this for weeks." Mavis threw her hands up in the air and sighed. "It's a simple request. Please don't disappoint me. This is a very important event. The monies raised will help many women who find themselves victim of an abuser. I don't have to tell you that, and…"

Rita put her arms around her mother's shoulders and drew a long sigh.

"You know I love you. Ever since I was a little girl, I wanted to emulate you in every way. I didn't turn out too bad. You've been a champion for this and that. You and Daddy were there for me when I needed you in the worst way and for that I will always be truly grateful. I commend you on the work you are doing at the Women's Center, and I would be the last person to leave you in a lurch, but I won't be able to be there. I'll support you financially or any other way I can."

"And you ran all the way to Oakland to help that no-count, lower-than-life ex-husband of yours the minute he came calling, but I can't get you to do something for me, your own mother, who's trying to raise money for a worthy cause."

"Don't be so dramatic, Mother."

Rita looked at her mother. They stood on the edge of the curb waiting for the officer to wave them across the busy thoroughfare.

"I'm going back to Oakland on Thursday."

Mavis gasped and abruptly turned her face away from Rita without uttering a word.

"Clyde needed a replacement for an act that cancelled and I jumped at the opportunity. The band could use the money."

"Does he mean that much to you?"

"This is not about a man, Mother. This is about a roof over my head…"

"That you never use… and you have plenty of money saved. And I know it because your daddy is on the board of the bank where your accounts are stored," Mavis hissed.

Ignoring Mavis, Rita continued, "…food on the table, a few pennies in the bank. I rely on these bookings, Mom. I'm not working a nine-to-five job, although I haven't done bad. I'll donate money, get someone else to sing if you like, but I've got to go to Oakland. I promise not to miss the next one."

Mavis Duncan kept walking until she reached the car. She hit the remote and got into the car, leaving Rita to put her own luggage into the trunk. Mavis knew she would get over it and certainly wouldn't love her child any less because of it. Even though she had not committed Rita for the gala, it was a forgone conclusion in her mind that Rita was going to participate.

Mavis was depending upon Rita to make her night a successful one. But Rita had a life of her own and could not answer every beck and call. Mavis rolled the window down and took a whiff of the fresh Seattle air. She twisted her ruby-red lips together, blew out a puff of air, and relaxed knowing she had no control over her grown daughter.

♪♪♪

Shenanigan's was crowded with late-afternoon patrons. They were dressed in casual to dressy wear—ladies in linen pantsuits, silk and rayon dresses; the men in open-collared, short-sleeve cotton shirts and polo pullovers.

Piped-in music met the trio's ears—a rhythm that was jazzy and a little rock and roll. The smell of freshly grilled fish met their noses. The hostess, dressed in a soft coral linen blouse and eggshell-colored linen pants with an eggshell, eel-skin belt wrapped around her waist, placed Charlie's name on the waiting list, promising a short, fifteen-minute wait.

Charlie, Graham, and Mary found seats next to a young couple. Mary eagerly sat in the middle of the group—two fine gentlemen at her disposal. They sat quietly, the only noise other than the music and the faint voices of the dining patrons was an occasional smacking of the couple's lips. It was a tolerable distraction in the wake of an awkward silence.

Mary shifted in her seat, occasionally tugging at the hem of her skirt. It dared to expose ample flesh that had both Graham and Charlie peering out of the corners of their eyes. Mary's legs were crossed at the ankles and her knees slightly bent to the right.

Mary was dumbfounded, unable to believe that two attractive males were fighting over her. Just last week they hadn't even given her a sideways glance. Graham said it himself, "If there was no Rita, he would give Charlie a run for his money." And Graham wouldn't have to work that hard. Mary would cut Charlie off in a heartbeat if she knew Graham would have her.

Things were beginning to crystallize right in front of her. Charlie was in love with Rita. She could feel it, and he was using Mary to make Graham jealous. She would not have believed it herself if she hadn't been in the play. Mary was enjoying this more and more and moved closer to Charlie.

"Ford, party of three," the hostess announced.

The trio stood and followed the hostess to a small, round table draped in imported starched linen. They sat next to a window that overlooked the marina. The interior of the restaurant had a rustic look about it—pictures and relics from the city's past hung on the walls adding to the nostalgia of the place. Charlie pulled out a chair for Mary while Graham eased into the one to the right of her. Charlie sat in the remaining seat, leaving only the hostess standing.

"The buffet is open, but if you'd like a menu, you're more than welcome," the hostess said.

"We'll have the buffet," Charlie announced. And the others nodded their approval.

The trio sat looking from one to the other, each uncomfortable in their destined setting. Anxious to get beyond the moment, Graham pushed back his chair from the table and stood.

"You all ready to eat?"

Both Charlie and Mary nodded their heads.

Graham promptly moved behind Mary's chair ready to pull it out, not wanting to be upstaged by Charlie. A smile rose on Charlie's face, wallowing in a small victory at Graham's small hint of jealousy.

"I'm ready. Mary?" Graham waited for Mary to rise from her chair.

"Oh, I've been ready. Been ready since yesterday. Just enjoying this view. You know, I never thought about sailing or going to the beach. It's always been a white thing, you know. But today when I looked out over the marina, I told myself, "*Self, you are going to learn to live. Yes, Mary Ross is going to learn to live a little*." Mary popped her fingers. "Yeah, that's what I told myself."

Charlie and Graham looked from one to the other. For whatever reason each man was there, Mary deserved a second look.

"I'm inclined to agree with you, Mary," Graham said.

Mary snickered and gave Graham a broad smile. "Yes, Deacon Peters, I'm ready to eat."

Graham pulled out Mary's chair and extended his arm for her to proceed. He walked behind her with Charlie bringing up the rear. They were a funny-looking group, and Mary relished and marveled at her good fortune. Not only one—but two—men were taking her to brunch and making a fuss over her.

♪♪♪

Charlie dropped Mary off and drove back to the church to retrieve Graham's car. The pair rode in silence. Charlie watched Graham out of the corner of his eye while Graham nodded his head like it was attached to his neck by a spring, catching glimpses of Charlie on the sly. They reached the church, and Graham got out and got in his car. As he passed Charlie, Charlie rolled the window down and leaned his head out of the window.

"I'll follow you to your house."

Graham sighed.

They arrived at Graham's house, and Charlie made himself comfortable on the overstuffed loveseat in the living room. He pulled out a toothpick and stuck it in his mouth and waited for Graham to return from the bathroom. A lot of memories were embedded in that room, the house, and the family that had occupied it. Charlie got up and went over to the fireplace. He picked up Graham and Amanda's wedding picture and stared at it for more minutes than he could account for—at least until he heard a grunt from Graham who had returned to the room.

"Some day," Charlie remarked with a grin and sat the picture back on the mantel.

"One of the best days of my life," Graham responded. "But let's talk about you."

"What ya mean?"

"Why Mary, and what are you up to, Charlie? That's a God-fearing woman."

"Hold up, now. Don't go and get all out of sorts. Sister Mary Ross done went through some kind of metamorphosis. And I saw how you looked at her—the same way I did."

"I won't deny that she looks more appealing, but Mary is not your type. I don't know what kind of game you're playing, but please, not at Mary's expense."

"Are we talking about the same Mary Ross that was asking for your ass to be thrown out of the congregation at the big church on Market Street? The same Mary Ross that you practically threw out of your house yesterday when she came parading up here only to find the lovely Ms. Rita Long had beat her to it and was dressed in a naughty nightie coming from what I suspect was your bedroom after a serious romp in your pleasure palace?" Charlie chuckled and rolled the toothpick that hung from his mouth over his tongue like a jazz pianist stroking the keys of a lover's melody.

"Yes, the same Mary, but that doesn't give you the right to disrespect her..."

"It sounds like you're worried that I might corrupt the God-fearing sister who seems to be exercising her faith to lure me to the house of God. Sounds like you need to get your house in order first, buddy."

"I love her, Charlie...Rita, that is. If I hadn't thanked you before...well, I'm doing it now. That Sunday when you got me out of the house..."

Graham lowered his head and took his time before continuing. "...and we started out at church and ended up at The Water Hole. The first time I laid eyes on her...the first time she opened her mouth and belted out that song, she dipped deep into the bowels of my soul.

"Sometimes I see Amanda's face—all angelic with a glow around it as bright as the noonday sun." Graham raised his head and smiled.

Charlie stared at Graham; not surprised at his revelation. He sighed and arched his eyebrows to their furthermost points. "Uhmm." Charlie sighed again and got up from his seat. The air was thick with Graham's sentimentalism, and Charlie was about to choke.

"Where's Johnnie Walker or Jack Daniel's? I could use either one of those boys. We need to lighten up the mood in here. Feels like we're at a damn funeral, immortalizing the dead." Charlie stopped short, realizing his Freudian slip. "Sorry, man."

"Don't worry about it. The bottle is under the sink."

Charlie nearly ran to the sink and opened the cabinet door. Charlie raised the bottle in triumph. "Here we are. Don't understand why you hide good liquor under there."

Graham watched as Charlie took down two small juice glasses from the shelf. Charlie picked up the bottle of whiskey again and held it. He seemed lost in his thoughts while his eyes roved throughout the kitchen.

"I remember how it felt when Amanda was alive—bustling about the kitchen; frying up a big skillet of picture-perfect, golden fried chicken; sprinkling a cup or two of cheese into her famous macaroni and cheese… and she always had a place at the table for me. Hey, the place looks much better than it did a few months ago."

Charlie and Graham shared a laugh. "I guess that's what a new woman in your life will do for you," Charlie continued.

"Maybe," Graham said slowly and in deep thought. "Thanks, buddy, for being there for me and shaking my lethargic bones from their rusty perch."

Charlie poured whiskey in both glasses and handed one to Graham. He lifted his glass and looked at Graham. "To my homeboy."

"To my homeboy."

They gulped down another swallow. "Homeboys," they said in unison.

Brrng, brrng. "Hello."

"Hey, baby. This is Rita."

"Hey, baby," Graham said quietly.

"Why you whispering? You got company?"

"Just Charlie. We're having a homeboy celebration."

"Oh." Rita snickered. "Don't drink too much."

Graham blushed. "So when and what time will you arrive in Oakland? Tuesday, seven forty-seven p.m., on American? Hold on. Let me get a pencil." Graham turned to Charlie and motioned for a pencil that was sitting on the counter near him. "Rita," he mouthed at Charlie.

A vast cloud covered Charlie's face. It seemed to signal a change in the climate—a storm looming over the horizon, a sudden drop in the temperature…the atmospheric pressure, an unexplained eclipse of the sun by the moon. He tipped his head slightly, nodding in comprehension of what Graham tossed at him so gingerly. Rita was returning to the Bay Area.

"Okay, baby…that was seven forty-seven p.m. on American Airlines, Tuesday the twelfth on flight 6771. Will be there…I love you, too."

Click.

"So the little lady will be here this week?"

"Yeah. Clyde needed the band to fill in for a group who had to cancel at the last minute. And it's right on time 'cuz I don't know if I could stand to be away from her for too long. Maybe we can double-date when she gets here—you and Mary, me and Rita. What you say?"

"Yeah, maybe. Look, I've got to go. Thanks for the drink."

"I'm glad we had this talk. I missed you, homeboy."

"Yeah, homeboys."

Graham embraced his buddy. Charlie forced a reciprocal handshake, then headed out the door.

CHAPTER 41

William nursed a shot of cognac. He sat back in the leather recliner, pulling the lever until the chair was almost at an 180-degree angle. He felt for the remote and clicked the power button. He took a few more sips and flipped the channel to ESPN. It had been a good day. Life was looking up. His horse had paid handsomely.

Fidgeting in his seat, William reached for his pocket, retrieved his wallet, and laid it on the small table that sat next to the chair. As he watched interview after interview, coaches and players who verbalized their thoughts on who would be the leading NFL team this season, he found the folded-up piece of paper with Angie's phone number written on it. William fingered it, folded and unfolded it several times, finally deciding to phone the digits that might lead to an oasis of possibilities.

He dialed and waited a few seconds until Angie's voice floated from her mouthpiece to his receiver. He stammered, "Angie?"

"Yes, who's this?"

"William. I've been trying to get up enough nerve to give you a call."

"It was good seeing you the other day."

"You looked well. Couldn't keep my eyes off of the black-and-white tweed suit you were wearing."

"Well…"

"I guess I caught you at an awkward moment…kinda like our conversation."

Angie sputtered, then let out a light laugh. "Wasn't sure you would call."

"Why, 'cuz you left me high and dry? I don't blame you, Angie. You had every right to do what you did…I might have done the same thing."

"So…things going well with you—job…?"

"Girl, I'm doing better than good. Things have started to look up for me. And believe me, they can only get better. How about dinner tonight…my treat?"

"Well…"

"Well, what's to think about? Oh, you're with someone," William pried.

"No." Angie lowered her head and turned her face away from the phone. "I was with someone, but we broke up. I'm by myself now."

"Say where and I'll pick you up. I'm still riding around in my broke-down Acura, but I'm going to take care of that soon. So what do you say?"

Angie smiled. "Sounds like a date."

"I won't disappoint you. And whatever else the night dictates, we'll play it by ear."

"I'll meet you at…"

"Don't trust the old guy with your new address?"

"It's not like that, William. I guess, I just want to be sure before I play all my cards."

"Don't blame you. Why don't we meet in the parking lot at The Water Hole at eight o'clock, and we can go from there?"

"All right. Can't wait to see you."

"Me either."

William hung up the phone and stared at the figures on the TV screen without really seeing them. He liked Angie. She was good people and a good lover, but his mind was on getting Rita back. It was very likely that he might have to be the one to orchestrate her return to his arms, even if he had to use a tangible object named Angie to do so.

♪♪♪

The parking lot was partially full when William pulled his Acura into The

Water Hole. Local talent was headlining, but Wednesday night was the time to unwind and break the monotony of the week. It was sure to be filled by the time the nine o'clock hour rolled around. Then he saw the marquee—*Rita Long and Midnight Express, Saturday at 8 p.m.*

Midnight Express this Saturday? William wasn't aware Rita would be back in town so soon. It only meant he had to accelerate his plan, and phase I was already in motion.

William drove on, searching for Angie's silver Toyota Camry. He made another sweep through the parking lot and finally spotted it just as Angie stepped out. Her lips tendered a perfect smile with about the same dip that showed off just enough cleavage at the scooped neckline of her black-and-rust silk dress. William couldn't pull his eyes from her.

The perfect gentleman, William got out of his car while it idled, opened the passenger door for Angie and closed it when she was safely inside. A faint grin crossed Angie's face like a digital marquee. They engaged in light conversation until they reached His Lordships on the Berkeley Marina. William was attentive to Angie's every need and treated her like the lady she was.

William told Angie to order anything she wanted on the menu and christened their meal with a bottle of Dom Perignon. They were seated at a cozy booth that overlooked the San Francisco Bay with a glimpse of the Bay Bridge that stretched from Oakland to San Francisco. Watergate, the island city that sat on a landfill with so-called skyscrapers of its own, was caught between the Bay Bridge and Interstate 880.

William brushed the top of Angie's slender fingers between sips of Dom Perignon and talked about their lives in Los Angeles, what went wrong, and what direction they were both headed. Angie had landed a great job, but she was born to sing. And she remembered Rita Long's promise upon her return to help get her career going.

"I think you're blessed to have Ms. Long in your corner."

"I can't believe how fortunate I was to run into her like that. And she'll be here this weekend. She is so real…unassuming. Most people who have it going on like her wouldn't have given me the time of day."

"She has an incredible voice and range," William's voice swooned as if talking about someone he had the distinct privilege of knowing in another lifetime.

"I wonder why she has never married? I've seen her with an older guy. She's so beautiful and classy. Let me stop. We didn't come here to talk about Rita Long."

When Angie looked up, William had a faraway look in his eyes. He felt her stare, and gave up his daydream.

"You don't have to stop," he said, as if he hadn't missed a beat of her speech. "I like watching your lips move when you talk about something you enjoy."

"You're making me blush. Let's order."

"That's fine. I recommend the blackened salmon. It's exquisite."

"I didn't think you knew words like…exquisite."

"The night is young. I have a whole bag full of words I'm going to use on you before the night is over. Thank you for accepting my invitation to dinner."

Angie smiled. "Thank you for extending the invitation."

♪♪♪

Dinner was only the appetizer on William's menu. It didn't take much to convince Angie to return to the mansion on the edge of the slum. She "ooh'd" and "ahh'd" as she passed through the foyer into the great room. She looked at her image in the tall mirror encased in oak. Admiring herself and the handsome gentleman at her side, who gingerly nudged her along as they gently stepped across glittering white marble tiles, encouraged thoughts of what could be. Large porcelain vases stood tall on either side of the mirror and stars fell from the sky when Angie looked up into the skylight.

Angie wanted to see everything, but William had other ideas—partaking of the main meal—then dessert. He swung Angie in front of him, and she took her hands and pushed his long dreads behind his ears. Now on the balls of her feet, she reached up to meet his waiting lips. He took them without hesitation and kissed her passionately—an air of familiarity, a flash of lustful moments that drove both of them crazy until they were out of breath. He pulled off her coat and encircled her waist, his hands draped over her shapely buttocks. She drank from his eyes until she closed hers and kissed him again while their bodies writhed in agony from want of each other.

William picked Angie up and cradled her in his arms. She blushed as he took her into Troy's sweetheart room—a circular room centered around a heart-shaped bed covered in a red satin spread. Large red-and-white satin pillows framed the bed.

"It looks like a giant box of Whitman's valentine candy." Angie giggled. William smiled.

The bed sat on a pedestal, and a two-step, cherrywood stool sat next to it. Mirrors circled the circumference of the room and an electronic drop-down movie screen, operated by remote control, was suspended in mid-air nearest the wall at the foot of the bed. A small bathroom with a mid-sized Jacuzzi, accessorized with red-and-white linen, could be accessed from the left side of the bedroom.

William pulled back the covers and laid Angie on the bed. He sat next to her and looked into her eyes. The longer he gazed at Angie, the face became Rita's. He forced himself to erase her image from his mind, but the image fought to stay. Rita, his one true love, held the key to permanent fulfillment that he failed to obtain on his own. Sweet, sweet Angie would take care of his immediate needs and in the very near future be the bridge to what he truly desired. William kissed Angie again and gently removed her clothes, then his own, and smothered her with kisses.

He sat up and brushed back her hair to see the fullness of her face. William's body longed for the tasty morsel that lay before him, but a silent alarm cautioned him to take it slow. He loved her once, but...

"I want to look at you, make love to you with my eyes." Angie's eyelashes fluttered. "Your face radiates like sunshine and your eyes, round as saucers, drink from the overflow of your sunshine. A still portrait in a museum of art is your body, laying in wait for passers-by to caress and behold your true beauty."

Angie frowned. "What's gotten into you, William? I've never heard you talk like this before."

"I told you my bag was full of words for you tonight. Your inner and outer beauty overwhelms me. Be still."

William's dreads cascaded about her face—a waterfall covering the madonna. He kissed her passionately, then released her lips—sweat pouring from his brow, stopping for only a second to wipe the sweat away. He lifted his head and took in the rest of her body.

"Your figure's delicate features fascinate me, console me, and send bolts of lightning to my loins. Your breasts…" he reached down and took her breasts in his hands, blowing on the now erect nipple, "are like golden apples in an orchard ready to be picked and suckled until the sweet nectar arrives. And the leaves that gingerly cover your fruit of passion whisper secrets that make men gape."

Angie tried to ease up, but he mouthed the word *no*.

"I just want to look at you," William said again. And he held her, kissing her gently here and there until he was ready to take her back to her car. He had her; he knew that for sure. Even in their silence, he knew. His whispers of love of lust were for her, but in the end, it would be Rita that he would have completely.

♪♪♪

Angie barely recognized this man who she would have given all she had at one time in her life. Surprises were worth the wait, but William was indeed the man she had been waiting for the last four years of her life, and tonight, he was the perfect escort. It felt like she was falling in love again, falling like a meteor that found itself in earth's gravity.

Angie watched William, a little spooked by his display of words. This was so unlike him, so uncharacteristic, and she wasn't sure where it was coming from.

CHAPTER 42

Rita Long sang her heart out. The crowd was wild. Not a vacant space remained on the dance floor and half-filled glasses dotted round tables like special occasion decorations. Everybody who was somebody was at The Water Hole to hear Rita Long throw down.

Fingers were popping, shoes clicking, some folks were singing along with the mistress of song. Bodies rubbed together and lips found their mates as a fast song moved to a slow song—elbows raised on lovers' shoulders trying to get a field goal.

"The joint's jumping tonight, Charlie," sang a happy Clyde. "My girl done turnt the house out. That's what I'm talking about." Clyde slapped Charlie five.

"Let's dance, Charlie. I didn't buy a new dress to be sitting on this bar stool all night."

"Can't you see that there's no more room on the dance floor?"

"You're about to get on my nerves."

"Shelly, please. Find somebody else. I don't feel like dancing."

"Maybe your friend Graham over there will let me have one itsy bitsy little dance. That's if he can tear his eyes away from Rita for two seconds."

"You just might have to find somebody else to dance with. The boy's in love."

"Please. I wanna dance."

It was hotter than the Mojave Desert. Sweat poured from brows liked they'd stayed up all night frying chicken to raise money for the church's annual building fund drive. But nobody cared. A couple here, then a couple there would drop out and seek the comfort of their seat for a breather, stopping long enough to finish off the drink they'd left on the table and order a refill. Then it was back to reclaim their spot on the dance floor.

"Sing, Rita. Sing the song, girl," someone would shout every now and then. "Talk to me."

"Party over here."

"Party over there. Raise your hands in the air…Party like you just don't care. Oh, yeahhhhhhhhhh!"

"Oh, yeah."

"I'm going to break it down real slow," Rita said in a sultry voice. "This next number is for my man, Graham Peters—the love of my life, my joy, my all. He's everything I've prayed for, everything I've ever wanted in a man. "He's a Beautiful Surprise" penned by the very beautiful India Arie."

Rita held the microphone like she was making love to it. She dropped her head and looked into Graham's eyes. He looked straight into hers. She slowly dragged her tongue across her bottom lip and made a circle with her mouth, throwing her man an exaggerated, sensual kiss that was only for him. And in time with the music, Rita slid her tongue along the bottom of her perfect white picket fence that sparkled from an extra coat of tooth polish.

"Yesterday, I didn't even know your name, now today, you're always on my mind."

There was no interrupting this moment. Rita sang the lyrics to the song like she meant it, like she knew they were written for her. And when the song was finished, when the last word left her lips, she struggled to place the microphone back in its stand—exhausted and drained to the bone.

A thunderous applause met her ears, begging for an encore, as she and Midnight Express stopped to take a set break. William Long stood in a far-off corner hidden from view by the capacity crowd—his eyes steady on the woman he would reclaim as his, regardless of her dedication to the old man who temporarily stood at her side. Angie was there, too, with a couple of her friends. He promised to meet up with her tomorrow because he was busy tonight. He couldn't risk her seeing him, but she seemed preoccupied with the swarm of well-dressed brothers who kept her heels clicking on the dance floor.

William watched Rita become engulfed in the gracious crowd who offered compliments and congratulations on her performance. She shook hands and gave side cheek kisses, but the main attraction was the man who gave Rita a personal standing ovation, clapping his hands together like a well-oiled puppet.

They embraced. The old man kissed her, and her lips kissed him back before a room full of people. No shame in her game. Unlike the timid Rita he knew. She wiped her forehead with a lace hanky the man handed her, and then accepted another kiss before partaking in a ritual of glass pouring, both clinking glasses together in toast to their love, and sipping on the bubbly that made them giddy and goo-goo-eyed. William had seen enough. He had to rethink his game plan to guarantee its success. He moved swiftly out of the room and into the night.

"Excuse me, Ms. Long." Angie extended her hand and nodded at Graham. "You were fabulous tonight, absolutely awesome."

Rita frowned, slightly annoyed. The stranger's face standing before her seemed familiar. "Thank you. I appreciate your kind words."

"I'm not sure you remember me. We spoke the last time you were here about my singing career, and you told me to get up with you when you returned."

"Yes, I remember now," Rita said, shaking her head in recognition. "I have your card somewhere."

"I just happen to have one in my purse. I would be so grateful if I could get together with you."

"We'll have to do that. Give me your card and I'll call you sometime next week."

"Thanks a million," Angie said, reaching into her purse and pulling out her card. "This is my work number, and you can call there anytime. I'm sorry for the intrusion."

"It wasn't an intrusion…" Rita glanced at the card. "…Angie. Anytime."

"It was an intrusion," Graham said, once Angie was out of earshot.
"Baby, we've got a lifetime…at least what's left of our lifetime."
"You're right. I love you, Rita Long."
"I love you, too, Graham Peters."

CHAPTER 43

Hurricanes Floyd, Isabel, and Fran couldn't rain on Angie's parade today. Neither the flash of lightning nor roar of thunder could put a damper on the downpour of good fortune that had finally found her. Her weather forecast had been fair and hazy with low-ceiling clouds hanging overhead, but in the last five days, the weatherman's prediction of nothing but sunshine for the days ahead was her dream come true.

The weatherman had predicted correctly. Angie and William were seeing each other again and had consummated their relationship, despite a strange beginning. There was more poetry but it was in stark contrast to the puzzling rhymes of the first night they were together. She and William had spent the last five days together—talking, dining in and out, and even taking in a movie, which was rare for William. And she liked the man she saw. He was courteous and attentive, obliging and gracious, and picking up the tab. But William's new image wasn't the cause of Angie's immediate celebration. Ms. Rita Long had called to ask when she was available to get together.

I'm beside myself. Rita Long called me at my job. I can't wait to tell William my great news tonight—Ms. Rita Long is coming to my house…yeah, my house next Monday. She'll be coming to my house to see me, to coach me, to give me tips and pointers so I can be just like her.

Angie pulled herself up out of her stupor. She waltzed to the kitchen to check on the meatloaf she had in the oven. It was William's favorite, and tonight was special. The smell of bell peppers tingled her nose. She tested the meat for doneness, tasted the sauce on top, and closed the oven door.

"Fifteen more minutes and it should be done," Angie said aloud. "All I have to do is mash the potatoes and make sure the wine is chilled. Angie, girl, watch out. You're getting ready to soar."

She picked out a short, sexy number—a black, form-fitting, A-line dress made of imported silk that fell just above the knees. William liked this dress, and she wanted to look special for him—to show she cared about all the effort he was making to put their relationship on sure footing. She floated on butterfly wings—her wings a kaleidoscope of colors, vibrant and alive that matched her heart whose broken pieces were being mended back together.

The powerful current of a raging Niagara Falls massaged her tense body. Angie's limbs began to loosen up as the water cascaded over her shoulders, down her back, over the curvaceous twin mountains of her gluteus maximus. Too much excitement bottled up in a small frame.

Steam poured from the bathroom when she opened the door. Angie looked like a sex goddess making her grand entrance onto a stage through a haze of dry ice. She felt on top of the world, and she stopped to admire her reflection in the large, floor-to-ceiling mirror. William said her body was perfection, and Angie kissed the tip of her finger and dotted a spot on the mirror, thanking her fairy godmother.

Angie had not told Latrice that she and William were back together. Latrice wouldn't understand, because she never understood their initial attraction and why Angie would support a washed-up basketball player who did nothing but make her life miserable. Angie would keep this to herself for a while, although she was anxious to show Latrice how people could change if you had a little faith in them. Right now, the only thing that mattered was sharing her wonderful news with her man and making love to him all night long.

Ding-dong. Ding-dong.

"He can't be here already." Angie peered at the clock. It was nearly 6:30. "He's thirty minutes early."

She grabbed her dress and slipped it on. *Ding-dong. Ding-dong.* She took a quick look in the mirror and brushed her hair back. She ran to the door before the bell rang again and opened it.

"For the lady."

William produced a half-dozen red, long-stemmed roses and gave them to a very surprised Angie. She took them, smelled each rose, and looked into William's eyes.

"Thank you," she said, in a voice just above a whisper. "They're beautiful."

"For a beautiful lady."

Angie broke into a smile. "I've got some wonderful news I've been just dying to tell you."

"Let me guess. Sniff, sniff. You've got my favorite food cooking in the stove."

"Right, but that's not the special something."

"Don't keep me waiting, girl. Tell me quick."

"Sit down, and let me get you a glass of wine."

William followed Angie with his eyes. He eyed her suspiciously, unsure where this was leading. He walked to the black baby grand and pecked one of the ivory keys before collapsing in one of the nearby red leather high-back chairs that complemented the rest of the mod décor.

"It must be special. I see you're wearing my favorite dress. You have to hurry and tell me, baby. I'm dying from the suspense. Special, huh?"

Angie returned to the living room with two glasses of chardonnay. She kissed William gently on the lips and handed him a glass. They sipped in silence.

"Okay. Out with it. What are you so excited about that you're having a hard time telling me?"

"Guess what happened to me today?"

"Baby, just tell me. I don't have any earthly idea."

"While at work today, I got a call. I bet you can't guess who it was from." William sighed.

"Okay, okay. I'll tell you. I got a call from Rita Long. She asked when it would be convenient for us to get together. Can you believe she called me?"

William stared and put his glass down on the coffee table.

"William, do you know what this means?"

"Yeah, you're meeting Rita Long."

"You aren't happy for me," Angie said flatly. She sat her glass next to William's.

"Yeah, baby, I am. I apologize if I didn't seem to share your enthusiasm. I think it's great. When are you getting together?"

"Monday. I can't believe it. She's going to take time out of her busy schedule to meet with me here. I want you to be here when she comes. I'm going to have a little spread—light refreshments. I want it to be real nice."

William listened as Angie went on and on about Rita. She was so animated, her hands going every which way as she described what she was going to do in preparation for Rita's visit. He was fifty miles away when he realized Angie was calling him.

"Are you okay? You seem…preoccupied."

"Just happy for you. So Monday is the day?"

"I'm excited."

"We've got a lot of planning to do. Congratulations, baby." He hugged her, although Angie could not see the face that was deep in thought and fifty miles away, salivating on his good fortune. He pulled himself away from his thoughts. Angie was whining again.

"I think it's karma that the two most important people in my life have the same last name. Some coincidence, huh?"

William didn't answer. Eyes fixed on Angie abruptly looked away when he saw her staring back at him. He was caught off guard. William went to her and put his arms around her. Theirs was a complicated relationship and he even felt a little remorse for using Angie to get to Rita. There was no other recourse, and Angie would eventually get over it. She had before.

"I'd say it's a coincidence, but you're just lucky." He looked down and placed a kiss on her lips. "You're lucky like that. Now, play something nice for me."

CHAPTER 44

Seventy-five degrees, the weatherman reported, dead in the middle of November and two weeks before Thanksgiving. The Westerners called it Indian summer. The leaves were painted in warm colors, falling across lawns like a blanket of Skittles in lemon-yellow, raspberry-red, and rich-brown fudge. The day started out with a little overcast, but the sun was shining bright in the cloudless sky.

Angie was on pins and needles. Everything had to be perfect for Rita's visit. Fresh-cut flowers were placed throughout the apartment. A tall, crystal vase full of cala lilies sat on the piano where Rita would sit. The room was warm and bright like the gorgeous day many Oaklanders ordered outside.

She was going to serve heavy hors d'oeuvres consisting of large meatballs in a sweet and sour sauce, fried chicken wings, smoked salmon and crackers, and fresh shrimp surrounding a bowl of cocktail sauce.

It was three o'clock; Rita was due at five. Angie had plenty of time. She had taken off early from work so that she could get everything just the way she wanted it and then be able to relax. Her clothes were laid out on her bed—a white satin blouse with long, sheer sleeves and a row of iridescent buttons running down the front with a bow that tied at the side, and a pair of black slacks.

Angie went to the piano and sat on the stool. She opened the door exposing the keys, running a finger across them. A melodious sound floated in the air, much like that of a harp when its strings are caressed by nimble fingers. With both hands on the keyboard, Angie struck a chord and began playing "Get Here" by Oleta Adams.

As Angie fell deeper into the song, her body began to sway from side to side. The back of her head was drawn back while the length of her back had formed a curve. She looked like a stunning black sailboat ready to take off if caught in a gust of wind. Then the melody that emitted from the piano and the melody that flowed from the hollows of her mouth merged together, taking the listener, if there were one, across the desert sands or up in a hot air balloon. She was lost over hills and mountains, admonishing her lover to get there soon.

She finished playing and opened her eyes. Searching for the clock, she found that only a half-hour had gone by. It was going to be a long hour and a half. If only William would come early. It would take some of her edginess off.

William seemed more nervous than he was about Rita's visit. He probably wanted the night to be perfect for her. Angie couldn't put her finger on it, but William's demeanor changed—almost resentful when she talked about Rita, especially when she mentioned the commonality of their last names. Maybe he was jealous. Basketball was a long time ago, and he was no longer a star.

Angie stopped and took another look at herself in the mirror. She picked her hair with her fingers, ran her tongue across her teeth, and smoothed down a wrinkle in her slacks. A small sigh followed by a smile said she approved. Now she was ready to meet the invincible Rita Long.

Bells were ringing, or so Angie thought. It was the doorbell, and the moment she anticipated had arrived.

Sweaty palms opened the door and before Angie stood a well-manicured Rita. She was smartly dressed in a crème-colored, satin, button-down blouse tucked in a pair of Tommy jeans. A lightweight, blue-linen, double-breasted jacket completed her outfit. Rita's hair was pulled tightly back on her face, the tension placed on her hair at the temples. Raspberry-plum lipstick was painted on her lips, and a quiet, reserved smile sat seductively on her face. Astonished by her beauty, Angie smiled timidly in return.

"Please come in," Angie said, her voice anxious.

"Thank you.

♪♪♪

Rita followed Angie into the living room. Rita admired the room. Warm colors were her forte, but the baby-grand piano that stood off in the corner made her smile the most.

"You didn't have a hard time finding me?"

"No, in fact, I took a taxi."

"Well, I'm glad you're here. Would you like something to drink? I also have refreshments."

"Just a glass of water with lemon would be fine for now."

"I'll be right back."

Suddenly alone, Rita hesitated, then rose from her seat. She sashayed to the piano and brushed the fingers along the keyboard. The place was cozy and she admired Angie's taste in décor. Rita walked to where the calla lilies sat on the piano and slid her graceful finger along the edge of the flower, stopping momentarily to inhale its fragrance. "Uhmm," she murmured to herself.

"Oh, there you are," Angie said, handing the water to Rita upon her return.

"Thank you. You have a lovely place."

"Thank you. Decorating is one of my hobbies."

"That's quite evident. So, Angie, tell me a little about yourself, what you like to sing, and what you would like me to do for you."

"I love to sing. Been singing most of my life but no formal training. I love contemporary jazz and gospel. I love sultry love songs, and Toni Braxton is one of my favorites."

"We have some of the same loves. I like Toni, too, but the sistah isn't good when you're hurting. She'd kill you—will take you slam out!!!"

They shared a laugh. Angie couldn't contain her smile. She was still in awe that Rita Long was sitting in her living room and letting her hair down.

"You've got that right about Toni. But me, I want to perfect my tone and my ability to make fluid transitions when, for instance, I come off a high note to a do-wa-wa or roll from one octave to another. I want to be flawless in my delivery so my listeners believe what I sing—like they do when you sing."

"Slow down, Angie, girl, one baby step at a time. You know what you want to do, so now you must take each task individually and perfect them one at a time. Perfect one, then move on. Sing repetitions every day. Since you play the piano, sing while you play. Sing while looking in the mirror. Feel your way as you do it. Have you performed anywhere?"

"Just some small hole-in-the walls in Los Angeles and special events like singing at friends' weddings."

A distant memory came alive for Rita. She was singing at a friend's wedding when she met William.

"So, you're from Los Angeles?"

"Yes, I came to Oakland about a year ago. I'm ashamed to say it, but I left because of a man."

Rita patted Angie on the leg. "Nothing to be ashamed of. We've all done something wild, crazy, and stupid because of a man."

"My man had been down on his luck…couldn't keep a job and gambled a lot."

Rita shuddered at the thought, Angie's life hitting so close to home.

"He stopped contributing to the affairs of the house…we lived together. I was out working every day, hitting the pavement to put a roof over our heads, food on the table and whatever else needed to be done. He was always lying around…no get up and go, and I just couldn't take it anymore. So, I decided I needed a change and moved lock, stock, and barrel to Oakland. My sister lives here and she was happy to see me out of that situation. She never liked my friend—the way he took advantage of me and all." Angie held her head down and sighed.

Furrowed brows raised on Rita's face. "It must be the singer's curse to have a man who disrespects them and thinks he can get by on your talents. I've felt your pain." And Rita understood all too well. Rita patted Angie's shoulder.

"I'm sorry for rambling on. Didn't mean to babble on about me like that," Angie said.

"It's okay. Everyone has a story."

"Well, my friend followed me to Oakland."

Rita looked disgusted. Angie turned her eyes away from Rita and continued.

"My sister wouldn't tell him where I was living. At the time, I had moved from my sister's to where I am now. But it was fate, I guess. I ran into my friend at The Water Hole. We have rekindled our relationship, and we are doing great. He's attentive, buys me flowers, and has grasped life. It must be the Oakland air."

"Gullible" was the word that came to mind after Rita heard the update on Angie's dysfunctional relationship. She wasn't sure if she felt pity or was downright mad at Angie's vulnerability and how easy she accepted her man back.

"Be careful of wolves in sheep's clothing," Rita heard herself say. "I'm not saying that your man is not on the up and up, and I hope he is, just be cautious and watchful in your dealings with him given his past. He may have another agenda and be schmoozing you along."

Rita looked into Angie's puzzled face.

"I didn't mean to sound so cynical, Angie. I want to offer you a valuable piece of information from Rita's chest of knowledge. Many of us have carried crosses, and we have to be wise the next time out. Now, why don't you go over to that piano, and let's get started."

"Thanks, Rita. If I don't get anything else out of our session, I thank you for that piece of wisdom. By the way, I've asked my friend to come by. He's a fan," Angie lied, given William's attitude of late.

"A fan? I can't talk bad about my fans. I look forward to meeting him, Angie."

Rita sipped her water and placed it on the coaster Angie had set on the piano. Rita moved to the piano bench, sat down, and began to play some chords.

"So, what do you play?

"I play classical music, jazz, and gospel. The church I belong to wants me to play for their choir because the current pianist has old ways, and they want to sing more current songs. As much as I would like to play, I don't want to hurt anyone's feelings or cause any dissension."

Familiar tunes floated in the air. Rita's eyes were closed—lost in her own world. Angie wasn't sure Rita heard a word she was saying.

"Do the right thing, Angie," Rita said almost in a sing-song voice.

Angie smiled. The woman who sat before her was a testament to elegance and grace.

"Why don't we warm up your vocal chords by doing a few scales? That way I can listen to you sing and note your range. There's an art to singing, and much of it is in how you control your breathing and your voice. Let's warm up."

Rita took a few more gulps of water and began playing. She stroked the keys so effortlessly. She played a scale in the key of "C."

"Sing 'do, re, me, fa, so, la, ti, do' several times and climb as many octaves as you can."

After warming up for a few minutes, Rita changed the pace.

"Sing, 'He has done marvelous, He has done marvelous, things…praise the Lord.'"

Angie sang the familiar hymn over and over until her eyes began to water. She had been singing so intensely that no one heard the knock at the door. At a pause before climbing another octave, Angie stopped abruptly.

"Did you hear that?"

"Yes, you have a wonderful voice," Rita replied.

"No, I mean a knocking sound. Let me check the door. It might be my friend."

Rita continued to play. She loved the feel of Angie's piano and she felt right at home.

Cold air entered the room. The sun had gone down and the temperature with it. Rita heard Angie say, "Hi, baby," after she closed the door, but it wasn't until Rita turned around and caught a glimpse of him that she became alarmed. She was paralyzed in her seat—a shrill chill moved over her body.

She saw his dreads first. They were slightly covering his face but moved away as he stepped forward. Angie's face was all aglow and full of excitement as she held a dozen red roses in her arms while another dozen roses lay in William's arm, apparently for her.

"Rita, I want you to meet my friend. Rita, this is William Long; William, this is Rita Long. I think it's ironic that you both have the same last name. Aren't these roses beautiful?"

"Nice to meet you, Rita. And roses for you, too. Angie has talked about nothing else but meeting you."

"Thank you," Rita said flatly, trying not to panic.

It was obvious that Angie did not know that William was her ex-husband. Too much of Angie's description of her boyfriend rang true to Rita's own unhappy experiences with William, but for him to be the one at this very time and moment repulsed her. And William allowed this charade to take place knowing how she felt about him.

She hated William. She couldn't tell if he was gloating. She was not going to give him the benefit of her uneasiness. No, he would not see her squirm. She'd play it out tonight and deal with William later.

Rita took the roses William held out to her. She held them like they were contaminated.

"I'll put the roses in water," Angie piped in.

Rita looked in William's eyes and attempted a smile. She looked at Angie who was like a helium balloon—so full at their meeting. A few weeks ago, William was begging for money; today he was passing out expensive roses as if they were as easy to come by as penny candy. William wasn't going to get away with this, and it was obvious Angie needed her lessons on wisdom if she was depending on the likes of William Long to be her knight-in-shining-armor.

Rita pitied Angie, who didn't have a clue what was going on, and to think she could see right through this sham. This was William's play, orchestrated and directed by William Long with Angie a pawn in the game. William used Angie to bring them together, but as far as Rita was concerned, he had another thing coming because she was no bofu the fool.

CHAPTER 45

Angie watched tension mount as the night wore on. Rita lost her zeal, and Angie lost the benefit of Rita's open heart. Eyes rocked and rolled while communication was reduced to a minimum. Angie wasn't sure when the night soured, but when she recapped the evening, she was able to pinpoint the moment to William's arrival. Her night was ruined.

Being polite, Rita ate two small chicken wings. William saved his healthy appetite for another day. The wonderful array of hors d'oeuvres that Angie took special care to prepare became cold on the serving tray. This could not be happening.

William jumped from his seat while Rita nursed the rest of her water. "Why don't you and Angie continue with your session? I'm going to step out of the room and give you both some privacy."

"You don't have to leave, Mr. Long," Rita said, enunciating each word. "I think I'd better be going."

"Please don't leave on my account."

"Don't trouble yourself. I'm not. I'm sorry I have to cut our time, Angie, but practice what I've given you so far, and I'll call you."

"Thanks, Rita. I really appreciate you taking out time from your busy day to see me. Look, since you took a cab, why don't you let William take you home? Maybe, you can get to know each other."

"That's a good idea, Angie." William smiled. "I would be more than happy to give your guest a lift home."

Rita's glass fell limp in her hand, spilling the remaining water onto the floor. The carpet absorbed it like a great big sponge, but left a spot in the shape of a gun. If she could have picked up that spot and turned it into a solid object, Rita would have blown William's brains out.

"No thanks. I don't want to be any trouble."

"It's no trouble at all, Ms. Long. It's the least I can do."

"Please," Angie begged.

Rita sighed. "All right. If you insist."

The mood in the room became even more somber, and Angie could not figure out why. Maybe if Rita and William had a chance to get to know each other on the ride home the ice would thaw. *It must be William's dreads*, Angie thought. *That's it. A classy lady like that is not used to being around a man with braids all over his head. Maybe William is intimidating. I probably shouldn't have given her that history lesson about William's and my life together. I won't invite William next time…if there is a next time.*

♪♪♪

Rita and William walked to his Acura in silence. He opened the door for her, and she got in without a thank-you or a smile. This was going to be just what it was intended to be—a taxi ride. Rita looked straight ahead when William eased into his seat.

"You look stunning tonight."

"Just drive the damn car."

"There's no need to get hostile," William said in a calm, soothing voice.

"I apologize."

"That's better."

"What did you expect to gain from this little meeting?" Rita inquired, ignoring William's attempt at sarcasm. "Didn't have the decency to tell your girlfriend why our last names are coincidently the same. You slay me."

"You're getting hostile again."

"I'm serious, William. What do you want? I've already told you I have nothing else to give."

"I want you in my life, Rita. I want us to be together. I'm a changed man…"

"Changed since when…changed how? Who do you think you're talking to, some bimbo that thinks just because you look good, you're all that? A few weeks ago, you were a beggar, and I gave you my last dime. And now, all of a sudden, life has changed for you. What about Angie who thinks that she has a relationship with a wonderful man? What about her?"

"Stop, Rita. Shouting doesn't become you. Anyway, Angie is just a good friend."

"How sad. You know she thinks you're more than that. The flowers, the dinners and whatever else, what is she supposed to believe? She introduced her boyfriend to Rita Long tonight, but you knew that before you arrived at the door."

"Angie is imagining things."

"Things you've led her to believe. She told me about having to move to Oakland to get away from you and how you followed her here. It sounds like a familiar scenario."

"Yes, Angie and I were lovers once. We've hooked up again, but it isn't serious. Where do I take you?"

"Drop me at The Water Hole. I can get home from there."

"Don't do this, Rita. I'm not some bum off the street. You and I were husband and wife."

"Right, we *were* husband and wife."

"Where is your old man? He should be escorting you around."

"Not that it's any of your business, but my rental was on a flat when I walked out of the apartment this evening. I didn't want to be late getting to Angie's so I took a cab. And for the record, my old man's name is Graham, and we're in love. There's no room to rekindle old fire…old flames. No room."

"You're making a mistake, Rita."

"No, I've learned from my mistake."

It became painfully quiet. Rita seemed agitated and shifted from side to side trying to get comfortable. William watched her from the corner of his eye, using his dreads as a shield. Although William had an agenda, he had fallen in love with his ex-wife all over again. He couldn't shake the feeling.

Yes, he wanted Rita. It was more than infatuation, more than her good looks. It was the woman—the woman he knew twenty years ago who had matured into the woman who sat next to him now. William began to breathe heavily. The thought of her with someone else made him cringe. He wanted Rita, and he'd do whatever it took to make her his woman again.

"Take me to Watergate instead," Rita sighed, not sure why she was letting William take her home.

William drove on until he saw Emeryville to the right and Watergate to his left. The freeway was lighter now that commuter traffic had died down. After a series of lefts and rights, Rita motioned with her hand and William pulled to the curb of an Extended Stay motel and turned off the ignition.

"Thank you for the ride."

"The pleasure was all mine." William hesitated, then continued. "You gonna invite me up?"

Rita casually turned toward William and pursed her lips. "No, and that's my final answer."

"Nightcap? Coffee?"

Rita turned her head and opened the car door before William could make it around to her side. He rushed, but she was already standing on the sidewalk poised to walk away. William hurriedly placed a kiss on her cheek and watched her walk away without looking back.

"I will have her," he muttered under his breath.

♪♪♪

Rita went into her furnished apartment and walked to the window overlooking the parking lot. William was still standing where she left him, lost in thoughts she would not help him to realize. She watched him with eagle eyes, vowing not to fall prey to one of his hidden land mines.

He still looked good, even better than he did the day they got married, but she was in love with a wonderful man who had not in the least bit misrepresented himself. He loved her and she loved him. She was truly happy for the first time in her life.

But something weighed heavily on her mind. She needed to tell Graham about William. And while she was afraid of what Graham might say, she was doubly afraid of the consequences if she kept silent. She backed away from the window and walked over to where the phone lay on the bed. She needed to speak to her baby, but she wasn't ready to reveal all. Not yet. She would pray about it.

CHAPTER 46

A week turned into two. Their contract was extended by a month as Rita and Midnight Express entertained packed-out houses at The Water Hole each night. They had energized the community of bar-hopping, foot-stomping, cigarette-smoking, fun-and-jazz-loving folks that came out faithfully to groove with their favorite nightclub act. It was rumored record producers had filtered in and out of the club in the last couple of weeks. But one thing was for sure, this sometimes damp and sweaty edifice filled with fun-loving folks was the place to be.

In the shadow of the crowd, with an unsuspecting Angie at his side, William lurked while he kept a watchful eye on the woman he vowed to make his again. And Rita kept him at bay, belting out song after song of love to her man, leaving no doubt on anyone's mind about the state of her heart and to whom it belonged. She was fed up with William's relentless pursuit, calling her day and night, begging for forgiveness, and vowing to love her from now until eternity. She had his phone number blocked, but he managed to elude that by placing a call from the manager's office. Rita had to fix things soon before the problem became unmanageable and her business became public knowledge—an advertisement on a highway marquee, high in the sky for everyone to see.

♪♪♪

Graham sat mesmerized by the beautiful, chocolate diva who had captured his heart and sung love songs to him. It made him hot around the collar. Sweat poured down his neck like sizzling candles whose flames travel up the length of the wick, creating a cavity of molten wax, and spilling its overflow down its own sides. Graham noticed Rita made other men hot, too, but they would not have the luxury of wooing her late into the night and the next morning.

"Do you mind if I intrude on your thoughts?"

"Hey, Charlie. Have a seat."

"She's beautiful...and a helluva set of windpipes."

Graham turned his eyes from the stage and looked at Charlie. "How could I be so lucky?"

"I asked the same question myself. My buddy, Graham...damn, you've had the best of the best. Every now and then I ask myself why Rita is with you instead of me. You know I loved her from afar, I guess I was afraid of a woman like that...you know...smart, elegant, classy."

"Well, my good friend, as long as you recognize that she's my woman now, we're all right."

"There's no mistake about that."

They laughed.

"Charlie, who's that guy over in the far corner—the one with the dreadlocks? You know everybody that frequents this place. He's been in here every night. It might be my imagination, but he seems to be watching Rita like she's some kind of Hollywood actress that he's fallen in love with—almost to the point of stalking."

Charlie looked in the far corner and spotted William. He had noticed him, too, but had not given it much thought until now.

"Don't know," Charlie lied. "The crowd gets newer and newer all the time. I'm sure he's an adoring fan like everyone else in here."

"Yeah, I'm sure you're right. Speaking of women, where's your apron string, Miss Shelly?"

"She's not my woman. Look, I've got an idea. Why don't you and Rita meet Mary and I for brunch tomorrow?"

"Are you crazy? Those two would have each other for lunch."

"Nothing like a cat fight to highlight the day. In fact, that would turn me on."

"Rita is too classy to act a fool. Besides, she's doing all the entertaining she's going to do now. Look at my woman."

"And now, I'm going to slow it down and sing a tune by Jill Scott for everyone who's in love like I am. The tune is entitled 'He Loves Me.'" Rita pulled the mike back and blew a seductive kiss Graham's way. Graham puckered his lips and kissed her back.

"You love me especially different every time. You keep me on my feet. Happily excited by your cologne, your hands, your smile, your intelligence."

Graham and Charlie sat with their eyes glued on Rita. *She looked like ripened watermelon ready to be devoured as she stood tall in her floor-length, strawberry-red chenille dress*, Graham thought. And the way she could take the words to a song and roll them over her tongue and mix it with love and throw it out in slow motion to all who would receive it caused Graham to squirm in his seat.

Halfway through Rita's song, Charlie risked a glance in William's direction. Finding him still in place, Charlie thought William's demeanor strange—a look of obsession written on his face that extended beyond mere fascination. William's eyes were stoic and steady, observing Rita's every movement. He wasn't caught up or moved by Rita's words that planted love tattoos on lover's hearts, and he stood in one place and didn't move an inch unless he was reaching for his drink that sat on a table close by.

For the umpteenth time that evening, the crowd roared and clapped as Midnight Express ended yet another set. Ten minutes later, Rita emerged exhausted, but she forced a smile as she reached Graham's table.

"Hey, baby, Charlie…"

"You were fantastic," Charlie said, as he rushed to be the first to speak. "You know you were singing to me."

Rita ignored his last comment and placed a kiss on Graham's lips. She turned to Charlie. "Thanks."

"I don't have to tell you how good you are, baby. You already know. Look, Charlie wants to know if you and I would like to join him and Mary Ross for brunch tomorrow."

"The Mary Ross…from your church? The Mary Ross that hates my guts, Mary Ross?"

"We don't have to. I already told Charlie…"

"No, no, uhh, wait a minute. Let me think…"

"I thought it might be nice to, maybe get…"

"Since Charlie suggested it, we'll go but only under one condition."

"What's that?"

"You put a gag in her mouth."

The trio laughed.

"So…Charlie…" Rita smirked, unblinking as she peered into Charlie's eyes. "So…is she your new girl? Is *Ms*. Holy and Righteous your new girl?"

Charlie grinned, excited by Rita's attention. "Maybe."

"Well, I can't wait," Rita returned, turning her head slightly and giving Graham an eye roll that caused him to chuckle.

Charlie blushed and turned abruptly away from Rita's stares only to find himself in the clutches of William's frozen gaze as he stood staring in their direction. Charlie jerked his head away once more, then pulled a toothpick from his pocket and put it in his mouth.

"Look, I'm going to the bar and get a drink. Mary gets out of church at one o'clock. Let's say two at Scott's Seafood on the Square."

"Sounds good to me," Graham hollered at Charlie's back, then softer, to Rita. "Glad to have you to myself for a minute."

"Me, too."

"I love you, Rita Long."

"I love you, too, Graham Peters."

CHAPTER 47

It was a beautiful day. The sun was bright for late November with the temperature teetering near seventy degrees. Churchgoers sat on the edges of their seat for the climax of the morning's sermon while the world outside was quiet except for occasional tourists on an early-morning sightseeing tour.

Rita woke up in Graham's arms, savoring their night together. The sheets rustled beneath her as she moved closer to him. She had not experienced love like this before—not even in her marriage to William.

The sound of the alarm clock startled Graham and he jerked quickly, and then smiled when he saw Rita was still next to him. He took two fingers and tickled her under the chin, and she grinned and turned to face him.

"Good morning," she said.

"Good morning to you. Did you sleep well?"

"I was in heaven."

They kissed and held each other for a long time.

"I guess we'd better get up so we can meet our challenge for today."

"If Mary Ross gets out of line today, I promise you, Graham Peters, I will hurt that woman."

"No you won't."

"I'm a lady, but I won't hesitate to take my dukes out and pop her upside the head."

Rita and Graham broke out into a hearty laugh. They laughed until they cried, and until those few tears had dried.

"One, two, three…the last one out of bed is a dirty dog," Rita screamed.

Graham held onto Rita. Rita tried to pull away. They tussled on the bed like siblings having a good time, and when they had given up on their child's play, they made love to each other like it was their first time.

♪♪♪

Graham and Rita arrived at the restaurant first and milled about the pier taking advantage of the beautiful day. Rita was dressed smartly in a two-piece black crepe dress and jacket ensemble that hit just at the knee. Graham wore a slick, black sports jacket by Polo Rita had bought on one of their excursions and tan khakis that ended in a cuff. He wore a long-sleeved, buttoned-down, tan-and-white-striped shirt that boasted a contrasting white collar and cuffs at the end of the sleeves. They were a handsome couple.

Rita spotted them first. Charlie wore a navy sport coat, a pair of khaki pants, and a white long-sleeved, buttoned-down shirt opened at the top. Mary wore a two-piece pantsuit the color of red Kool-Aid—the watered-down variety. That suit had been in the rinse cycle one too many times. *Jezebel*, Rita thought.

Eyes shifted between the couples with Rita and Mary almost in total combat. Charlie extended greetings but couldn't take his eyes from Rita. Graham was the only sensible one as he led the pack to the demilitarized zone. No pleasantries seemed forthcoming from Mary.

Silence ensued until they were shown to their seats.

"Nice color on you," Rita lied to Mary.

"Too much lipstick," Mary replied.

Rita looked to Graham for support, but he was desperately trying to hide a grin.

Meal orders taken, Graham and Charlie made small talk. Rita and Mary resisted the temptation to look at each other, and it was Mary who made the first move.

"Why do you sing in a nightclub? Don't you know God is not pleased when you sing songs to the devil?"

This is it, Rita thought. *The woman has pushed her last button and now she was going to have to get black on her. All of her mother's teaching was about to go out of the window, and turn the other cheek meant getting this heifer told before the devil in her really showed out.*

"Mary," Rita found herself saying, "where I choose to sing is really none of your business, but if you must know, I'll tell you. I've always loved jazz. My mother used to sing many years ago. She and my dad would go to all the jazz festivals, and when I was old enough, they took me with them. I was in awe of the greats like Hugh Masekela. I was brought up on this, and this is what I know.

"There are some great gospel singers, and many of them derived their music from jazz. But before you judge me, know this. I am a good person raised to know right from wrong, raised to know people will come across my path to tear me down and scandalize my name. My parents carried me to church and taught me to be an upstanding citizen. I love God, and I know He loves me. But more than that, I know who I am."

Everyone sat still, the ball in Mary's court. Her eyes were moving around in their sockets, gathering her thoughts. She looked at Rita and let her head fall slightly forward. A faint smile was forming on her face like a child drawing a line with an Etch A Sketch.

"I appreciate you telling me that, Rita." Mary's head dropped. She grabbed the glass of water the waitress had placed on the table. She looked back at Rita as if she were embarrassed by something. She took a sip of water, dropped her head, and proceeded to speak again. "I was jealous of you and Graham. I've had a crush on Graham for years, even when he was married to Amanda."

Eyes shifted from one to another while Mary kept her head down.

"I feel like a fool, acting the way I've been acting over a man that doesn't feel the same way I do about him."

"It's okay, Mary," Graham said, embarrassed by her confession.

"I must apologize to you too, Graham. I can't even look at you, although I got a goooooood look a few weeks ago."

Graham's laughter was infectious, touching each one differently, but laughter all the same. The tension eased as everyone let out a wail.

"You didn't look bad yourself, Mary," Graham said bashfully.

"And to think I busted in on you and Rita at the most inept time."

Now, there was a roar at the table. Mary, Rita and Graham were convulsing with laughter. Charlie seemed to be on the other side of the moon—far, far away.

"Back to earth, Charlie," Mary snapped. "I laid my pathetic life on the table a few minutes ago, and you didn't even have a comment."

"I'm glad you were able to purge yourself." Everyone looked in Charlie's direction.

"Look, Rita," Mary charged again, "why don't we start over?"

"Okay," Rita said hesitantly.

"If you can find the time, I would like for you to come to church one Sunday. Maybe you can sing a song for us."

"Whoa, Mary," Graham said. "Back off."

"I'm ashamed of you, Graham. This is an opportunity to minister and draw someone to Christ. You've been *away* too long. Now, how long is it going to be before they bring our food out? I'm starving."

"I'll be happy to go to church one Sunday," Rita said after a moment. "It has been my intent all along, but with your prodding, it's going to happen a lot sooner."

"Amen. And Charlie, you come along, too."

"Yeah, yeah, yeah."

CHAPTER 48

"Hurry, Graham. I don't want to be late for Martha's birthday party."

"Now don't you look nice," Graham said as he hurried into the living room. Rita was wearing a two-piece, pumpkin-colored sweater and pants ensemble. The sweater sported a faux fur collar that ran around the neck and at the base of each sleeve with ten buttons the color of honey dotting the length of the sweater. Rita complemented her outfit with a lacy shell of the same color.

"I think it's great that her birthday fell on Thanksgiving Day. She'll be surrounded by family, and hopefully, everyone will be in a festive mood."

"I love that woman dearly. You know she became my surrogate mother when I came to California so many years ago. With both of my parents dead, it wasn't hard to accept Martha and Elroy as my own. I think it was awfully nice of her to invite the both of us for dinner, despite the fact Deborah hasn't come around."

"I feel bad about that, but I'm not going to let Deborah's dislike of me spoil Martha's day. After all, she invited me personally, and I'm going. I happen to like the old woman myself. I'm sure Momma is a little jealous in Seattle right now, but as soon as this gig is over, I'm going to go home and pamper my parents. And I'll be back."

"Maybe I'll go with you."

Rita stood stock-still. She was afraid to trust what her ears believed they heard. She exhaled and smiled, thanking God for placing this wonderful man in her life.

Graham saw how pleased Rita was to hear him say he might go. And he made up his mind right then and there that he would. And if the chance arose, he wanted to have a heart-to-heart with her dad. He went to Rita and held her tight.

"A penny for your thoughts."

"We better get out of here before we're late."

"Okay, baby. I love you."

"I love you, too."

CHAPTER 49

A small gust of wind blew leaves across the sidewalk and into the street. Some swirled in the air while others danced in perfect formation, forming a line, then breaking into smaller groups like a well-choreographed ballet. The parade of leaves were momentarily interrupted as Graham and Rita got out of the car and made their way to Martha's front porch. Crispy crunching sounds came from under their shoes as they threatened to break up the ballet. But the leaves soon regrouped and continued their dance while Graham and Rita stood on the porch ringing the doorbell. Laughter and excited voices met their ears when Martha opened the door.

"It's Graham and Rita," Martha announced, happy to see the two of them.

Graham and Rita followed Martha and Elroy into the living room. The smell of roast turkey and other delectable foods met their noses and conversation stopped in mid-air when they entered.

♪♪♪

"Hey, Granddad," Elise and Riley, Jr. said as they ran up to Graham and gave him a great big hug.

"Hey, Dad," Liz said, coming up behind her children.

"Hey, babies," Graham said in return, kissing Liz and his grandchildren on the cheek, then stopping to rub Liz on the top of her head. "Where's Riley?"

"He's in the kitchen with Deborah and Grant."

Liz turned to Rita. It was obvious her dad was in love. She sort of liked Rita, too. She was classy and seemed intelligent. "Hi, Rita."

"Hi, Liz."

"These are all kin in here," Martha said to Rita as she commandeered the conversation. "Over there in that corner watching TV are Elroy's grandnieces and nephews. Y'all say hi. And in the other corner are Elroy's niece, Wanda, and her husband, Junie, and Sister Hattie Mae Johnson from the church. The pastor and his wife are due any minute. Deborah and Sister Betty Boyd Floyd are in the kitchen getting ready to set the dining room table for Thanksgiving dinner, and the kids are just all over the house."

"Daddy," Liz said gently to Graham, pulling him aside, "You and Deborah need to talk. You know she loves you…she's just a little stubborn… a lot like you."

"I know, baby. And today is Grandma's day to shine, and we must do everything to make her day perfect."

"Your house is decorated so nice," Rita said.

"Rita, my granddaughters fixed it up for me. You ought to see my birthday cake. They got my picture and name on it."

"I can't wait to see it."

They walked into the dining room that was dressed for a holiday feast. An oblong table covered with a cream-colored, satin tablecloth sat in the middle of the room. A mahogany china cabinet sat on one of the side walls, laden with antique china plates, cups, and saucers—a collector's delight. Sparkling, crystal stemware was arranged smartly on the shelf below along with a crystal candy dish. Turning slightly to her left, Rita saw a beautiful mahogany serving buffet that probably housed Martha's good china. Beautiful runners with autumn leaves and branches covered the length of the buffet. Martha and Rita moved to the table and Rita picked up a silver fork and examined the fine handiwork on its base.

♪♪♪

"Why don't we go into the kitchen to see what's holding up progress? Liz and Graham will be along in a minute."

"All right," Rita said, not sure she was ready to see Deborah again.

"Who left the water running?" Martha called out when she and Rita entered the kitchen.

All eyes turned toward Martha and Rita. Silence. Deborah rolled her eyes, then looked Rita up and down. Rita stared back at the woman who wore a long-sleeved chemise the color of an overripe cantaloupe.

"All right, it's my birthday, and I'm not having any stuff in here tonight. For those who don't know this young lady, let me introduce her. This is Rita. She's a friend of Graham's. Now make like you got some sense and show your manners."

"Hello," Rita said to everyone.

A series of quick "hellos" were heard except from Deborah. She turned her back and began to place ham on the platter.

"Can I help you with that?" Rita asked.

"I've got it," Deborah said flatly.

"Don't worry about her, baby," Martha cooed as she rubbed Rita's arm. "She'll come around after while."

Rita wasn't sure she would be around that long, but tonight wasn't about Deborah. They were there to give thanks for all that God had been to them, and if Deborah thought she was going to wear her down, she had another thing to think about.

"What's going on in here?" Graham said as he and Liz entered the kitchen. "It sure smells good. I know you made your mouth-watering mac and cheese, Deborah."

Deborah placed the last piece of ham on the plate and turned to face Graham. "Yes, Daddy, I've baked macaroni and cheese just like Mom used to make it."

"I can't wait to taste it," Graham said solemnly and walked over to Rita. "If we can't be of any help, we're going into the living room."

"Hold it. I guess I'm going to have to pray before the big prayer," Martha said. "Children, we have come a long ways in this life, and God has been good to us. We have so much to thank Him for—life, the activity of our limbs, a good job, a good husband…wife…so much to thank Him for that we don't have time to spend looking like we've lost our best friend or our reason for living. God loves us so, that in spite of ourselves…our little undeserving selves, that *think we all that*…if that's how you say it…that He finds favor with us over and over again. Here we are together to celebrate how good God has been…Thanksgiving, they call it, and y'all got the nerve to turn your back to God and say kiss my…"

"Grandma!"

"You the main one, Deborah Ann Peters-Hill. Stubborn as the devil. Got so much hatred in you, you done forgot how to love."

"Grandma, you're not being fair."

"Fair? I thought it wasn't fair when God took my only child from me… my child that I loved so much. But she's in a better place now, happy as a lark, singing in the angelic chorus, looking down at us and shaking her finger because we are just one big mess down here. Your daddy and Rita have done no wrong. Your dad is guilty of a having a broken-down heart, and Rita was sent to help mend it again."

A small sniffle, then a loud "boo-hoo" met everyone's ears. Deborah's head fell forward as she let all of her pent-up emotion ooze forth. Chairs shuffled across the floor as hands reached toward Deborah. Grant scooped her in his arms and held her tight and Graham put his arms around her and rubbed her back. Liz and Riley made a circle around them and put their arms on Liz's and Graham's shoulders. They looked like a huddle of saints getting ready for some serious prayer.

Rita stood back and observed the group, looking between them and Martha. Martha's eyes were shut as she began to pray for the group. The sobs were coming and going, getting louder when there was a group hug and lower when Martha's utterance outdid the group. There was love and compassion here, and Rita knew in her heart that it would be well.

As the group peeled away from each other, Graham and Deborah were left linked together. Deborah's sobs were faint, but yet audible, and Graham held onto his oldest daughter for dear life. He lifted his head and grabbed Deborah under the chin, lifting her face upward as he looked into her eyes, "I love you, baby—always will."

"I love you, too, Daddy."

Smiles erupted from everywhere. Father and daughter were back together again. Deborah couldn't seem to let go of Graham, and he hugged her some more. Then Deborah abruptly lifted her head and turned toward Rita.

"I'm sorry, Rita." Graham reached out and brushed Rita's hand.

Rita started to speak, but Deborah held out her hand.

"Let me get this out. I know now that you aren't trying to replace my mother, but it's going to take some time to get used to seeing you with my dad. They were always so happy."

"Hmmph, they had their moments," Martha muttered under her breath.

"What I'm saying is, give me time to get used to the idea of you and Dad."

"I will."

"Now, let's have Thanksgiving," Martha said. "That bird is tired of lying up on the platter waiting on you folks to finish this long, drawn-out conversation. I can't wait to dig into my Deborah's mac and cheese and Liz's sweet potato pie."

"Slow down, Martha," Elroy admonished. "You gonna tire yourself out. We still have to celebrate your birthday after we eat."

"All right, baby. Dinner is served!"

♪♪♪

Deborah came into the dining room and stood behind Martha's chair. "It's time to say happy birthday to the woman of the house, my grandmother, Martha Carter." Everyone around the table clapped their hands. Liz and the others joined Deborah in the dining room, and the women quickly cleared the table for the birthday celebration.

Teeth packed in smiles ready for an audition for a minstrel show prepared to sing. "Happy birthday to you. Happy birthday to you. Happy birthday, dear Martha, Sister Carter, Grandma, happy birthday to you."

"Praise the Lord," Martha shouted. Everyone clapped and chanted,

"Martha, Martha, Martha." The children shouted, "Go Granny, it's your birthday."

Tears streamed from Martha's face. "Thank you, everyone. This is a day of Thanksgiving. God has blessed me to live on this earth eighty-four years today." Martha stopped, overcome with emotion. "And I thank Him every day for all His blessings, my wonderful husband, family, and friends. Where's the knife so I can cut this cake? All right, somebody sing, make some noise."

Liz turned to Rita. "Would you sing us a song, Rita?"

Rita froze. All eyes were looking at her, waiting for her response.

"No, let someone else sing."

"Rita, sing me a song," Martha interjected.

How could Rita deny this woman her request? She looked around the room. The smiles were warm. And Graham was grinning like a Cheshire cat.

"Please sing," Deborah said without sarcasm in her voice, surprising everyone in the room.

Rita pushed back her chair, got up from the table, and moved to where Martha sat. She placed her hand on the old woman's shoulder, closed her eyes and began to sing.

"I believe for every drop of rain that falls, a flower grows. Out there in the dark somewhere, a candle glows. Every time I hear a newborn baby cry or touch a leaf or see the sky, I believe, I believe… "

Everyone clapped their hands, including Deborah and Liz. But Graham was paralyzed in time—a distant memory of his wife as she played that very song on the record player and asked him to dance.

♪♪♪

"You ought to be singing in a church choir," Reverend Fields exhorted. "We could use another beautiful voice like yours."

Rita didn't answer Reverend Fields, but nodded her head to let him know she heard what he said. Rita bent down and kissed Martha on the cheek. "Happy birthday, Martha."

"Thank you, baby, for that beautiful song." Martha lowered her voice. "Follow me into my room."

♪♪♪

"Grandma pulled Rita into her room," Deborah said to Liz. "I wonder what that's all about?"

CHAPTER 50

"Pull up that trunk and sit on the chaise next to me, Rita," Martha said.

Martha opened the trunk that Rita placed before her and took out two beautiful embroidered hankies and a set of monogrammed sheets and pillowcases. The handkerchiefs were made of soft cotton surrounded by a lacy border with Martha's initials, "MC, "embroidered in fuchsia and lavender in one corner. A large, cross-stitched "C" was at the top of the flat sheet with the letters "E" and "M" cross-stitched to either side of the letter "C."

"My Amanda made these for me with her own hands. Every now and then, I open up this trunk and take these things out and hold them to my face thinking about my beloved Amanda. She was a beautiful woman. Never gave me or her daddy any trouble when she was a child. Met Graham during a church meeting. It's funny now, but that was his first time going to church and his first night in California."

"They're beautiful, Martha. Amanda was very talented."

Martha reached into the trunk and pulled out some jewelry Amanda had given her that she no longer wore and then some old photographs of her granddaughters that were taken at school.

"Now look at this, Rita. This is Deborah…," Martha turned the picture over, "when she was eight years old. And this is Liz when she was six. Little darlings. I would keep them when Amanda and Graham needed a night out."

Rita took the pictures and looked at each one. "You know, Martha, it's as if I can see into their souls. I understand their feelings, although it has not been a pleasant experience being the target of their animosity." Rita sighed. "But it is not hard to understand the love Deborah and Liz shared with their mother, you and Elroy, and Graham. I'll admit it has made me realize the one thing I've missed—not having my own child, something I've desperately wanted at one time in my life.

"Martha, can I confide in you about something?"

Martha's brows furrowed. "What, child?"

"I'm not sure where to start, but I remember your words about not disappointing you, and I want to share something I've not even shared with Graham."

"What is it, baby? Go on and spit it out."

"I was married to a basketball player years ago whose playing days came to an abrupt end because of injuries. Even before he was no longer able to play, my husband was abusive, a womanizer, and a gambler. It was in small doses at first, but when he no longer shared the spotlight and life was over as he knew it and thought it should be, his exploits became unbearable. I asked for a divorce and went my way.

"We've been divorced for over twenty years. During that time, I may have seen him once, maybe twice. Now, after all these years have passed, I recently received a call from him asking for ten-thousand dollars and to sign off on some old insurance papers he held on me. He claimed it was a life and death situation, so I obliged—against my parents' protests. I thought it odd, but I thought I'd honor him this request.

"I come to find out he is living in Oakland and has been here for some time. He came here following a woman after a failed relationship. He spotted me singing at the club, and I believe formulated a plan to get money from me. A couple of months ago, I met him in Oakland and gave him the money. But I think he is stalking me. This girlfriend of his is also a singer, and while she doesn't know that William, that's his name, and I are divorced, he used her to get me to come to her house to help her with her singing career. I was shocked when William showed up at her house while we were practicing. He wants to get back with me, but that's only because he knows Graham and I are very good friends. I'm at my wit's end and don't know what to do."

"You have to tell Graham, Rita. You have to tell him before things get out of hand. If you are going to have a relationship built on trust, you have to do the right thing. I'm sorry about what you're going through, but you need to put your trust in God. Let Him guide and direct you as to what you should do."

Rita moved closer to Martha and gave her a big hug. She clung to Martha like an unripe peach fastened to a tree in a California orchard, then broke down sobbing. "Thank you."

Martha rubbed Rita's head. "Let me pray for you, daughter. God, I ask You to be with this, Your child right now. She is in need of Your help, Lord. She is being pursued by someone who does not mean her well and desires to threaten her happiness. We bring this petition before You and ask that You see that no harm befall this child and that her adversary fall by the wayside. You said You'd make our enemies our footstools. We believe in the name of Jesus, that You are a God that has power and dominion over all the earth and that nothing is too hard for You to do. Bless this child, be with her. Let her know that You have authority of all, and if she has faith like that of a mustard seed and believes that You will do what she asks, everything will be all right. We pray this prayer in Jesus' name. Amen."

Rita brushed away a tear. "I love you, Martha. And thank you for being you."

"Just trust in God, baby. He'll see you through."

♪♪♪

"Are you spying on Grandma, Deborah?"

"No, I'm just trying to figure out what's going on. I could hear Grandma praying, but not what about. I think Rita is crying."

"Well, get away from that door before somebody smacks you in the head with it."

"Liz, the pessimist." Graham watched as his daughters stood outside of Martha's door. He walked up behind them, putting his arms around their shoulders and startling them for a moment.

"Rita still with Grandma?" Graham asked.

"Ask Deborah. She's been spying on them." Deborah made a face.

CHAPTER 51

The wind outside picked up, howling and hurling loose objects against the house. Elroy turned the heat to seventy degrees to knock off the chill that had entered the house. Lively conversation was still taking place throughout the house. Pastor Fields and his wife said their goodbyes.

"Baby, get Deborah." Martha leaned slightly forward toward Rita. "I have a terrible pain in my chest."

"Martha, oh my God. Sit still, Martha. I'll run and get Deborah."

Rita jumped off the bed and ran to the door, tripping over the trunk. She looked back and saw Martha holding her chest.

"Deborah!" Rita yelled at the top of her lungs when she snatched the door open and almost bumped into Deborah. Now was not the time to figure out what Deborah was doing. Martha needed her.

"What's wrong, what's wrong with Grandma? Grandma."

"She says she has a terrible pain in her chest."

"Grandma!" Deborah shouted running toward her. "Call 9-1-1, Rita."

"My chest hurts, baby," Martha said to Deborah. "Hand me my nitro tablets off the nightstand."

The phone shook uncontrollably in Rita's hand as she tried to dial 9-1-1. She closed her eyes and opened them when she heard the dispatcher's voice.

"Nine-one-one, may I help you?"

"Yes, the lady of the house may be having a heart attack. She says she's having severe chest pains."

"We will send someone out right away."

"What's wrong?" Elroy shouted as he ran into the room followed closely by Graham, Liz, Grant, Riley, and children. "Baby, what's wrong?" Elroy picked up Martha's frail hand and held it, afraid to let go.

"Think she might have had a heart attack, Granddad. I just gave her a nitroglycerin tablet."

"Jesus."

"She's going to be all right, Elroy," Graham said, putting his arm around him. "She's in good hands. Nurse Deborah knows what to do."

Deborah scooped Martha's hand in hers. "She's got a pulse and she's still breathing. I think the nitro tab is helping. Help me hold her up, Liz."

Desperate and worried faces appeared in the doorway. Martha's eyes were closed as she sat on the bed flanked by Deborah and Liz who held her around the waist. Mother Hattie Mae Johnson barged through the crowd so she could lay hands on Sis. Carter.

"Grandma needs some air," Deborah said. "Some of you will have to leave."

"Riley, take the kids into the living room," Liz said.

"She was praying for me, and all of a sudden..." Rita let her tears flow. "I feel so helpless."

"It's all right, daughter," Mother Hattie Mae Johnson said. "Jesus is on the throne. He's a healer and a doctor in the sick room. I command that demon to loose Sister Carter right now."

The room was silent except for Mother Johnson, whose voice boomed like thunder in the distant sky. Martha opened her eyes and everyone, especially Elroy, was grateful for this miracle. The sirens wailed outside. Grant rushed to the door to let the paramedics in and pointed the way to Martha's room.

"Coming through," a paramedic shouted.

The paramedic put the cold stethoscope on Martha's chest and listened for a heartbeat. Then he took two fingers and placed it on her wrist. "She's got a weak pulse. Let's move."

Sweat covered Deborah's face. She watched the paramedics strap Martha to the gurney. Liz's eye twitched at fever pitch as anxiety and nerves began to rule her body. It hadn't been a year since their mother had died.

"We're going to Mercy," the paramedic said.

"I'll drive," Graham shouted. "Dad, you come with me. Deborah, Liz…"

The girls stood in the middle of the room and looked from one to the other, finally resting their eyes on Rita. She still held Martha's hand, giving it a quick rub before the gurney was pushed out.

"All right, Daddy," Deborah said. "Grant and Riley can take the kids home."

"The kids want to go to the hospital, too," Grant said. "You and Liz ride with your dad. Riley and I will follow you."

Cramped in the backseat of Graham's car were Rita, Liz, and Deborah with Elroy in the front. It was deathly quiet and everyone wore somber faces; Graham looked in the rearview mirror, glancing first at Rita, then at Liz and Deborah. With no words exchanged, the cast of four continued to lay their heads back while Graham raced toward Mercy.

Rita sat up when she heard her name called. "Thanks for being there for Grandma," Deborah said. Liz moved slightly forward in her seat with a smile on her face.

"She's a beautiful woman." Rita sniffed. "I'm glad I was there." The car was silent again.

CHAPTER 52

It had been a long night at the hospital, but Martha was resting peacefully. She was not yet out of the woods and was being held in ICU overnight for observation.

Rita sighed as she exited the cab, weary from the day. She admonished Graham to stay with Elroy at the hospital. It was going to be a long day tomorrow and she needed to get some rest. Ordinarily, she would have been at the club on a Thursday night, even on Thanksgiving, but she had wanted to be with Graham to help celebrate Martha's birthday.

The wind whipped around her almost causing Rita to lose her footing. The temperature had dipped down into the low fifties and the shrillness of the wind cut like a cerated knife.

Rita could hear the phone ringing as she put the key into the lock of her apartment. *It might be Graham with a report from the hospital.* Rushing to get the key out of the lock, she hit her forefinger on the door.

"Damn, broke a nail. Hold on, I'm coming," she hollered at the phone. "Hello."

"Hey, Rita. I've been calling and calling. Where have you been?"

"What is it, William? What do you want?"

"My, aren't you testy tonight?"

"I'm tired, William, and I don't have any time for your foolishness."

"Hear me out, Rita."

"I told you, I'm tired. Graham's mother-in-law just had a heart attack and nearly died in my arms. I'm in no mood for any of your..."

"Rita, stop. Please. Just calm down. I'm sorry about your mother-in-law."

"Graham's mother-in-law. Where's Angie?"

"She's with her sister. Look, I want to run something by you. I'd like to come over and show you a proposal."

Rita gritted her teeth. She was in no mood for a fight, but she was not about to fall into any of William Long's traps. "No! I don't want any company and I don't want to see any proposal you've got."

"Rita, I won't take much of your time."

"Do you realize what time it is? Why can't you tell me on the phone?"

"It's a little more complicated than that. Look, Rita, I have your best interest at heart, and I think you're going to love this."

"Umm-hmm," Rita said under her breath. "One minute, and then you're gone."

"I'll be right over."

"I was afraid of that." And she hung up the phone.

Although the apartment was small, it was cozy. It was perfect for the short visits without the cost of an expensive hotel stay. The thought of an intruder, especially at this hour, threatened her comfort zone—even if it was William. Rita flung her long sweater over a chair in the living room and kicked off her shoes. Then she walked into the kitchen.

Rita ran water into the tea kettle. She put it on the stove and turned on the burner. She rubbed her neck as a throbbing pain ran the length of it. A puzzled look crossed her face. *What was so urgent that William had to come tonight?* she thought. *It was probably not a wise decision to allow him to come over.*

It was too quiet in the room for Rita. She sat on the couch with her feet tucked under her and picked up the remote from the end table. The late news was still on, wrapping up the Bowl highlights for the day.

The whistle from the teakettle startled Rita. She had dozed off so quickly. As she got up from the couch, she thought she heard a noise. *Buzzzzzzzzz.* It was the door.

Rita sighed and walked nonchalantly to the door in her bare feet. She peered through the peephole and was instantly disgusted at the face staring back. She opened the door and hugged it with her body as William sought entrance.

"You did invite me, Rita."

"No, William. You invited yourself. And I might add that you were very persistent that it be tonight. You got one minute. Start talking."

"Don't be that way, Rita. May I come in?"

William slithered in as Rita moved to the side. His silhouette against the midnight sky elicited an excitement she tried to deny—a twilight mood that makes you want to do things you would regret in the morning.

Rita looked away from the man who was once her husband and now stood at her door with the scent of Giorgio Armani oozing from his body. Her soft, brown eyes roamed the length of him while the portion of her brain that controlled her emotions worked overtime. *He was handsome*, she admitted to herself. His long, ruddy-colored dreads blended with the color of his quarter-length leather coat. He wore a drab, olive-green, double-knit turtleneck sweater and a pair of olive-green pleated slacks belted at the waist. A slick pair of brown Stacy Adams rode his feet like a luxury limousine.

"What do you have that's so hot that you couldn't wait until tomorrow?" she said in a voice that was much too sexy.

William hesitated. "I've been talking to some record producers who are really hot about your sound. In fact, they've already caught your act at The Hole."

Rita was not amused and stood while William plundered through his presentation.

"You may not believe this, but I have your best interest at heart...and Midnight Express', too. May I have some water?"

"Don't think about getting comfortable. I agreed to listen to what you have to say...and after that, brother, it's good night. Just a minute, I'll get your water."

Rita returned to the living room and found William tucked into the corner of the couch with his coat lying neatly over its arm. His legs were crossed as if he belonged there, sitting in his favorite chair. The semi-pleasant expression present on Rita's face earlier evaporated and was slowly replaced by a cold wall of steel as she debated whether to throw the glass of water in William's face.

Rita handed William the glass of water. "Make this quick. I'm tired and I've got to get up early in the morning."

William took a sip of water and put the glass down on the end table. "My connections can get you and Midnight Express in some upscale clubs and possibly Vegas. Imagine your name along with Lola Falana, Wayne Newton, and Freda Payne. And some nice comfortable change will come along with the package."

William picked up the glass again and took another sip. He could tell Rita was a little interested. "I could become your manager—secure your bookings, look out for your interests."

Rita sighed aloud and sat down on the couch. "You dreamin', boy. I couldn't trust you when we were married, and what makes you think I would trust you now?"

"I've changed, Rita. Let me prove it to you. We can get married again and start fresh. Maybe have some kids."

Rita jumped off the couch and started to swing her arms. "That's it, William. Get out!"

It was a moment frozen in time. William couldn't control himself and leapt from the couch. He moved swiftly up to Rita and encircled her with his arms and covered her mouth with his, then backed away.

"Stop it!" Rita screamed as she struggled to get away.

William continued to kiss Rita while she clawed at him, her fingers entangled in his hair.

"I want you," William said between breaths, pressing his body roughly into hers. "You look so sexy with one hand on your hip and the other pointing the way to the door. You belong to me."

She felt his throbbing hardness as he pressed against her body. It repulsed her to no end, but William had no intention of stopping. The more she tussled, the more aggressive William became. Rita slipped, and they fell on the couch.

William grabbed her hair and gently pulled it back before sealing his lips around the circumference of her mouth. Rita tried to push away, but William had her in a death grip as he moved a leg between hers for better control. He turned her slightly so she was on her side, and a strong hand began to stroke her spine, slowing down at her buttocks and taking the scenic route to her thigh.

Rita's thoughts were running rampant like a planet spinning out of orbit. Should she call the police? *What should I do*? were her thoughts as she struggled to get away from William.

"Hmmm, you feel good, girl," William said, his eyes closed and relishing the moment. He could hear Rita's shallow breathing as she lay non-responsive.

Whack! William clutched his jaw, and Rita got up from the couch and hovered over William. "Get out!" Rita screamed, shaking where she stood. "Get out!"

Still holding his jaw, William slowly got up from the couch. Before he could say another word, his coat was flying in the air. Rita was seething and her eyes were like coals of fire. William reached down and picked up his coat and looked back at Rita. She stood with her hands on her hips and dared him to utter a word. He turned around and headed for the door.

William turned around once more and felt his face. "You gonna call Lover Man? What do you think he'll say if he knows I was with you at one in the morning?" William managed a weak laugh.

"Get out and take your lousy proposal with you."

Slam! And the silhouette returned to the vast darkness, but not before leaving a memento, a fresh reminder that the past wasn't so long ago.

Rita stood shaking in the same spot for several minutes. She encircled her body with her arms and pondered the last half-hour. What just happened? "I've got to tell Graham," Rita sobbed aloud. "I've got to tell him about William before it's too late."

CHAPTER 53

Morning light filtered through the blinds as Graham lay exhausted on the bed. Sleep had come easy for him when he finally made it home at four in the morning after dropping Elroy, Liz, and Deborah home.

Graham woke easily not sure of the time. He stretched out his arms half expecting Rita to be there. They hadn't spent as much time together as he would have liked with her rigorous schedule, but he planned to change all that.

Lying in bed felt good. Lord knows he needed the rest. Graham had a slight headache and touched his forehead. He was a little warm, and when his hand came to rest on his chest, he noticed that his body had amassed a thin layer of sweat.

He lay there without moving. Seeing Martha lying on the paramedics' gurney last night brought back a myriad of nightmares. There was a vision of Amanda as she lay dying on a hospital bed after she suffered a severe heart attack. Mother and daughter…life was so fragile, but thank God, Martha was going to pull through this one.

A chill ran through Graham. It was time to get up. He could not lie in bed any longer for fear the dreams would consume and swallow him up once more. He looked at the clock.

"My God, it's already eleven o'clock. I need to call Rita."

The wrinkled khaki pants from the night before lay at the end of the bed where Graham left them when he hurriedly jumped into bed. He picked them up and staggered to the bathroom in his bare feet to brush his teeth and wash his face. When he finished in the bathroom, Graham stumbled back to his room, rubbing the silver hairs on his chest that he planned to hide with a pullover shirt.

Brrng, brrng. Graham rushed for the phone.

"Hey, baby," said the voice at the other end of the line.

"Hey, sweetheart. I was just getting ready to call you. I just got up."

"I know you must be tired. Have you heard how Martha is doing today?"

"No, I'm going to pick Dad up and take him to the hospital in a little while."

"Okay. I'm going to the club at noon. The band and I need to rehearse for tonight's show. I'll see you later tonight?"

"Yeah. Are you all right? You seem distant."

"I'm fine. Yesterday was a long day. I didn't rest well."

"Well, you're going to spend the night here with me. No ifs, ands, or buts about it."

"We'll see. I love you."

"Love you, too, sweetheart."

Bang, bang, bang. Ding-dong. "What is it now?" Graham said aloud. He had hoped that this would be a quiet morning. "I'll be there in a minute!"

Remembering the last time he opened the door to an uninvited Sister Mary Ross, Graham snatched a white polo shirt from the dresser drawer before answering the door. He didn't need a repeat performance, and Mary Ross wasn't going to get another chance to salivate over his body.

Bang, bang, bang. "Open up the door," a voice called out.

"Damn, it's Charlie."

Graham opened the door, and Charlie rushed past with a fifth of Chivas Regal in his hand.

"How long were you going to keep me waiting on that porch?"

"You could have picked up my newspaper and brought it inside," Graham said, as he stepped outside to pick up the paper. "And I'll have you know that I might have been in bed with my woman," Graham retorted as Charlie followed him into the kitchen.

"But you weren't, were you?"

"How do you know? You been spying on me? Sit down."

"I rushed over when I heard about Martha. How is she?"

"Her prognosis is good. I was scared, man. I kept seeing Amanda lying on that gurney instead of Martha. I wouldn't be able to take it if something happened to Martha. It's only been a few months since Amanda's been gone."

"I'm glad Martha's going to be all right. Have a shot. Might take the edge off."

"Charlie, you're on your way to being drunk, and it's only eleven-thirty a.m. Why don't you put that stuff down?"

"Man, don't start on me this morning. Just came by to shoot the bull with my good friend, Graham, and see about sweet, dear Martha."

"Well, I appreciate that."

The room was suddenly quiet. Charlie nursed his Chivas while Graham flipped through the paper. "Man, those Cowboys beat the crap out of the Bears. Look at this score—forty-two to seven—a blowout."

"I hung out at Manny's house. Had Thanksgiving dinner with him and the wife. Thirty years they've been married."

Graham looked up from the paper. "Amanda and I shared forty good ones."

"Yep, you had all the luck—a good life with a good woman, beautiful children, and now, another good woman. Humph. Life ain't fair."

"Come off it, Charlie. You are way too hard on yourself."

Charlie sipped his drink and sat in silence reminiscing about his life—a kaleidoscope of mishaps and misfortunes that equaled too much of nothing. He was still good-looking, had charm, money in his pocket, but it could never buy him love. His friend sitting across the way was blessed with two good women in his life...and...

"Umph. They got an article in the paper about gamblers and athletes. Pete Rose's name probably heads the list. Listen to this."

Charlie took another sip straight from the bottle. "I'm not the least bit interested in what some overpaid athlete was doing with his life."

"Listen anyway. Says that it is becoming a growing trend among athletes to lose thousands and even millions of dollars at the game tables or the racetracks."

"They pay 'em too much damn money and turn around and condemn they asses for what they do with all the money they don't know what to do with."

"I guess that makes some kind of sense…and lay off that bottle. It says Ronnie Calhoun spent thousands of dollars in Atlantic City for sport…"

"Now, that boy just got too much money. They ought to let me be in just one Nike commercial. I'd buy eve-r-y b-o-d-y in Oak…town a *drink*."

"What about that Pete Rose betting against his own team? The paper goes on to talk about ex-basketball star, William Long…William Long… Rita's ex-husband, William Long?" Charlie's ears perked up at the mention of William's name. "Says that he was a compulsive gambler and never got over his short stint in the NBA. Played the tables in Vegas and Reno and owed some people over $50,000. I wonder if Rita knows about this?"

"Probably why she left him."

Graham put the paper down and stared at Charlie. "You act like you know something."

"Man, I'm just speculating. Makes sense to me. She left him soon after his basketball career was over, and it wasn't a secret that he liked cheerleaders…I mean any woman who would cheer him on."

"Shut up, Charlie. You're drunk."

"Relationships. Remember when you and Amanda got married?"

"No comparison, and what made you think of that?"

"Just sitting here going over my life…my life. You and Amanda were a big part of my life. I was there in just about ev-e-r-y as-pect of your life." Charlie put the bottle of Chivas down. "I was there when you and Amanda got married. I was at the kitchen table just about every time you were."

"We've come a long way together…you and me. Homeboys. What's mine is yours."

Charlie pondered that a moment. He crunched his face—creases dividing his face into three equal parts. He looked up and continued.

"I was there when Deborah and Liz were born. I attended their weddings as Uncle Charlie and rode their babies on my knee. Remember the day Liz met Riley? I was all up in Riley's face, giving him the third degree like it was my baby girl having her first date."

Graham smiled. "You're right. Those were some good memories, Charlie."

Charlie plundered on like he was on a 747 bound for Paris and the whole world was his stage. Even Graham sat back and reminisced on the wooden chair that sat under the table where so many breakfasts were eaten, stories of how Barbie couldn't stand Ken were told, where backsides stayed glued to their seats until all homework was completed, and nobody would ever know about the lap dance Amanda gave her husband that turned into a sizzling hot, freaky-deaky sex marathon that lasted nearly two hours.

"Graham, do you remember how I met Ernestine?"

"Yeah, Amanda introduced you. She and Amanda went to the same hairdresser."

"Yeah, you asked me to pick up Amanda from the beauty shop that day because her car was in the shop. She was talking to Ernestine, and I guess Amanda thought I would be a good catch for her. What a mess I made of Ernestine's life. But I did love her."

"I smell Amanda's fried chicken. Dang, that woman could cook. Had the whole church house over for Sunday dinner. That was about as close to the Lord as I ever got."

"My baby could sho' 'nuf fry some chicken. Yes, siree. Why don't we change the subject? I was doing all right until you smelled the chicken. Shit, I mean shoot, I smell it, too."

"Those were some good days—me, you, and Amanda."

"If I didn't know better, I'd swear you were sweet on Amanda." Charlie picked up his bottle of Chivas and took another swig. He looked at Graham, then lowered his eyes. "I remember back in 1970," Graham continued, "when you took Amanda to the James Brown concert at the Oakland Auditorium. I had to work overtime that night. I wasn't complaining 'cuz the money was good, but I wanted to hear ole James say, 'I'm Black and I'm proud' just one time."

"Yeah, we were all into it. We'd repeat right after him, 'Say it loud, I'm Black and I'm proud.' And the more he said it, the louder we got. Our tall Afros sat on our heads like crowns while we bopped to the beat. Everybody wore dashikis and had Black Power buttons, and buttons with Huey Newton sitting in his favorite wicker chair pinned all over them. We were on a high when we left the concert. We were expressing our new identity. We were no longer Negroes. We were Black!!

"When we left the concert, we went over to Slim's barbeque near Seventh Street. A big crowd ended up over there, and we were singing and carrying on. You remember Larry Graham of Sly and the Family Stone. Well, I believe his momma owned that joint.

"We were having such a good time I didn't want to go home. If it wasn't for Amanda, being the lady she was and trying to get home to her man, I would have kept her out all night."

Charlie had hit a nerve. Graham watched Charlie, but didn't say a word.

"Do you remember when you asked me how I got that scratch on my face?"

"I'm listening." Graham rubbed his stomach. He felt queasy and wasn't sure why.

"Well, I didn't tell you the truth about it. I believe I told you I stumbled into the house with no lights on 'cuz I was drunk and cut my face on the edge of the bookcase in my living room. Truth is, I did something very bad that night, something I'm ashamed of. Never told a soul and never repented for what I'd done."

Fixed eyes gazed upon Charlie while he hemmed and hawed around with his story all slow and deliberate. Graham wasn't feeling any of this, not sure what trip Charlie was taking him on. Then Charlie opened his mouth to continue with Graham giving him his undivided attention.

"Have you ever wanted something so bad and knew you couldn't have it because it belonged to someone else?" Charlie looked at Graham and did not flinch. Charlie felt in his pocket for a toothpick, and when he found one put it in his mouth. "I recalled wanting this Panama hat so bad that sat on a mannequin in H.C. Capwell's window when we were young men, and I didn't have enough money to buy it. I thought of different ways to try and get that hat—down to just out and out stealing it. I wanted it because I thought I should have it, and I loved the way it looked. I know that hat would have looked good sitting on top of my head.

"Well, I went for the forbidden." Graham squirmed in his seat anticipating Charlie's next words. "I had loved…loved…wanted Amanda for a long time. I watched her, I watched the two of you together and couldn't understand why she didn't see the same thing in me that she saw in you." Charlie looked up into Graham's seething face. He ignored the look and continued. "And now Rita. How is it that you are able to pick the best fruit on the tree?

"When we left Slim's, I had every intention of taking Amanda straight home. I took a detour and drove around Lake Merritt and parked. Amanda was anxious and begged me to take her home, but I had to tell her how I felt."

Graham jumped to his feet.

"Please let me finish." Graham sat down and fingered a napkin that lay on the table.

"I tried to tell Amanda how I felt, but she wasn't hearing any of it. I touched her and tried to kiss her, but I never anticipated her striking back. She clawed at my face until she was able to get in one good slap. Nearly gauged my eyes out. I was drunk and defenseless."

"She should have killed your ass, nigger, like I'm getting ready to do. I can't believe she didn't tell me."

"If I didn't respect her before, I had more respect for that woman after that night. She told me she would go to her grave with this secret because I was your best friend and she didn't want you to think any differently about me. But she promised me that she would kill me if I ever so much as looked at her or touched her in any way that was not befitting my best friend's wife. And I kept my word."

Tears began to stream from Graham's face. Such a pathetic story from a pathetic man—a man whom he'd have given his life for only moments earlier. But right here and right now, he hated the very sight of him. Charlie was the epitome of all the Sodom and Gomorrah's—a worthless piece of swine in a corrupt city full of vile and vulgar people that weren't worth saving.

Graham swiped at the tears that now ran fast down his face. No longer able to endure his pain, he took the edge of the table in both hands and lifted up one side. All the contents slid onto Charlie's lap like one big water slide. It scared Charlie and he pushed back from the table scrambling to get on his feet. His bottle of Chivas crashed to the floor—its liquid content crawling over the floor like it was on a secret mission.

A loaded fist slammed into the wall as Graham charged at Charlie. Graham's five-foot-eleven-inch body towered over Charlie's six-foot cowering frame as he ducked an angry Graham.

It didn't take much effort to pin Charlie against the wall when he offered no resistance. Graham held him by the collar, squeezing it tight around his neck. He wanted to punch him, hit him until the death rattle came, but Charlie stood against the wall lifeless, ready to accept whatever punishment he deserved.

Time and again Graham had put up with Charlie's antics and some of his crazy, wild and whacky ways. Now he had the audacity to tell him that he had put the moves on his wife—that he'd tried to touch her in ways that were inappropriate—ways that could get a man killed. Graham hated Charlie at this moment, hated him so much that even his tears hurt. The only thing left to do was to throw him out of his house, his life. He didn't even have the strength to beat him down, but the sad truth was, Charlie wasn't even worth it.

He took Charlie by the collar and dragged him to the front door and opened it. He knew he should call a cab, because Charlie wasn't in any condition to drive. Maybe Charlie would just get in the car and kill himself and he could wash his hands of him. Graham pushed him out of the door with little effort. He slammed the door and watched Charlie stumble to his car. This was the only way to deal with it at this time, short of taking a gun, aiming it at Charlie's head, and blowing his damn brains out.

♪♪♪

Charlie jumped behind the wheel of his car and took off without looking back. He deserved what he'd got, and yet, he didn't believe that his best friend had thrown him away like yesterday's trash. Hell, he, Charlie Ford, was the one who had picked Graham up from his stinking pit of hell, and now he was banished from the little house on Chester Street where he had just as many memories as Graham. He was livid, and Graham was going to pay for it.

No cops were in sight and Charlie barreled down the street going twenty miles in excess of the speed limit. The Chivas was wearing off fast and instead of being angry at himself, Charlie was mad at the world. He pulled into a side-street and turned right at the next corner. His tires squealed as they rubbed against the curb.

He sought refuge at the little white stucco house with the neatly arranged bed of marigolds running along the walkway. Charlie paced back and forth until Mary opened the door with a surprised look on her face.

"Hi, Charlie," Mary said with a seductive look on her face. She stood on the porch dressed in a cotton, snap-down housedress made out of yellow print seersucker with a field of white daisies growing wild in the background. "What brings you here? I was getting ready to go out. Pew…what have you been drinking? I smell you from here."

Charlie entered and kicked the door shut and took Mary in his arms, ignoring her questions. Instead, he answered her with a passionate kiss, and Mary reciprocated the best she knew how. Charlie opened one eye and spotted Mary's brand-new leather couch that now sat under the picture of Jesus. He dragged Mary with him and fell upon the couch, panting and kissing her all about the neck and mouth like a dog in heat.

♪♪♪

Heat seared through Mary's body. She closed her eyes. All of a sudden, she felt cold air on her breasts as they lay exposed after Charlie ripped open her housedress. He began to kiss her breasts through her lacy bra, making it impossible for her to resist.

Mary began to cough, trying to catch her breath as she lay on her back. But Charlie overpowered her, placing kisses here and there—and she was a river of melted butter, floating on a bed of hot steamy potatoes ready to be stirred, tasted, and eaten.

Some dreams held stark revelations, and Mary couldn't be sure if she was or was not dreaming. Her eyes were shut tight, standing at the door to the twilight zone. Charlie pulled up her dress and tore at her pantyhose, pulling them down halfway. He touched her lightly on the fleshy part of her stomach and ran his hand across it, slowly moving his hand downward across her nylon panties, down her left leg while lavishing kisses all over her body. Mary was tingling all over.

One eye popped open but closed abruptly as she felt Charlie outline the contour of her panties with his fingers. Mary shuddered at his touch but offered no resistance as he inched his way into her lush garden. She wasn't sure how she was to feel—maybe embarrassed, but at any rate, she remained still as Charlie continued his probe.

And his fingers were little antennae—touching, feeling, scouting, taking notes, and planting mile markers for his return trip. And then his fingers became rugged and forceful as if the speed limit had suddenly increased and he was anxious to get to where he was going, discovering and redis-covering new and wonderful sights along the way.

It was more than Mary had bargained for. She tried to clamp her legs shut, but not in time as her body began to convulse and tremble like the great San Francisco earthquake. She was not ready for this, and tried un-successfully to pry herself from Charlie's grasp. The more Mary resisted, the more determined Charlie was to get what he came for.

Charlie's body was heavy on top of Mary, and he continued to ignore her pleas for him to stop. She kicked and screamed, but Charlie covered her mouth with his to muffle the sound.

This was not what Sister Mary Ross had envisioned sex would be like. She thought it was going to be soft and gentle in an angelic kind of way. She imagined soft kisses, soft words passing between them. And finally, there would be the gentle acceptance of her man into her womb that would make her feel all fuzzy and warm—not violated. Hell and damnation she'd brought on herself. Would the Lord ever forgive her?

"Stay still," were Charlie's first words. "Shut up, and be still."

Mary lay still as Charlie continued to kiss her roughly on the mouth, his breathing becoming more labored. She was frightened at the Charlie she didn't recognize—a Charlie who seemed to be so filled with anger and resentment.

Charlie raised his head and looked down at a frightened Mary. "I love you, Rita. And he's going to pay for what he did to me. Pay, I say."

A stone face replaced the frightened one. Charlie gazed down at Mary. She didn't utter a word or move a limb. She had passed out. Charlie rose and took her arm, trying to elicit a response as he shook it. Suddenly, Charlie was embarrassed at his behavior and how he had treated Mary. He couldn't believe that he had blundered twice in one day.

Mary shifted on the couch. She looked like Cinderella waking up from a deep sleep, but without Prince Charming to make her day right. Like a coward, Charlie ran to the door, briefly looking back to make sure Mary was all right. When she appeared to be moving of her own accord, Charlie rushed from Mary's house, nearly missing the two steps that led to the sidewalk. He recovered his footing, headed for his car, got in and drove away.

Mary had never felt so humiliated in her whole life. Even the standoff at the church was a mild happening in comparison. Love definitely wasn't for the lonely.

CHAPTER 54

Bile rose in his stomach at the thought of Charlie touching Amanda. Graham paced back and forth, his blood pressure rising the more he thought about Charlie. He'd trusted this man with his life. He'd go to the ends of the world for Charlie. Now a small confession that sneaked its way out of Charlie's mouth had interrupted and destroyed in an instant the bond two friends had for each other.

Tears of hate formed in Graham's eyes. He understood what the old-timers meant when they said that hatred was a killer and a flapping tongue was like a two-edged sword. It made you want to hurt somebody bad. It gave you the license to kill and beg God's forgiveness later. It made you want to do things that you never thought of doing before—things that caused people to get twenty-five to life without parole.

Graham sat down on the overstuffed chair and threw his head back. He didn't want to kill anyone or go to jail. He just wanted to know why his best friend had betrayed their friendship. And Graham was a little miffed at Amanda for not telling him, but that woman was so full of wisdom. She let Charlie get away with his vile act to save a friendship, because she knew it meant so much to Graham.

"Amanda, you always knew the right thing to do," Graham wailed. "You were my sunshine on a rainy day, spreading cheer when there was sadness." *Sniff.* "I love you, girl. But I better stop this crying 'cuz your momma needs me now. No, she ain't ready to come…tried to, but the doctors say she's going to be around a little while longer. …I miss you."

Graham wiped his face and got up from the chair. It was one o'clock, and he was late in picking up Elroy for the hospital. He grabbed his coat and headed for the door.

Brrng, brrng. "I don't have time to get this phone." *Brrng, brrng.* "Hello?"

"Graham, this is Mary Ross."

"Mary, I was on my way out to the hospital to see Martha."

"Martha? Martha…in the hospital?"

"Yes, but she's going to be all right. She had a mild heart attack last night."

"Jesus. I'll send a prayer up for her."

"Thank you, Mary, but I must go. I've got to pick up Deacon Carter."

"I understand. This won't take but a minute."

"What is it, Mary?" Graham asked.

"Uhh, uhh, it's Charlie."

Graham sighed. He paused for several minutes before he could go on. "What about Charlie?"

"Is Rita there?"

"No, she's at the club. What's up, Mary? I'm not in a good mood."

"Charlie just left here. He…he had been drinking. He was really upset about something. He just showed up at my house, and I thought it…it was…you know…he wanted to be with me."

Graham was silent, then leaned forward in his seat. "What happened, Mary?" There was concern in his voice.

"He was a wild man, Deacon Peters. I've never been so scared in all my life."

"What happened, Mary? Did he hurt you? Tell me."

Mary held the phone tight and tried to tell her story without all the gory details.

"Damn him," Graham said aloud.

"Deacon Peters," Mary said hesitantly. "Are you all right?"

"Did he hurt you, Mary?"

"Not really. My ego was more bruised. Weird, I tell you. He was some-one I didn't recognize. The strangest thing happened. He called me 'Rita.'"

Graham was stone silent. The walls of his head throbbed as he absorbed what Mary had said. Charlie was a jealous fool. Graham twisted his neck in a figure-eight motion to loosen the kink and began to breathe heavily as he contemplated his next statement. "Did he say where he was going?"

"No. He left in a hurry. I think he was embarrassed. You're not going to do anything crazy, are you?"

"No, Mary."

"I've never seen him like that, I tell you. Frightened me good. I was scared he might do something crazy to me, especially with me living alone and all. But I'm all right now."

"Well, I'm glad you're all right. Thanks for calling. If you need me, give me a call. I mean that."

"I appreciate that, Deacon. I really appreciate it."

Graham dropped his coat on the couch and dialed The Water Hole. The phone rang and rang, and it made Graham irritable. Finally, after six rings, a friendly voice answered the phone.

"Hey, Clyde, Graham. Rita there?"

"Yeah, buddy. They getting ready to rehearse some more—took a short break. Hold on, I'll get her for you."

"Thanks, man."

Nerves were the order of the day. Graham tapped his foot in anticipation of hearing Rita's voice. He was being overprotective and zealous for his own good, but he had to know that Rita was all right.

"Hey, baby. Clyde said you sounded urgent."

"Hey, sweetie. Just wanted to know you were okay."

"Why wouldn't I be? The guys and I are rehearsing. Not too many folks hanging around. Probably too much turkey," Rita said.

"Just making sure no crazies or lunatics are messing with you."

"What are you talking about, Graham?" Rita asked hesitantly. "You aren't making any sense."

"Nothing, sweetheart. I guess with all the frenzy surrounding Martha last night, I'm a little anxious. I just miss you, that's all."

A sigh of relief tumbled from Rita's mouth. "I'm fine, baby. Are you coming to the club tonight?"

"Depending on Martha's condition and how long Dad wants to stay. I want you to come and stay the night with me tonight."

"We'll see…I didn't sleep well last night. Now, I've got to run. The band is warming up."

"All right, sweetheart. I'll chat with you later."

Graham hung up the phone somewhat relieved. His mind was racing, and he hated Charlie for it. The drunken fool had absolutely ruined his day, but he wished he had handled it differently. Pacing the floor, Graham grabbed his coat off the couch and headed out the door. Charlie was probably off somewhere drowning in his sorrows.

CHAPTER 55

There was a slight chill in the hallway of the hospital as Elroy and Graham stepped from the elevator on their way to ICU. No hustle or bustle this afternoon, just an occasional beep of a monitor as they passed several doorways before approaching the nurses' station.

"Room 23E," the station nurse told Graham and Elroy. "Only family members allowed."

They nodded their heads in acknowledgment.

A noisy sigh of relief escaped Elroy's mouth when they entered Martha's room. Martha was sitting up with her eyes open. Although encumbered by a series of tubes and wires that hung about her, she managed a faint smile at the sight of her two favorite men. She was a sight for sore eyes as tears welled up in the corner of Elroy's tiny eyes.

Elroy and Graham, hands clasped together, walked the few feet to Martha's bedside. Graham was happy for the support, too, but released his grip so Elroy could enjoy the first moment with Martha.

"How's my man?" Martha said in a voice so low it was almost inaudible.

"Save your breath, girl. Your man is doing fine now. You gave me a big scare."

Martha smiled and mouthed, *I know.*

"I love you, girl. Lord, I don't know what I'd do if you left me here."

"Probably find a new woman like our son Graham." Martha smiled and then raised her hand slowly and waved her fingers for Graham to come near. "What you standing back there for? Trying to make me holler?"

Graham walked to the bed and stood next to Elroy. He leaned over the bed and planted a kiss on Martha's forehead, then looked longingly after her. "No, Mother, just wanted to give you and Dad some time. I'm so glad to see you in such good spirits."

"I'm fine, now. In fact, I'm ready to go home."

"I told you to stop talking, girl," Elroy cut in. "I want you to get completely well. I have a special pill for you if you be good."

Graham sputtered into his hand as he tried not to laugh out loud. But it was too late. Martha began to laugh, although her voice was no louder than a whisper. Then Elroy laughed. A nurse passing by heard the commotion and walked in.

"I don't know what's going on in here, but you two are going to be evicted if you upset my patient in any way."

Martha couldn't stop laughing, and soon everybody was in stitches holding their sides with their hand while covering their mouths with the other. The nurse looked at all three of them and began to grin even though no one made her privy to the joke.

"Behave," she admonished again and left the room still grinning and chuckling about how funny they all looked.

"Well, keep me company so I can hurry up and recuperate. I want to test out that pill you keep talking about." The trio looked from one to the other, then covered their mouths again, trying to stifle their laughter.

♪♪♪

Parking was at a premium. Friday nights were always popular at The Water Hole, but it seemed that tonight everybody wanted to shake off the turkey, ham, and sweet potato pie they had eaten the day before. It was the long weekend and there was no other way to start it off right, with the exception of feeding their faces on Thanksgiving, then with some good, finger-popping music at the Hole. Cadillacs, Lincolns, and Mercedes dotted the parking lot like a late-night auto show at the Cow Palace.

Rita was tired, but she gave the crowd what they wanted to hear. Dressed in a sassy, powder-blue, chenille, form-fitted dress that fanned at the bottom and highlighted the swell of her breasts held up by a pair of spaghetti straps, Rita empowered the audience with her riveting tunes. They held onto lovers so no one else would steal them or kicked up their heels and gyrated their bodies in three/four time. Mascara and makeup was smeared on lovers' collars or made track marks on female faces as the temperature soared upward along with the frenzy of the dancers who kept the dance floor hot.

It was the musicians' time to shine. The four other members who made up Midnight Express went into action. Johnny, the bass guitarist, led the pack. He stood up and performed a short solo number. His body began to gyrate, dipping his guitar toward the floor and then up again as he jumped into the air and then into a perfect split. Gerald, the cello player, took over. His fancy finger work plucked into the soul of the listener. Adonis, the pianist, began to play a soft melody that ended in a crescendo. His fingers rippled over the keys as they went up and down the scale causing the audience to cry out for more. And Rico, the drummer, brought up the rear—a little swish of the snare drum, a tinkle on the cymbals, ending in a series of well-orchestrated moves that highlighted his skill as a drummer. Then the four sounds blended together—couples stopped on the dance floor to take notice, pop their fingers, and sway to the beat. The sound of Midnight Express was so smooth and electrifying, it was a wonder they hadn't gone on and made a name for themselves.

As the band played, Rita searched the audience. No sign of Graham. She spotted Charlie holed up at the bar nursing a drink with Shelly at his side. He never raised his head to look at the stage. Just as Rita was about to go back to the mike, she spotted William sitting at a table in the corner. Angie was hovering nearby. She gasped and turned away.

♪♪♪

William watched Rita until their eyes connected. He saw the look on her face. She seemed frightened. Rita had nothing to fear from him.

A napkin lay on the table in front or him. William picked it up, took out a pen and wrote something on it. He folded the napkin in quarters and proceeded to the front of the room as Angie stood back and watched. William found Clyde and whispered something in his ear, gave him the paper and returned to his seat without ever saying a word to Angie.

William watched Rita read the note he had given Clyde. Rita fumbled around with the mike, glancing again at the note. The audience stood patiently and waited for her to sing, but she stood and stared into the crowd with a blank look on her face, clearing her throat repeatedly as if it was the cause of her delay. Even the band seemed confused. Suddenly Rita swung around and looked dead into William's eyes, ripping the mike from its stand.

"I have a special request…from…my ex-husband, William Long, who is in the house tonight," Rita began. "He wants me to sing his favorite song that he on many nights sang to me—'My Funny Valentine.'" Rita continued to look straight into an amused William's eyes while Angie's jaw dropped as the words flew from Rita's mouth. A hush fell over the room after the last *ahh* had died down. "Funny thing, he was my valentine once, but that was over twenty years ago. He broke Cupid's arrow in half, and now he thinks he can just waltz back into my life because he's a miserable…"

"You don't have to sing, Rita," Clyde hollered from backstage.

Rita was on a roll.

"Oh, I'm going to sing it, but just not the version he remembers. My funny valentine," Rita began.

"Stop, Rita," Clyde called out to her.

With her eyes shut tight, Rita ignored Clyde and continued to sing as she gripped the microphone tight with both hands. She belted out the words mechanically, like the tin man in the *Wizard of Oz*, crying out for love with an empty heart, changing and rearranging the words to suit the mood she was in. "Don't change your hair for me…"

Not able to stand any more, William got up from the table, knocking his chair over as he did and headed for the door. A bewildered Angie watched William's back disappear while tears slid, then rained, down her cheeks. William had humiliated her for the last time.

CHAPTER 56

Rita was drained and the weight of the evening was heavy on her. She lost control in front of a crowd of people, her adoring fans, to get back at a trying-to-get-back-in-her-life-no-good-ex-husband who wasn't worth the time of day—time she wasted and could never recover. She looked out at the near empty club—patrons pulling themselves from their seats while others tipped glasses trying to sip the last bit of alcohol before hitting the night air, and hung her head.

She doubted anyone would care in the morning what had happened tonight. The grapevine would be busy for a few hours at the beauty shop, and then the topic of conversation would jump to something else—story-tellers bored after recounting what went on at The Water Hole for the fifth time.

Rico and Johnny passed Rita in the hallway and offered to take her home. Rita didn't know what she would do without the band. Midnight Express was more than just a band that showcased her work. They were a big family glued together at the seams. Rita waved the guys on, wanting to be alone, while her mind drifted back to the evening's wrestling match—Rita versus William.

Rita turned at the sound of Clyde's feet brushing the carpet as he came toward her.

"Let me take you home, Rita," Clyde consoled, rubbing her back with soft feathery strokes. "I see your boy didn't show up tonight."

"His mother-in-law had a heart attack last night, and he's been at the hospital with his father-in-law most of the day."

"Well, let me take…"

"No, Clyde. I'll get a cab. That way you can finish up."

"May I ask you a question?"

Rita's brown eyes, with their long wispy lashes, penetrated Clyde's face as she went on the offensive. "You may. I'm sure I have an idea what you're going to ask me."

"Rita, I love you like you were my own daughter. What happened out there tonight? I've never in all the times you've performed here seen you act like you did tonight."

"When I saw him come up and bring that piece of paper to you…with that smug look on his face…and then seeing his handwriting on that piece of paper asking me to sing that song, I lost it. I just completely lost it, Clyde."

"I'm sure you've seen him here before. He's been coming for a long time. What was it about tonight that made you go haywire?"

"Look, Clyde. My relationship with William…my marriage to William was a very rocky one. I suffered a lot during that time, but I bounced back. It took a lot of love, and most of all, understanding parents who took care of me when I didn't think I could take care of myself. I fought back and took my life back in my own hands, and no one, I don't care who they are, will take away my dignity and self-respect ever again. I've come too far.

"I have a good man in my life, and it's such a shame that whenever some-thing good begins to happen in my life, something tries to destroy it. But I'll be damned, I tell you…I'll be damned, Clyde, if Mr. William Long is going to slide his way in here and think he's going to take residence in my life. Not on your life."

"I hear you on that. What about Graham?"

"What about Graham?"

"Does he know your ex is in town?"

"No."

"After tonight, he's going to know."

Rita's head flopped forward until it touched her chest. then brought it up again, looking into Clyde's concerned eyes. "You're right. I've got to talk to Graham."

A wide smile crossed Clyde's face. "Well, baby girl, you be careful. I worry about you. I'm going to call you a cab, and you better call me as soon as you get in the door."

"Thanks, Clyde. You're so good to me."

Rita walked the few feet to where Clyde stood and placed a kiss on his shiny, bald head.

"Girl, you made my day."

♪♪♪

The air was crisp but refreshing when Rita emerged from the club. She draped her wrap over her shoulders and drew it tight about her body. Looking around her, she suddenly gazed heavenward and smiled at the blanket of stars that were sprinkled across the sky like little white Christmas lights. With her feet apart, she raised her arms high to grasp as many stars as she could, finally picking out the brightest one and pretending to pluck it from the cluster of other stars. She gave it a big hug and kiss and thanked her lucky star for sending Graham her way. With some reluctance and after one more kiss, Rita flung her arms upward and placed her lucky star back amongst the other stars in the constellation.

As if on cue, a yellow taxi drove up to the front of the club and stopped in front of Rita. A young man in his early twenties, lean with a close-cropped, precision haircut, jumped from the cab and hurried to the other side and opened the door. Rita smiled and proceeded to get in, taking one more glance upward before she did.

Rita rode in silence, looking up every now and then, passing a nod to her admirer in the rearview mirror. The streets were virtually empty, save a few people who found their way to a twenty-four-hour restaurant to fill the void dancing all night had induced.

Rita took out her cell. Graham had called twice. She punched in the number one and listened as the transmitter recalled the pre-programmed number for Graham. A groggy voice met Rita's ear.

"Hey, baby," Rita said, her admirer glued to the rearview mirror.

"Hey, baby," Graham muttered. "How was tonight?"

"Okay as nights go. Were you sleep?"

"Yeah, baby…It was a long day." Graham yawned. "Elroy and I spent most of the day with Martha. Looks like she's going to be all right. By the way, Mary Ross called wanting to know where you were. It was a…strange phone call."

"Baby, go to sleep. I'll come over first thing in the morning. We'll sit and talk then."

"All right baby, I'm tired. Are you on your way home?"

"Yep. I had a long day, too. I'm in a cab."

"Be careful. I love you."

"I love you, too, Graham Peters. 'Bye."

The face in the mirror vanished and the rest of the trip was in total silence. Scattered clusters of light illuminated the street as the cab drove through the heart of West Oakland into Emeryville, but most of the city was at rest, lying between cool sheets and a warm blanket.

A swift turn made Rita's neck jerk. Her head nodded forward, but she was alert now that her apartment was in view. The cab pulled to the curb—the taxi driver once more surveying his now departing guest. And Rita was flattered as she tried to pass the driver a ten-dollar bill that fell onto the seat because his eyes were fixed on her. She doubted he heard the words, "Keep the change."

The driver scrambled to open Rita's door, and she smiled again. She thanked him and headed for the entrance to her building with keys in hand, looking back at the sound of tires squealing as the cab driver drove off.

An eerie feeling came over Rita. She jumped just as a car drove by. Uneasiness crept in like a slithering snake, but it could very well have been her tiredness. Rita looked into the heavens but was unable to locate her star for the heavy fog that had just rolled in.

Silence enveloped Rita as she walked up the stairs to her apartment and put the key in the lock. Out of nowhere, long spindly fingers connected to sweaty palms grabbed her wrists, unlocked the door and pushed her in. Rita jerked her arm and kicked at the shins of the intruder, but the hand tightened its grip on her wrists, pushing her up against the back of the couch with the back of the other hand. Using her elbows, Rita tried to push away. Rita lifted her face slightly to the right, and her mouth fell open and made a giant circle at the sight of the intruder.

"What are…?"

"Shut up. Don't say a word."

Rita's chest heaved in and out as she continued to pull away. "Keep your hands off of me. Stay away."

"I said shut up, little lady. I don't want to hurt you."

Rita could smell his stale breath—a brewery that stank to high heaven. His speech was slurred, and his grip was tight on her arm. Rita's eyes became wide as saucers, but the vicious face of her attacker meant every word he said.

"I…I…I want youuuuu, Rita. I've wanted you, only you…only youuuuu from the first day I saw you." Whispering in Rita's ear, her attacker continued. "When I hear you sing, I…I…I pretend you're singing those… those…those love songs to me. 'I Can't Live Without You,' 'You're My Everything,' 'Ain't Nothing but the Real Thing.' I've dreamed for years, months, weeks, days, and minutes that I carried you off in a coach drawn by six white horses to a place far away from civilization—just you and me. I…I…didn't have to share you with anyone, and you just sang and I made sweet…ahh…love to you over and over and over again."

Rita cringed at the thought.

"Oh, baby, the moment has finally come. No-o-o Graham to rescue your heartbeats—only me. He is a greedy fool. Had the best woman this side of the Mississippi all those years. He loses her to death, and he thinks he can just pick up where he left off…picking new fruit from the vine like he had the number-one draft pick. I hate him for that. You know, I loved Amanda, too. Sick, huh? She wouldn't give in to me, though, and she never told Graham what I had tried to do to her. She loved him too much."

A frown streaked Rita's face. Her mouth turned up at the corners in disgust. "My God, what kind of animal are you? Graham is your best friend for goodness' sakes. How on earth could you violate his love and trust? He talks about you as if you were his brother—closer than a laminated piece of paper. You disgust me. Take your hands off of me."

"Be still, little one." Rita cringed as Charlie attempted to rub her arm. "Don't be afraid. You're…you're sooo beautiful."

Charlie's words were again slurring and his eyelids seemed heavy. Rita raised her right leg and plowed her knee into his stomach. Charlie heaved and let out a small scream. Rita headed for the door, but in her haste, the fringe from her wrap caught onto a piece of metal strip on the armoire that held the TV. Rita tried to jerk it off, but decided to throw the wrap from her body. But Charlie was right on her heels by the time she reached for the doorknob.

Charlie pulled Rita to him and tried to force a kiss. Rita fought back. This infuriated Charlie, but Rita was not about to give in to the advances of this monster. Her nails became pointed spears and lodged an attack on Charlie's face. Then Charlie picked Rita up and took her into her bedroom and threw her on the bed, but not before she hit the wall. A small amount of blood began to ooze from over her eyebrow. Rita pulled the comforter from the bed and wrapped herself in it, thwarting off any further blows. But Charlie was like a wild man in a hellified stupor, and he fought the she-lion tooth and nail.

There was a knock at the door. No one answered the incessant knocking. Charlie pulled a lamp from the dresser and smashed it on the floor while Rita cowered in a corner. From the corner of her eye, Rita saw Charlie stop. He looked in her direction, wiped his face, and walked briskly toward her and yelled, "I love you, Rita. I love you, Rita."

And one moment Charlie was yelling *I love you, Rita*. And in the next, there was an eerie calm, then a loud thud after Charlie fell backward from a blow sustained by a vase to the base of his skull. Rita stared wide-eyed as her vision blurred and cleared. William was standing before her, offering his hand. She dabbed at the small amount of blood that trickled from over her eyebrow and mouth, mixed with snot and tears. William was a sight for sore eyes.

"You all right?" William asked.

"Yeah, just scared as hell." Rita looked at the clump on the floor and covered her mouth with her hand. "What about him? Is he dead?"

"I don't think so. Let me check his pulse."

William kneeled down and checked Charlie's pulse. It was faint but there was one. "Don't move," William said to Rita. "I'm going to call 9-1-1."

"Thanks, William. I mean that."

♪♪♪

William smiled, then looked away. It occurred to him that Rita had suffered enough. She deserved some happiness in her life. Who was he to disrupt what she so truly deserved? When he had the chance, he failed her. And now he wanted back in her life only to use her.

Just like that, he finally saw her for what she really was…a priceless gem. She was more precious than rubies and diamonds, silver and gold. Rita was a portrait of a virtuous woman—a woman made to love and be loved. And yes, William still loved her. He pushed the three numbers on the keypad.

"Nine-one-one, may I help you?"

CHAPTER 57

The ambulance arrived waking everyone within a four-mile radius. The paramedics appeared sleepy and lethargic. Two heavy-set white males, one tall and one short, and a tall, red-haired lanky woman with a gurney rushed past William into the interior of the apartment. Rita was guarding the doorway to the bedroom and the paramedics looked from one to the other in a confused state. It was easy to see that Rita was a victim of some type of domestic dispute—her hair matted, dress wrinkled and tossed, and dry blood caked over her eye, but she didn't seem to be the victim that required their immediate services.

"Are you all right, ma'am?" the tall woman asked.

"Yes, I'll be okay. But…but…but him…"

Rita raised an arm and pointed in slow motion to a corner of the room. The trio followed the direction of Rita's pointed finger and spotted a large body lying on the floor. They raced to the corner and the taller of the two males dropped to the floor to check Charlie's vitals.

"He's breathing," the tall paramedic said. "Sammy, take his vitals."

The tall, lanky woman turned to Rita once more—her red hair swinging with her movement. "I need some information. Can you tell me what happened here?"

Rita rocked back and forth where she stood. She turned her head in William's direction, the tall lady following her gaze, and slowly brought it back to meet the woman's eyes.

"He…he was stalking me, and he came out of nowhere when I tried to open my door. He pushed me in the room and..." Rita began to sob. At first, they were soft sobs, but her body shook as the full magnitude of what had transpired became real. William came and stood by Rita's side and put his arm around her shoulders.

"Were you here, sir, did you see what happened?" the tall lady asked, turning her attention to William.

"I came to see Rita...Ms. Long, about fifteen minutes ago. I kept knocking on the door, but no one answered. I could hear noises...loud talking. The tone of the man seemed hostile." William became animated, his dreads crawling about his face with his movement. "The door was slightly opened, and I pushed and came on in. The voices were louder, and from what the man was saying, I knew Rita was in trouble. I rushed to where I heard the voices..."

"In the bedroom?" the lady asked.

"Yes, the bedroom. He..."

"By 'he' you mean the victim lying on the floor," the lady interrupted once more.

"Yes, that he," William said sarcastically. "He was trying to thrust himself on Rita, and...and I picked up a vase and hit him on the head from behind. I only wanted to get him away from Rita."

"And how are you related to Rita...Ms. Long?"

"I'm her ex-husband."

"Thank you, Mr. Long?"

"Yes, I'm Mr. Long."

"Thank you. The police should be here any second."

William nodded.

"Ms. Long, it might be a good idea if you go to the hospital and let them check you out."

"He threw me into the wall, and my back aches."

"Like I said, you need to get that checked out."

The red-haired woman looked around the room with a puzzled look on her face. "Ms. Long, are you acquainted with the intruder? Why would he be stalking you?"

Rita frowned. "If I knew he was stalking me, don't you think I would have called the police? And why are you asking all these questions? You're just a paramedic. So do your job."

"It's all right, Rita," William cut in, frustration in his voice. "Lady, my ex-wife has been through an ordeal." Rita looked quickly at William with a scowl on her face and turned her head quickly away. Ignoring Rita, William continued. "The man's name is Charlie Ford."

"How do you know Charlie?" Rita stammered, her eyebrows bunched in little clouds.

"Does he have next-of-kin?" the redhead asked.

"We'll wait for the police," Rita declared.

"Rita!" William sighed.

"I'm not sure, but he has a best friend who I'm sure would know." Rita dropped her head, then raised it, looking from William to the paramedic. "His name is Graham Peters. I'll call him from the hospital."

"Thanks, Ma'am."

Knock, knock, knock.

"It must be the police," Rita said.

She walked the two paces to the front door and opened it. Two black policemen stood at the door.

"Hey, Gladys. What we got here?" one of the policemen asked.

The redheaded lady gave him her account.

"Okay, Gladys," yelled the tall, heavy-set paramedic. "We're ready to roll. Sammy, you take the lead. Folks, we're taking this fellow to Kaiser."

Rita and William watched as the paramedics rolled Charlie from the apartment.

"Got to be more careful, Ms. Long. Just spoke to the paramedics, but I need to get both of your stories."

"What's up with that lady paramedic?" William asked. "She acted as if she was the police."

"She's trying to get into the Academy. Wants to right the world. I'm Detective Bell and over there is Sgt. Lenny Smith or Smitty. Let me get your account of the story."

William and Rita repeated their stories for the policeman who made notes, took measurements in the bedroom, and took pieces of the broken lamp. They dusted for fingerprints and took several photographs.

"Please fill these forms out. And by the way, Ms. Long, here's an extra blank report form. Would you autograph it for me?"

"I'd be honored."

"Mr. Long, I'll ask that you not leave the city. The victim may press charges against you. Also, the police may need you for further questioning."

"All right."

The policeman looked at his notes and back up at William. "You're not William Long who used to play for the Lakers back in the day?"

William chuckled. There was a time when he couldn't produce a chuckle about his short stint in the NBA and why he was not sitting in the Hall of Fame. But he smiled, and said, "Yes, old, washed-up William Long."

"Man, you were bad. If you hadn't had the leg injury, you would have had a record that Magic or Michael Jordan couldn't touch. Give me five. And while you're at it, would you give me an autograph? I have another blank report form in my car. Smitty, go and get it for me."

"I'm going to get one for me, too," Smitty said.

The officer and the former NBA star slapped five while Rita stood off in a corner and contemplated what she would tell Graham. It was do or die because everything was getting ready to come out in the wash.

♪♪♪

"Some night," William said, letting out a sigh.

"Yeah. Who would have thought it would turn out like this?"

"Maybe…maybe if I had come just a few minutes earlier."

"Then what? It would have been you instead of Charlie except Charlie was drunk and not in his right senses."

"What are trying to say, Rita?"

"Not that I don't appreciate you being here at that moment, God knows I'm thankful, but why were you here, William? I thought I made myself perfectly clear that you were no longer a part of my life. And that stunt you pulled tonight at the Hole."

"Seems you were the one that made an ass of yourself."

"Hold it. Don't you even…"

"Not now, Rita. I'm sorry. I was wrong."

CHAPTER 58

Rita checked on Charlie. He was still in emergency waiting to be wheeled to a room. The doctors had to sew twenty stitches in the back of his head. Between the pain and the withdrawal from his bottle guzzling high, Charlie would thank the Lord that Kaiser Permanente Hospital was his home for the next couple of days. If he had to depend on anyone else, he would probably be out of luck.

William stayed at Rita's side during her check-up. The doctor examined her bruises and cuts and determined that a little bedrest and a cold compress should be her friend for the next day or so. Rita's body ached from her tussle with Charlie, and she trembled slightly from nerves.

She had to call Graham, and she had to muster all the courage inside of her to do it. Sunrise was only a short hour away, and before long he would be heading this way to see Martha.

"I think you better go, William. I'll talk with you later. I really need to talk with Graham alone."

"I don't think that's a good idea, Rita. You don't need to be by yourself."

"I think it will be better this way."

"What are you going to say when he asks you where I am? You're going to have to tell him what happened. I know if it were me, I would be mad as hell. I'd think you had something to hide, and I don't think I'd be able to trust you."

"You are a work of art, William. You kicked me to the curb when I needed you most, and now that my heart has healed, you have the audacity to show up twenty years later with some fly-by-night, gonna-make-me-a-star scheme to benefit your sorry-ass pockets, pretending that you love me when you don't know the first thing about love."

"But I do love you, Rita."

Rita pushed William lightly on the chest. "Don't do this, William. I love Graham. I'd marry him if he asked."

William turned his head and stared off in another direction. He couldn't look at Rita, because he hurt like she must have hurt when he rejected her love. "I'm going to wait, if you don't mind. It will be for the best."

Rita was quiet. She couldn't make William leave, and he was probably right. But she knew that Graham would not appreciate what she would tell him despite her love for him.

♪♪♪

Nothing like a good night's sleep, Graham thought, as he yawned and stretched his arms high above his head. The bed felt so comfortable that he hit the snooze button one more time.

Rita had consumed his dreams, and he couldn't wait to see her. He had not seen her since Thanksgiving Day and that was a blur. Passionate kisses covered his queen in his dreams—so real that he could almost taste her cologne on his tongue. Rita embodied everything he liked in a woman, and though she and Amanda were two different people, there were many similar qualities that endeared Graham to them both.

Graham didn't wait for the next wake-up call. He sprang from the bed as if it was on fire—flames licking at his heels and hurried to the bathroom. His reflection nodded back at him while his toothbrush moved east and west across his teeth in a cloud of toothpaste. Next he turned on the water to take a shower, quickly drawing his hand back after touching the very hot water. He adjusted the water and began to take his shower, whistling as the water cascaded over his body blazing trails through the thick ashen forest that covered his chest. Graham flexed his muscles, grinning with thoughts of what he was going to do to Rita.

He felt refreshed and in a good mood. After a short visit with Martha today, he was going to take his baby out to lunch, love her up, take her out to dinner, love her up some more, and enjoy whatever else the evening held in store for them. He scrubbed, whistled, and smiled at what his day was about to bring.

Graham opened the door to the bathroom and a large vapor of steam escaped. He hurried to his bedroom and rummaged around in his chest of drawers for underwear. He pulled out a pair of boxer shorts and a thin, scoop-neck T-shirt.

There was a slight chill in the room, and Graham shook his body to chase the cold away. He found the remote and turned the television on. Oddly enough, a commercial was on advertising boxer shorts, and a crazy guy was dancing in his shorts, telling the world how free he felt in them.

This tickled Graham. He laughed aloud and mimicked the guy on the television screen and began to writhe around the room as if he were in pain. He hopped on one foot and then the other, raising his hands in the air like he was climbing a ladder. He looked much like the dancing baby that flooded computer screens when graphics first emerged as small video clips.

Lost in his crazy antics, Graham suddenly jerked his head to the right when the phone rang, bringing him out of his reverie. He rushed to the phone, almost tripping over his shorts that he had dropped on the floor. Trying to take control of his breathing, he took a deep breath and answered the phone.

"Hello," Graham said, out of breath but in a rather sexy voice.

"Graham, is that you?"

"Well, what other man would be answering my phone like that?"

"I...I...you didn't sound like yourself."

"Well, I rushed to the phone hoping it was you. I've been having nothing but sweet dreams about you, baby."

"That's wonderful, baby," Rita said in a non-committal voice.

"What's up, where are you? Are you all right? You don't sound like yourself."

"I'm okay. I'm at Kaiser Hospital."

"What's wrong? Is it Martha? Please, God, don't tell me something has happened to Martha."

"Calm down, Graham. Martha is resting fine. I checked on her a few minutes ago."

"Well, what are you doing at the hospital?"

"It's…it's Charlie."

"Charlie? What about Charlie?"

"He's in the hospital. He had an accident. You better get down here as soon as you can."

Graham was silent. He had heard Rita correctly. Charlie was in the hospital, and it might be his fault. He'd never forgive himself if something happened to Charlie, no matter how angry he was with him.

"I'm putting my clothes on now. I'll be right there. How is he?"

"He's going to live."

"I'll be there in a few minutes."

"Hurry." And the line was dead.

CHAPTER 59

Pacing the floor, Rita held her head in the palms of her hands. She periodically rubbed her temples to relieve the pressure. Walking was the only thing she could do. If she sat down, her nerves would become more unraveled than they already were.

What would she tell Graham? And then there was William sitting over in a corner refusing to go home. She had to tell Graham the truth no matter the consequences. And she would not be able to put it off another minute.

Rita looked up at the sound of footsteps. Graham rushed toward her, a jacket dangling from his arm. He embraced Rita when he got near, kissed her tenderly on the mouth and held her again—glad to see her. Graham pulled back and noticed the small cut over her eye and examined it a moment before he spoke. He brushed her hair away from her eye and noticed her hair was somewhat matted. A puzzled look came over him, but he didn't say a word.

"Where's Charlie? What happened to him? What happened to you?"

Rita flinched, not sure what to say first. Surveying the room, Graham noticed a man who seemed quite familiar staring in their direction. The man wore dreads that snaked across his head with a free-fall to his shoulders.

"Let's go sit down over there, Graham," Rita said, pointing her finger at the cluster of chairs that comprised the waiting room.

Graham looked at Rita thoughtfully and then followed as she led him to a row of seats. He looked up and saw the same guy watching them—his eyes passing back and forth between he and Rita as if observing a ping-pong tournament. It was unnerving, and it was getting the best of Graham.

Still standing, Graham moved close to Rita's ear and whispered. "There's a guy watching us."

"Where?" Rita asked.

"The guy sitting in the corner. Don't turn your head right away because he'll know we're talking about him. His face is familiar, but I can't place it."

"Sit down, Graham."

Graham continued to stand, his eyebrows arched and his mouth turned downward. He reached out and touched Rita's elbow, and she turned to face him. "What is it, Rita? What is it you're not telling me? Where's Charlie and how does he figure in this?"

"Sit down, Graham. Please sit down."

Graham searched Rita's face and let out a sigh. He relented and sat down, throwing his jacket on the back of the chair.

It was hard to look into his face, and she avoided that as long as she could. Graham's patience was growing thin. Rita could tell by the way his eyes became slanted and his jaw line moved up and down. She looked up and stared into his waiting eyes.

"Charlie attacked me last night."

Graham's mouth flew open, and his breathing became labored. He jumped from his seat and jabbed at his temples with the points of his fingers. He sat back down and looked into Rita's pleading eyes.

"Charlie attacked you? When? Where? Oh…it's my fault. It's my fault." He reached over and held Rita. "You could have been hurt and I wasn't there to protect you."

"It's not your fault, baby," Rita said, pushing him back a little to keep from being smothered.

"It is my fault. Yesterday Charlie told me something that disturbed me about Amanda."

Rita's eyes became wide as saucers.

"We said some terrible things to each other, and I threw him out of my house. I knew he had been drinking, and I still let him get behind the wheel of his car and drive away while secretly hoping something bad would happen to him. He went over to Mary's house and tried to take advantage of her. She was frightened but he must have come to his senses and left. She called looking for you. That's why I called you at The Water Hole yesterday to see if you were all right."

"But why would Mary be looking for me?"

"Seems Charlie may have called out your name while he… I was so stupid to let him go out by himself all liquored up. I don't believe this."

Graham paused and turned his head slightly to the left, catching a glimpse of the man in the corner. "And that guy is still looking at us."

Rita kneaded Graham's fingers. The right words were not coming, and she could feel her pressure rising. She fidgeted in her seat, and finally looked in Graham's eyes—eyes that were sorry…sorry for not protecting her when she needed him most. He held her hands tight not wanting to let go.

"Tell me what happened, Rita. How did it happen? Where? And how did Charlie end up in the hospital?"

Looking away and then back at Graham, Rita began to recount her story, promising herself not to leave out any details. She mashed her lips together and let out a little sigh. She needed all the courage she could muster.

"I was coming home from the club…" Still holding Rita's hands, Graham looked at her and noticed for the first time that she was still wearing her clothes from last evening. "…I was unlocking my door when someone came from behind and opened the door and pushed me in. It was Charlie." Rita stopped and watched Graham's face—eyes flat, not moving, almost fixed like he was dead. The muscles in his arms began to flex—thick veins protruding along the length of them. Graham looked straight ahead as Rita continued her story.

"He," Rita began, "he tried to kiss me. We fought and he picked me up and threw me up against a wall. He was ranting and raving and saying he loved me."

"Stop! I don't want to hear any more." Graham jumped up from his seat and started pacing back and forth and in circles. His fists were clenched and he gritted his teeth, occasionally hitting one fist into the palm of the other hand. After a minute or two, he sat back down, reached for Rita's hands, and held them.

"You've been through a lot, baby. I'm sorry I wasn't there for you. But what happened to Charlie and why is he in the hospital?"

Before Rita could respond, William got up from his seat and headed in their direction.

"That guy is coming toward us," Graham said, catching a glimpse of William in his peripheral vision. "Who is he?"

Rita caught her breath. In a voice that was barely audible, Rita said, "He's my ex-husband. He's the one who saved me."

Graham released her hands.

"Please let me finish. If it hadn't been for William showing up when he did, I don't know what would have happened. I don't know if I could have stood up to a drunken Charlie. William found my door open, heard the noise, saw the commotion, picked up a vase and hit Charlie on the back of the head."

Words were lost on Graham. He jumped up from his seat in disgust. "Your ex...ex-husband, your ex-husband? You're telling me that your ex-husband just happened to stop by to see you at two or three in the morning?" Graham's lip began to quiver and his nostrils were flaring like a raging bull. Both hands went into the air, his fingers pointed straight— then he raised and lowered them as he tried to get his point across. "And what was your ex-husband doing at your apartment that time of morning? That's what I'd like to know."

Before Graham could turn around, William was upon them. William extended his hand. "I'm William Long."

A distorted frown was etched across Graham's face. He looked at William, surveyed his face, glanced down at his outstretched hand, rolled his eyes around in their sockets and let them rest on Rita. "What room did you say Charlie was in?"

Graham grabbed his jacket from the chair and walked away before Rita could answer, leaving the two demons to their own devices. His haste left a dust cloud, and the inseams of Graham's pants rubbed together, creating a noisy and thrashy beat, like a cricket's mating call.

Rita hugged her chest and shook her head. He hadn't given her a chance to explain.

CHAPTER 60

Where he was walking didn't matter at the moment. He had to distance himself from Rita. Life had a way of punishing you for your sins, and he hated to think that his girls had been right about Rita all along. Just to think that he was ready to commit heart and soul to her. Now it turned out that she was seeing her ex-husband on the sly. *The Bible says that your evil doing will come to the light*, he thought.

At that moment Graham was ashamed...ashamed that he had let his family and church down. He was ashamed because it hadn't been two months since Amanda was buried that he was burying his sorrows in another woman's bosom. He was ashamed because he fought his daughters on principle—it was his life and he was going to live it as he saw fit. He had been insensitive to Deborah's and Liz's feelings about the loss of their mother.

To think Rita pretended to be innocent in front of his in-laws! They could have denounced Rita and Graham, too, but Martha took up for him at a public church meeting and let Sister Mary Ross have it. Graham smiled at that thought. He would have given anything to see that moment.

Realizing that he had been walking in circles, Graham saw the information desk and asked for Charlie's room number. Graham hunched his shoulders when he got near the room, trying to push the dread out of his mind. When he came upon the door to Charlie's room, he hesitated, looked at the card on the door with Charlie's name on it, and pushed it open.

Graham had hoped Charlie would not be awake, but there he was in the hospital bed with a large bandage on the back of his head. He looked like a mummy wrapped up in all of those white blankets, propped up watching television. Charlie the mummy turned the volume down when Graham approached the bed.

They stared at each other for a moment. Charlie motioned for Graham to sit in a chair beside the bed. Graham plopped down in it, smirked and looked up at Charlie.

"Why?"

"I'm a miserable old man. I can't do anything right. I've lost my best friend." Charlie hesitated and started again when Graham didn't say anything. "I've made some terrible mistakes in my life…and some that I'm not too proud of. If I could erase the slate clean, I would this very minute. If I had life to do all over again, I would be a different person. But I can't, we only get that one chance at life, and I've blown it. I can only ask those who I've committed an injustice against for forgiveness.

"There's some things about me, Graham, you may never know. I want you to know that you've been the best friend a guy could ever have." Charlie paused and looked in Graham's direction. "You were the brother I never had. We were tight. We did everything together. I could always count on you. You and Amanda treated me like one of the family. I am your girls' godfather, and I love them so much. I love you, too, buddy." Charlie tried to smile. "And I hope you will forgive me. I know I don't deserve your forgiveness, but all the same, I'm asking."

Silence was more painful than the twenty-one stitches that ran around the base of Charlie's head. He could hear Graham shuffling in his seat, his feet sliding occasionally across the floor, but no words to provide relief seemed forthcoming.

Graham looked down at the floor, taking in all that Charlie had said. It wasn't going to change anything. Charlie had made his bed and he was going to have to lie in it. Graham wanted a reasonable answer for Charlie's misdeeds, and he wanted to understand how and when he had become the despicable person that he now was.

"You don't have to say anything," Charlie said, sensing Graham's reluctance. "Maybe someday we can…"

"Why, Charlie? Why Amanda and Rita? Can you answer that for me?"

"I don't know, Graham. Maybe I was jealous because life seemed to favor you instead of me. Maybe I felt cheated."

"You had every opportunity that I had," Graham interrupted. "You came from a loving home. You did all right in school. All the women loved you. You had your pick of the litter. I settled down, but you didn't. I joined the church, you preferred the night life. I got married and settled down. You got married and divorced. But through it all, I was always there for you... like a brother.

"Our home...was open to you. And there's no excuse on this earth for you to violate my trust, violate the only two women that I've ever loved."

"I'll agree with you on most of what you said, but I'd rather not talk about this anymore. If you don't mind, I would like for you to do me a favor. I'll be in the hospital for at least another day or two—mainly for observation. Would you go by the house and get some things for me? I'll need my insurance information; I'll tell you where to find it. I'd appreciate it very much if you would do this for me."

"No problem." Graham looked up at Charlie and smiled. "I thought back to the day you nearly kicked my door down and told me to take a bath and get my act together or you were going to call the police on me."

Charlie smiled. "It took a lot to get through to you, but you did. And the next day you saw Rita."

Graham's smile disappeared from his face. "I'll get your things. I have your spare key on my key ring. I'm going to go and see Martha first, then head out to your place. I'll be back in a little while."

Graham stood up to leave.

"Thanks, man. I hope you can find it in your heart to forgive me. I'll wait."

Graham nodded his head and left the room. He had committed to all that he was going to commit to for one day. He headed toward Martha's room.

♪♪♪

Martha and Charlie were on the same floor—Martha on the east wing, Charlie on the west wing. Graham walked slowly allowing the morning's events to seep in. He had never been so disappointed in all his life, and now there was no one he trusted or could go to and vent his frustrations.

As he approached Martha's room, he tried to put on a happy face. The last thing he wanted to do was upset Martha and get her blood pressure boiling. He would handle the situation with Rita. It was better that he found out about her now rather than later.

A great big smile met Graham when he opened the door. Martha was eating the last bit of her lunch and offered to share.

"No, you eat. Umm, mashed potatoes and meat loaf."

"It was delicious. Not as good as mine, but good all the same. Did you come by yourself?"

"Yes, Charlie's in the hospital."

"Oh my word. What happened to him?"

"It's a long story."

"Well, I've got time. Sit in that chair and let me have it. They say my heart is as good as new. With a little exercise and better eating habits, I'll be fine."

Graham sat in the chair and laid his jacket across the back. He looked at Martha and then at the floor and decided he needed to talk. Forty-five minutes later, Martha looked at Graham.

"I want you to listen to me and listen good. Rita is a good girl. No matter what you've just told me, I like her very much…in fact I love that one."

Graham began to protest.

"Hush. I said my heart was in good condition, but it doesn't need any undue stress. Do you remember Thanksgiving Day?"

Graham nodded his head.

"After all the festivities, Rita and I had gone off by ourselves—to my room. I took out a trunk and showed her some of Amanda's things. That's when she confided in me about her ex-husband who has been trying to extort money from her. She believes that he has been following the two of you. He had no contact with Rita for years, and somehow he ended up in Oakland…and of all places, that club called The Water Hole. He must have seen the two of you together and hatched some scheme to get to Rita."

"Rita confided all of this to you? Why couldn't she have come to me?"

"She wanted to, baby. Scared was the word. She was afraid of what you might think, especially since all of the commotion with the girls. She was trying to handle it all by herself, but the more she did, the more motivated that scoundrel became. That's what we were talking about when I had my heart attack."

Lowering his eyes, Graham began to shake his head back and forth.

"No time for that, son. You need to get up from here and find that girl. Don't let her out of your sight. She loves you so much and would never intentionally hurt you."

"Did you give her a chance to explain?" Martha shook her head. "Figures. She's been through a traumatic experience from what you told me. Men just don't know how to get it right. You don't think. At the first sign of trouble, you go running off with your tail between your legs."

The bulge in Graham's eyes didn't get past Martha.

"Yes, that's what I said."

And they laughed. *The wisdom of this woman*, Graham thought.

"You're right, Mom. I've got to find Rita. Maybe *I'll* get a chance to save her."

"Well, get on. You're wasting time."

Graham kissed Martha and headed for the door, running into Reverend Fields on his way out.

"Hi ya, Graham. How's Sister Martha today?"

"Good, Reverend. She's absolutely amazing. You better watch out, she might have a good word for you."

"Heh, heh, heh." The Reverend smiled. "Now where's that pretty young filly you had over to the sister and deacon's house the other night? You need to bring her to church. We need us a songbird like that in our choir... and she don't look bad, either."

"I'm on my way to find her right now, Reverend. Reverend Fields, there's someone else in the hospital I'd like for you to stop by and see—Charlie."

"I sho' will, Brother Peters. Just write down his room number and I'll make sure I stop by on my way out."

"Charlie will appreciate it. Now good day. I'll bring Dad by later on," he added, looking in Mom's direction.

"All right, baby. Just go and take care of business, now."

A big smile covered Graham's face. After leaving Reverend Fields the number to Charlie's room, he practically ran back to where he had left Rita and William. There was no trace of them. Graham walked the corridors and after not finding them, went to the nurses' station to inquire about their whereabouts. The nurse at the window looked at him with a silly grin on her face and hunched her shoulders like, *How am I supposed to know where they went?*

There was no need to waste any more time there. The obvious place to look was at her apartment. He would go and pick the few items up at Charlie's first and then go to Rita's. The thought that William might be with her hastened Graham's resolve to find her as soon as possible.

CHAPTER 61

It was a warm day in December. Twenty-five more days until Christmas. In another few short months, a year would have passed, marking the first anniversary of Amanda's death. Graham shook the thought from his mind and tried to replace it with something more upbeat.

Graham could see the tail end of his Buick Regal in the parking lot. It desperately needed a bath. There was nothing worse than driving around in a dusty, dirty, black car. Graham had been under the weather with being out in the night air so much—seeing after Martha and making sure Dad was all right. He would take it to a car wash before he drove to Rita's. He couldn't have his baby sitting up in a dirty car.

Signs of Christmas were everywhere. Lampposts were decorated with Christmas lights and garland and billboards advertising the hot-pick item for Christmas loomed from every corner.

Graham drove on until he got to Charlie's street. He hooked a sharp left and two rights before he came upon what Charlie called his one-room bungalow. It was a small, two-bedroom starter house that was built in the early sixties. Charlie led an easy life and purchasing anything beyond this modest A-frame house would have been a waste.

Although in need of a little paint, the mint-green stucco house had stood unceremoniously at attention for the past thirty-eight years and had served Charlie well. If the walls could talk, there would be enough volumes to fill the Library of Congress. A stray cat walked lazily across the lawn, a local homesteader without exemptions and looking for the few morsels Charlie took the liberty to leave it every now and then.

Graham got out of the car and used his key to get in. It was neat inside—everything placed just so and not a dish left in the sink or dishwasher. The blinds in the house were partially open and a fourth of a bottle of Chivas sat on the kitchen table next to an empty glass.

The mere sight of the liquor got Graham's adrenaline going. He tapped lightly on the table until the drumming became loud enough to hear next door. Graham picked up the bottle and threw it across the room, hitting the stove and finally crashing to the floor. And the glass was next. Now Graham had a mess to clean up, but it made him feel better.

He cleaned up his mess and walked into the living room. There were pictures of his family...Amanda, Deborah, Liz, Martha, Elroy, Graham. Not just one but dozens. There was a picture of Uncle Roc. He was a good man but died too early from drinking and women.

Graham was done sightseeing. He was ready to get out of the house. The bedroom was next to the kitchen and Graham went about retrieving the items Charlie wanted.

More pictures cluttered the dresser top, and once again, they were pictures of Graham's family. He opened the top left drawer as instructed and thumbed through the papers until he found what looked like Charlie's insurance information. Just under it was Charlie's birth certificate.

Graham pulled the birth certificate from between the other papers and brought it out into the light so he could read it. He began to read and stopped short, not believing what was printed on the certificate. He coughed, then grabbed at his chest, bracing at the revelation that promised to change people's lives once again. Mother: Eula Mae Perry Father: Harvey Ford. Mother: Eula Mae Perry. Mother: Eula Mae Perry. His mother's name was Eula Mae Perry Peters.

Graham sat on the floor and began to cry out loud. "He's my damn brother. He wanted me to find this. Ohhh, God. All this time and he didn't say a word, not one freakin' word. Kept it all bottled up inside until one day the cork could no longer contain its contents. And the anger and rage pours out, venting hostilities where it might hurt me the most. I'll be damned," he said, the paper in his hands now crumpled. "But now I understand."

The front of his shirt was wet. Graham sighed and looked once again at the piece of paper that was more than sixty years old. He held it there, staring at the name of his mother unable to take his eyes away. Why had he not been told? More tears like raindrops fell. He wasn't sure whether he should be mad at his mother or Charlie.

He remained in a heap on the floor another fifteen minutes. Slowly lifting himself to an upright position, Graham tucked the piece of paper back in the drawer but not before taking a last photographic picture of the text. He developed the image in his mind and ran it through the rinse until he could see all parts clearly. "EULA MAE PERRY" blinked at him like a yellow traffic light, warning him not to go there or at least proceed with caution.

Turning toward the nightstand, Graham picked up the telephone and began to dial out. He wasn't sure he remembered the number—it had been quite some time since he used it last. But as his fingers tickled the illuminated buttons, the numbers quickly came to him, and he drummed them out on the phone pad.

"Hello," said the tiny, feeble voice.

"Aunt Rubye?"

"Yes. Ya gonna have ta speak up so I can hear you."

"Aunt Rubye, this is your nephew, Graham Peters."

"Who?"

"GRAHAM," he shouted.

"You mean Eula Mae's boy?"

"Yes, auntie."

"My, my, my. It's been a long time since I heard ya voice. Yo sisters told me Amanda died. Lord, so much happening in deh world. How ya doin'?"

"Fine, doing just fine. Look, Aunt Rubye, I need to ask you a question about something that happened a long time ago. I hope you can remember. It would be very important to me if you could."

"Now, I hope I can too, son." A high-pitched cackle came from somewhere deep in Aunt Rubye's nostrils. "I don't 'member too much these days."

"It's about my momma, your sister."

"Oh, I see."

"This is hard for me, but I guess I'll just come out and ask. Did Momma have another child before me? A baby boy?"

There was a long silence. Graham wasn't sure if Aunt Rubye had been caught up in the rapture or the cat had her tongue.

"Are you still there, Aunt Rubye?"

"Yes, dear. I…I'm still here. Now what you knowed about Eula Mae havin' a baby boy?"

"Remember my best friend, Charlie?"

"Yeah, it's been so many years ago. But, I 'member that tall, slick-talkin' fella that couldn't keep his hands off the gals and kept you in trouble."

"We've been best friends, Aunt Rubye, since we were in junior high school. Well, he's sick and in the hospital. He asked me to pick up some records from his house, and in doing so, I stumbled upon his birth certificate. Imagine seeing Momma's name on his birth certificate—Eula Mae Perry; place of birth: St. Louis, Missouri; hospital: Parklane General. And all of this a year before I was born in the same city, in the same hospital, to a woman with the same name. Uncanny?"

"Un-who?"

"That's all right, Aunt Rubye. I just need to know if you know something."

"Well, since ya put it like dat…yo momma was pregnant by this good-looking fella named Harvey. Harvey Ford was his name. I see 'em clear as a crystal bell. He staid after yo momma, and she kept runnin', but finally, she gave in…just one time was alllllllll it took. She tolt me, but we couldn't tell Momma or Poppa what she'd done. See back in those days, you couldna say stuff like *my baby's daddy this or that*, shoot yu's better not say yu's was pregnant. That broke a family apart back then. Sho' did. But we had to tell Momma 'cuz she'd keep up with 'r' cycle and all. Yes, she did. Knowed it better than we did. We told Momma and Momma told Eula that she would have to put that baby up for 'doption. First, she had to go live with Aunt Frankie and Uncle Jasper. Tore Eula Mae's heart up to have to give dat baby up, but there was no way 'round Momma and Poppa, and we were sworn to secrecy."

"Did Momma ever try and find her baby…or even care what happened to him?"

"Now, watch yo mouth boy. It weren't yo momma's decision to give up dat baby. She had to do what Momma and Poppa told her to do or there would be conse…consequinses…you knowed what I'm tryna say. Anyway, I believe Eula Mae knowed who had her baby. Momma and Poppa make the 'rangements, you see. It was someone twice removed from the family but could keep a secret. Me and Eula didn't talk about it much, 'specially after she married yo daddy. A shame…I hope that boy fared well. I knowed it hurt Eula to her grave that she didn't get to love and care for that baby like she did you and yo sisters."

"Well, Aunt Rubye, I think you've answered most of my questions. I only wish I had known that I had a biological brother—maybe some things would have been different between me and Charlie. In my heart of hearts, I believe Charlie resented me some, but he never let on until it was too much for him. Well, I thank you, Aunt Rubye."

"Dat all right, son. Maybe Eula Mae can finally rest in peace. Now, when yu's coming home? Whens the last time you come home? Better not let me die and I ain't looked on your face 'fore I go. I'll come back to haunt you, boy."

For the first time that afternoon, the phone felt light. Graham let out a small giggle and Aunt Rubye let out a high-pitched cackle. A smile radiated across Graham's face.

"How about I come home for Christmas? I'll contact my sisters, and we can all enjoy the holiday together."

"Yu's better not mess up. I'll be waiting for you 'cause we gonna have Christmas St. Louis style. Love ya, boy."

"I love you, too, Aunt Rubye." Graham hung up the phone, retrieved Charlie's belongings, and headed for Rita's. He needed her more than ever.

CHAPTER 62

Adrenaline flowed in heavy doses through Graham's veins. He pulled away from the curb in front of Charlie's house smoking at forty miles per hour. It would take approximately twenty-five minutes to get across town to get to Rita's.

The drive down E. Fourteenth Street was scenic—people loitering and hanging out in the streets like it was summertime. An occasional rumble from the Bart train as it tore through the middle of one of the busiest streets in Oakland caused few heads to look up as the train whizzed by on the rail. Graham squinted his eyes and shook the kink out of his neck before finally producing a smile. It had been a long day, although it was only early afternoon, but it was a day full of revelations that put so many misplaced puzzle pieces into perspective.

♪♪♪

Graham headed straight for Rita's. There was no evidence that anything happened earlier in the day—no crime scene tape or curious neighbors conducting their own investigation. Wobbly knees knocked together as Graham proceeded to Rita's door. *What if she didn't want to see him? What if she didn't give him a chance to explain, as he had not given her the opportunity?* Martha's voice boomed in his ear. *You need to get up from here and find that girl. Don't let her out of your sight.*

Graham folded his fingers over into his palm, exposing his knuckles. He rapped lightly on the door and waited. After a minute, he put his ear to the door, and not hearing anything, knocked harder. A few moments later, light filtered from inside as the door was cracked slightly. Rita peered from within the shadows—a portrait in charcoal on black canvas. A look of surprise was etched on her face.

"You have company?" Graham asked.

"No," was Rita's flat reply.

"May I come in?"

"If you like."

"I'd like that very much."

The charcoal still vanished when the room became illuminated with light as Graham passed through the threshold. Rita watched him as he passed in front of her—her face drawn tight and eyes downcast. Graham stood at her door and looked at the sight that lay before him.

Clothes were strewn neatly throughout the living room. Long gowns in garment bags hung on hangers that hung from several doors. Shoes of various styles and colors lined the floor several rows deep. The room gave the appearance that a brand-new store was getting ready to open—the owner making last-minute preparations for the big event.

Graham's eyes darted throughout the room. "What are you doing?" he asked with a frown on his face.

Rita went about what she was doing. She didn't look at Graham, still unsure why he had come.

"Packing. I'm going home." She looked up at Graham who stood in the middle of the room staring at her. "I'm going to tell Clyde today that I'm canceling the rest of our engagement."

"Have you told the band yet?"

"Not yet, but they'll understand. I need to lose this town." Rita paused and drew her lips back not sure she wanted to continue her thought. But she did. "There is one thing William was right about...I need to expand my horizons."

A frown appeared on Graham's face and his eyelids lowered when he looked at Rita. "Are you and William getting back together?"

Hands on her hips, Rita turned and looked at Graham. And with movements as fast as a stealth bomber, she was on him…up in his face, waving and pointing her index finger right between his eyes.

"I recall that not even two hours ago you walked out on me without giving me the benefit of an explanation. And now you stand at my door all meek and humble like you've lost your last friend, like you've suddenly realized the error of your ways. I don't understand your unpredictable moods and I'm not sure this relationship is worth the effort, although my heart is saying otherwise. You look at me in mock contemplation and ask whether or not William and I are getting back together. No, Graham, it has *never* been my intention to be with him." Rita threw her hands in the air out of frustration. "I have…sit down, sit down…let me explain this to you."

"I know, Rita, I know all about the extortion attempt. I know about the stalking."

"Who told you? Martha? Did Martha tell you?"

"Yes, Martha told me. She gave me a good lashing, too."

Graham reflected on that moment in Martha's hospital room. That wise old woman knew how to get his attention. He looked back into Rita's eyes, wanting to touch her hands, but thought better of it.

"I'm sorry, Rita. I'm so sorry. I'm sorry that I didn't take the time to listen—to understand what was going on." Graham took a deep breath. "So many things have been going on these past few days, and my mind has been in turmoil. Finding out that your ex-husband was in the neighborhood, that he was at your home that time of morning—me not knowing he was in town and that you had seen him, sent me in a tizzy. I'm not proud of the way I acted, but you don't know what I've been through these last few days."

"I don't blame you for being upset. It's what you did with the information when I gave it to you. So many days and nights I was plagued with when to tell you. Both my mother and Martha agreed that I needed to tell you."

"Your…"

"Shhhh…let me finish. I had hoped William would just go away. My mother knew all along that he was going to be the death of me. Even last night at The Water Hole, he tried to intimidate me, and I got darn near ugly, too. I'm sure that's why he showed up last night to explain.

"I want you to know, Graham, William is not a part of my life and hasn't been for the last twenty years. I believe he has finally grown up and come to realize some of the frailties of life. For sure, he finally realized Rita had taken the last of his crap." Rita got up from the couch, picked up a blouse, and began to fold it.

Watching her, Martha's words shot at him again like a two-edged sword. "Are you going to unpack your clothes now?"

"Why?" Sadness covered Rita's face as she continued to fold another piece and put it into a suitcase. "What happened to trust?"

Suddenly, Graham jumped up and was at Rita's side. She could feel his breath against her skin. He stood so close it made her tingle inside.

He kissed her neck, and a sigh escaped Rita's lips. "I love you. I love you, Rita Long. I don't want you to go. We have a lifetime of memories to make. I want to marry…" he paused, "marry you." Now he said it, and he could feel Rita's body become taut. "I was going to tell you today. I had planned to take you to lunch and a movie…movie and dinner…until this stuff about Charlie surfaced." Graham threw his hands in the air. "I was feeling so good when this day started out, and I thank God I have a chance to make this day right. Whew."

"Slow down, baby. You're all out of breath. Enough of that. What I want to know is did you just ask me to marry you? I mean…did I actually hear the words or was it my imagination?"

"I love you, Rita, and I want to marry you."

She hugged Graham and he put his arms around her. Their lips came together like cake and frosting until Graham pulled away.

"Baby, I've got something else to tell you…something I found out a little while ago."

Here goes, Rita thought as she stared back at Graham. She tried to hide her disappointment. It was like coming off a high too fast and bracing yourself for another painful episode.

"Charlie is my half-brother."

Rita let out a "How?" as the words seeped in. "Your what?"

"Yes, Charlie is my half-brother, and he's known a long time but never said a word." There was a long pause. "It's a little scary."

"Wow," was all Rita could say and sat down on the couch.

Graham sat down and continued. "He had me to go over to his house and pick up some things for him today, and I think he had hoped I would find that document. Well, I did, and when I saw my mother's... hmph...my mother's name," Graham sighed, "my mother's name on it, my heart jumped out of my chest. I didn't know what to think. All this time, and I didn't even know."

"Well, that explains some of his ranting and raving. It didn't make sense to me then, but this certainly explains some of it."

"That doesn't excuse Charlie's behavior. Charlie and I have a lot of talking to do, and it's going to take the Lord to get me through it." Graham rested his chin on the back of his hand. "You know, Charlie and I have got lots of memories—too many to count. From St. Louis to California. Back in the day, we were a team, the mack daddies of our day..."

"Yeah, right."

"We were. We were close as brothers could be without at least one of us knowing it. Maybe that's why he stayed so close. Hmph. What am I going to do? What are we going to do? The police are going to take him to jail."

"You're going to acknowledge your brother, forgive him, and work things out." Rita paused. "I'm not going to press charges. Charlie went over the edge, although I don't understand it. I don't want to see him, Graham, but he's going to understand that this is not over. What about Mary Ross?"

"I don't think we have to worry about Mary Ross saying anything. No wonder Martha is fond of you. You're just like her. Now, I want you to take those clothes out of that suitcase and grab your purse, because you're going with me. First, we're going to pick up Dad and take him to visit Martha. I'll have Deborah or Liz pick Dad up from the hospital. Then I need to see Charlie to iron out some things. Then, you and I have a date. We are going out to dinner, restaurant of your choice, and for dessert— well, how about back to my place?"

Rita couldn't contain her smile. "My baby is trying to take control of the situation. Listen to you...you're so cute and funny. Anywhere you want to go, my love."

"I want to be with the woman I love."

Rita's eyes glistened as she continued to listen to Graham. Graham sensed she was overcome by his humility. He stood several feet from her and then she moved toward him with her arms outstretched, intertwining her arms with his like a Gullah woman weaving her baskets.

"I love you, Graham Peters. I love you with all my heart, soul and mind. And, I want to be with you, forever."

♪♪♪

Drip, drip, drip. Charlie lay still on his back in the dimly lit room—the IV drip marking time. *Drip, drip, drip.*

Charlie gazed at the ceiling and crawled across with his eyes. He suddenly grabbed his stomach and squeezed, rolled his eyes upward, and began to shake. He felt cold all over and began to shiver. Vomit rose from his stomach into the mid-section of his throat and he pushed down on his chest to make it recede.

A door slammed, Charlie thought, his mind and body too weak to respond. He continued to squeeze his shivering and convulsing body, then opened his eyes slightly. With all the strength Charlie could muster, he sat up straight.

"It can't be!" a delirious Charlie wailed.

Before him stood Amanda all dressed in white. Her hair was flipped at the ends, and she peered at Charlie as if he were a child.

"Why, Charlie? I thought you learned your lesson years ago."

"Amanda...Amanda, is that you?"

"Charlie, why did you have to go and hurt Graham? I protected you from him all those years ago because you were like brothers. Didn't want to break up the family—yeah, I considered your pathetic little self as family—but you just couldn't leave well enough alone. You had to go and try and rape Mary and Rita. Why, when you had your pick of just about any woman in town? And if you had treated Ernestine halfway right, you would have known what true love was all about."

"Amanda, I don't know why I did all those things. I...I...guess I wanted what Graham had...a loving wife..."

"Don't go there, Charlie. You had a loving wife."

"You're right, I did have a loving wife. But you and Graham had the perfect family—two beautiful daughters, grandparents for your children, wonderful friends who adored you."

"You could have had that, too. But you must ask for forgiveness, Charlie. You must make amends with all of those people you have hurt along the way or you'll never find peace or happiness. You'll continue to be a dreary old man on your own island. It's time for you to stand up and be a man."

"I want to ask for their forgiveness, but it's so hard. Amanda...Amanda, where are you?" Charlie cried out. "Amanda! Please come back. I need you."

And Amanda was gone.

"Oh, God, what am I gonna do?" Charlie cried, his body shaking.

"You're going to ask for forgiveness," came another voice, "like I'm going to ask you for forgiveness."

"Momma, is that you? Why did you give me away? Why, why, why?"

"Charlie, baby, I'm sorry. I was so young back then, and while I wanted to keep you safe in my arms, I had to do what Momma and Poppa said do. It was hard back in those days when you had a baby and you weren't married. But know this, my son. I've always loved you. You were always in my bosom...my heart and I loved you until the day I died. I watched you grow up right under my eyes, and you and Graham were so much alike. There were times when I could barely stand to watch the two of you together."

"But why didn't you say something to me so that I would know that you loved me?"

"That was my mistake. I should have gone to your momma, my distant aunt, and told her that I wanted you to know who I was. To tell you the truth, I was frightened what the truth might do to my family. But it was unfair to you, my firstborn. I don't blame you if you never forgive me for what I've done, but don't hold it against Graham. God sent Graham to you. I can only ask you to forgive me like you must ask Graham for forgiveness for what you have done. You have a brother. Go and get it straight with him before it's too late."

"I'm the one who's been in pain, but nobody seems to care about that. I've been in pain for the past thirty-five years—ever since the day I got my birth certificate so I could marry Ernestine. Ernestine was a good woman, but I couldn't get over the fact that my very own mother was also my best friend's mother and that I actually knew who you were. I let it eat me up inside, destroying a good woman and what might have been a good marriage."

"I'm sorry, son. I hope you can forgive me. I've got to go but know that your momma has always loved you."

"No, don't go. Please don't leave me now. You just got here."

"Forgiveness lifts every heavy burden. Forgive."

"Momma, don't go...don't go!" Charlie cried out loud.

The door to Charlie's room opened.

"My God, what's going on in here?" the nurse questioned, rushing toward Charlie. Charlie was convulsing and sweat poured from his body. The nurse checked the monitor, felt Charlie's head, and pulled Charlie's chart from the foot of the bed.

Charlie made an attempt to smile. His eyes were glossed over and he continued to shiver while the monitor made erratic noises.

"I need assistance," the nurse yelled into the intercom on Charlie's bed. "The patient may have had a reaction to a drug." She turned to Charlie. "Let's pull these blankets around you and try to get you stabilized.

Two nurses rushed in and prepared to pump Charlie's stomach. Charlie began to cough and did so until he purged himself of the impurities in his body. The doctor arrived and ordered the nurses to replace the saline drip with a new bottle. Charlie settled down as if nothing had happened and fell into a light sleep.

"Forgive," squeaked through Charlie's tight lips, and the nurses looked at each other wondering if the message was for them.

CHAPTER 63

Their lips lingered and their eyes studied each other. Graham held Rita tight as he pressed his lips against hers—his reassurance that the woman he loved was in synch with him.

"Thank you, Graham, for a wonderful evening," Rita said, as she released her lips for a breath of fresh air.

"I don't know what I would have done if you walked out of my life."

Rita placed her hand over Graham's heart and held it there. She looked into his eyes and smiled.

"It meant a lot, Graham, that you came looking for me—to save your damsel in distress."

"Shhh," Graham pleaded. "I'll always be here."

"But," Rita stuttered, "but, but I knew then I had not made a mistake about the man I had given my heart to."

"I love you Rita, and I'm going to prove it to you until the day I die."

"Silly man. Hmph, no need. I know you love me. Kiss me again."

They embraced and brought their lips together again, saluting each other. After a moment, Graham backed away with a frown on his face.

"All right now, what's with the frown? Just a minute ago…"

"Come and sit down, baby. It's Charlie. I can't get him out of my mind. All the appalling things he's done to you and Mary…even Amanda all those years ago. And then…I find out he's my brother. I can't get over it. After all these years, my best friend turns out to be my own flesh and blood."

Rita remained quiet.

"What ya thinking?"

"Graham, sweetheart, I have every right to hate Charlie, and I do hate him for what he tried to do to me, but I want to forgive him. I know I can't face him right now, and I'm not sure I even want to be anywhere near him. I checked on him at the hospital—that was all I could do. But you have to confront Charlie and get things out into the open if you ever hope to have some kind of resolve within your own soul."

"He makes me so angry and then I stop and remember the times that weren't so bad. I remember the day he told me to get my crusty butt up and get on with my life. If he hadn't been there, I would be in the grave next to Amanda and I wouldn't have met you." Rita blushed.

"I need to understand why he did what he did to you and Mary. What kind of low-down dirty person would resort to such—how could he hurt the people he loved and cared about."

"Charlie flipped a switch. Something happened that caused those demons inside of him to take over. I hope he has learned his lesson this time, especially since I'm not pressing charges."

"Stay here, sweetie, until I get back. I've got to go to the hospital tonight and see Charlie. I can't let another minute pass without me having a word with him. He was sleep when I slipped his insurance information in his room. By now, he knows I've been there and may know about the birth certificate. That was what he wanted me to find out by sending me out to his house. Don't you move; I'll be right back."

"I'll be here."

♪♪♪

Graham raced to his car, got in, and sped toward Kaiser Hospital. The day was almost over—a day full of happiness and misfortunes, discovery and surprise, forgiveness and caution. Whatever the day had been, Graham needed to bring closure to all the questions that were galloping across his mind. His spirit was in conflict with his soul and Graham wanted to afford

Charlie every opportunity to explain his behavior. Graham wanted to understand, although he already knew they would never be the same.

♪♪♪

When Graham reached for the door, a nurse was on her way out and held the door open for him to pass. Graham saw the doctor and a second nurse checking Charlie's vitals.

"Is he all right?" Graham asked with a hint of concern in his voice.

"He is now," the doctor responded. "You are…"

"I'm his brother, Graham Peters."

"Well, Mr. Peters, Charlie had a reaction to one of the drugs we gave him, and he had a bit of a rough time. We were able to stabilize him, and he's a little groggy, dozing off and on."

"He's…" Graham hesitated, "Is he going to be all right?

"I think so," the doctor said. "He's been talking out of his head."

Graham stared at a sleeping Charlie, angry with himself for waiting too late to tell Charlie what he thought of him.

CHAPTER 64

The bright-yellow taxi pulled to the curb and Charlie slowly stepped out. He stood on the sidewalk as the cab sped away, then turned and looked at the mint-green stucco house he had lived in for more than three decades. Not much had changed in the week that he was in the hospital, and like everyone else, Tinkerbell the cat, hadn't been there to welcome him home.

Charlie entered the house and looked around. He moved to the kitchen and noticed the bottle of Chivas was not on the table. Charlie sighed.

While he felt much better and the bandage to his head had been removed, he moved with very little energy. He walked into the living room and slumped down onto the couch and flicked on the television. He picked up the remote and walked through several stations, but there was nothing on worth investing his time.

It was Graham, his brother, who had saved his sorry hide once again. He probably deserved the jail cell that he narrowly escaped by a miracle that had reduced his unsavory antics to probation and rehab.

The telephone lay on the table next to the couch, and he reached over and touched the receiver. He removed his hand, then thought better of it and picked it up. Before he changed his mind, he dialed Mary's number, the digits coming back to him the faster he dialed.

He heard Mary's voice, but he was afraid to say anything. He listened, and there she was again.

"Hello."

"Mary?" And the line was dead.

It would be a few more days before Charlie dialed Mary's number again. He was met with the same answer—no response. After the sixth try, Charlie gave up, remorseful for all he had put Mary through. He would ask her and Rita for forgiveness in time. No one had come around to visit, but he remembered the words of Amanda and his mother, *forgive*.

♪♪♪

Several months later…

"My Lord. Son, what brought you to the church house?"

"Pastor Fields, do you have a moment to speak with me? I need to talk to someone."

"Come on in, Charlie, I'll make time for you. Son, we've been praying for you."

"I thank you, Pastor. I'm not sure I deserve your prayers, but I appreciate it anyhow."

"As Christians, we are supposed to pray for everyone, no matter what the circumstance. Now tell me, what can I do for you this fine morning?"

"I need help with that word called *forgiveness*."

"All you have to do is get on your knees and ask the Lord to forgive you, and he will."

"You don't understand, Pastor Fields. I've hurt a lot of people, and I have to tell them I'm sorry and that I didn't mean to do the things I've done."

"We've all sinned, Brother Charlie, but God forgives us if we ask."

The tears began to roll down Charlie's cheeks. "Ohhhh, Pastor," Charlie cried, "I've done some terrible things. Oh God, help me. I betrayed my best friend, my brother. Graham and I are brothers. He had the mother I never had…I mean he had everything that I wanted. I wanted him to suffer like I suffered because my mother gave me away and he had the best of her. If she could have just told me she loved me."

Charlie released all the hurt that was inside of him.

"Charlie, it's not too late to get things straight with Brother Graham.

It's not too late for you to get it right with yourself. You have to ask God for forgiveness. Once God has forgiven you, you can go to those you need to address. Let them know how you feel and why you're coming to them now. God will do the rest. Trust me, son. It's going to be all right."

"I wish it were that simple."

"It is. Repeat after me."

"Lord…"

"Lord…"

"Forgive me."

"Lord, forgive me."

"That how it starts. We're getting ready to begin church service in a few minutes and I'd like for you to stay. You want help? The doors to the church are open. Now, son, I've got to run. I'm praying for you."

Pastor Fields left his study before Charlie could say thank you. Charlie stood there a minute, contemplating what he should do. He pushed the door open to Pastor Fields' study just as the choir marched by. He saw Rita as she passed by and Charlie darted back into the study for safety. He wasn't ready for any one-on-one confrontations with the people he had hurt and loved, especially since he had not made any attempt to contact them.

Ten minutes passed and he felt it safe to exit the study. He was on his way outside when he got a glimpse of Mary in her white usher's uniform, helping an elderly woman to the restroom. She didn't resemble the woman he had come to know, more the plain Mary from before. But there was something about Mary Ross that Charlie couldn't deny.

So Charlie seized the moment when Mary wasn't looking and went inside the sanctuary. He took a seat in one of the back pews where no one would recognize him, where he didn't feel out of place, and where he could watch Mary from a safe distance.

"And let the church say…Amen!" one of the deacons shouted at the end of morning prayer.

Tambourines took to the air with their golden rings clashing like cymbals in an upbeat tempo, their skinned backsides beat by the outstretched palms of human flesh. The piano and organ competed for the melody while Nine

West, Enzo, Coach, Stacy Adams, a pair of Marc Jacobs, and a pair of Ferragamos kicked up dust on the worn-out carpet in their quest to win *The Best Fancy Footwork Contest for the Lord Award*. Fans moved in synchronized rhythm either to the beat of the fast-paced, hallelujah-shouting music or to cool down the sweat of the "private summers" the young fifty-something women had found themselves entrenched in. Whatever the pleasure, praise and worship was mighty high.

In one row of pews sat Deborah and her family, Liz and her family, and Graham. Graham sat forward as the choir prepared to sing. Rita, dressed in a long purple robe with a shiny gold collar, came forward and took the mike. She closed her eyes and raised her head toward Heaven and began to sing the first verse of "The Battle is Not Yours" by Yolanda Adams.

Hands throughout the congregation were lifted toward Heaven and there wasn't a dry eye in the house. Rita sang with conviction and knowing because this was her testimony. "The battle is not yours, it's the Lord's."

"Thank you, Sister Long, for that beautiful song," began Reverend Fields. "The battle is not yours, it's the Lord's. How many of you have tried to fix things by yourself without any result?"

The entire congregation raised their hands.

"Well, I'm telling you today, try Jesus because He's all that you need. He's your doctor in the sick room…"

"He sure is," Martha sang out, sitting next to Elroy in her gold-brocade, two-piece suit with rabbit fur looped around her neck to form a collar.

"He'll be your lawyer in the court room, He'll be whatever you need," Reverend Fields hollered into the microphone.

Shouts of "Yes, Jesus, Yes, Jesus," and "Hallelujah" were heard all over the building. Hands up in the air, Reverend Fields slowly brought them down to quiet the congregation and continue with his sermon. And at the conclusion he opened the doors to the church and asked Sister Rita to come up to the microphone once more and sing.

Rita walked up to the mike and looked out into the church. "Reverend Fields sent us a timely message—a message that never gets old. The Lord wants to be a part of each and everyone's life. None of us has been good all of our lives, but it was God's mercy that kept us. We fall down, but we get up…for a saint is just a sinner who fell down and got back up."

The choir stood up and backed Rita up on the song Donnie McClurkin made famous. There was no doubting the power of the message or the messenger, and after a minute or two, one person stood up, then another.

Charlie watched as people got up and moved toward the front of the church. He felt naked on the pew, but he knew the words of the song were meant for him. He slowly got up and shuffled to the end of the row and took what seemed like a long walk to the front to dedicate his life to Christ.

Fingers touched his and Charlie opened his eyes to find that Graham had joined him at the altar. Before long, the whole pew where Graham sat was empty—Deborah and Grant, Liz and Riley, Martha and Elroy had joined the others, praising God for the prodigal son who had returned home.

CHAPTER 65

Spring 1990

A sweltering heat had come through Oakland. Ice cream trucks were busy on every street filling little and big kids' tummies full of ice cream. Children took turns jumping in and out of water sprinklers to cool their body temperatures down. Lemonade stands became prosperous service ventures.

Rita placed silverware next to the stoneware plates that sat on the table. She was fixing Graham's favorite meal, fried chicken. You could smell it a mile away.

Rita stood over the stove and took the last piece of chicken from the fryer. She wiped her forehead that had been dusted with flour and a little sweat and was about to place the rice in a bowl when the doorbell rang.

"Graham, get the door."

"I'm in the bathroom, you'll have to get it."

Rita's eye began to twitch and she gave a deep sigh. She walked to the door and opened it. There stood a polished Charlie, dressed in a tweed jacket and brown slacks. He was carrying a bouquet of flowers in his hand and offered a smile.

"Come in, Charlie. We're almost ready."

"Just like old times," Charlie whispered, sniffing at the aroma that permeated the house. "I remember that a week didn't go by without fried chicken being served in this house. And I was always here," Charlie paused, "just like today. These flowers are for you."

"Thank you," Rita said, taking them from Charlie. "Come in and make yourself comfortable. Graham will be right out."

Charlie strode into the living room and walked straight to the mantel. He surveyed the pictures that littered it—Graham's family, his extended one.

"How are you doing, Charlie?" Graham asked.

Charlie jumped and turned around, startled at Graham's voice.

"Not bad. It's been three months without alcohol, and I'm feeling pretty good. I want to thank you for asking me to come over today."

"I talked it over with Rita. She's not totally comfortable with it, but she wants to try."

"I understand. If it's too much, I can leave."

"No, we want you to stay. You smell that fried chicken, brother?"

Charlie was surprised as much as Graham seemed to be at the word "brother." It was music to Charlie's ears.

"I can't wait to sink my teeth into it."

"Rita is a little uncomfortable cooking in Amanda's kitchen, but after we're married, I think we'll move into a place that we could call our own."

"Oh," Charlie said with surprise in his voice. Then he remembered the words of Amanda and his mother's spirit when they visited him in his hospital bed. Charlie promised to keep their visit to himself. "I'm happy for the two of you."

"Well, go wash your hands and prepare to eat," Rita cut in. "Graham and I have a couple of surprises for you."

"She's doing better than I thought," Graham said to Charlie, then winked.

The men washed their hands and proceeded into the dining room.

"Where would you like for me to sit?" Charlie asked with a puzzled look on his face. "Looks like the table is set for four."

"Sit right there," Graham said and winked at Rita.

The doorbell rang again, and Rita hurried to answer it. She moved quietly from the door to the dining room followed by Sister Mary Ross. Mary smiled and Charlie smiled back unsure what to say. He and Graham rose from their seats, Charlie pulling out Mary's seat so she could sit.

The house had never been this still. Even the clock on the stove made more noise than the four adults who sat at the beautifully set table, waiting to devour the meal Rita had prepared.

"Hello, Mary," Charlie said.

"Good to see you, Charlie. You're looking well."

Eyes darted back and forth across the table. Dinner was moving a lot slower than Graham would have liked. He would have to liven up the place before the whole night became a disaster.

Graham blessed the food and they took turns filling their plates. The women made small talk while the men listened—Mary occasionally taking a peek at Charlie and he doing likewise.

"Rita and I have a surprise for you."

"You finally set the date," Mary blurted out.

"Yes, but that's not the surprise," Graham said.

"Well, what is it?" Charlie asked, concern written on his face.

"Graham and I would like the two of you to be our best man and maid of honor," Rita said.

"Oh," gasped Mary. "Rita, are you sure? I'd be honored!"

"Yes, Mary, I'm sure. You've turned out to be a very good friend."

"What about you, Charlie? You up to being my best man?"

"I'm honored that my brother chose me to be his best man. How can I say no? Of course, I will."

"You've made me and Rita the happiest couple in the world. I can't wait for her to be a permanent fixture around this house or wherever we'll live. You only have two months to get ready. Rita wants to be a June bride."

"I'm so excited," Mary said. "I'm excited for the both of you."

"Me, too," Charlie said. "What about us?" Charlie asked as he turned to Mary, her eyes bulging from their sockets.

"I'm not ready for anything, Charlie, I don't know if I ever will be. Why don't we get past dinner first?"

"That sounds like a good idea, Mary."

♪♪♪

The church was decorated in lilac and white. Lilies in several varieties adorned the vases that sat near the altar. The flame of the candles sparkled against the stained-glass windows, while two Love birds perched in a cage under the flower-covered arch chirped happily.

Seats filled fast—the first two rows reserved for the family. Invitations were at a premium ever since Rita and Graham's engagement was announced in the society page of *The Oakland Tribune*.

The wedding party was small. Deborah and Liz were the bridesmaids and their husbands the groomsmen. Mary Ross looked lovely and Charlie was the perfect best man.

The congregation rose as Rita and her father walked down the aisle. Rita wore a simple, silk taffeta strapless gown and a crown of Swarovski crystal jewels circled her head. Her French-manicured fingers gingerly held a bouquet of lilies.

As Rita glided past rows of spectators, she saw Clyde and the guys in the band. She smiled as she passed Martha and Elroy, but right in the midst of all the well-wishers sat William, giving her the thumbs up.

She trembled at the sight of him, turning her head forward and never taking her eyes off of Graham. Rita willed the minister to move forward with the nuptials so that she and Graham could be pronounced man and wife. But the moment came and the minister asked the infamous question: "Is there anyone who finds just cause that this couple should not be joined together in holy matrimony?"

William stood and Rita's worst fear was coming to pass. Worried looks crossed the faces in the congregation and the minister raised a calming hand to bring the matter under control. Before the minister spoke, Rita's father stood tall and statuesque, Rita's mother at his side.

William looked from Rita to her father. He walked into the aisle, raised his hand, and saluted the bride. He turned on his heels and walked out of the sanctuary.

"No!" boomed Rita's dad. "No one objects to this marriage. "Take it away, preacher."

The congregation laughed and Rita's smile returned to her face.

Graham wore a smile on his face. It brought back memories of a time forty years earlier, but new ones were being made this day. His bride was beautiful and love had conquered all.

ABOUT THE AUTHOR

Suzetta Perkins is the author of her riveting debut novel *Behind the Veil*. She is also a contributing author of *My Soul to His Spirit*, an anthology that was featured in the June 2005 issue of *Ebony* magazine. Suzetta is the co-founder and president of the Sistahs Book Club in Fayetteville, North Carolina and is Secretary of the University at Fayetteville State University, her alma mater. Visit suzettaperkins.com and www.myspace.com/authorsue or email to nubiange2@aol.com

DISCUSSION QUESTIONS for *A Love So Deep*

1) Where did Graham meet Amanda?

2) How did Amanda's death affect Graham? Was it healthy?

3) What did Charlie do to rescue his best friend, Graham, from the depths of despair?

4) Graham found strength to live again in the most unlikely place, although he initially did not want to go there. What was the name of the place and what made him feel alive again?

5) Do you feel that Graham's daughters were justified in being upset that he was seeing another woman so soon after their mother's death? Why or why not?

6) Do you feel that if Graham was to be with anyone that it should have been Sister Mary Ross? Why or why not?

7) What do you believe Rita saw in Graham? Do you believe she portrayed herself as an opportunist? Why do you believe Martha, Graham's mother-in-law, took a liking to Rita?

8) Was William, Rita's former husband, ever a threat to Rita? If yes, why?

9) What was Charlie's secret? How did his secret affect his relationship with Graham?

10) Love can be painful and oftentimes people make sacrifices for love, do crazy things in the name of love, and even forfeit love for love's sake. What did the following people do in the name of love?

Graham
Rita
Charlie
William
Mary

11) Do you believe Mary Ross understood what was really happening when Charlie turned up on her doorstep and tried to take advantage of her?

12) It took a lot of soul searching and prayer to accept Charlie into their home. Why do you believe Graham and Rita forgave Charlie for what he did to Rita even though forgiveness didn't come right away?

13) What do you believe was William's intention at the end of the story?

Sneak Preview! Excerpt from

Ex-Terminator: Life After Marriage

by Suzetta Perkins

Coming from Strebor Books

Day of Reckoning

The clock sat quiet on the nightstand, its green fluorescent numbers shouting out three a.m. Heavy breathing was muffled under the layers of bed linen that draped the large mass that lay in the middle of the bed. Every now and then the large formation would shift and a new pattern would occur.

In an instant, the still formation erupted—the mass tossing and turning under the bed covers that sang like a robin as the silk fibers rubbed against each other.

"No, don't go, please don't go," the voice cried out in the darkness. Then quiet.

The dreams were coming again, and Sylvia St. James let them play in her subconscious.

"What did you say, Adonis? I know I didn't hear what I thought I heard."

"I want a divorce, Sylvia. I can't say it any plainer than that."

"But why, Adonis? When did you decide this? I didn't know that our marriage was in trouble."

"That's the problem with you. You're always too busy to notice what's going on right under your nose. Too busy trying to kiss the boss' behind. Too busy trying to be something you're not. Think you're better than everybody else, and if you remember before we got married, I told you I didn't like fat women."

"I'll get on the treadmill tomorrow, I promise, but can we talk about this…try to work it out? We have invested so much of our lives into this marriage. Our daughter, what is she going to think?"

"Sylvia, I'm unhappy. I've been unhappy a long time, and now it's my time. I've got to go."

"But…what about me? What about…?"

"What about you? Look, Sylvia, the love slipped out of our marriage a while ago. Of course, you were too busy to notice. I don't have a lot of time left on this earth, and I'd like to enjoy a little happiness before I go."

"Time left on earth," Sylvia muttered to herself. "What are you talking about? Where are you going? No one will ever love you like I do, Adonis."

"Sylvia, please don't sound so desperate. You'll do fine. You always do."

"Don't go, Adonis. Don't leave me like this. Noooooooooooooo," Sylvia screamed.

The cream-colored, silk comforter slid to the floor as Sylvia's body continued to roll from side to side.

"Nooooooooooo," she screamed once more into the early morning. "No. No."

Pulling her hand from underneath her, Sylvia began to beat the pillow on which her head rested. She pounded into the soft down until her hand tired. She peeled her eyes open, then sat up slowly, sweat pouring from her brow. She scanned the dark room, her eyes out of focus. After a moment, Sylvia was able to make out the outline of a "T"-iron that Adonis had left behind, his winning golf club that he had nicknamed "Tiger."

Sylvia sat upright for a few moments, then slowly brought her hands to her face to catch the stream of water that ran from her eyes and threatened to soak her nightgown. Her breathing was labored and sobs, soft at first, became loud wails. She sobbed and sobbed, then grabbed her throat to keep from choking. Still sitting, she wrapped her arms around her chest and shook herself from side to side.

"Why, Adonis, why? Why did you leave me? I loved you with all my heart and soul. Why, why?"

Then there was quiet…an occasional sniff. Sylvia unfolded her arms and drew her knees up to her chest and wrapped her arms around her legs. She laid her head on the bend of her knees and began to rock back and forth. She willed her dream to recede. She sniffed again.

Sylvia lifted her head and turned toward the nightstand that held the clock. It was 3:55 a.m. She threw her legs over the side of the bed and stood up, almost slipping on the comforter that had fallen to the floor. She moved to the bathroom and relieved herself, washed her hands, then looked into the mirror.

Rough hands circled Sylvia's almond-shaped eyes set apart by high-arched eyebrows. Even in the dim light, her skin seemed blotchier than it was the day before. It had discolored her face something awful, and the older she got the more defined the blotches became.

Sylvia's reflection stared back at her, daring her to speak.

"You don't need him," the reflection sputtered. Sylvia put her hand to her mouth not sure whether it was she or the reflection that had spoken.

"Yeah, I don't need him. Get a hold of yourself, girl, and grab the world by its axis. It's time to take my life back and leave this pity party at the doorstep. "

Sylvia was sure this time that the reflection in the mirror was not doing all the talking, but the face that stared back meant serious business.

D-Day

"Where's my purse?" Sylvia shouted to no one, moving from room to room, looking in corners and closets, pulling on her too-short, linen dress every two seconds. "I've got lots to do and I want everything perfect before the ladies come. Ouch, darn! Not my stockings. This was not the time to get a run. Now I've got to stop and change them.

"Here's my purse," Sylvia continued to ramble out loud, her stockings making a swishing sound as her legs rubbed together when she trotted back to her room to change them. "Hiding from me again. I don't have time for this. I've got to get to the beauty shop by ten and I still have to stop and get gas before I go. Damn."

Brng...brng.

"Whoever it is, I don't have time to talk." Sylvia let out a sigh as she walked to the phone to see whose name was registered on the caller ID. "Aw, it's Mom."

"Hello, Mother. I'm in a hurry right now. Getting ready to go to the shrink."

"The shrink? I thought you were having a men-hating party today? And hello to you, too."

"I'm sorry. Just got a lot to do and I'm running behind time. This will be our first meeting, and I've got to look good for the occasion. Arial, my shrink is going to give me a touch-up. And I can't wait to get to the shampoo bowl to partake in the divine five-minute head scrub that causes you to have the most wonderful multiple orgasms."

"Sylvia St. James! I know you didn't just say what I thought you said."

"Mom, I'm a forty-five-year-old, good-looking woman albeit lately my attention grabbing curves have become a series of bumps on a line, hidden in my extra layer of body fat."

"Stop beating yourself up. Just need to lay off some of those carbs and get some exercise."

"You're right. And today is the first day of my real healing. I've got a reasonable portion of my health and strength and I know that there is a world of somebody's out there waiting on me."

"Be careful what you ask for."

"A baby and twenty years of my life, Ma, and he had to go and…"

"Let's not talk about it."

"That's the problem. I need to talk about it." Sylvia paused. "I had one of my dreams last night."

"I'm sorry, baby. I wish I could be there for you. Let him mess up your your mind and he ain't even thinking about you."

"Thanks for the support, Mom. That's why I'm having this meeting. Now, I've gotta go. Love you."

"Love you, too." And the line was dead.

Sylvia stood in the middle of the room with hands on her voluptuous hips—gold bangles dangling from one arm and surveyed her surroundings. In one corner stood a wooden African fertility statue that looked as lonely as she did. Six months had passed since the judge declared that the marriage of Adonis and Sylvia St. James was dissolved, but today, Sylvia made her own declaration that she was ready to live again.

Sylvia looked down at her watch. It was almost ten o'clock and she had to go. Her adrenaline was high, excited about the prospect of sitting with other women who were divorced and sharing ideas about how to move on.

"Aw hell. Broke a nail."

Sylvia stuck her finger in her mouth to soothe the writhing pain. After a couple of seconds she put the key in the ignition of her silver BMW 530i sedan and headed for the gas station two blocks away.

Five minutes away, Sylvia thought. She would still be on time. She looked in her purse for her gas card but remembered she had taken it out and put it on the nightstand. Sylvia shook her head in disbelief. Her road to healing had some major obstacles.

She looked in her purse again and rummaged through her wallet that was crammed with receipts. Adonis was always telling her that her purse was going to get stolen one day, and the robber would know her life story. She sifted through until her fingers pulled up a folded twenty-dollar bill. "Thank you God, You're so good. And I promise to pay careful attention to what I'm doing from now on."

XXX

Arial's mouth was moving a mile a minute when Sylvia walked into the beauty shop. Hair piled high into a ponytail that fell to the nape of her neck, Arial's petite frame was dressed to the nines. She wore a pair of caramel-colored, kidskin leather slacks and a white starched, short-sleeved blouse with lacy scallops running around the collar. Two-carat diamond studs dotted each ear lobe, and her feet were stuffed in a pair of Dr. Scholl's comfort sandals made for standing long hours. Although Arial was in her late forties, she could easily pass for thirty. But more than that, the girl could hook up some hair. Arial had the gift.

"Be with you in a minute, sweetie…kiss…kiss." Sylvia blew a kiss back and picked up a hairstyle book to pass the time.

Mane Waves was Arial's baby. The shop had grown from a small clientele to one whose clients sometimes drove an hour or two for Arial's services. The decor was befitting the queens the ladies believed they were—plush gold carpeting running the length of the shop and exotic plants standing or leaning in their foliage as if their presence demanded attention. A black lacquered chest of drawers stood next to a large palm tree just inside of the main entrance, displaying samples of facial and nail products Arial also sold. A six-inch curved bar that served as the guest registry and stood to the right of the chest was handsomely decorated with porcelain beauty shop motif whatnots along with business cards that sat in a black-lacquered holder.

"Sylvia." Sylvia jumped. "What have you been up to, girl?" shouted Arial through the noise of the blow dryer as she put the finishing touches on Ms. Jenkins.

"Preparing for a coming out party."

"A what?"

"I'll explain later."

Fifteen minutes later, Arial took the towel from around Ms. Jenkins' neck.

"Looking good, Ms. Jenkins," Sylvia said.

"Thank you, baby. I've got a darned good stylist."

Sylvia gently slid into the chair vacated by Ms. Jenkins.

"How have you been, sweetie? I know you've been through some rough times." Arial picked through Sylvia's hair. "And you know you needed a perm three weeks ago. Next time you come in we've got to put some color in your hair, too."

"You're right. But to answer your question, I'm fine, Arial. In fact, I feel better than I have in the last year. I'm meeting with some other women tonight, and we're going to talk about life after divorce."

"A support group."

"Yeah. I'm looking forward to it."

"Whose in the group? I don't know about sitting around talking with a bunch of women…having them all up in my business, especially sistahs. You sure about this?"

"It's going to be a good thing, Arial. Sometimes your friends get tired of hearing your troubles over and over again. Some days you're up but there are many down days. Being able to connect with women who share the same experience and who may need me as well is the answer to my prayer. God knows I need this. Rachel Washington is going to be there. You might want to stick your head in and join us."

"You didn't have to go there. Lawrence and me are prehistoric news. I've been single for darn near fifteen years. Don't need no counseling, and I sure don't need a support group. Back to Rachel. It was a damn shame how her husband messed all over her, but that woman don't know how to pick a husband. Isn't this her third divorce?"

Sylvia turned around to look at Arial. "See, that's what I mean. So what if it's her third? Rachel is a sweetheart and one of my best friends. It's not her fault that these men take her kindness for weakness."

"I know you better hold your head up while I put this perm in your hair."

"You better not burn me, either. I'll take this shop from you like I took the house from Adonis." They laughed.

"Girl, you know I'm always here for you. Have you heard from Adonis?"

"You mean since he went to live with his ex-wife?" Sylvia hesitated. "No, I haven't heard from him."

"You still love him, don't you?"

"I don't love him like I used to love him. We've got history. We were married for twenty freakin' years, Arial!"

"Shhh, don't get yourself so worked up, sweetie."

"I'm sorry. Lost my head for a second."

"My next customer won't be here for another thirty minutes. I figured you and I need some down time."

"I gave that man a beautiful daughter and the best years of my life. I still can't believe he just got up and walked out on me like that—without a decent explanation. Do you know that the self-confident, independent, woman I was has turned into a whining, bitter, angry..."

"It's okay, sweetie."

"But, Arial, it hurts to love a man as much as I loved and adored Adonis. He stabbed me straight in the heart. Declared that he was no longer in love with me and marched straight into another woman's bed."

Tears began to fall, and Sylvia let her head drop.

"I think it's time for your shampoo." Arial took off her latex gloves and with both hands kneaded Sylvia's shoulders. "I'll make it extra special today. We'll make it a ten-minute massage."

"You always know how to make a girl feel good."

"I love you, Sylvia. And I don't want you to take my shop! If we wait another minute, your whole head might be on fire."

Laughter ripped through the near empty shop.

"I think you're gonna be alright, sweetie. And the way you're wearing that dress—showing all the thighs you own, Adonis might have to come back and rescue you from all the players that will be buzzing around the honey-bee."

"Stop. I threw this dress on real quick because I didn't feel like ironing anything. Although, the meeting is going to be at my house, I'm going to be wearing my eggshell print, chiffon napkin blouse and an almond-colored silk tank under it. I'm going to slide into a pair of off-white kidskin leather pants that will lie on my perfect forty-two-inch curves just right. And girl, I've got a sharp pair of off-white Franco Sarto ankle-high boots that are to die for, and when you finish my luscious, reddish-brown mane, I'll be swishing my head from side to side, moving my hair like it was a merry-go-round."

"Girl, you're crazy. Knock 'em dead even if it is going to be a bunch of cackling women."

"I see it like this, Arial. If we are going to get our lives back, we have to act as if we want change so we can close our Ex-files for good."

"I'm with you, sweetie."